LOST IN CRETE

LOST IN CRETE

LAURIE STRANGE

Troubador Publishing Ltd
Unit E2 Airfield Business Park,
Harrison Road, Market Harborough,
Leicestershire LE16 7UL
Tel: 0116 279 2299
Email: books@troubador.co.uk
Web: www.troubador.co.uk

ISBN 978 1 80514 543 1

British Library Cataloguing in Publication Data.
A catalogue record for this book is available from the British Library.

Printed and bound by CPI Group (UK) Ltd, Croydon, CR0 4YY
Typeset in 11pt Minion Pro by Troubador Publishing Ltd, Leicester, UK

For our Cretan family and friends

PREFACE

The first seeds of this story were sown while helping with the grape harvest for my newfound family on the rocky slopes of Crete. It was the summer of 1983. I had married my wife two years earlier in the tiny church of the village of her birth.

Attracted to Crete in the first instance by its glittering ancient past, it was history of a more recent kind that had begun to occupy my thoughts. Despite already knowing Greek hospitality to be legendary, I was totally unprepared for the warmth and gratitude seeming to come from one and all, purely because I came from England. The legacy I was benefiting from was due to Allied wartime aid as Crete tried to repel the airborne invasion that eventually led to German occupation

With the sun blazing above, heavy baskets cutting into each shoulder, I slithered once more down the narrow path, vines to one side, a sheer drop to the other, and began to empathise with those men. Evacuated from the mainland, they fought on here again until forced to retreat and march across the mountains in the desperate hope of yet another naval evacuation.

What if I had been among them and couldn't reach the ships in time? What if some kindly family had sheltered me and I had tried to repay them with my labours? What might I discover in this ancient land? What about the pretty girl laying out sultana grapes to dry…?

The first drafts followed later that year, life then intervened, as it does for everyone. But as each successive draft was dusted off, and the story grew, it became like meeting up with old friends every few years. I hope you enjoy their company as well.

ONE

A murmur of appreciation rippled across the lecture room of the Archaeological Institute as Vangelis Xenakis brought up the penultimate slide of his presentation. The involuntary expressions of wonder unleashed from each member of his audience confirmed his instinct to allow them a few moments more to absorb the beauty of the intricately worked Minoan jewellery that now filled the screen, bathing the room with a golden glow.

The lecture had gone well. Vangelis was justifiably pleased, as indeed were his audience. Though some may have feared, given his name, that a struggle might be looming to understand their guest speaker, they soon discovered that any such reservations were without foundation, for his English was faultless. For that, among many other things, he had his mother to thank. His looks he shared with his father. A classic Cretan combination of dark hair that framed a noble, bronzed face — his mother's gift in this respect being only the grey-blue eyes that glinted in their swarthy setting, as did the lapis lazuli inlays set in their golden surrounds, still shimmering upon the screen.

Reflecting that even he was still incapable of remaining

immune to the palpable charge of excitement flooding through the audience as they gazed, mesmerised by the image displayed before them, it now seemed almost unbelievable that it had been his fortune to have held these fabulous treasures in his own hands. The very same treasures that had shaped not just the fate of those born to a far distant past, but the fate of his own family as well. For Vangelis, these precious jewels were not just a link to a lost Minoan history. For him, they also held the secret to his own history.

Cueing the final slide, Vangelis watched together with his audience in silence as the garniture of jewellery displayed before them slowly dissolved into a final close-up of one single earring from the set.

'That's my boy,' whispered Jack, 'plug that book!'

Anne silenced him with a sharp nudge, quickly turning her attention back to her husband's closing remarks.

'As we have seen, it has now been over thirty years since this solitary piece first gained global recognition. A lifetime for some! But it has taken that lifetime, infinitesimal as it certainly is when weighed against the millennia that distance us, to fully appreciate the significance of this and the later finds that have now finally given us a key. A key that could help to unlock those ancient times and resolve the controversies surrounding the true date of the Santorini eruption … a date which has for so long plagued historian, scientist, and archaeologist alike.

We may never truly know for whom these beautiful gifts were fashioned, but that should not deter us from using that most powerful weapon in our armoury … our imagination. With that we can escape this rainy London afternoon, leave behind the present of our own fledgling millennium, and step across the boundaries of time, to breathe new life into these fragile survivors of the past. As precious a gift as any I have shown you tonight, I leave you then with the most precious of all ... your imaginations!'

As Vangelis assured his audience that they would soon be free to head to the bar, Anne held Jack back in his seat to hear the vote of thanks now being given to her husband on behalf of the Institution. She caught his eye, sharing in his happiness, for she knew how much this invitation lecture had meant to him.

Holding her gaze, he waited on the rostrum for the closing formalities, only barely concealing a smile as he noticed Jack escaping Anne's clutches to head for the bar.

Tomorrow would bring the book launch and he had much to be grateful to Jack for. That their friendship went way back certainly helped, but he had always known that it would not be taken for granted that Jack would publish him. Academic publications were not his usual fare, and any financial return would be modest.

Some twenty years his senior, Jack had taken Vangelis under his wing following their first meeting at the Oxford and Cambridge, but the friendship had developed since with a natural ease regardless of the disparity in age. Jack had known Vangelis's grandmother, but then Jack seemed to know everybody, young and old alike. This publication would be no bestseller, but for Vangelis it meant a great deal more. For him, the reward would come in knowing that his work would finally be recognised, and would also help to resolve some, at least, of the many discrepancies that still defied a definitive dating of the massive volcanic blast that had ripped out the heart of the tiny island of Santorini and sealed the fate of Minoan civilization.

Vangelis gathered up his presentation material, thanked his hosts for their help, and tried to make his way through the gathering towards Anne. Even this was no longer a simple task, obliged as he now found himself to acknowledge a heady mix of queries and congratulations enroute. The limelight was an unfamiliar place for Vangelis Xenakis.

Jack saw his struggle to reach them and recognising his unease sailed through the crush to rescue him.

'Excellent Vangeli. Superb presentation that'll get the launch off to a flying start! Now, we still need to discuss a few details about tomorrow ….'

With that he flung an authoritative arm around his friend, flagged his intended return passage with a raise of the other, and waited for the seas to part. Scooping Anne up on the way, he ushered them both into a suitably quiet corner.

'What details?'

'None whatsoever. Just getting you out of there. Now … red or white … though I think I already know the answer to that one …?'

Vangelis nodded and turned to embrace Anne as Jack went off in search of the wine.

She and Vangelis had met at university several years earlier. Both had been in their early twenties, and after the freshers' merry-go-round had slowed to a halt, they began to find themselves increasingly in one another's company — set slightly apart as they were from the younger mainstream. At first shared interests and companionship were all they needed. They had both already enjoyed their fair share of good and not so good relationships. Neither had any intention of leaving university without a first and it had taken until the start of their second year to realise just how close they had become.

The summer break had seemed endless and while neither had been under any illusion about the physical attraction they knew existed between them, it had taken this period of forced separation for them to see each other anew. The intimacies they shared had combined the tender thrill of long-anticipated discovery with the deep warmth of familiarity. Suddenly there were no longer enough hours in the day. Lectures were missed. Deadlines passed. The new year finally brought some sanity and they both eventually achieved their goals.

After graduation there had followed the usual dilemmas, until separate offers of work dictated their choices. There had been time together and time apart: holidays in Crete, Christmases in England, family introductions, redundancies, and new appointments, until Vangelis finally made the decision to settle back in Crete to concentrate on securing an excavation there.

Anne had thought long and hard about whether to join him. He had made it very clear he would like her to do so, but there had been no mention of marriage, and while that had not greatly concerned her since she had given it scant thought herself, she was unsure whether she was prepared to give up the work and independent lifestyle she enjoyed in London for an uncertain future in Crete.

Since Vangelis's mother was English, and her daughter equally fluent in both tongues, she knew there would at least, if only family, be someone close she could relate to. Yet as welcome as she had always been made on her visits, she knew it could prove a challenge adapting to a much smaller, closer-knit community. For a while they drifted apart, neither completely severing the ties, neither prepared to fully commit.

Then one day there was the phone message from Jack. 'Annie! Haven't seen you in ages … bit of a do on Saturday evening … sure to be some people you'll know ….' Jack's 'dos' were legendary. The rest of the week slipped by without any decision on or consequent reply to his invitation.

Come Saturday evening, with dresses strewn across the bed and still no fully binding decision having been made, Anne realised she had spent far more time in front of the mirror than she could ever remember doing before, staring at the auburn-haired woman before her.

She picked up a framed photograph of herself and Vangelis, taken the year they had graduated and compared the likeness with the reflection. Her hazel eyes examined those of the carefree girl in the photograph, before looking back at the woman she had become. She allowed herself a pout at her reflection, swivelled into profile, and assessed the curves: a little fuller perhaps than her former self, but everything still thankfully in the right places. There was only one thing missing.

Later, as the cab drew up to Jack's door, a moment of indecision had gripped her — what if he wasn't there? But her worries were soon dispelled. The door was flung wide and Jack, being Jack, enveloped her in a bear hug of a greeting before promptly marching her in and through the fray to join Vangelis. Within seconds he had uncorked champagne — filled their glasses — placed the bottle on the mantelpiece and left them to their own devices by the glowing fire.

Since then they had been inseparable. They had married later that year, and both had been relieved to find that it did not prove to be the kiss of death that each had secretly feared: knowing it to have accounted for the demise of several of their friends' long-standing relationships. The magic was still there. The bond even stronger. So much so, that at this moment, as the buzz of the reception continued behind them, no words were necessary. The loving embrace and tender expression of admiration that now shone in his wife's eyes, told Vangelis far more than he needed to hear.

Jack returned with three full glasses, to find Anne loosening her husband's tie.

'My God, she can't keep her hands off him. Leave your husband alone woman!'

'This isn't my husband,' she joked. 'He doesn't wear ties!'

Vangelis was happy to let Anne rid him of the unfamiliar constriction, and he undid the top two buttons of his shirt. Anne provocatively slipped open a third to wind Jack up.

'Ah but he has his public to consider now. He's no longer just yours!' Jack decided to use the mood of playful banter to bring up a familiar theme. 'I'm still relying on you to persuade this man to give us the *whole* story. Now that *would* make a book!'

Anne smiled wryly and they both looked to Vangelis, who refused to be drawn. Jack changed tack.

'I know. You wanted to keep it academic … objective. Well, I've kept my side of the bargain. You'll now sit shoulder to shoulder to gather dust with your peers on the reference shelves of every archaeological library there is.'

Vangelis still would not be pulled in, knowing full well there was no remaining unkept part of any bargain outstanding on his side. He gave them both a good-natured smile of non-committal and took a welcome swig of wine. Therein, of course, lay the root of the problem: too many evenings spent by Jack's fireside, enjoying the Cotes du Rhone Villages and the conversations that ensued, as his friend had teased out detail after detail of his family's past and the roles they had played in the tangled history of the Minoan hoard. Anne broke the silence.

'*I* don't even know the whole story,' she complained, reflecting that Jack might very well know far more about her own husband than she herself.

For the most part, Vangelis was as open and uncomplicated a partner as she could wish for, but something had clouded his past and it was a territory she had come to avoid. She had tentatively raised the subject with his parents and had met the same reticence, with equally similar evasions to any question which probed too deeply. Not wishing to rock the boat, she had let the matter be.

'Then you obviously need to spend more time with Diane before it's too late.' Jack immediately regretted his clumsy choice of words. 'I'm sorry. How is she, Vangeli?'

'Oh, she's better. Been out of hospital now a couple of weeks or so.'

'Longer,' Anne corrected him, 'and she's determined to make the launch tomorrow.'

'That's wonderful.' Jack relaxed a little. He knew though that one day in the not-too-distant future, he would miss the longstanding friendship of a mentor — under whose wing he had often sheltered in his college days. Now in her eighties, Vangelis's grandmother was as sharp as ever, but a recent string of operations had left her frail and weary. He tried to recall when exactly it was that they had first met and cast his mind back to the summers of his late teens when, at the tennis club, they had bartered their skills: she agreeing to help him with his studies, he divulging the secrets of his backhand. It had been 1978.

TWO

Diane led a triumphant march to the clubhouse bar. 'Two St. Clements please, young man.' Her innocent air did little to conceal an inner pleasure as Jack, whose turn it was to staff the bar, reddened slightly, teeth clenching as he served the drinks. She knew full well that the last thing Jack wanted was to be considered a 'young' man. It was one of her favourite teases for boys of his age: desperate to shrug off the last of their teenage years in the race to be considered a man. It was a term she also employed with equal success for men of her own age and older, for quite different reasons.

Still flushed with her victory, she turned to the losing pair and relayed their orders to Jack. He handed the St. Clements to her partner, whose expression, in contrast to Diane's was more one of relief to have the match over. He could sympathise. Diane took no prisoners on court. To be drawn against her was always a challenge, but infinitely preferable than to partner her. He had done so in a mixed doubles not that long ago, and her withering comments when he had netted a simple deciding volley set up by her serve were still seared in his mind.

She gave him a warm, genuine smile now, however, as she settled for the drinks. 'Have one yourself Jack.' She was coming down from her high. Off-court, Diane was a completely different character. Jack watched as the four took their drinks out into the late afternoon sun. Diane turned, framed in the doorway, the sunlight casting an aura around her tennis whites and gave him another reassuring smile before joining the others, leaving him alone in the otherwise empty clubhouse.

He turned back to the Evening News crossword, not as he well knew that he would now have any chance of concentrating on it. For God's sake — not only was she old enough to be his mother — she had a daughter already several years older than him. Struggling to put her out of his mind, he stared at the crossword once more, but found himself thinking instead of the tennis-girl poster from the previous year's *Athena* calendar that hung on his bedroom wall. Caught between the image of her cheeky rear and scenes from *The Graduate* that now began to form in his imagination, his attention was brought sharply back into focus as he realised he was no longer alone.

'No luck?' Diane had returned for peanuts.

'Not in the mood' he said, putting the paper aside to deal with her request. Then, finding none to hand and grateful for an opportunity to conceal yet another bout of blushing, explained, 'I'll just get some more from the back.'

Diane smiled, put the change on the counter and picked up his paper, glancing idly at the headlines before thumbing through the pages. Jack returned in time to see the flicking of pages come to an abrupt halt as something caught her attention. She stared at the article in disbelief.

'You look like you've seen a ghost!' Jack quipped.

Her trance broken, she smartly closed and folded the paper before Jack could see what it was that had so upset her.

'Do you mind?' she said, holding up the paper like a starting flag.

'Sure,' he shrugged.

Within a second she and the paper had disappeared, leaving Jack alone again with both the peanuts and the change in front of him.

Turning the key in her front door, Diane prayed once more that Catherine would indeed be out with Ellie, as she had so fervently hoped during her hasty rush home. She needed time alone. Eddie, she knew, would still be up at the Prince and probably would be for a good while yet.

'I'm back!' She paused for a moment to catch her breath, welcoming the silence that greeted her. Throwing her racquet case down by the hallstand with uncharacteristic disregard, she headed past the stairs, oblivious of the hard crack of press meeting tile, continuing on through the kitchen where she checked the back garden, half expecting to see her daughter nursing Ellie on the lawn. The garden, however, was empty. She breathed a sigh of relief and steadied herself against the sink for a few moments before relaxing her grip on the newspaper. Setting it aside, she poured a glass of water and drank deeply. Then, topping up her glass, she grabbed the paper once more and went up to the bedroom.

Sitting on the bed, Diane unfolded the Evening News, smoothing away the creases in momentary hesitation, before composing herself and finding the article. It was not the caption that had caught her attention 'Heraklion Museum Thanks Donor for Golden Find,' nor the picture below of the museum director shaking hands with said donor, alongside an official from the Antiquities Department. There followed a body of text, the detail of which even now she could not fully settle to take in.

Below that, however, was the image she had instantly recognised. She stared at it now almost in disbelief, tracing the fine swirls of the delicately wrought earring. Her earring! She had to set her mind at rest.

Laying the paper aside on the bed, she opened the oak wardrobe door — looked up to the top shelf and reaching up and inside — began to rummage behind seldom used hats and bags until she found what she was looking for. Suppressing a curse as one corner of the old confectionery box split under its rough withdrawal, she nursed the box and its contents down onto the bed. Again, there was a momentary pause before she felt able to open the lid and face what lay within, knowing that to do so would stir up a host of memories.

Shaking off the apathy, she set aside the lid and looked at the jumble of mementoes and ephemera. Instinctively pushing aside the all too familiar telegram, she leafed through the assortment of faded black and white photographs that now seemed so incongruously tiny, save for the occasional enlargement. Pushing deeper into the box, she found the small bundle of letters with their customary blue censor's labels, still tied in ribbon. As dear to her as these might be, it was still not what she was looking for and she continued the search, her fingers eventually finding the small box — instantly recognising the feel of the rough utilitarian cardboard.

Withdrawing it, she looked once more at the plain, square, brown box. Pasted on the lid was a label affirming the contents as glass slides; falsely, as she well knew. Opening it in turn, she took out the stained and yellowing field dressing kit. Finding the slit that had been cut into one side of the battered packet, she teased out the earring, which even now in the fading light glinted again as if new. She lay it upon the newspaper, side by side with its photographic counterpart. She had not been wrong. It was identical.

For some time, Diane sat there trying to decide what this would mean. She read the article and reread it. Still her brain would not work properly. She had always suspected the design was unique and this was now being confirmed by the museum in Crete, but she had never dreamt that it could be so old. She glanced back at the article to be sure she had not misunderstood. '… Neo palatial / Late Minoan era, approximately 1500 BC ….' She had not misread. It made sense of course that the earring had to have a twin — but how could she be holding one, when the other had only just been unearthed in Crete?

She had no time to calculate the odds of this unlikely event, however, for the slam of the front door downstairs brought her rapidly to her senses. Ordinarily, the first rasp of key in lock would have alerted her, so wrapped up in her thoughts had she been. She glanced down briefly at the crumpled field dressing and its disguise that had brought the unexpected gift into her life so many years ago, before replacing the earring and hastily gathering everything up.

'Mum? We're back!' came the familiar cry from below.

'Yes darling … I'll be down in a moment.' Replacing

the box in the wardrobe, she slipped the newspaper underneath it and closed the door. Any further speculation on the mystery would have to wait. Going out onto the landing, Diane saw her daughter lifting Ellie from the pram below.

Catherine looked up. 'Still in your togs … must have been a long game?'

'Match.' Diane corrected automatically, 'Sorry! No, well … yes, it did go on a bit. I just needed a bit of a lie down.' She realised her contrived excuses were wasted on Catherine, who was far too pre-occupied with her own daughter. 'I'll just change. Be with you in a minute.'

What should have been a relaxing family evening had dragged on interminably. Though the circumstances of Catherine now being a single parent were obviously regrettable, it had meant that Diane had seen a lot more of her recently and both had begun to explore a different relationship than just that of mother and child. And of course there was her grand-daughter Ellie: all of eleven months and a constant source of delight as she sought to explore the world around her.

On this occasion, however, she could not wait for Eddie to tire of bouncing his grand-daughter on his knee — have the evening meal out of the way — and pack her daughter off to her nearby flat. Fortunately, there had been a bottle of wine in the larder which she had opened for the meal, calculating that it would guarantee an early night for her husband.

She had been proved right and now, sitting up in bed staring at the unread novel in its pool of light, she waited for

Eddie's breathing to slow and settle into the steady rhythm she knew so well before pulling out the Evening News from under the bed. She had felt stupid, retrieving it earlier from the wardrobe — after all it was just a newspaper. Deep down she knew she would have to show it to Eddie sooner or later but at this moment she had no idea what she should do next, or indeed what this discovery might mean to her — to Eddie — to her family.

Rereading the article did not give her much solace either. Beyond naming the donor, one Michaelis Serides, described as a local entrepreneur — a brief mention of the involvement of the antiquities department — and the following transfer to the Heraklion Museum of Archaeology, there was no explanation whatsoever of the nature of the earring's discovery.

Diane settled back into the nest of pillows and closed her eyes, allowing her weary mind to travel back. Reluctant for the moment to dwell on the receipt of that innocent brown box and its accompanying correspondence, she pushed back further still — back through the Blitz — back to happier, carefree days of adolescence when she, Eddie, and Richard had been inseparable. But her anxiety would not let her linger for more than a brief few moments in those halcyon peacetime days — inexorably pulling her on through the whirl of preparations for war — conscriptions, imminent separations, and their consequent, hasty decisions.

In a way, she had always known it would be Richard she would marry, but as she had come to realise in the brief time afforded them between wedding and first posting, it was the indefinable chemistry of the camaraderie the three had shared that had been the most potent stimulus. They had known each other since their schooldays. All three living no more than a street or two apart from each other in Stoke Newington. Always the tomboy, Diane quickly grew apart from other girls of her age, preferring instead the rough and tumble company of her two chums.

Leafy Clissold Park had hosted their summertime adventures, its cafeteria sheltering them in rainier days and all the while the tall, grey, stone spire of nearby St. Mary's had kept watch over them. The bond stood firm throughout their teenage years, though the park was soon left behind as evenings at the cinema and weekend forays into town were now needed to satisfy their growing curiosities.

It was of course curiosity of a different kind that eventually began to test the strengths of that bond. Whether, had there not been a war breaking out around their heads the decisions would have been made so rapidly, Diane would never know, but Richard had proposed and she had accepted. Eddie had taken her decision on the chin — it had, after all, not been entirely unexpected. Whatever he might have felt deep down, he had congratulated them warmly and agreed to stand as Richard's best man. It was natural they should be married in St. Mary's.

They shared a brief honeymoon weekend at an inn on the outskirts of Epping Forest, trudging peacefully through the beech leaves in the last of the autumn sun before returning to face the inevitable compromises. Since it was obvious Richard would be called up sooner or later, it had been decided that for the time being he should share a room with Diane in her parent's house. It was not an ideal start to their marriage, but one that was familiar to many.

Almost a year older than Eddie, Richard's call-up would naturally have come first had he not already decided to enlist. By joining The King's Royal Rifle Corps, and therefore London based, he managed between exercises to keep in reasonable contact with Diane until, training over, the posting finally arrived. His battalion, the 1st Rangers, were bound for North Africa.

The three had said their final farewells together and, as Diane had then stood alone with Eddie on the station platform, the friendship between them seemed equally awkward and incomplete.

'Cheer up girl…' Eddie had struggled to find the right words.

Diane's eyes remained fixed upon the departing train.

Neither for the first, nor the last time, would Eddie wish that he was the focus of her attention. 'You mark my words, I bet the jammy little beggar will be sunning himself by some oasis in no time!'

Diane had laughed. That was the thing about Eddie — he could always make her laugh.

THREE

Pressed into the thorny bush of the rocky hillside, Richard shivered as the chill wet breeze funnelling down from the mountains ahead sliced through his hastily improvised rifle pit. It had snowed all night and now in the steely grey dawn, the steady drizzle began to snake its way inside the ripped rain cape, soaking the rough wool of his battledress jacket that clung like an icy mantle across his shoulders. He shuffled in his position and tried not to dwell on the absurdity of the situation, but it was difficult not to. It was less than three weeks since he and the rest of the 1st Rangers had sweated their way through desert training exercises in Camp Quassassin, fully expecting to then be dispatched from Egypt to support the recently captured fortress port of Tobruk in the ongoing push to drive the Italians from Libya.

Instead, attached to the 1st Armoured Brigade, the Rangers had become part of the hastily assembled British Expeditionary Force and found themselves rapidly dispatched to Greece to counter the imminent threat of German invasion through Yugoslavia. Contingents of British, Australian, and New Zealand forces already sorely needed in the North African Campaign would now fight alongside the Greeks.

Having already defied all the odds, the Greek army had succeeded in turning the tables on Mussolini's opportunist attack on their country, pushing the invading Italians deep back into Albania, but this had left them vulnerable to Italy's far more deadly Axis partner from the north. Hitler was already known to have amassed formidable forces in Romania and Bulgaria and was pressing the Yugoslavs to join the Axis.

The Rangers had first been deployed to the Vardar Plain, where there were already two Greek divisions guarding against an attack on Salonika, but as war was finally declared on Yugoslavia and Greece, the main impetus of the invasion seemed likely to come first from the Monastir Gap in the mountains to the west. And so they were ordered westwards to join the Australian 19th Infantry Brigade already stationed in the Vevi-Kozani sector, leaving the Greeks to hold their line.

Even to the untrained eye, it was clear their antiquated weaponry would be hard put to hold back Hitler's Panzer divisions. Their courage however was in no doubt, as the Italians had already paid dearly to discover.

Leaving the plains, the Rangers marched up across the foothills. Passing through one tiny village after another they were met by well-wishers, many giving them what little food they could spare. An old grandmother shuffled towards Richard, her lined and weatherbeaten face breaking into a beaming smile as she pressed two boiled eggs into his hands.

'*Sto kalo na pate paidi mou,*' wishing him well for his journey, before suddenly remembering to unfold her apron, withdraw a crust of hard bread, and clutch his one free hand as he pocketed the eggs with the other. '*Paximadia*,' she had explained '*paximadia*' enfolding his fingers around the bread with a final squeeze of her leathery hands. He had smiled in gratitude as, being drawn on by the others, he noticed her give a final heavy sigh before brushing aside a tear.

With the fall of night came the rapid drop in temperature, and it grew colder still as they pressed up higher, on and over the rocky trails. The mules they had been given for the heavier equipment slithered across the frozen moonlit paths which threatened to vanish altogether as sleet set in. In the early hours they reached the crossroads of Vevi, where other troops were gathering. To the north lay the brooding mountains of Yugoslavia and the Monastir Gap, to the south the road led on into the heart of Greece. Cold and weary, they sought what food and shelter they could find and rested for a few hours before their orders finally came.

They were to head south along the winding road that cut through the valley, there they would join the Australian anti-tank regiment and New Zealand machine gunners to hold the Klidi Pass.

As they had prepared to leave, another company of Australian infantry began to arrive having also marched through the night, their complaints as bitter as the freezing weather itself — and not without reason — for the greater majority had no warmer clothing than their desert shorts and jackets. The lucky few had blankets.

Thankful at least that they were not in that situation, the Rangers set off down the road that wound through the steep valley, amid the growing traffic of civilians seeking refuge further south. It was not long before the hills closed in on either side and as they rounded a bend where the road came to its narrowest, they found the 1st Australian Anti-tank Regiment placing their forward guns high up on the hillsides. It was these they were here to support.

While their superiors briefly discussed the general plan, Richard and the other Rangers chatted with the Australian gunners, exchanging news and banter as the train of refugees spilled past them along the road. It would not be long they realised, looking back up the road, before the traffic would be of a very different nature. They had little time to dwell on it, however, as the orders were soon given. Any mechanised assault from the enemy would have no other option but to use this road through the pass. Looking back in the direction of Vevi, their positions were agreed upon.

Two companies of the Rangers took the left flank of the pass. Climbing up the foot-slopes past the guns they pushed forward, high along the ridge that curled above the bend of the road ahead, overlooking the route they had just travelled.

Richard's company took the right flank, again climbing high up, but concentrating on the pass itself. There was precious little natural cover on the steep hillsides, but Richard had spotted the bush from below and on closer inspection found the hollow of its gnarled roots that clung to the rocky hillside provided him with a decent brace to keep watch through the coarse foliage. He settled in, wondering as time slipped by just how long he might have to stay there.

On the road down below, the steady stream of displaced humanity wearily trudged by. Mostly on foot, sometimes leading mules or donkeys, laden with whatever they had time to collect, they pressed resolutely on. Now and then, a horse-drawn wagon or caravan would pass, and as the beasts struggled to haul their heavy loads over the unmade road, so chairs, tables, and all manner of household goods joined the detritus of abandoned handcarts, perambulators, and the like that lay strewn along the roadside.

Rarer still were the occasional truck or antiquated car, their suspensions straining to carry opportunists clinging to running boards or perched on cab roofs. At first they had been mostly Yugoslavs fleeing their homelands. Now many Greek families swelled their numbers and the odd straggle of retiring Greek soldiers with antiquated mortars lashed to mules and bullock-drawn gun carts bore witness to the rapidity of the German advance. Their preparations in place, they could do little more than dig in and wait. With night came more snow, and brief, uneasy snatches of sleep.

And so came the dawn, with the sleety drizzle that had penetrated both his slumbers and his clothing. Peering ahead Richard could now make out once more the mountains looming in the distance. Further up the hillside to his right, he could see Stan, tucked into the rocky outcrop, scanning the murk ahead. All quiet so far. From behind, lower down, he could just catch Don's sporadic muttered curses, while on the road below them the motley trail of refugees had thinned to a trickle.

A tiny waft of smoke caught Richard's eye on the opposite hillside. One of his number he knew was sneaking a crafty, last minute fag.

Low rumbles of complaint from his stomach reminded him that aside from being half frozen from the all-night vigil, he was now extremely hungry. Remembering the kindly Greek woman he had met the previous day, he reached inside his jacket pocket. The eggs were now a jumble of broken shell fragments still clinging to their scattered contents. Even so he enjoyed the welcome breakfast, patiently picking the tiny pieces of shell away from the thankfully, hard boiled eggs.

Almost breaking his teeth on the rock hard bread, he gathered some snow that blanketed the bush and nursing it and the bread together under cover of his cape, encouraged the one to melt and soften the other. It chilled his fingers to the bone but was worth the effort.

'*Paximadia*!' Now he had another word to add to his meagre Greek vocabulary.

Up to his right, he noticed Stan stiffen a moment before setting aside his field glasses and training his rifle ahead. Was this it? The approaching rattle of the engine that had first alerted Stan, now reached Richard's ears as well. He steadied himself. This would be his first experience of combat. Eyes fixed on Stan, he waited for a signal. Stan's eyes in turn were trained on the forward left company, dug in on the opposite hillside. Further forward, it would be they who would get first sight around the bend of the winding road ahead. The hum of the motor engine grew and was soon accompanied by another of different tone.

Before long the sound became an ominous chorus. Richard glanced briefly back down below. The stragglers on the road had heard the approach as well and one by one they now melted into the hillsides. The Australians guarding the road pulled over a barricade and took up their positions behind. Others climbed up and forward, into the foot-slopes, to back up the Rangers. Richard steeled himself. The weeks of training and exercises were finally at an end.

The wind had picked up, now driving the sleet into his eyes. He saw Stan raise his field glasses again, focused across the divide. From the sound of the engines, they must be almost at the bend ahead. Sure enough, Stan turned and signalled down to him. But it was not the signal he had been expecting. Relaying it in turn down to Don, they both watched as two of their own armoured patrols returned from reconnaissance — one New Zealand, one British.

After a brief exchange of conversation, the barricade was drawn aside and the patrols disappeared behind it heading down to HQ. With the barricade left aside, the band of refugees hastily reappeared from the hillsides and continued on their way, wary of being left behind. No move, however, was made to replace the roadblock and a trickle of new stragglers began to appear. Richard relaxed a little, amid a curious mix of feelings: relief, on the one hand, while on the other lay an uneasy sense of disappointment, of not having got it over with.

'Looks like we've got a bit of a breather still,' Don called up to him. 'Why don't you nip down and see what's going on? I'll keep an eye on Stan.'

In half a mind to tell Don to 'bloody well do it himself,' Richard decided that he would welcome the chance to stretch his legs and warm up a little. Climbing up first to check with Stan, he then slithered back down and slipped past Don.

'Bring us back a cuppa!'

'Fat chance!' Richard made sure his retort was loud enough to warn the Australians below of his imminent arrival. The last thing he wanted was to end up skewered on an Aussie bayonet for want of a password. Instead he was greeted with a cheerful,

'Going walk-about mate?'

'What's the news?'

'Jerry's definitely on his way! Reckon we've still got another couple of hours yet. Have a word with Mick ... bombardier over there ... he spoke to them,' the Australian nodded towards his countryman leaning on the barricade.

As Richard crossed the road, he saw a familiar face appearing from the bushes on the opposite slope behind the bombardier. It was another Ranger obviously on a similar quest for news to relay to his flank. When the Ranger made his final descent, slithering down through the loose scree, the startled Australian bombardier spun round.

'It's alright ... one of ours,' Richard reassured him.

The news the bombardier gave them was in essence exactly what he had already been told — the Germans were indeed on their way. The patrol had run into two motorcyclists sent forward from the head of the main column of tanks and motorised troop carriers that was coming their way. They were keeping the road open for another hour or so to allow the last few stragglers through, but then it would be barricaded.

'Our boys have already laid a few surprises for Jerry up ahead,' he explained. 'And your lads are going to blow the road once we've shut up shop.'

Suddenly a shout from the road caught their attention and all three turned to see a lone Greek soldier among a small cluster of refugees levelling his pistol at one beside him. Those in front hurried on, while the queue behind recoiled, forcing the horse-drawn wagon right behind them to halt with an abrupt slither as the driver hauled back on the reins, prompting bitter complaints from the horse, whose clattering hooves struggled to hold back the impetus of the wagon, scattering those directly in its path.

Finally at a standstill, the horse pawed uneasily in its shafts, just behind the two men left alone in the middle of the road, its nostrils pumping wreaths of steam about them in the chill morning air.

The Greek soldier stepped aside a little from the other man, his pistol still firmly aimed at the other's chest. Barking out commands in his native tongue he gesticulated wildly at the other man, and as he realised his words were not understood, entreated those around him to recognise the threat. For his part, the refugee shrugged his own ignorance and made as if to move on but was halted by the tone of the Greek's latest outburst, which all understood. He was about to fire.

Within a moment, a ring of Australian gunners had formed, weapons now also drawn, entreating the Greek soldier to lower his own. He slowly raised his other hand to show his acknowledgment, then pointed down at the other man's feet. Their gaze, having already taken in the traveller's bedraggled attire, passed on down from his blanket-swathed body to the baggy, nondescript trousers, there to settle on the stout, black jackboots he wore.

Jerking his arms aloft in response to a vigorous prod of a bayonet, the ragged blanket he had gathered around him slid to the ground. Another probe to the tightly buttoned shirt below revealed the uniform of the German scout concealed beneath. The infiltrator was rapidly stripped of his disguise before being disarmed and led back for questioning, as also, much to his disgust, was the observant Greek soldier.

'It'll be fine,' reassured the Australians, but 'they had to check.'

Richard chuckled with the other two, as the steady torrent of the Greek's outrage faded into the distance. 'Time to get back.' He gave a nod to the other Ranger, who began to pick his way back up the slope.

The disrupted train of refugees now began to move once more and Richard waited for the covered wagon to pass, oblivious to the earnest sideways glance the driver directed at him as he slowly eased the horse on. As he started to cross behind the wagon, a canvas flap to the rear was flung open, the loose rope tie lashing into his face. Cursing, he caught hold of the flailing rope and looked up into the wagon.

The sight of a figure about to leap out from the rear momentarily startled both parties. Each froze for a second. The figure inside had not expected anyone to be crossing in between and hesitated for a split second more, assessing the obstacle to his freedom before resolving to leap upon Richard in any case. That split second gave Richard a chance to sling his rifle around in an effort to protect himself, but as the figure crashed down upon him, he felt the side of the rifle-butt smash hard into his cheekbone before the wind was knocked out of him, landing on his back with the man on top of him.

Pinioned by the weight, Richard struggled desperately as his assailant tried to seize the rifle, grinding the butt hard into his face again. He felt the cold steel of the bolt cut into his windpipe as the rifle was forced down across his throat. The man had a grip at either end of the weapon and his efforts to push the rifle back up were in vain. Instinctively he brought his knee up into his opponent's groin and the moment of surprise allowed him to loosen the stranglehold enough to force a return swipe with the rifle butt.

Suddenly the grip loosened altogether, and he could see from the man's eyes, as they shot upwards, that he was no longer the sole focus of his attention. Two Australian gunners appeared above him, hoisting the assailant up.

'That sure put his balls in a knot, mate!' The bombardier he had been talking to at the barricade now hauled him up as well, as the two gunners unmasked their second prisoner of the day.

Richard met the steel-grey gaze of the German soldier's eyes once more, now standing face to face. They were of similar age. A wry smile spread across his opponent's face as each looked the other over; both reluctant to acknowledge any discomfort from their injuries. Richard readjusted his uniform, while the fair-haired soldier epitome of the Aryan ideal, arms held casually aloft, patiently allowed himself to be disarmed and searched, as unruffled as if he were at his tailor's being fitted for a suit. Noticing the bombardier's interest in the insignia of his uniform, he proudly satisfied the Australian's curiosity.

'*Erste Liebstandarte SS Adolf Hitler.*' before adding in impeccable English, 'You may perhaps have heard of our division?'

'I couldn't give a tinkers' cuss, Adolf!' The bombardier nodded to his men to take the prisoner back. 'It's the end of the line for you anyway!'

'Oh … I shall be reboarding the train sooner than you think,' he parried, with an unsettling nonchalance before being hustled away.

The covers of the wagon were thrown back for a full search, but only the terrified faces of women and children appeared. Behind them, the driver's face was one of exhausted relief. The Australian bombardier turned back to Richard.

'You alright?'

'Yes thanks, fine,' Richard nodded. In truth, he felt far from it. 'I'd better get back.' He held his hand out in thanks to the bombardier. 'Richard.'

The Australian grinned and pumped his hand vigorously. 'Alan. Now bugger off, before you get into more trouble!'

Richard was happy to take his advice and headed back up the hillside, pausing to give Don news of the German approach, before passing it up the line. Settling back into his position at the now welcome if sparse shelter of the bush, he reflected on his first encounter with the enemy — which had not been as he had expected — through the sights of his rifle.

FOUR

Catherine glanced down at Ellie, nursing quietly now at her breast. The urgency of her demands was passing, and contentment would soon bring sleep. At eleven months her daughter was all but weaned, yet there were still moments when no other comfort would suffice. This had been one of them and had been expected. Through all the last-minute preparations — the taxi, booked in advance and still forty minutes late — the stomach-churning race to Heathrow, checking in just in time, only to be informed of flight delay. Ellie had viewed all this with quiet interest, her grey-blue eyes straining to focus on all these new and busy sights.

Even take-off, which Catherine had felt sure would be the final straw had passed without complaint. But then as the tedium of the flight wore on, the long-awaited storm had arrived. Catherine had slowly worked through her flight bag, packed in anticipation of this with a wide assortment of carefully planned distractions, but all were in vain. Ellie knew what she wanted and both parties considered she had earned it. In any case Catherine was happy to oblige. Not every woman she knew found the experience enjoyable, but it gave her a deep pleasure to feed her child. It was a feeling she knew she would miss in time.

One of the stewardesses hurrying to a call at the rear of the plane, still found time to pause briefly, for a wistful glance at the pair before continuing with her duties. A familiar surge of pride filled her, also bringing a sense of reassurance, for not every member of the crew had viewed them so warmly. Not that she was likely to lose any sleep over their opinions. Tucked away in her window seat, no one was obliged to pay them any interest.

The captain's announcement interrupted the piped music, prompting her to peer out of the window. True to his word, they were indeed passing over the Alps. She watched them for a while, far below, appearing and disappearing again through each flurry of cloud that rolled off the silvery wing. Ellie had now finally succumbed to her exhaustion, and untangling her still-clenched, tiny fist from her hair, Catherine smoothed her daughter's own wispy locks and settled her for sleep.

Easing her seat gently back, Ellie squirmed briefly before burying herself into Catherine's embrace. Her duties fulfilled, Catherine was free to ponder once more why it was that she was now several thousand feet up in the air on a plane bound for Crete, when her desk at home was still groaning with unfinished assignments. She turned to look at the culprit beside her, but found that Diane, like Ellie, was also asleep.

Taking advantage of the opportunity, she studied her mother's face for a moment or two, conscious of the fact that she so seldom took the time to step back from life's continual demands and really look. She had aged, of course, but some strain seemed to etch its mark there far more than age itself, which had generally been kind to her. A drawn, pained look permeated even her sleep, if indeed she truly was asleep. Catherine knew of old her mother's habit of feigning sleep if she needed time to think things over.

She wondered what thoughts filled her mind now and pushed aside her own fears that perhaps there was some illness? Her mother was so active. Whatever it was that troubled her, she felt sure that in some way this trip was part of it. It had been so uncharacteristic of her to suddenly announce that she had booked a last-minute trip to Crete for the three of them. Ordinarily, her mother would have everything planned months in advance, down to the very last detail. This had come completely out of the blue.

Ostensibly the trip was for Catherine's benefit. A respite, an escape from all her worries, a chance to put the breakup with Robert firmly behind her. She gave Ellie an involuntary squeeze and pushed Robert from her mind before the floodgates could open. Perhaps that was all there was to it. Her mother was simply troubled by their break-up, though she had dealt with it all remarkably calmly so far. 'Crete,' she had explained — not altogether convincingly — had always held a fascination for her, but most importantly the holiday would do Catherine 'a world of good.' Strangely, there had been no question of her father coming with them. 'He's too busy,' had been her mother's only comment, though Catherine knew that to be untrue.

An idle thought crept through her mind that perhaps her parents were also experiencing difficulties in their own relationship. It seemed unlikely, but who was to know? Inevitably, such a train of thought brought her full circle to Robert. He was never far from her thoughts. Even after so much pain and bitterness, the simplest recollections of their time together could evoke such strong emotions within her. Predominant among these now was a desperate sense of futility, knowing she could only choke back the tears their remembered joy gave rise to.

Ellie wriggled in her lap, a sleepy complaint telling of her discomfiture. Engrossed in her thoughts, Catherine hadn't realised how tightly she was hugging her daughter. Relaxing her grip she settled her, watching until sleep once more calmed her face. Robert's face. Everyone said so. There was no forgetting.

At thirty-six and with eight years of what had seemed a rock-solid relationship behind her, Catherine had been unable to delay the longed-for conception of her child any longer. Though they had never married, they had always been sure that they would have children, but later. One by one the years slipped by. They had been good years, and she had no complaints.

As a freelance graphic designer, she had built up a strong clientele over the years and even though the closed shop squeeze of the print unions had meant the loss of some of her contracts, the demand for her services was such that she often had to burn the midnight oil. She enjoyed the work, which also occupied her during the times when Robert would be away on location, which as a lighting rigger on film productions was more often than not.

At first she hated being parted from him and often forsook her own commitments to travel with him, but then as time went by, she found the periods of separation kept a freshness, a keen edge of wanting in their relationship. Of all the moments in their time together, his returns were the clearest for her — dawns on station platforms, waiting for the night sleeper to arrive — or meeting rigging trucks on their weary journeys back to London late into the night. Candlelit homecomings for a precious day or two, before work called once more.

These and the memories of a score of halfway houses were milestones in the course of the relationship for her. Every so often in the breaks between productions they would talk of the future together — of a farmhouse somewhere — of the family they would have, but the time was never right. There was always another film to be shot. 'Later … later.' The word had rung through Catherine's ears a hundred times. And with each hearing her anxiety grew. How much later could she leave it?

At first, she had ignored the plethora of friendly advice and endless magazine articles that warned against delaying too long. Then, insidiously, their arguments had begun to take hold: the longer she left it, the greater the odds might be against a problem-free birth. But most telling of all had been the yearning deep inside her that would no longer be quelled.

Their discussions deteriorated into arguments. She even pleaded with him. For nothing else had she stripped herself so bare of self-respect.

Finally, she had made her decision. Confident that she could take care of the child without interference to his career — convincing herself also that once she was pregnant, he too would welcome the prospect of a new life — she waited only for the right moment. With their special meaning for her, she had wanted it to happen on one of his returns and persuading him against arriving at an unpropitious time with excuses of extra work, she had steered a return visit towards the moment that suited her best.

It had been some time since she had taken so much trouble for one of his homecomings. Fond memories of past occasions sped her through the chores in anticipation of this special return. The candles alight, the food prepared, she chose a flimsy white cotton voile dress, dispensing with any underwear that interrupted its light hold on the contours of her body.

Smoothing her dress, she wondered if perhaps she was being too obvious. Its transparency left little to the imagination. But then she had never been backward at coming forward, as her mother had often reminded her. She turned her attention to her hair, deciding to wear it up for the evening. Robert, she remembered, had made appreciative noises the last time she had done so. She had good hair, though to her mind its colour left something to be desired. Robert referred to it as ash-blonde. She was happy enough not to contradict him. Choosing a necklace that drew attention to her cleavage, she just had time to fasten it before Robert's arrival.

Though earlier than she had expected, having caught a lift with another of the crew, he looked nevertheless tired and drawn from the journey. He had headed straight for the drinks cabinet oblivious to her charms. Undeterred Catherine had pressed on with the dinner. Robert had seemed unusually preoccupied with his thoughts. Twice she had asked what was troubling him and only after some lengthy consideration at the second asking had he seemed ready to unburden himself, but then had thought better of it, and turned his attentions to her instead.

That he was about to remedy his neglect of her was sufficient for her to press him no further on the subject of his problems. And indeed, the frenzied passion of his lovemaking that followed seemed to exorcise whatever haunted his thoughts.

When Catherine's doctor finally confirmed her hopes, she broke the news to Robert. In all the anxious weeks of waiting she had imagined his every reaction. From the unlikely, but still she hoped possible, melting tenderness of the father to be, to the outrage of the tricked man — her imaginings had ranged the spectrum of his possible moods, yet what she had not expected was the curious depression with which the news affected him.

The long-awaited arguments followed, but her oft rehearsed assurances fell on deaf ears. It was his turn to plead. 'This was not the time. She must do something about it.' But she had resolved at the outset that she would never resort to that. Her resolve still held, when three weeks later he left. By then the truth had come out — it was no longer just a question of the baby — there was someone else — and had been for some while. Her world fell apart.

'Come on darling, leave Richard behind.' Her mother's voice broke Catherine's train of thought. Opening her eyes, she now found herself the one under observation.

Her mother smoothed away the furrows that had begun to knit her brow. Catherine smiled and closed her eyes again, relaxing to the gentle ministrations, but something nagging in her mind would not let her succumb. Suddenly it flashed onto her lips, 'Richard!'

'What darling?'

'You said Richard.'

'Did I? How silly, you know I meant Robert. Now you really must try not to dwell in the past. What's done is done. You have to think of the future.'

Catherine closed her eyes once more under the onslaught of good advice. Diane, however, continued to liberally dispense her platitudes until quite sure that her daughter was thoroughly fed up with the subject. She had let her guard slip and was now desperate to paper over the cracks. God knows her daughter had problems enough of her own without her mother adding to her burdens.

It was hardly surprising though, that she had mentioned Richard's name. Her thoughts had been filled with nothing else since seeing that newspaper. She must be more careful. Ellie was once again occupying her daughter's attentions. The mistake had, she hoped, been forgotten.

Thankfully their arrival at Athens airport soon gave them both plenty to think about as they joined the scramble to retrieve their cases for the transfer to domestic departures. Their delay in leaving London meant they had missed the connecting flight, and it was some while before they were reassured that they would be able to take a later one on to Crete.

Looking out from the glazed front of the airport terminal, Catherine spied a café across the road beyond the taxi ranks.

'If we've got a couple of hours to kill, that looks as good a place as any to do it.' She pointed out the rows of tables nestling under gaily coloured awnings.

'Looks fine ... but what about these?' Diane nodded towards their cases.

'We must be able to check them in now,' her daughter responded airily. Her confidence, however, seemed in danger of being proved unfounded as they quickly became embroiled in a lengthy argument at the counter. Only a well-timed complaint from Ellie saved the day.

'Well done my darling.' Catherine congratulated her daughter, as their baggage was reluctantly accepted ahead of time. 'It looks as if you're going to prove very useful. And to think your granny wanted me to leave you at home with boring old Aunt Alice.'

'I only wanted to make sure you get a decent rest. And your Aunt Alice wasn't so boring when she took care of Ellie while you and Robert tried to make a go of it again.'

Catherine winced at the memory of the disastrous weekend they had spent at one of their favourite halfway houses of the past: a small guest house in Gloucestershire. She had urged they try a reconciliation, but whatever fire had burnt between them in happier times, no warmth stirred in the cold ashes of that final visit.

'Not fair Mother,' she said, emerging from the cool of the airport building into the heat of the early afternoon sun. 'In any case, I thought we weren't talking about Richard?'

'Quite right dear.' Diane ignored the bait and proceeded to carve a path for herself through the taxi cabs, declining their offers, Catherine mused, with something of a regal air.

Their first foray onto Hellenic soil proved uneventful, as well they might have expected, watching the endless procession of taxis and their occupants. Airports and their environs were much the same wherever you went. Time nevertheless slipped by, and they found themselves once again being ferried out across the tarmac to board their flight.

As they disgorged from the crowded bus, Catherine deciphered the Greek script, painted on the nose of their plane.

'Ariadne.'

Both women recalled the sad tale of Ariadne and her misplaced affections, each now finding some separate significance in it that related to their own circumstances. Diane wondered whether the ball of thread she had grasped would indeed unravel itself to provide a solution for the predicament that now beset her. And would there be for Catherine, some Dionysus to rescue her from her abandonment? Hoisting Ellie astride her hip, she rather doubted it. The prospect of being carried off by some Mediterranean lover brought a smile to her lips nonetheless. But like her mother, she kept her thoughts to herself.

Once aboard, they began to sense the excitement of being in a foreign land. The smaller aircraft, packed now with locals, resounded with the unfamiliar rapid chatter of Greek. Airborne once more, Catherine eyed Ellie warily, but the flight was short, and they soon found themselves peering down at the scorched browns of the island of Crete. Their landing was smooth and troubled only by the steady drip of viscous liquid that had begun to issue from the overhead luggage stow of the seat in front of them.

As they came to a halt, the Greek executive upon whose smart, grey suit the liquid now spread its growing stain shot up issuing a stream of expletives. Stewardesses rushed to the scene. The man continued his diatribe. Fellow passengers began to throw in their own opinions and with the aisle now blocked, arguments began to erupt.

The woman in the neighbouring seat quietly stood up

— an elderly Greek widow dressed in the ubiquitous black of her permanent grief. She motioned for the man to sit and allow her access to the stow. Struggling with its weight, she withdrew a large plastic carrier bag. Lowering it onto the armrest of the executive's seat as he recoiled in noisy disgust, she then untied the ends with painful slowness to reveal the glistening plastic gallon can of olive oil she had brought with her. Indicating the leaky stopper, she gave a shrug of her shoulders that explained everything and, without further ado, made her way to the front of the aircraft to join the first of those disembarking, leaving the unfortunate businessman to complain in both Greek and English to any who would listen of the old woman's ignorance. 'Didn't she realise Crete was swimming in olive oil … why bring her own? *Peloponnese!*'

'Sounds a bit like a case of 'coals to Newcastle!' Diane helped Catherine gather the last stray belongings into Ellie's bag.

Their baggage regained, Catherine and Diane found that progress through customs was thankfully a speedy affair and once outside they had no difficulty finding their hotel bus. The driver insisted on making a fuss of Ellie. But after her strange and tiring day, Ellie was in no mood for foreign tongued babytalk and made her feelings abundantly clear.

Annoyed that her labours had been wasted and unsure whether the driver's real interest lay in Ellie or herself, Catherine whisked her child from under his nose, and stalked to the back of the bus. Her mother's expression confirmed the regret she instantly felt for her hasty reaction. She too was probably more tired than she realised. At any rate the driver seemed not to have taken any offence and was once more cheerfully stowing cases and guiding the rest of his passengers on board with broken snatches of English and German, or just the occasional self-explanatory gesture.

'Relax,' Diane said simply. But this was easier said than done; the bus was uncomfortably hot. Mercifully, they were soon on their way and a refreshing breeze from the driver's door — left open for the purpose — helped to cool tempers. Entering Heraklion, the bus paused in Eleftheria Square to collect other hotel guests. Catherine watched with amusement as the red necked tourists clambered aboard, some laden with the fruits of their shopping expeditions, others clad in beachwear, squealing as their raw legs met the hot plastic seats. Would she seem the same to others in another few days, she wondered? She hoped not but considered that doubtless each saw his or herself as the only lone intrepid traveller, surrounded by a throng of 'tourists.'

The driver, she noticed, had ambled across to the centre of the square where groups of tables and chairs were arranged underneath the plane trees. Waiters were skilfully negotiating the steady flow of encircling traffic that separated them from the surrounding cafes and tavernas, weaving their orders to and from the square. He was now cheerfully settled at a table, immersed in conversation with friends. Testily, she remarked on this to her mother.

'Whole different pace here honey,' confided the American lady who had seated herself behind them. 'Either you relax and enjoy it … or it drives you crazy!'

So, for the second time in the space of a few minutes she had been advised to take things more easily. There seemed nothing for it but to comply.

The driver soon returned, and they were once more on the coast road heading out of the centre. Looking back they could see the Venetian fortress that dominated the harbour basking in the late afternoon sun, the sandy stones now painted a dusky pink. The beauty of the scene aided the process of Catherine's relaxation, and this was helped further still when a short distance from the town they arrived at their hotel. The brochure had made great play of the tasteful design. Catherine tried to remember the wording. 'Fashioned in old whitewashed monastery style … the apartments nestle among gardens of near tropical splendour …' had been something like it. They had not been idle boasts and their rooms were no less disappointing. Both women felt that were it not for the growing pangs of hunger they could easily go straight to sleep.

'Funny how travel makes you so hungry,' Catherine noted a little later, ordering a dessert. They had opted for a meal in the hotel restaurant rather than travel back into town on their first night 'What have you got planned for tomorrow?'

'I don't know really … take it as it comes, I suppose,' Diane replied vaguely.

'Well, what things do you want to see?'

'Oh … I don't mind. The museum maybe … Knossos perhaps ….' Diane struggled to remember what other places of interest the brochure said Crete had to offer. Catherine had already realised that for someone who professed to have had a longstanding desire to visit Crete, her mother seemed to know precious little about the place. 'Anyway,' Diane continued, 'there'll be plenty of time to decide about all that. I really have had enough for one day. I think I'll turn in if you don't mind.'

'Of course not Mum. I'm going to do the same anyway.' Catherine decided not to pursue the matter. 'It'll be the beach for me first thing in the morning, I think. No sense in coming all this way and ignoring that beautiful sun.'

'Good idea. Look Cath, …' her mother paused awkwardly searching for the right words. 'Please do as you feel on this holiday. I don't want you to feel you're tied to me you know?'

'What's that supposed to mean?'

'Just what I say. I simply want you to feel free to do as you like.' Diane got up, ending the conversation. 'I'll see how I feel about the beach in the morning … you go ahead if I'm not up and about.'

But tired as she was, sleep did not come easily to Diane that night. The unaccustomed heat and unfamiliar bed did little to ease her mind's incessant quest for reconciliation: a resolution she had struggled with for three-and-a-half decades now. Only half-achieved at the outset, it had lain dormant all the while just beneath the surface, occasionally resurrected by some chance conversation or random memory, but now brought back into unquestionable immediacy by that damned earring! Was it possible — could he still be alive?

Sleep, when it finally came, still brought no respite: all too familiar dreams continued to twist and contort the real and the imagined, known and unknown, the pain and the ecstasy. And always surfacing above the maelstrom of emotions would remain the lingering sense of guilt and betrayal.

FIVE

The glint of sunlight piercing the tightly shuttered Cretan window eventually roused Diane from her troubled night's sleep. Shrugging off the rapidly fading fragments of her dreams, she checked her watch, surprised at the lateness of the hour given that she had already adjusted it for the time difference. Pulling back the shutters, she let the morning sun flood her room and took in her surroundings. Outside two gardeners went about their chores as a sprinkler lazily rotated, spurting erratic jets of sparkling gems across the broad leaved grass. A knock came at the door.

'Mum … are you awake?'

Diane chose not to reply.

'I'm taking Ellie down to the beach … see you later, alright?'

Diane waited until she heard Catherine's footsteps diminish along the corridor. It was nine-forty, she wound her watch and wondered how long Catherine might stay on the beach. Two or three hours at best maybe, probably much less. She could make a start, nevertheless.

In so short a time that she surprised even herself, Diane was ready and boarding the hotel bus for her trip into Heraklion. She had left word for Catherine at reception that she was visiting the shops and would return during the afternoon. She didn't relish the idea of deceiving her daughter, but hoped that perhaps once the day was through, the whole matter might be resolved, and she could devote her energies to her daughter and granddaughter once more.

Catherine had thought she would limit her first day's sunbathing to a couple of hours of the early morning and spare Ellie the fiercer warmth of the later sun. In the event it was Ellie who seemed quite content to continue raising her bare behind to the sun's rays, endeavouring for the hundredth time to eat sand, while Catherine was the one beginning to feel generally disgruntled in the heat.

Whether it was because of her fruitless attempts to keep Ellie under the shade with healthier things than sand for her digestion, or simply the unfamiliar heat that had tested Catherine's mood, she didn't know, but she suspected that beyond both of these factors, the truth lay in her unaccustomed idleness. Since Ellie's birth, there had hardly been a moment's rest. Now, with time on her hands, she found it difficult to relax and more difficult still to keep her mind free from thoughts she preferred to forget.

Gathering her belongings, she scooped up Ellie and decided to see if her mother was up and about yet. Not finding her in her room, Catherine decided she would probably be in the dining hall. But later, having showered and made Ellie respectable once more, she was unable to find her there or indeed anywhere else in the hotel grounds. Then she thought to check at the reception desk.

'Ah yes, there is a message from your mother. She has gone for shopping in Heraklion and will return this afternoon.'

Odd that she didn't wait, thought Catherine, as she thanked the receptionist, *she must have known I wouldn't stay long on the beach.* The prospect of a hotel lunch alone with Ellie didn't appeal — she had quit the beach for much the same reason and now felt in need of either company or diversion.

It was shortly after twelve and having no idea what time her mother intended returning, she decided to do the same and travel into town. If she ran into her mother, all well and good, if not she would look around herself — have some lunch perhaps. She was after all, as her mother had already taken pains to remind her, free to do as she pleased. Collecting Ellie's carry sling and sunhat, and throwing a few other necessities into her beach bag, Catherine rushed out just in time to catch the bus.

Knowing the bus would drop her in the main square, Catherine had decided to catch her breath at one of the tavernas she had seen the previous day. Seated now under the welcome shade of the trees, she viewed the scene from a very different perspective, watching with both amusement and admiration as the waiter emerged from the taverna opposite, a full tray held aloft on the one hand, a fistful of bottles in the other, barely pausing a moment before committing to his course through the swirling jumble of traffic, oblivious to all complaints. She half expected to see him hop on the rear of the circulating vehicles, like a fairground barker at the dodgems. It had taken some considerable time for her to make the same journey with Ellie.

The waiter began dispersing his orders then brought Catherine's to her table. She decided to settle the bill at once, so that she could be free to move on when she liked and familiarised herself with the various denominations of the drachmae notes she had exchanged. Feeling it had been too early for lunch, she had settled for tea and toast, but now regretted not being more adventurous as the toast proved to be a dry, toasted ham sandwich, while five minutes of prodding failed to extract any further colour from the tea bag that swam listlessly in the lukewarm cup. Best to leave England behind she decided, resolving to seek out local fare from now on.

A cool breeze blew through the plane trees, bringing with it a refreshing calm and for a while she was content just to sit and watch the world and his wife go by, but soon the itch of unaccustomed time on her hands grew too much to bear. It was time to explore.

Disentangling Ellie from her endeavours at peeling apart the remains of the sandwich, Catherine settled her into her carry sling, gathered up her bag, and took advantage of a lull in the traffic to dash back across the road. She had noticed a steady throng of people turning into one of the side roads that led off the square directly ahead of her. Away to the left, past a row of tavernas, she had also seen another less populated exit and decided to head for this, her general plan being to make a clockwise loop, to end up hopefully back at the square.

The road itself though a busy thoroughfare for traffic was less crowded with pedestrians, clearly the attractions of this route did not match that of the other. She was happy though to walk free of the crowds for a while, knowing that her planned route should bring her round eventually to whatever the main draw might be.

Walking had always been a source of relaxation for Catherine, and knowing there was nothing she could do about her unfinished assignments, she banished them from her mind and gave herself over to the enjoyment of her surroundings. She could see welcome greenery ahead and was soon presented with a choice of routes. She could either continue on the present road or take the right fork that skirted the open space. Feeling she ought not to venture too far afield on her first exploration, she opted for the latter, which also fitted her general plan. Her choice was soon rewarded as she came upon a thriving market area lining the triangular space that led into a busy street of tented stalls and shops. Catherine felt content now to join the throng of local shoppers and tourists: Ellie had already nodded off.

The stalls were a riot of colour — split watermelons, huge deformed tomatoes, hosts of exotic and unfamiliar fruits, myriad hues of tanned and untanned leather goods, bright clothes and beachwear — and interspersed among them, the mundane requisites of life everywhere, plus of course the inevitable profusion of postcards and souvenirs. Further down, as the street narrowed, butchers' shops vied with each other for attention, row upon row of chickens, hares and rabbits hung above the larger carcasses, the dressed cuts proudly displayed beneath.

The ripe odours of the meat and offal gave way to a medley of scents now emanating from several stalls that followed, where every imaginable herb or spice was laid out both loose and packeted amid profusions of nuts, sultanas, and other dried fruits. Bottles of local raki or ouzo nestled among them. Catherine paused awhile, content for the moment just to breathe in the spice laden air, heavy with cinnamon and nutmeg, before a murmur of wind supplanted the heady mix with fresh aromas of thyme and sage.

Arriving at a busy junction at the end of the street, she guessed that the main road to her right would be the one leading back to the square, but from across the road, the tantalising smell of roasting meat carried her eye to a small stall.

Halted temporarily by the indignant whistle of a traffic policeman as she tried to cross against the busy stream, she waited with the growing huddle of people until the lights changed, before crossing and joining a small queue that had formed at the stall.

She watched as those before her were served — the stallholder slicing thick chunks from the spit into a doughy, circular pitta, before topping it with fresh salad and a creamy yoghourt dressing, deftly twisting the contents into a paper cornet. Content to order the same, she strolled on, looking for somewhere to sit and enjoy her first *gyropita*.

Coming upon the first place she actually recognised from the brochure, *Liontaria*, Lion Square, Catherine settled by the eponymous, if sadly dry, fountains. She counted her blessings that Ellie was still fast asleep and she would therefore be able to enjoy her feast in peace. Assessing her surroundings at leisure, she wondered why the brochure had insisted on calling it a square, since its shape was plainly triangular. *Place*, she concluded, obviously did not carry the same ring in English as its French counterpart, which seemed the closest equivalent to the Greek sign she guessed to be *Platea.*

Idly watching the steady flow of tourists milling in and out of the shops and tavernas, Catherine satisfied the hunger that had crept up on her until, savouring the last salty mouthful, she spotted her mother among a huddle of tourists heading towards her from the apex formed by the diminishing rows of tavernas ahead. She watched as Diane stopped now outside a small bookstore. It looked as if she was asking for directions — referring several times to a piece of paper she held. Seemingly getting no satisfaction, she moved on to the next shop. Catherine was about to call out to her, when her view was blocked by someone's presence.

'*Yassou!*'

Peering up into the man's face, she was forced to squint against the harsh aura of sunlight behind him.

'I'm sorry. Did I frighten you?'

Catherine realised that the combination of her squinting and the total incomprehension of who was addressing her must have formed quite an alarming picture.

'My name is Antonis …'

The voice was vaguely familiar, but still no bells rang.

'From the hotel … your driver?'

Now she remembered. It was the poor man she had so rudely snatched Ellie from the previous evening. It had been a different driver on the bus today.

'Oh yes … hello. I'm sorry, I didn't recognise you.' She declined his hand with an embarrassed display of the greasy serviette and wrapper she was still clutching.

'It is very hot here in the open. Perhaps you would like something to drink?' He gestured towards the shaded tables of a nearby taverna. The thought was tempting, but Catherine's eyes were rapidly searching for her mother, who was no longer to be seen.

'What? Oh, no I'm sorry I can't … it's my mother … she's gone!' With that, she darted off in the direction of Diane's last stop. Turning briefly, she shouted a final apology to the bewildered man, before pressing on with her search.

'He must think I'm mad,' she muttered, as much to herself as Ellie, who was beginning to stir from her slumbers.

Checking one shop after another proved fruitless until, entering an arcade to her left, she caught sight of her mother again — at the opposite end — emerging from its dark confines into the brilliant sunshine of the main street. With a shock she also realised that her mother was not alone. The man now standing with her was trying to hail a taxi. Moving slowly through the arcade, Catherine continued to watch as he opted for a better chance across the busy road, ushering Diane through the traffic with a solicitous steer of her elbow.

Reaching the end of the arcade, Catherine resisted the urge to shout out to her mother and she hovered awhile instead in the shadowed entrance, unsure of what she should do. She didn't know what to make of it all and suddenly felt incredibly guilty at spying on her own mother.

Pretending to examine the contents of the corner shop window at her side, she backed out a little into the street, gazing blankly at the displays of glassware, her attention instead focused on the reflection of her mother and her mysterious companion mirrored upon the pane. She saw the taxi pull up and a thousand thoughts raced through her mind as she tried in vain to piece together the ill-fitting jigsaw. Was the paper her mother held just the travel brochure? Did she simply want to get back to the hotel? If so, why was the man now getting into the taxi with her?

From her manner, it didn't seem as if her mother was being abducted. Catherine didn't know what to think, but Ellie now fully awake gave full voice to her own needs, and before Catherine could make any further decision, the taxi sped off, leaving her feeling hot, bothered, and very foolish.

Later that afternoon as Catherine lay resting on her bed, she heard her mother's door being unlocked and closed. Leaving Ellie to her slumbers, she tiptoed out and knocked hesitantly upon the door. There was no reply. She knocked harder and called out as loud as she dared without waking Ellie. Her mother's voice greeted her at last, reassuringly.

'I'm in the shower darling … won't be a minute. Door's not locked.'

'Well, it should be!' Catherine muttered, letting herself in. She sat down on the bed to wait, saying nothing more, content for the moment in her relief that her mother was back safely.

Diane's bag lay on the bed. Protruding from it was the paper Catherine had seen her mother referring to earlier; clearly now, a folded page from a newspaper. Unable to resist the temptation, she withdrew the page and unfolded it, noting its familiarity as the Evening News from barely more than a week ago. It would have taken no great feat of further detection to establish which article was of interest to her mother even had Diane not underlined two names. Catherine read for herself about the donation of the golden earring to the Heraklion Archaeological Museum. Her mother had underlined both the donor's name and an official of the Antiquities Department who had supervised the transfer to the museum.

What Catherine had hoped might be the answer to her mother's mysterious behaviour served now only to further confuse her. Her mother had never shown more than the normal passing interest in archaeology or antique jewellery, and she had never heard of either of the two men. What did it all mean? Her mother appeared at the door, towelling wet hair.

'Did you see how prettily the maid has arranged my nightdress?' Diane saw that her daughter had found more to interest her than the carefully arranged nightdress, pleated into a fan upon her pillow. Catherine still said nothing but sat patiently awaiting an explanation: the newspaper article an open accusation upon her lap. Diane vigorously resumed the drying of her hair. 'Did you enjoy the beach darling?' She struggled to keep up an air of normality.

'Heraklion was far more intriguing,' Catherine replied drily.

'Heraklion? Yes … isn't it an interesting place? I found it fascinating, time just flew by.'

'Oh, come off it mother. I want to know what's going on … and for heaven's sake stop drying your damned hair … you'll pull out what little you've got left!' Despite the instant regret she felt for the unkind remark, Catherine pursued the matter. 'Who was the man you got into the taxi with this afternoon?'

Diane said nothing, desperately trying to assess just how much her daughter knew or suspected. What could she say?

'I want to know,' Catherine insisted grimly.

'He is a cousin of Michaelis Serides.'

'Michaelis who?'

'Michaelis Serides … the man in the article. I assumed you'd read it. He's the one who found that earring.'

'Then you've never met him before … the man in the taxi?'

'No ….' Diane noticed her daughter visibly relax a little, though her puzzled look remained. 'Oh darling … you didn't think … that he and I …?

'I didn't know what to think. I still don't.'

Diane saw that the pressure was not yet off her. 'I was trying to find Mr Serides … instead I found his cousin and he offered to take me to see him.'

'And …?'

'And nothing. We didn't find him. He runs a night club. He'll be there tonight.'

'And you're going to see him … why?'

'I … it's a family matter Cath …' Diane struggled on despite her daughter's snort of derision at her own ill-concealed prevarication. 'I truly can't explain more now, but I promise you I will soon. Please believe me when I tell you that there really is nothing for you to worry about … I'm not in any trouble … nor am I planning to leave your father.'

'Does he know about this?'

'Yes.'

'Then why can't you tell me? In case you hadn't noticed I stopped wearing gymslips and pigtails quite a few years ago.' Failing to draw anything further from her mother, Catherine pursued the inquisition, 'You've never met either of these men before?'

'No.'

'Then what's your interest in this earring? You know nothing about archaeology.'

'I've told you already Cath, I'll explain everything to you when I know the answers myself. Now I'm sorry, but that's all I intend to say about the matter.' The argument had at last reached its stalemate and both women felt somewhat relieved to hear Ellie's complaints from the adjoining room — like a bell her cries brought the round to an end. Catherine paused in the doorway. 'I'm coming with you tonight!' she announced before smartly closing the door on any possible reply.

SIX

Such a short span of time, yet he had journeyed so far. Richard could now scarcely recognise the mere boy who had scuffled with the German scout on the Klidi Pass road barely two weeks ago. Battered, bloodied, and now burdened by his own blood-stained hands, three-hundred-and-fifty tortuous miles of rearguard fighting lay behind. But as many miles as might lay ahead, Richard would forever struggle to recognise the stranger's eyes he now saw mirrored with each and every new day.

From the outset, it had been a pattern of holding positions, delaying the enemy for as long and as dearly as possible until one fighting withdrawal after another saw successive lines give way under impossible odds. With only a handful of planes and unfinished airfields to give fighter protection, the RAF fought until there was nothing left to fly, leaving the Luftwaffe to cruise the skies at will, bombing every position and strafing every column they could find. The screaming sirens of the Stuka dive bombers had been constant and deadly companions. Their banshee wail echoed still in Richard's ears. Gaping yellow beaks of gaudily painted engine cowlings and thrusting undercarriage claws swooping down upon them, ever present by day, returned again to plague his dreams in what little sleep there was to be found at night.

There had been moments of pride — even elation — amid the terror and revulsion as he had acquitted himself with the Rangers, but it had been difficult not to eventually succumb to the constant fatigue and general mood of demoralisation as the rearguard fighting eventually became cover only for the inevitable evacuation, leaving a trail of shattered and abandoned equipment strewn in its wake, as weary soldiers now followed in the footsteps of the refugees fleeing south before them.

Provosts and Military Police — usually avoided — now became welcome saviours as their hurricane lamps guided their paths through the night: 'First in, last out!' their motto. Soon what little transport was left carried only wounded. The fate of the ill-starred British Expeditionary Force now lay in the hands of the Royal Navy. Ships that had brought them from Egypt only a matter of weeks before would now have to run the gauntlet once again to evacuate them from the beaches and harbours around Athens.

As dusk finally brought respite from the aerial attacks, Richard had left the sheltering olive groves to join the columns of men winding down to the evacuation beaches. Naval beach masters organised the men into orderly queues — some bound for the quayside some for the beaches — in order to get as many men away as possible in the cover of darkness.

Finding himself directed to the beach at Rafina, where amid the acrid stench of diesel fumes, he witnessed the engines of trucks, transports, and a solitary light tank whose tracks had not already been shattered on the rocky roads now being destroyed. The high-pitched racing of engines battled with a cacophony of metallic clanging as weapons were rendered useless, until the sand that had been poured into fuel tanks finally brought the screaming engines to a smoking, shuddering halt.

This they learnt was now the third night of evacuations. There might not be another. The ships would not arrive until after dark and had to be away well before dawn to keep out of the Luftwaffe's reach. Failure to do so had already cost some dearly. The flickering glow now tingeing the evening sky over the nearby harbour bore witness to their deadly aim. There would be no time to load equipment, hence the destruction. Personal arms only. No materiel to take precedence over men.

Richard surveyed the wreckage about him. Vehicles that had been nursed for so many miles — equipment that had been in such woefully short supply were now cast aside. And what of the men — how many of them would not return? Only a handful of his company stood with him now. How many more from how many nations would there be? Gunfire in the distance behind reminded him of those still holding off the advance. What chance for them? What had it all been for?

As darkness set in, so the chatter began to subside among the assembled groups of waiting men, most simply grateful to rest awhile under the inky, moonless sky lulled by the rhythmic pulse of waves on shore below them. Eventually a stirring of men spread up the beach and everyone made ready as the subdued motors of approaching landing craft slowly became audible. Hidden along the coast by day, they now emerged to ferry the men out to the waiting ships, whose stealthy arrival now found them anchored a mile or so out in deeper waters. The naval beach masters took charge once more, marshalling groups down to the craft.

Advancing in fits and starts, Richard finally found himself at the water's edge, only to watch the last of the craft head out across the swell into the darkness. A general anxiety spread through the gathered men, until a degree of calm was regained by assurances from the beach master that they would be back for more.

Time dragged by however and distant explosions triggered further speculation as to whether they were fuel dump disposals or imminent, unwelcome company. Again the beach master tried to ease tensions, explaining that the heavy ground swell out by the ships meant it would take some time to get everyone up and aboard.

'Just be ready,' he warned, 'toss your rifles up first … wait for her to lift … then jump for the ropes!'

Richard had little time to ponder on these instructions, however, as the returning craft began to appear from the darkness gliding as gracefully as boxes can to a halt on the shore in front of them.

The ramps lowered, and men scrambled aboard, past the bulkhead and into the well of the craft. Moving quickly along by the central bench, Richard took a seat tucked under the overhang of the deck. In a matter of moments, the craft was full, the ramp raised, and they were slapping out across the waves.

Before long the familiar form of a Glen ship loomed clear and large before them. Small fishing boats and caiques now also became visible, bobbing alongside the giant, bringing still more men from the harbour. Finally — lurching alongside — it was time to put the beach master's advice into practice.

Ropes snaked up above them towards an open hatch in the hull, from which, further short wooden ladders were fixed. Richard could see now why he had to wait for the landing craft to rise on the swell — a well-timed jump would get you to the ladder — get it wrong and you just had the ropes.

'Rifle first!' came the cry from the bluecoat above.

Up went the rifle — Richard waited for the lift — but as it came, so the craft began to swing away from the ship. He hesitated for a second.

'Go! Go! Go!'

He leapt for the ladder, feeling the deck of the craft pushing out further still. His right hand just caught the bottom rung — the left missed — hitting hard into the hull. He struggled to hold onto the slippery rung. Having insufficient grip with the one hand to swing his other arm up, he struggled to catch one of the nearby swinging ropes.

Desperately clutching on to one with his left hand, he fought to steady himself, boots clattering against the hull, until finally he was able to get a firmer grasp on the wooden ladder.

Looking down at the giddy swell below, he saw the landing craft slap up against the hull again beneath him, and swiftly putting aside thoughts of what might have happened had he missed the ladder he scrambled up to safety.

SEVEN

Waking with a start, Richard lifted his head from the cradle of his arms and blearily took in his surroundings. The mess deck was crammed with battle-weary men. Like him, most had fallen into an exhausted sleep wedged together at the tables. At their feet, those not lucky enough to have found a space on the benches filled the gaps in between. A sickly tang of burning rubber and diesel still clung to the back of his throat, its stench lingering on in his battledress.

The burning pyres and wreckage they had left behind dwelt on in his mind, subduing the harsher and more painful memories of bloodshed, terror, and loss. Memories that would emerge much later, pulled out by chance, like stitches from a half-healed wound.

Trying with little success to ease the ache in his back, as neighbouring grunts of complaint persuaded him to give up the attempt, he settled his head back down again, grateful at least to succumb once more to the snug warmth and general torpor that surrounded him. The constant drone of the ship's engines deep below, resonated through the table, lulling him briefly back to sleep: their throb, like some mighty pulsating heartbeat, urging them on in their flight from Greece. But it was not long before remnants of a never-ending nightmare soon began to steal back into this fitful sleep and, lingering once more on the borders of waking, he looked to replace them with more comforting memories.

Diane of course was never far from his thoughts, but even these were somehow troubled. Picturing her now, as she had stood by his side in St. Mary's, he struggled to see the face behind the veil. All else he could remember with complete clarity. It was a moment he knew he would never forget. But his memory, like the church that contained it, was imbued with a strange, indefinable coolness — there was an appreciation of the beauty of the moment, yet it lacked passion. Passion there certainly had been in the days that had followed. Exultation even, as the years of adolescent frustration they had shared found exquisite release.

He had marvelled, as his new bride had lain asleep by his side, that it had been he and not Eddie she had chosen. He had always assumed it would be otherwise. That she should look beyond the triumvirate was unthinkable. Like some benevolent but omnipotent matriarch, Diane had held court, her two young suitors vying amicably for the bestowal of her absolute affection.

For some time, he had taken a backseat in the friendship. To Eddie, all things came easily, or at least to Richard's eyes they seemed to. With consummate ease Eddie could reduce Diane to tears of laughter. He it was who always knew how to please her in the where to go and what to do of their days together.

Reluctantly, Richard had begun to accept that Eddie was to be the man in her life. They were too well suited for it to be otherwise. Both held a frenzied zest for life within them, possessing an ability to abandon themselves totally to the spirit of the moment. It was a gift that each knew the other possessed, and one that Richard sensed with every organ of his body, yet invariably found himself unable to fully experience with them.

Thus, it had been a complete surprise to him when Diane had begun to make it clear that it was his company she preferred. At first he had tried to keep things as they had always been, adopting Eddie's role of masterminding their excursions together, but these outings had proved uncomfortable and awkward. The wind of change had arrived, and he had either to bend with it now in this unexpected diversion or break. Within days he had proposed. Diane accepted as if there had never been any question that it should be so.

Yet in the months that followed, Richard could not help but notice a subtle difference in his bride. Something he could not define was lacking. There was nothing he could complain of and everything he had to be thankful for, yet he felt their marriage was somehow incomplete.

The Diane he had always known seemed so distant from him now. It was as if by choosing him she had sought to bring about some wished for change in herself — a change that neither found comfortable. And while she was still as lovely, as charming and beautiful as before, Richard came to realise that this was now a very different Diane. But there had been no time to explore these subtle alterations.

Unable to drift back to sleep, Richard decided to finish off a letter, though what he could tell Diane that would not fall prey to the censor's blue pencil was as ever so constrictive as to reduce all to the banal and mundane. Still, at least he could let her know he was alive. It made sense to take advantage of the opportunity and did not take long to complete the hamstrung discourse.

The drowsy warmth of his surroundings that had formerly been so appealing now began to stifle him, and gingerly extricating himself from the table of still sleeping men, he weaved his way up and out onto the open decks.

Stepping out into the cold light of dawn, a breathtaking headwind threatened to force him back down the steps, bringing his awakening to rapid completion. Moreover, its strength gave him some idea of the speed at which they were carving their way through the elements. The scene that greeted him was little different to that which he had left below, only here its impact seemed far greater. The gangways ahead of him, as with every other available space on the massive craft, were crammed with men sleeping as best they could. Raised on their davits now, even lifeboats cradled sleeping stowaways.

A turmoil of men on the deck below were stirring from their slumbers: Māori, Australian, Cypriot, Palestinian, New Zealander, Briton. But among their numbers were only a handful of Greeks — to the majority of their compatriots would fall the task of facing the grim realities of surrender and occupation.

Looking out, he could see another transport ship joining their convoy, its decks also laden with the fruits of evacuation. Escorting the new arrival was the sleeker form of an anti-aircraft cruiser, holding position on the port beam, while to the starboard the grim outline of a destroyer watched over them. But impressive as the massed convoy was, Richard's eyes were nevertheless soon drawn skywards as he, like many others around him, now began to watch for the first glimpse of an enemy plane. He had noted with some relief the absence of land beyond the destroyer that brought up the rear but doubted they had yet slipped the Luftwaffe's reach. Their ship already bore its share of scars that told of recent bombardments.

An unmistakable waft of cooking brought up by the breeze broke his train of thought and confirmed his suspicions as to the reason behind the movement down below. The men were gathering around several Soyer stoves, set up by the ship's cooks. He wasted no time getting down and joined the queue. He could hardly remember when he had last had a hot meal.

As he waited, so his previously forgotten hunger now began to gnaw at his insides, sharpened by the sea breeze and the sight of passing mess tins laden with breakfast sausage, soup, or stew. His own kit at the ready and just one to go, Richard heard the familiar ring of an East End accent, as the sailor at the stove addressed the soldier in front of him.

'Lost yer kit too mate? It'll have to be yer titfer then, we're fresh out of silver service!'

Looking around, Richard now noticed others also without kit, cradling their tin hats abrim with stew.

'Always knew it would pay off ….'

'What's that?'

'Having a big head!' the Geordie quipped, handing over his helmet.' Hoy it in, lad!'

Richard cut in uncoupling his own mess tins. 'Here … share mine … I doubt they'll be filling both.'

'You're right there my son … pass them over!' The sailor

grinned and ladled generous helpings of the steaming stew into both mess tins, handing one to each.

'Cheers canny lad. All as ah need now's a table with a sea view!'

The queues had freed up coveted spaces and both settled down around the foot of the gallows crane, briefly exchanging names before attacking their meal, Richard with spoon, Jim with a loan of his fork. Its unsuitability for the stew made little difference to Jim, who rapidly demolished the welcome meal, swigging back the remaining juices. Eventually he broke the contented silence.

'Amazing what they can do with bully beef.' Wiping out the last remnants from the tin, he handed it and the fork back. 'Thanks Dick.'

Richard nodded, too busy with his own last mouthfuls to bother with any discussion about 'Dick.' Jim watched him finish off.

'Ranger eh … up from the smoke?' Nodding with Richard, he continued, 'Northumberland Hussars, me, 102nd Anti-tank. You were up there at Vevi as well weren't you … certainly gave the bastards something to think about didn't we? Too bloody many in the end though.'

Richard gave his mess kit a final wipe. 'Where's home for you, Newcastle?'

'Tynemouth. Wish we were headed there now, Ah could murder a good pint!'

'I guess it'll be back to Alex again …' Richard's suggestion was cut short by the Australian beside him.

'Crete first they reckon.' The Australian nodded up to his source, a young sailor manning the anti-aircraft gun above them. 'Gives them a quicker turn around for the rest of the boys.' They watched as the gunner and his companions scanned the skies. 'Good as weathercocks those lads!'

True to his word, they saw the gunner's attention suddenly switch focus — the weapon's aim now trained directly over them to the port horizon. They stood up to follow the course. At the same instant the ship's alarm sounded and all at once seemed chaos as ship's ratings rushed to man their posts, colliding with soldiers eager to be out of their way and in any shelter available. They could now see the approaching planes and stood for a moment, transfixed, as two inky black dots rapidly expanded into recognisable form. Instinctively the three reached for their weapons — Richard for his rifle — Jim picked up his bren gun — and neither were able to suppress a belly laugh as the Australian hauled up an anti-tank rifle from behind him.

'How the bloody hell did you get that on board?' grinned Jim.

'Told em I wasn't going anywhere without it mate!'

They looked back to the planes and braced themselves against the gunwales, but between them and the planes was the anti-aircraft cruiser. It had also spotted the pair of Junkers 88's and the sky around the planes was suddenly filled with a barrage of fire, its din rattling out across the water to them moments later. The planes dipped and circled a couple of times, probing, but seemingly unwilling to engage in a serious attack until, discouraged by the continuing firework display, they disappeared once more.

An uneasy calm slowly returned to the troubled decks as everyone settled back to watch and wait, for none doubted that the danger was far from over. Conversation now was muted, their attentions focused on the skies above, but neither they nor the young gunner spotted the first planes. The ship's alarm startled them from their thoughts and onto their feet as once again the decks seethed with activity. Then, by sudden contrast, all action ceased as they waited, frozen in readiness for the attack to begin. Silence reigned as every ear strained to catch sound of the approaching planes, but only the monotonous drone of the ship's engines answered them.

Finally they saw them. High up and removed by the distance, Richard found himself thinking how innocent they appeared now, like a flock of tiny birds. But from bitter experience, he knew better. So too did the gunner, who entertained no such fanciful notion: his weapon trained in keen anticipation of the grim flock's descent.

Suddenly they were upon them, pride of the Luftwaffe, the deadly Stuka dive bombers. One by one they peeled off to swoop upon their prey, the all too familiar, boastful wail of their sirens blaring out, as they plummeted towards the ship. A thunderous roar of anti-aircraft and machine gun fire filled the air, but above it all blared the sirens. They carried a message that Richard and the others had come to understand only too well.

It was one that brought them to their senses, and flinging themselves down among the rest, they hit the floor as the first bomb exploded in the water close by, showering the decks. Having pulled out of its sickening dive, the aircraft banked sharply away, allowing the rear gunner to deliver a salvo of parting shots. His staccato gun beats were swiftly echoed as the bullets raced across the decks, giving off harsh metallic rings as they ricocheted from the armour — alternating with soft telling thuds, as one after another they found their mark on the crowded decks.

As the siren's blare diminished, Richard hauled himself up from the huddle, giving himself a push up on a neighbouring shoulder. 'Cheers! ....' But there was no reply.

Glancing down, the neat hole in the centre of the man's back gave the explanation. In answer to the question forming in his mind, both Jim's and the Aussie's heads appeared reassuringly above the melee — but beyond them and at regular intervals, a ragged line of writhing bodies told its own story. There was no time to savour the relief, as the next group of planes screamed into their attack. Once more it hammered down around them and again, they saw the planes climb steeply from the thunder of the AA guns.

Richard watched the young sailor follow the sweeping ascent of one plane, conserving his limited ammunition until — as the aircraft banked to rejoin its squadron — presenting him with the opportunity he had been waiting for, he unleashed a brief salvo. He turned immediately to concentrate on the next group already sweeping down upon them. Richard's eyes stayed with the tracers that sped now after the retreating aircraft until, with deadly accuracy, the hurtling shells claimed their prize, biting into the fuselage. The explosion wrenched the tail from the craft, leaving both the remnants and the unhappy occupants to plummet amidst a black, flaming spiral into the sea.

A rapid swiftening in the gunner's tempo and the deafening shriek of another diving Stuka cut short the momentary flush of victory. An explosion rocked the ship.

'Time we lent a hand!' Jim loosed off with the bren gun, spinning around as the next plane screamed by. He was not the only one venting his anger. Many now stood defiantly blasting their last rounds at their attackers. Richard gave the

Aussie, now wielding his anti-tank gun a wide berth as the muzzle flared, deafening all nearby.

'Watch out!' came a cry from behind them. 'That's one of ours up there!'

The unlikely sight of a lone Blenheim briefly scattered the flock. The Aussie turned to face the voice of the pilot behind him.

'Ahhh ... our Ruddy Absent Friends have finally decided to get out of bed, have they?'

'Give us the bloody planes and we'll fly them!' the pilot snapped. 'There's another.'

They looked up and could clearly see the gunner in the snub nosed turret of the Blenheim as he engaged the diving Stukas, bringing one down, but several others now swarmed in around him.

'Just aim at the right ones!'

Then as the ship lurched from another near miss, everyone's aim was thrown off and those about them begged them to stop, for their own safety. But Jim was not to be discouraged.

'Brace me against here Dick!' He leant back against the gallows crane mounting and Richard pinioned him to it as the harsh chatter of his bren rejoined the cacophony of the ship's defences.

Suddenly, appearing as if from nowhere and seeming larger than life, a lone ME 109 loomed upon them. While the ships' gunners and everyone else's attentions had been focused above, this lone wolf had hugged the waves from afar, staying unnoticed until now.

Hauling his weapon into line, the young sailor opened fire, starting the head on confrontation. The attacker's reply followed instantly, the two guns haranguing each other until the plane filled their vision. In chilling detail, they watched the bomb slip the shackles of its rack to nose gracefully into its dive — its course this time unmistakably bound for them.

'Jesus! I think this one's got our names on it!' Jim relaxed his grip on the bren's trigger, hypnotised by the lethal explosive plummeting towards them.

Confusion boiled around them as everyone scrambled to avoid its impact. Hauling Jim with him, Richard flung himself aside as the bomb hit the deck. An ear-splitting clang deafened them as they winced in anticipation of the blast — but none came. Instead the bomb rolled noisily about, clattering across the deck with every sway of the ship. Everyone stared in disbelief, until the Australian, throwing down his anti-tank rifle, broke the spell.

'Come on you dumb bastards ... let's get it overboard before it goes!'

For a moment no one moved but the burly Australian, who struggled to get a grip on the slithering cylinder, then Richard found himself bending down to help lift the bomb. Their eyes met. Both knew only too well the folly of this moment that could so easily be their last. Hands sweating and slipping on the grim, cold steel, he took the weight with the Aussie and together they tottered towards the rail — but then, as they heaved it up for the toss — the ship swerved once more, and it came to rest with a sickening clang upon the rail. Jim jumped up to help them and together they flung the bomb into the swirling waters below.

'Good on you mates!' The Australian slapped both Jim and Richard on their backs as a rumble from the deep told of the bomb's ultimate fate.

'It's not over yet,' shouted Richard as he saw the ME 109 returning. Pushing the bren back into Jim's hands he urged him back into position. Again the plane came in low, its machine guns spitting fire. Jim responded, as did the young gunner up above, pounding away as the pilot with equal determination relentlessly kept to his course.

A rapid volley of screams pierced even the din of the relentless machine gunning as the plane roared overhead, its final round scoring Richard's neck before embedding itself in Jim's shoulder, setting off a string of expletives from both. Still cursing the pilot's escape as the plane continued out past the ship, low across the sea, they waited in dull anticipation for the plane to climb up in readiness for the next attack, but the ascent never came. Slowly the craft began to lose height, creeping lower and lower over the sea until its belly seemed to skim the waves. Then suddenly one wing dipped too low. The liquid snare grasped at its prize and the plane cartwheeled giddily across the surface until, with a last fiery explosion, it dissolved into the watery grave. A cheer rose up from the men and Richard looked up to congratulate the young lad on his success, but a different gunner now ranged the skies.

'Made a bloody garden sieve out of him … poor bastard!'

They followed the Aussie's gaze and watched in silence as the shattered body of the young gunner was taken below.

'Made a fair mess of you two as well!'

As suddenly as the attacks had started, so they ceased. The skies were now eerily silent.

'Must be beyond their range,' Jim reasoned, inspecting his wound.

'You'll live!' joked the Aussie, as he took a look. Then turning his attention to the gash on Richard's neck, 'Ahhh … nothing but a fleabite mate!'

EIGHT

It had been an uneasy journey in the taxi — both women totally preoccupied with their own thoughts — neither one able to find a scrap of small talk between them. Their driver, having abandoned initial attempts at breaking the silence, now consoled himself with sporadic curses at passing drivers and the occasional stray pedestrian foolish enough to cross his path. True to her word, Catherine had refused to allow Diane to embark on her rendezvous without her.

Thankfully the hotel offered a baby minding service, but perhaps because of the heat, Ellie had taken much longer than usual to settle despite the lateness of the hour. Nine o'clock would be the earliest she could expect to find Michaelis Serides at his bar, Diane had been told. Now, as they stepped out from the taxi into the neon glow bathing the entrance to the Aphrodite Paradise Club, it was approaching ten.

Diane looked around her as she settled the fare, secretly thankful that Catherine had insisted on coming with her. The club, while still on the seafront, was nevertheless somewhat removed from the busier central areas, adjoined by small shanty houses to the one side and a gloomy industrial site to the other. Though she had no specific reason to be fearful, she had hoped that the club would at least be in among the general throng. Considering whether to book a return trip with the taxi driver — in case calling one from the club became a problem — suddenly ceased to be a possibility as he sped off in response to a call. Still, keeping her bearings had not been difficult and she knew it would be a simple enough matter to follow the coast road back into town and hopefully pick one up on the way. They both regarded the entrance to the club. Pleasantly decorated, palm trees to either side of the swing doors, the unique strains of Cretan music emanating from within.

'Well,' Catherine finally spoke, 'I hope you know what you're doing!'

'So do I,' admitted Diane. 'Perhaps I really should try and explain first…'

Her attempt was promptly cut short, as a side door to the club was thrown open, spilling a pool of light across the pavement some twenty yards away from them. Clearly audible above the raised volume of the music, an argument could be heard. Though they could not understand the language, it came as no surprise to them to see a figure being hustled out. What did surprise them, however, was the dress and bearing of the person being ejected — rather than the young rowdy reveller they might have expected — they saw a frail woman, conservatively dressed, and at a guess some ten years older than herself, Diane surmised. Continued argument from behind the door clearly expressed another's concern at the woman's treatment, before he himself emerged berating two others who now stood guard over the door.

Clearly younger than the woman, Diane guessed him to be her son and she and Catherine watched, as first he checked to see that his mother was alright, before turning back to continue his complaint. But by now, the elder of the two had ushered the other back inside and spitting out a final warning ended any further discussion by firmly slamming the door.

The pool of light vanished, and the music dropped back to its earlier muted level, leaving the mother and son only dimly visible now alone in the street. Catherine and Diane heard him question his mother about her well-being, though there was also a tone of remonstration in his voice, Catherine thought. A strangely familiar voice too. She watched as he escorted his mother away across the street.

'Let's get this over with!' Diane took Catherine's arm as she plucked up the courage to enter the club.

'Just make sure you behave yourself!' Catherine's retort was not entirely humorous. She glanced back briefly towards the couple, only to find that the son was now also looking across directly at her. He was about to cross back towards them, when a tug on his arm from his mother dissuaded him. Instead he gestured a warning to Catherine against their entry. As he did so, Catherine realised she now recognised him, it was the second time she had seen him that day — Antonis, the driver from their hotel. She was about to acknowledge him, when a firm tug on her own arm from Diane pulled her through the club doors. A curious sense of guilt now mingled with her general apprehension.

An unmanned foyer led directly to a further pair of double doors. Expecting a dimly lit scene, both women were surprised by the stark lighting of the large smoky room they entered. Ahead, on a slightly raised stage was the source of the music: a small group of lyra and laouto players. Seated in front of them were several boisterous groups of diners gathered at joined tables, variously eating, arguing, or toasting one another with glasses that were then slammed back onto the table.

Further back and closer to them were some empty individual tables and Catherine and Diane instinctively headed to one close to a bar that ran alongside the wall to their left.

'I'll ask at the bar,' said Diane, as Catherine settled herself at the table. 'We'd better order something in any case … what would you like?'

Catherine surveyed the busy tables, which seemed to be dominated by local wine amid several bottles of Johnnie Walker Black Label. What she really felt like was a cold beer.

'I'll just stay with a soft drink for now.'

'Good idea,' agreed Diane sharing her daughter's caution. She returned shortly with the drinks. '*Gazoza* apparently,' she explained as Catherine inspected the unfamiliar bottles. 'Should be like lemonade …?' Catherine nodded her approval. 'The barman says Mr Serides will be over in a while.'

'Well, how about making a start on that explanation Mum. I want to help you, whatever it is, but if I don't know anything ….'

'I know darling. I shouldn't have been so secretive and I'm really glad you're with me. It's just difficult … it was so long ago.'

'What was?'

'During the war, I…'

Diane's explanation was again cut short by the arrival of the owner. Both women recognised him from the altercation they had recently witnessed and now as he stood above them, Diane knew it was the man whose photograph had led her here. Around her own age, shorter than she had imagined, balding. The remaining hair, left untrimmed, formed two wiry tufts to either side of his head — a vain declaration of undiminished virility she felt.

'Mr Serides?' She was about to stand for the introduction.

'Michaeli ... please ....' He pressed her back into her seat. 'English ... no?'

'Yes. Thank you for agreeing to see me.' Diane offered him a seat, noticing as he circled the table that he walked with a slight limp. Briefly massaging his knee, he sat down.

'How can I be of assistance?' He cast an admiring glance at Catherine. 'You would like to book the club for an engagement perhaps?'

'No! No ... you have a lovely establishment Mr Serides, but that's not why I am here.'

'Michaeli' he repeated, patiently waiting for her to come to the point. Diane felt completely tongue-tied, her own daughter as much a stranger to her at this moment as this unknown man, now idly fingering through a set of worry beads. Instead of speaking, she reached for her bag, placed it on the table and withdrew the newspaper article opening it for him to see.

'This is why I'm here Mr Serides ... Michaeli ....'

'Ah ... I see my fame is spreading!' he announced proudly. 'If only it paid the bills. You are interested in archaeology?'

'No, but I am interested in how you came by this earring ... you see I have the other one of the pair.' Diane found herself under the scrutiny of two pairs of eyes as the conversation briefly fell silent.

'I'm sure you are mistaken. Here on Crete we manufacture many replicas of pottery and of jewellery. This …' Michaelis stabbed at the photograph, 'this is an authentic piece of Minoan jewellery, not something manufactured ten years ago!'

'I don't doubt that for one minute Mr Serides. And mine certainly wasn't manufactured ten years ago either … it came into my possession during the war.'

The casual clicks of Michaelis' worry beads came to a halt and all pleasantries slipped from his face.

'You're with them, aren't you?' he demanded suddenly.

'Who?' Diane responded with genuine puzzlement.

'Those troublemakers earlier. That Xenakis bitch and her bastard!'

'I'm sorry I have no idea what you're…'

'Mum, we're going!' Catherine sprang to her feet, but Diane restrained her.

'No Cath, no … look, I'm truly sorry Mr Serides … I don't know what it is that I've said to upset you. Please believe me … I'm not accusing you of anything if that's what you think … and I certainly don't know anyone else here on this island. I've never been here before. I have come here because of this article, to try and find out what happened to my husband.'

Catherine found herself persuaded to sit. Michaelis weighed up the situation, then signalled to his barman. Seeing both Catherine and Diane's nervous glances, he tried to reassure them.

'My apologies ladies … village matters … nothing more. Of course you could not possibly be involved.' And as the barman brought over a tray of glasses and a bottle, 'Ouzo …

please … you will forgive me?' He poured three glasses and added a little water to his own. Diane and Catherine watched as the clear spirit turned milky white. He gestured for them to join him. Waiting until they had followed his example, he raised his glass. '*Yamas!*'

'Cheers,' Diane responded weakly, as she and Catherine sampled their first ouzo. Initial surprise at the unexpected flavour of aniseed gave way to an appreciation of the strength of the spirit, which both now felt in need of.

'Tell me about your husband.' Michaelis settled back in his chair, flipping the beads back and forth across nicotine stained fingers.

Catherine said nothing, but her eyes repeated the invitation: *Yes Mother, please do!*

'He fought in Greece during the war, and I know he was here in Crete, when the troops were evacuated from the mainland, but then there was a letter from Egypt and we … I … thought that …'

'Many died in the war.' Michaelis quietly slipped bead after bead through his fingers.

'I was hoping you might have known him?'

'Why would you think that?'

'Because the earring came with the letter.' Diane saw Michaelis' fingers come to rest on a single bead, that was different from its amber counterparts: metallic. Noticing her gaze, Michaelis spread the circlet of amber beads on the table in front of him.

'We call them *komboloi*. They help us to … see things more clearly. And this one …' singling out what was clearly now a spent bullet threaded among the beads, 'helps to remember.'

'Then perhaps my husband's name would also help?' suggested Diane. 'Richard ... Richard Forrest?' Michaelis shrugged impassively. Diane pressed on. 'I could describe him, better still, I have a photograph ...'

'It would make no difference.' Michaelis stopped her. 'I'm sorry to disappoint you, but I never fought with any of the British soldiers, I was too young.'

'And this?' Diane pointed to the bullet.

'That was later.' Michaelis scooped up the beads. 'Nazi reprisals.'

Diane felt uncomfortable pursuing the subject but felt that time was running out on their audience. Fortunately, Catherine came to the rescue.

'You were going to tell us how you found the earring?' she smiled engagingly at their host, leaning back with her drink.

'I didn't. It was my father's.'

'Perhaps he might...'

'My father died a short while ago. It was among his possessions. I thought I might be able to sell it and raise more money for this place, but when I took it to be valued ...' he paused momentarily to stab another accusatory finger at the antiquities official in the newspaper article, 'I was told I would be obliged to 'donate' it to the museum!' Noticing that Diane had underlined the official's name as well as his own, Michaelis asked, 'You're thinking of going to see this man?'

'I tried today, but he's away at a conference for three days, I thought he might be able to tell me something.'

'He wasn't there.'

'I'm sorry?'

'He doesn't come from this island. He can't help you.'

'Well, he might at least be able to tell me something about the earring.'

'You have it with you?' Michaelis' eyes travelled to Diane's bag on the table.

'No,' Diane lied, determined not to glance down at her bag. 'I thought it best to leave it in England. No, I was hoping he could tell me more about how it was discovered. You've no idea how your father came by it?'

'I'm afraid not.' Michaelis' eyes remained on Diane's bag. 'It is as well you did not bring the earring with you. If it is as you say a genuine relic then I trust you are aware that you would not be allowed to take it out of the country? There are severe punishments for exporting such items.'

'Just as well it's safe in England.' Diane reiterated, smiling as she stood up. 'Thank you for your time.'

Michaelis shrugged. 'It's nothing … I'm sorry I wasn't able to help. Please, let me call you a taxi.'

'No, it's fine really, we can walk.'

'I insist. On the house as you say.' Michaelis brushed aside Diane's protests and called over the barman. 'Which hotel are you staying at?'

'The Astoria.' Diane lied again, praying that Catherine would not contradict her.

'I expect you'll be visiting the museum?' enquired Michaelis.

'Oh, of course.' replied Diane.

'Then when you see the real thing, I'm sure you will see you have been mistaken.'

'Yes, I daresay.' Diane conceded, willing the taxi to arrive soon. 'Might as well get some fresh air while we wait.'

She ushered Catherine out through the doors, Michaelis followed.

'It won't be long,' he reassured them, 'I use a man nearby, he knows better than to keep me waiting!' He was proved right, as a sleek silver-grey Mercedes soon pulled up, putting an end to the awkward small talk. 'Ladies.' Michaelis escorted them to the vehicle and spoke quietly to the driver in Greek.

'Please Mr Serides … we will pay!'

'Nonsense … you are in my country now!' With that he slapped the roof of the Mercedes. 'Astoria!'

Diane looked back as the taxi whisked them away, leaving Michaelis to watch their departure, the *komboloi* beads flicking back and forth in his hand. For the second time that evening the two women spent a taxi ride together in complete silence, but not this time for want of something to say. On their arrival at the Astoria Hotel, Diane once again offered to pay the driver, but her attempts were firmly refused. Seeing that he was making no attempt to leave, Diane took hold of Catherine and steered her into the hotel.

'Come on, we'll have a drink at the bar until he's gone.'

'He's probably just hanging around for another fare,' Catherine reasoned.

'I'm not so sure!' Diane found a spot at the bar where they could just see the rear end of the taxi, still waiting outside.

'Well, I think you owe me a bloody stiff drink and one hell of an explanation!'

'I know!' Diane ordered two large brandies and settled back onto a bar stool, one eye still on the waiting taxi. She winced at the taste. *If this was five star, what must the three star be like?* Catherine waited for Diane to regain her composure, until her own impatience became too much to bear.

'Let me help you out here. You've come here looking for a husband you've never breathed a word about, and unless I'm mistaken, you don't even know if he's dead or alive?

'I know it doesn't look good, but…'

'Good? Oh, it gets better. Not only do I have a mother with a secret past, she's also walking around with a national treasure in her handbag! I'm right, aren't I?'

'Well, I couldn't leave it in the room.'

'Christ!'

The conversation fell quiet as both women absorbed the situation.

'It's gone … the taxi ….' Diane pointed with her brandy glass before taking a relieved swig. 'I don't trust him though … something he said ….' She tried to run through the conversation again in her mind. 'I'm sure he's hiding something.'

'I'd say he's used to hiding all sorts of things.'

'He wasn't there! That's what didn't seem right. He said, 'He wasn't there …"

'Who?'

'The antiquities man he doesn't want me to meet. Wasn't "where"?' Something happened, I'm sure of it. He's lying … I'm sure he knew Richard.' Diane finished the glass, as she considered the alternative, casting a nervous glance to her daughter. 'Or knows him?'

'I think the brandy's getting the better of you Mum. We'll sort it out tomorrow. Come on, let's get a taxi back to the hotel, there are plenty outside.'

'Yes, but they're all grey Mercedes!'

This time Catherine did the steering, and both were relieved to be greeted by a different driver as they took the first in the queue. They settled back into the comfortable leather seats.

'It'll be fine Mum.' Catherine squeezed her mother's hand and both women relaxed a little, but neither noticed the sleek grey Mercedes pull out from the rear of the queue.

NINE

An irritating trickle of blood continued to work its way down past Richard's collar from the makeshift dressing the ship's medics had applied to his wound. The gash on his neck was painful enough, but the persistent trickling annoyed him more. Tired of dabbing at it, he pulled his collar tight against the bandage and shuffled to a more comfortable position propped against the side of the forecastle. Jim snored blissfully by his side. The medics had dressed his shoulder wound, given him a shot to ease the pain, and said they would get the bullet out as soon as the surgeons had dealt with the worst cases, already overflowing from the ship's operating theatre. More than likely they would reach land first.

Idly watching the sun slip slowly back and forth as the convoy kept up their zig-zag course and with Jim's snores rumbling on hypnotically, Richard's eyes also closed in the drowsy warmth. Soon he was back in Clissold Park, the three of them sailing Eddie's new pond yacht. It had lodged against the little island in the centre where the ducks nested and, while Richard and Eddie discussed ways of retrieving it with string lassos, Diane waded out into the shimmering water, her skirts tucked into her knickers.

A kick at the soles of his feet shattered the image.

'Land ho, mates!' The Aussie, anti-tank rifle still propped warily against the superstructure, was pointing out ahead of them. 'Crete!'

The name echoed in Richard's mind, stirring half forgotten, schoolboy imaginings of the mystical home of the Minotaur. Imperceptibly, the land ahead began to spread before them. With size came colour, as dark, mottled patches of green emerged amidst reds and browns, fired by the glow of the afternoon sun. Bringing a welcome relief to the vista, these earthy tones lent new vitality to the blues of sea and sky — provided now with contrast, they were no longer endless washes of monotonous colour. Gradually the rusty hues sharpened into distinct features, gleaming white pinpricks became towns — then houses — until at last, the zig-zagging motion of their course suspended, the great ships fell into line as the arms of Souda Bay slowly opened to enfold them.

But any notion that they were to be cradled in some carefree caress here was quickly dispelled. A black pall hung in the air above the bay, and appearing from within this shroud, they could now see the charred, smoking vessels that littered the anchorage. As they slipped past these ghostly skeletons, an air of despondency began to fall upon them and Richard found it difficult to brush aside the notion that some vast, invisible net was closing around them.

Men were now pressing against the rails, pointing and peering at the waters below.

'What's going on?' Richard asked one of the sailors now readying to dock.

'Probably spotted some of their mates.' came the grim reply. 'Jerry hardly gives them a minute's peace here, so the dead have to wait. I'm amazed we've made it straight in … place is usually buzzing with planes.'

Shouts from afar drew their attention to the hills surrounding the harbour. It was as if the landscape suddenly dissolved and reformed in front of them — like some shifting, hazy mirage — until they realised that the entire scene was filled with their fellow soldiers camped among the olive groves. Many were now standing to give them a rowdy welcome, lifting their spirits. At length the huge ship was manoeuvred up to the wharf, the hawsers rattled, berthing lines were tied off, and with the gangplank lowered from the block, so the disembarkation began.

Even with their prime position on the main deck, it still took some time before Richard and Jim found themselves trundling down the railed steps by the side of the ship to the welcome sight of a trestle table laden with enamel mugs of tea. 'Grab one quick and keep moving lads,' they were told, 'and bring the bleeding mugs back when you're done!'

Taking in their surroundings, they could see large gatherings of men from earlier disembarkations already settled around the area, mostly seated on the ground in distinct groups. The cause of their separation becoming obvious as they saw the hastily erected signs.

'Looks like it's the end of another fine romance boys!' The Aussie grinned, heading off towards the one marked: 'Anzac Troops Report Here.' A raucous cheer soon confirmed that he had found some of his mates.

'And this looks like our lads,' said Jim, 'hardly need a sign to know this lot, man!'

'We ought to find someone to get your shoulder seen to first.'

'You're not looking so tidy yourself Dick.' Jim pointed to the steady trickle of blood, still seeping into Richard's shirt. 'Let's have our brew first, I daresay some of these lads will know where the field ambulance is.' He headed off towards a group of men settled around some packing crates. 'Let's have a seat for the walking wounded!'

Richard followed in Jim's wake as he badgered a couple of spaces on the crates from their occupants. And as Jim continued to banter with the others, Richard fell to watching the stream of weary men continuing to disgorge from the ship. All would be eternally grateful to the Navy for their rescue but, like him, they could not help but wonder what lay ahead.

Diane settled into the window seat of the little café that had been the trio's favourite haunt, stirred the thick brown tea and stared out of the taped glass windows at the still smoking wreckage of the little cobbler's shop farther up the street. Having arranged to meet up with Eddie, on leave from his training, she wondered now if they should have chosen somewhere else. Their happier memories seemed so distant now, their dreams, like Mr Benson's whose shop had taken the direct hit, shattered in this changing world.

Her mood brightened though with the sight of Eddie's familiar jaunty figure approaching, and she rose to give him a hug as he swung open the door.

'Blimey! Where am I going to get soled and heeled now, eh ducks?'

'Is that all you can think of?' Diane chided.

'Left me best pair of dancing shoes in there!' he carried on teasing her. 'You alright for tea? Just one for me then Betty ... and a slice of whatever that is there, if you can get a knife through it!' Ducking Betty's dishcloth, Eddie joined Diane at the table. 'Now, what am I going to get our Alice for her birthday present? She'll be turning fifteen this week.'

Diane was grateful to have her thoughts diverted and suggested a few things she thought Eddie's younger sister might like. She listened to him chatting about his training for a while, smiling as he amused her with impersonations of his superiors.

Inevitably the talk came round to Richard. Not having seen each other for some weeks, Diane brought Eddie up to date with his movements, what little she knew of them. Knowing his pal was now in Greece, sobered Eddie somewhat, as they both reflected on recent official broadcasts that had recounted the withdrawal of the Allied troops, heading for the southern ports. With an elder sister working in one of the RAF operations rooms, Eddie occasionally benefitted from stray snippets of information that should not have come his way.

'I've heard Cunningham's fleet are taking them off. You saw how he dealt with the Iti's at Matapan. He'll be getting them away alright... they're getting what fighter cover they can to them.' Eddie squeezed her hand. 'He'll be alright, Di ....'

'I know.' Diane forced another, weaker smile. Idly stirring the tea, her mind's eye roamed the swirling seas.

'Bet you ten bob our boy's got his backside parked on some sandy beach this very minute with a glass of bubbly in his hand!'

This time both she and Eddie laughed out loud at the notion, but as Diane watched the first drops of rain spatter the taped glass of the café windows, the happy prospect rapidly began to dissolve, as did the dusty grime of the previous night's bombing under the steadily increasing rivulets of rain now streaming down the cracked panes. She turned her gaze once more, down to the far off world she held in her cup.

The shadows were lengthening over the busy wharfside as Richard drained the last of his tea.

About to return their mugs, he spotted a medical truck draw up nearby. He nudged Jim,

'Come on let's get you seen to.'

'Just let me finish this one …' Jim was keen to get to the punchline but seeing several others also getting up to head for the truck, he decided it was wise to join him. 'You'll just have to imagine what she did next boys!'

Several men were gathered around the truck, where the medical officer began assessing their injuries, passing minor cases to the nursing orderlies who attended to their dressings.

'Still in there is it?' He said to Jim, inspecting the bullet wound in his shoulder. 'Jump up then.' Jim climbed up into the truck. The officer turned his attention to Richard, peeling aside the sodden dressing. 'You can count yourself lucky to be alive son …' he said after a moment, 'Any deeper and that artery would have been cut in half. We'll need to close that up properly. Up you go as well!'

Before long, the truck was full and they lumbered off into the dusk, winding up the dusty road that climbed above the bay, until they reached the makeshift field hospital. Richard eyed the line of tents.

'Looks as though we could be getting our first night under canvas at long last.'

'Not a chance ...' chuckled the orderly, 'once we've patched you up, you'll be back under the stars again!'

And so it proved, as a few hours later, both men lay under the trees, grateful at least for the camp beds they had been given gazing up at the night sky. Richard watched the rhythmic wane and glow of Jim's last cigarette melding with the stars. As sleep beckoned, he no longer knew or cared if the billowing white shapes he saw were the cigarette's smoke or distant clouds, but he still clearly heard Jim's final words as he settled back for the night.

'Welcome to Crete!'

TEN

With Ellie now contentedly dissecting the remains of their hotel breakfast, the second pot of coffee began to fuel the post mortem of Catherine and Diane's adventures of the previous evening. Sensing that her mother was still not ready for a full heart to heart discussion about her revelations, Catherine bided her time, adopting a practical approach.

'So, what do we do next?'

'Well, I don't see that there's much we can do really, not until the antiquities man gets back from his conference. I might as well go to the museum, I suppose … I want to see for myself … just to be sure.'

'Well, I've had an idea, Mum. Why do you imagine Mr Serides would think we had anything to do with the argument we saw outside the club?'

'I haven't a clue. As he said … it was just some village matter.'

'Exactly! So if they're from the same village and there's something he doesn't want us to know about, maybe they would be able to help us?'

'Even if they could help, how on earth would we find them? We don't know which village they're from.'

'We don't need to Mum!' Catherine had the bit between her teeth. 'I recognised the man. He's the driver here at the hotel. We spoke yesterday in Heraklion … he wanted to buy me a drink.'

Diane could see where this was heading. 'I'm not so sure ….'

Catherine, however, was not going to be dissuaded. 'Look. Why don't you head off to the museum and I'll hang around here at the pool with Ellie? If he and I should happen to bump into each other, well …' Seeing Diane about to object, she insisted, 'I'll be fine Mum, don't worry. I'm a big girl now!'

'That's what worries me!' Diane surprised herself with the comment, but the levity eased the tension between them. 'I really shouldn't have got you involved.'

'Too late for that now! What's the worst that can happen? We're in a busy hotel. Anyway, I've got my trusty chaperone to take care of me.' She tousled Ellie's locks. 'You'll throw up on him if I need you to, won't you darling?'

Diane worked her way through the airy rooms of the museum, surprised to be almost its sole visitor. Case after case of pottery, from the tiniest of fragments to huge earthenware storage jars, charted the island's ancient history. Even without translations of the tiny, typewritten labels, she found little difficulty in understanding the progression of the various periods and marvelled at the colour and ingenuity of design on reaching the Minoan era.

Initially eager only to find the earring, she now found herself entranced by the grace and beauty of the fragile bull leaper — suspended in air — the beast long since vanished. There was the majesty of the intricately chased steatite bull's head with golden horns and then the natural elegance of the little, rock crystal rhyton, and beyond that, the sheer exuberance of the writhing octopus, swimming across his painted world on the loop-handled wine jar. Playful dolphins writhed around vase stems, and exotic blooms competed for attention everywhere.

Pausing by a tiny clay model of a child on a swing, her mind was drawn to Ellie and Catherine, and a wave of guilt spread over her. She should hurry on and get back to be sure they were alright.

But she was rapidly seduced back into the realm of the Minoans, fascinated now by the snake goddess, an asp in either hand, bare breasts proudly uplifted by her bodice, her layered skirts cascading below. There were golden-handled daggers, double-headed *labrys* axes, and finally she came to the beaded necklaces and delicate golden jewellery. Two wild bees embraced over an orb of pollen, droplets of nectar suspended from their wings, or were they golden suns? Necklaces of coral, lapis lazuli, and then her eye first catching the newly printed label — conspicuous among its yellowing neighbours — came finally to rest upon the earring. Her earring.

She looked at it now afresh: as if for the very first time. Displayed alongside its contemporaries, she could now see the similarities in design. The tightly coiled, golden spirals and delicate links suspending the finely wrought basket with its lapis centre.

She had agonised that morning over what to do with its twin. Reluctant to involve the staff, with Michaelis Serides' dire warnings still ringing in her ears, she had avoided Catherine's suggestion of the hotel safe. Neither had she wanted to burden her daughter with the responsibility of looking after it. Once more, it burned a hole in her handbag.

Looking around the deserted room, the temptation was almost too great. She longed to lay it down on the glass of the display case to see it alongside its partner. Not that she now had the slightest remaining doubt of its authenticity, but rather, she knew now that this was where it truly belonged. But first she might still need it — there were other answers yet to be found.

Galvanised once more, she barely paused to appreciate the magnificent frescoes on her way out, knowing full well that this would not be her final visit.

Catherine checked her watch. Just a few minutes more and the hotel bus would be returning from Heraklion ready for the one one-o'clock trip back into town. She had not wasted her morning. Enquiring earlier about a 'missing' pair of Ellie's water-wings 'left' on the bus, she now knew from her lengthy chat with the receptionist that Antonis would shortly be handing over the afternoon shift to another driver.

She had set up camp by the hotel pool, commandeering a table and two chairs, towels and playthings strewn across them to prevent re-appropriation, a soft drink nursed to the point where it was clearly still in use and not abandoned, paperback spread open, spine up: 'Hands off — I'm coming back!'

Hoisting Ellie up onto her hip, she slung her bag over her shoulder and headed back past reception and out to the drive, where she knew the bus would pull up. Pointing out the bright pinks of the oleanders planted along the driveway, she endeavoured to keep Ellie amused as she strolled up and down waiting for the bus to arrive.

The minutes ticked by, and she sensed Ellie's growing disgruntlement in the heat as she tried to dislodge her sun hat. Fortunately, a pair of gaily painted butterflies danced by, distracting her for a while as Catherine checked her watch again. Concerned now that there was no queue waiting for the bus, she wondered if she had mistimed her plan. *Had the bus already left?*

A family of four suddenly tumbled out from the hotel with similar worries, but all were relieved as the bus turned into the driveway. Catherine promptly resumed her inspection of the oleanders and other nearby shrubs. As Ellie reached out for the butterflies, the bus slowed to a halt behind her. She heard the engine switch off and a pair of elderly guests thank Antonis for their safe return. Recognising his cheery reply, she timed her continuing botanical exploration to bring her alongside the bus as he stepped down.

'*Yassou!*' He beamed a smile on seeing her.

Catherine found herself taken aback. She had been so preoccupied with Ellie and other matters on their earlier encounters that she had not realised just how handsome this man was. His easy, natural smile revealed perfect teeth, appearing all the whiter against the nut brown tan. Taking in the slight, wayward curl of his hair, she also registered a happy spark in his twinkling hazel eyes that seemed to confirm the sincerity of his smile. All now combined to make her aware that the butterflies were not only in the air around her. She completely forgot her carefully prepared fiction of the water-wings.

'Hello … *Yassou!*'

'Are you going into town? Pavlos will be out in a minute.' Antonis waved the waiting family on to the bus and turned back to Catherine. Cocking his head at Ellie, he asked, 'Are we friends today young lady?'

'No.' Catherine replied, before hastily clarifying: 'No, we're not going into town … and … yes … I think Ellie's changed her mind.'

Ellie reached out for Antonis' sunglasses, glinting in his shirt pocket.

'Careful, she'll break them …' Catherine warned as he handed them over. Antonis shrugged happily. 'I wanted to apologise for the other day … and yesterday … it was very kind of you to offer me a drink.'

'*Tipota* … it's nothing,' he shrugged again, still smiling as Ellie attempted to pull apart his glasses.

Catherine rescued them and put them back in his pocket. 'I was wondering … if I could return the favour?' She struggled to backtrack and make the invitation seem casual and unplanned. 'I was just having a stroll. A change of scenery … but I do have a table by the pool. Would you like to join me for a drink, if you're finished now?'

'I would love to … but my bosses wouldn't! Unfortunately, they don't like us using the facilities.'

'But you would be my guest.' Catherine didn't want to let the chance slip away, but she saw Antonis was not comfortable with the idea.

'We could meet on the beach,' he suggested, 'there's a small bar...'

'It's just so sandy ...' Catherine found herself saying.

'You don't like sandy beaches?'

'I do ... well I did ... but trying to keep suntan lotion on this one without her ending up looking like one of the sugared doughnuts they sell here was a nightmare yesterday!'

Antonis laughed and Ellie giggled, now also captivated by his smile. 'I have an idea,' he said, 'if you don't want sand, there is a beautiful little beach just five minutes away. There is no sand ... only tiny little stones. You just brush them off. I can take you there!'

Catherine's mind raced. This would take the situation out of her control, and it wasn't just herself she had to worry about, though it was clear this man seemed to be as enchanted with Ellie as she was becoming with him. 'I don't know ... I'm not sure what time my mother will be back, she will be expecting to find me here ....'

'We can leave a message for her at the desk. I have to be back here later this afternoon for my evening shift anyway. And you won't have to walk ....' Antonis pointed to the rear of the car park, where an open backed pickup truck was parked. 'I know it's not what you're probably used to ... but it works!'

'No, no ... it's fine really, it's just...'

'*Yassou Antoni!*' Pavlos hailed his friend as he headed for the bus.

'*Yassou Pavli!*' Antonis waved him on his way. Again, Catherine noticed the infectious, genuine smile he gave his friend: subconsciously reassured that it was not the smile of the cat about to get the cream. Antonis turned back to her. 'I'm sorry, I understand you must be cautious. I should not have suggested it. Perhaps we can arrange to meet another time … with your mother if you would like?'

Catherine shot him a look of surprise. 'That's either very brave of you, or an excellent bluff!' She found herself agreeing. 'I'll need to get my things from the pool, and as you say, leave a message for my mother.' They headed towards the reception desk.

'There is only one condition.' said Antonis. Catherine halted. 'You must first tell me your name.' This time it was Catherine who smiled.

At the desk, Antonis took charge, explaining to the receptionist where they were going and when they would return.

'Did you find the water-wings?' asked the girl.

'They were in the bottom of my bag all the time!' Catherine improvised, feeling herself colour up as the girl gave them both a wry smile. 'I'll need to get some water.'

'I'll deal with that.' Antonis insisted.

'And I need to grab a couple of things from my room.'

'No problem … take your time. I'll be over there.' He nodded towards the seats of the reception lounge.

Catherine gathered her things from the pool and raced up to her room. Parking Ellie in the safety of her cot, she tried to think what she might need — quickly threw a few things into her bag — then headed for the mirror. Fifteen minutes ago, she couldn't have given a damn what she looked like, supremely confident in her charms, interested only in what Antonis might be able to tell her about Michaelis Serides. Now it was different.

'What the hell is your mummy doing Ellie?'

Neither Ellie, nor her reflection had the answer, so she primped and preened as quickly as she could, changed Ellie

— which she knew full well would mean changing her again in five minutes — threw another couple of nappies into the bag and headed back down to reception, simultaneously trying to compose herself and ignore the battle of wills that still raged in her head over her decision.

Antonis as promised was waiting in the lounge. Rising he opened the door for Catherine.

'The water?' she reminded him.

'Yes, we will collect it now.' As they walked alongside the hotel towards his pickup, Antonis knocked on a side door. Catherine glimpsed the busy kitchens inside and laughed as he was handed two large carrier bags. He held them up proudly. 'You call it a picnic, I think?'

'We do!'

Thankfully the pickup was partially shaded by trees. Antonis swung the carrier bags into the open rear and opened both the doors to let the breeze through. 'We should wait for two minutes, it will get cooler,' he suggested.

'No problem.' Catherine relaxed, leaning against the pickup, enjoying the pine scented breeze as Antonis rolled back the raffia beach mats shielding the windscreen from the dappled sunlight.

Soon they were driving out along the old coast road, leaving Heraklion behind them. Catherine gradually became aware that Antonis' notion of five minutes bore little relation to the reality of their journey time, but clearly, she just had to adapt to 'Cretan' time. She settled back to enjoy the view, grateful of the cooling sea breeze.

After a short while he took a small slip road that led downhill to their right. With the coast disappearing to her left, a momentary wave of panic coursed through Catherine's body. Had she misjudged this man?

The pickup was now rumbling along a rocky, tree lined trail in the shade of the road above. She could see a small group of run down houses beyond the trees on her right. She had felt so sure about him, his manner, his smile, his openness with the receptionist. She clutched Ellie close, a shiver tingling in her spine. She was about to call out his name, when he swung the pickup hard to the left and into darkness.

'Antonis!' the name shot out of her lips now startling Ellie awake. Suddenly she was dazzled by the sunlight, as they emerged from the underpass, the beach clearly visible ahead of them.

'What is it? Are you alright?' he asked, bringing the pickup to an abrupt halt.

'Yes … yes, I'm sorry, I thought …' she breathed a sigh of relief and tried to settle Ellie. 'It's nothing … please, carry on. The beach looks beautiful.'

He drove on a short distance, then pulled up close to a path that led down to the secluded bay. Gathering up the bags and the beach mats, he led her down past a small rocky outcrop, overgrown with succulents. A green cascade that tumbled down to the beach below studded here and there with purple flowers.

Catherine soon understood what he had meant about the tiny smooth stones that made up the beach. Throwing off her sandals, she luxuriated in their feel now, as they slipped between her toes. To their left, the rocky outcrop rose higher up encircling the bay. In the distance to her right, beyond a small promontory, she could see the busier beaches of the seafront hotels. Here though, there were scarcely a handful of people.

Antonis rolled out the beach mats and spread out a small, woven blanket for them, placing the carrier bags in the middle.

'Let me help.' Catherine laid the now sleeping Ellie down, sheltering her with the portable parasol from her bag, and began unpacking the picnic.

Antonis' friends in the kitchens had done him proud, and it was easy to make small talk over the food. But sometime soon, somehow she would have to bring the conversation around to Michaelis Serides. She didn't want him to think that she was here just for that, and as she began to reflect now, nor was she. There was plenty of time. It would keep. Instead, she found herself saying, 'You must be boiling in those,' looking at his dark trousers and long-sleeved shirt, his only concession to the full heat of the day having been a roll up of the sleeves.

Antonis shrugged, looked up at the sun, assessed it for a moment and nodded. 'Yes, it's probably warm enough today. *Ena lepto* ... one minute.' He got up and strolled back to the pickup. Catherine tidied away the remains of their feast and settled back on the beach mat as Antonis reappeared. Now dressed in swimming trunks, he threw a towel over to their blanket. Catherine wondered how, if he drove a bus all day, he had managed to stay in such good shape. She was also aware as he sprinted down to the sea that her interest in his lithe, tanned body was far from academic.

She watched him dive in — emerging moments later — to swim with clean, powerful strokes towards a group of rocks. Encouraged by his own relaxed manner, she now felt more comfortable about slipping out of her own top and shorts, to the bikini she wore underneath.

Ellie was stirring. Catherine had packed a bottle and hoped Ellie wouldn't kick up a fuss, demanding the real thing. But in the event, she seemed much more interested in the fruit that had come with their picnic, and proceeded to spread as much as she ate, around her face.

'Time for a paddle my girl!' Catherine had decided a splash in the sea would be the easiest way of cleaning her up and set her down at the water's edge, amid squeals of surprise as she sat in the cooling waters and struggled to get to her feet again, the waves gently lapping around her.

Antonis had swum across to another shallower group of rocks, and now seeing them up and about, turned back towards them. He arrived amid a shower of spray, drawing more squeals from Ellie as he sat on his haunches beside her.

With one hand, he scooped out a hollow in the wet shingle and as the waters filled it, unfolded his other to reveal the purpose of his visit to the shallower rock pools. Dropping a little crab into the improvised pool, he continued gently thwarting the crab's attempts to burrow down to safety for Ellie's amusement. Eventually Ellie's interest waned, and the little crab was allowed to scuttle off to freedom once more. Reaching up to Catherine, Ellie made it clear what she was after.

'I'm sorry ...' she grimaced awkwardly, 'I'm going to have to ...'

'No problem, I understand.' Antonis smiled reassuringly, 'I need a walk to dry off.'

She watched him stroll away along the beach, pausing occasionally to flip a bit of driftwood over, as she made her own way back up to their mats. Drying Ellie down, Catherine let her suckle, but after a couple of half-hearted attempts, she began to nod off. Drawing a towel around her, Catherine encouraged her to snuggle down beside her and before long she too found her own eyes closing in the now more comfortable warmth of the afternoon sun.

Diane had also found it difficult to stay alert after lunching on the hotel terrace. Her concerns about Catherine and Ellie's whereabouts and well-being had been somewhat mollified by the receptionist's earnest assurances regarding the character of their trusted driver Antonis, and she had allowed herself a glass of white wine with the late lunch. Perfectly chilled, it had quickly led to another in the balmy heat of the afternoon, and so to the requisite nap in her room.

Relaxed now, the only sound permeating the silence of the siesta being the rhythmical hiss of the lawn sprinklers drifting up from below, Diane put aside her worries and in her mind's eye wandered once more through the galleries of the archaeological museum, reliving the wonder of the precious artefacts she had seen and wondering indeed what their lives must have been like, these bull leapers and snake goddess worshippers. So strange, so very different — and yet in many ways so similar — men still drinking from the same vines, their wives bejewelled, children playful.

Diane pictured again the little clay model of the child on the swing, and as sleep began to transmute her imaginings into dreams, so the gentle *swish, swish* of the sprinklers carrying still upon the breeze became the swing's rope, creaking and straining on the bough above the little girl.

The girl's clothes, like the low terraced villa beyond with its painted columns, were from a different time. Her dusky face, which should have been the face of a stranger, so clearly of different race — was in many ways so achingly familiar — yet how could it be otherwise, for in this dream, she knew this child was hers.

'Higher Daddy, higher!'

Diane struggled to speak out, desperate to urge caution, but was unable to make any sound in her dream and found herself able only to watch as the child's father gave in to their daughter's request.

One sandal slipped from her daughter's foot as the swing lurched higher. Father and daughter laughed together, the whites of their teeth sparkling against dusky skin, the afternoon sun glinting off the gold adornments in their flowing black locks. Again, her daughter's skirts billowed as the swing flew higher still — the remaining sandal also flying loose.

Again Diane struggled to cry out for the child's safety, but instead a voice from the villa beyond halted the play. It was a voice whose absolute authority she instinctively recognised. One that propelled her from onlooker to full participant in the crystal clarity of this dream.

She rushed forward to catch her daughter — now tumbling from the swing that her father held arrested in the air — his attention focused on the source of the cry behind. A woman's voice. A familiar and assured voice that expected to be answered.

The child flew into Diane's comforting embrace. She could smell the jasmine in her daughter's hair, feel the wetness of her tears as they fell on her own bare breast. Diane looked up to her lover, but she had always known this day would come and both knew what the return of his wife would mean for mother and daughter.

He rested a comforting hand on her shoulder now, as she gazed at the woman standing in the colonnaded terrace, surveying her new home. Around her spilled a retinue of attendants laden with her belongings. Diane felt the hand on her own shoulder give one final squeeze as he left her.

Her daughter struggled to join him, but she held her tight, silencing her complaints. They watched together as he walked back through the lemon grove to his wife, returned for good now from their homeland of the Nile.

A deep rumble grew below their feet. It shook the earth and the lemon trees swayed. Shaken from their branches, a rain of fruit tumbled to the ground. He turned to look back — not at them — but past them at the mountain in the distance. They followed his gaze. An ominous plume of smoke spiralled above its heights and now as they all turned to stare, they could see a faint glow begin to tinge the rising clouds, but this was not the work of the sun.

An unfamiliar sound filtered into Catherine's own dreams, triggering her conscious mind to query its origin. An irregular scratching told of some light labour nearby. Shrugging off her drowsiness, she turned to find Antonis seated on a rock at the foot of the slope, quietly carving away at a piece of driftwood.

Seeing that he was now dressed, left Catherine feeling exposed. Easing Ellie aside, she slipped her top back on and drew up her shorts. Alerted by her movements, Antonis ambled over and squatted down beside her, burnishing the piece of wood with his hands.

'What's that?' Catherine whispered, one eye on Ellie.

'For your daughter,' replied Antonis softly, handing her the carving. 'A souvenir.'

The gnarled and weathered piece of driftwood now had a permanent visitor climbing over its twisted roots: A tiny crab.

'That's amazing! How did you do that … is it stuck on?'

'No, no … it is one piece of wood … you just have to cut back underneath … so.' Antonis demonstrated for her, tidying up a remaining claw, before handing back the finished carving.

'Thank you, that's so kind.' Catherine cradled the carving, genuinely impressed, but her mind was also racing once more with her original mission: How best to strike up a conversation about Michaelis Serides? She was sure Antonis would soon need to be getting back to the hotel. Probably best just to wade in, she concluded.

'Yesterday evening … at that night club…'

'Yes, I apologise,' said Antonis unexpectedly, 'I have been worrying about that. I hope you did not think I was interfering?' Catherine could not hide her confusion. 'Warning you not to go in there … it was not my business.'

'No … no, really, it's quite alright … I'm glad you did.'

'Why, did something happen?'

'No … well … yes in a way,' Catherine realised the door had been thrown wide open for her. 'You see, my mother had wanted to see the owner, Mr Serides.' A look from Antonis did little to conceal his opinion, but he let her continue. 'She came to Crete, to look for … a friend. Someone who went missing a long time ago. She thought Mr Serides might have known him.'

'And did he?'

'He says not, but my mother doesn't believe him.' Catherine changed tack, 'He seemed very rude to you last night outside the club?' inviting him to explain.

'Serides!' The name was explanation itself as far as Antonis was concerned.

'Was that your mother with you?' Catherine pressed on as Antonis nodded. 'It seemed an unlikely place for her to be. What was the argument about?' Sensing he was unwilling to explain, 'I'm sorry that's very rude of me, it's none of my business!'

'It's nothing …' he shrugged, 'just village matters!'

'You're from the same village?' Catherine feigned surprise. Antonis nodded. 'Up in the hills.'

'I suppose it must be difficult living so closely to one another?'

'He lives in Heraklion now. His family came from the mainland, before the war.'

'So, they're outsiders really?'

Antonis gave a bitter laugh, 'It is us they have made the outsiders!'

'For some strange reason Mr Serides seemed to think that my mother's enquiries had something to do with your argument.' Catherine hoped Antonis would be drawn into an explanation. 'He got very angry for a moment ….'

'Why did your mother think Serides knew her friend?'

Catherine knew this was the moment to sink or swim. 'He was in a newspaper article … it was about the discovery of a Minoan earring … ' From his look, Catherine could tell Antonis knew exactly what she was talking about. He listened intently, but said nothing, forcing her to divulge more. Wary of a similar response to last night's outburst, Catherine began to improvise, 'I think the friend she is looking for might have been an archaeologist who knew something about the other earring … she hasn't explained it to me properly … says it was a long time ago.'

'How long?' queried Antonis.

'During the war … before I was born, I suppose.' A shiver coursed down her spine the moment the words had left her lips, and her brain raced to assess the ramifications of what she had just said. She sensed that something of vital importance lay just beyond the grasp of her faculties, but her speculations were abruptly cut short.

'We have to go.' Antonis began gathering up the mats. 'My shift,' he offered by way of explanation.

Catherine scooped her belongings back into her bag, and cradling the still sleeping Ellie in her towel they headed back to the pickup in silence. It was not just the atmosphere that had chilled. The heat of the day was passing, and with a strengthening breeze bringing cloud, she was grateful to get into the warmth of the pickup cab. The journey back passed quickly and quietly, Ellie snuggled into one arm.

Catherine toyed absently with the driftwood carving in her free hand, unable to think of any comfortable way to probe for further information about Michaelis Serides. Besides, a burning question of a very different nature was now circling endlessly in her mind.

As Antonis pulled up in the hotel car park, she struggled to salvage something of the afternoon. 'Thank you for this afternoon, and for Ellie's present. Listen, I'm sorry if I said...'

'No problem!' Antonis smiled, but Catherine noticed that this time, his eyes remained far away in thoughts of his own.

ELEVEN

The fleeting satisfaction of swatting the irritating insect, though ending its persistent, dancing attentions about his collar, served only to remind Richard that the wound on his neck had still not fully healed though it had had a good three weeks to do so.

All in all, it had been a pretty depressing day. The bombing and strafing had been particularly heavy. There had been a steady build up in intensity over the past week. The much anticipated invasion could not be far away.

The only incident to brighten their day had been the arrival, late in the afternoon of two boxes of grenades that Jim was now cheerfully demonstrating how to prime in front of his captive local audience. Their brief sojourn together in the field hospital had meant that both had missed the onward embarkations of their respective companies and in the push to organise a hastily improvised defence of the island, they now found themselves assigned to train and assist a group of local irregulars, as part of the recently formed 'Creforce.'

Looking north from their encampment towards the sea, the low, flat plain of Maleme airfield was clearly visible as, with the aid of field glasses, were the Bofors guns emplaced to defend it from enemy use. One battery overlooked the mouth of the Tavronitis river below them to the west, the other guarding seaward to the east. Lacking any natural cover, they had proved to be a favourite target for the daily bombing raids, but they had survived thus far.

Between the airfield and their encampment, rose the hill that had been designated 107 in the midground below them to their right. A high spur, ideal for the anti-aircraft emplacements now crowning it, while the dry riverbed of the Tavronitis continued its journey inland down the slope to the left. Situated in a clearing in the higher ground above, they were well placed to assist in any invasion that may develop, but the brunt of any such attack would be borne by the New Zealand companies, spread out over the terrain below.

Across the island, similar strongholds at Rethymnon, Chanea, and Heraklion were also being guarded by whatever forces were available. Once again, fighting units were formed from the remaining elements of the evacuated British Expeditionary Force. Once again Greek and Briton stood beside the Anzacs and their other allies, and once again they did so with pitifully few armaments or air cover. They knew that a massive build-up of enemy air transport had been reported on the mainland and there was still the danger of invasion by sea. It seemed only a matter of time.

Richard surveyed their own loosely knit company. Among them were a small group of Greek soldiers from the mainland. Survivors of various regiments, their drab uniforms hung in ill-fitting, antiquated fashion upon the weary and disillusioned shoulders of their occupants.

Their mood, he noticed also, was markedly different from that of their Cretan cousins, older men, whose sons had been sent to fight at the Albanian front. They waited now to defend their country with a grim determination. But these men with their proud spirits seemed even more firmly rooted in the past, many with antiquated pistols that had last seen service during the Turkish occupation, tucked into their breeches.

Richard's eyes came to rest upon Manolis, a Cretan whom both Jim and Richard had recognised as being something of a leader among his compatriots. He stood now, keenly following Jim's every movement in the continuing demonstration. Like his compatriots, Manolis wore the distinctive Cretan breeches, tucked into long, black leather boots. A loose shirt and the traditional *sariki*, his knotted black headscarf, completed the attire save for the one other seemingly compulsory Cretan adornment, his splendid walrus moustache.

Richard would have put the man's age in his fifties, but wouldn't have laid any money on a definite guess. There was a majestic air to the man, with which time did not interfere. He leant upon one of a few captured Italian rifles that had been distributed among his men. Some had lashed bread knives to the barrels to serve as bayonets, none had more than a handful of rounds to use in them. Yet they were the luckier ones, for many had only knives and hastily improvised weapons that had seen better service in the fields and vineyards.

The Greek soldiers were armed with rifles of various provenance, but they too lacked any suitable quantity of ammunition. Communication to HQ was by runner, there were no remaining field telephones or wireless sets. Even the larger, better equipped companies struggled in this respect.

Richard and Jim realised they would be very much left to their own devices

'Well ... reckon they got it?' Jim asked, his demonstration over.

'There'll be a job for you on the halls when this is all over!' joked Richard.

'Universal language that lad. Got to ham it up a bit, they don't speak a word of the lingo.'

'Thank you Capitaine.' The deep, gentle voice of Manolis interrupted their conversation, disproving Jim's assertion somewhat. 'My men not ...' he struggled for the word, 'disappoint you. We ... owe you.'

Brushing aside their demurrals, he continued to explain in broken English that he wanted the 'Capitaines' to go with him, and at length it became clear that there was to be a gathering that evening at his house to celebrate his niece's engagement. Expressing his disbelief that such an event was to be held in the present circumstances brought Richard only a shrug from Manolis.

'Why to wait? Not good to leave our *raki* for them ... the Germanos to drink.'

Richard realised that Manolis, despite his proud and avowed determination to fight for his land, sensed the true seriousness of the situation confronting them.

'Not far ... come ... you will like!'

The prospect of any enjoyment that would break the dull monotony of the long evenings they had spent with only dawn bombing raids to look forward to was naturally appealing.

'Might as well,' said Jim, 'looks as though he's already sorted out who's staying on guard and who's going!'

'Anything happen ... my men tell me ... quick!' He

reassured Richard. 'Not far.' He gestured further up the hillside and began to move off, accompanied by several others, turning as the 'Capitaines' hesitated, '*Ela* ... Come!'

'Well, I don't know what the form is for engagements in these parts, but I'd say there's one young lass who's going to be a bit surprised at the guest list!' Jim headed off into the rapidly fading dusk.

'I'm amazed it's happening at all.'

They followed the motley group up along a rough track, which narrowed as it cut through two vineyards banked up on either side of them. The chatter diminished as they fell into single file, but at their head, Manolis could still be heard chanting an old Cretan *mantinada*. Bringing up the rear, Richard tried to push from his mind the nagging fear that this would prove to be the very night their presence would be needed at the camp, when he became aware of a rustling of leaves above him. But looking up, he could only see the twisted black silhouettes of the vines, clinging to their rocky perch. He paused warily, but there was no sound now save for Manolis' song and the tread of diminishing footsteps.

He was about to continue when he heard it again, a heavy rustling up among the vines — then came a sharp snap — followed by a stumbling scuffle of sounds. A fine spray of dirt spattered down around him.

Flattening his back against the rocky wall, he readied his rifle, no longer in any doubt. Someone was up among the vines. Ahead, Jim and the last of the others rounded a bend that took them out of sight, leaving him alone in the gloomy gully.

A rapid review of his options was swiftly brought to a halt as, alerted by another fall of soil, he turned in time to glimpse the dark form of a figure leaping down onto the track behind him. Swinging fully round, he levelled his rifle at the man, and hardly recognising his own voice, croaked out the request for password. But barely had the sound left his lips, than from his other side came the ominous thud of a second pair of boots hitting the track.

Instinct told him to shoot now at the first man, but as his finger tightened around the trigger, the latter called out to the first and the language he used arrested Richard's motion, for it was Greek. A wave of relief coursed through him, but his training still held him in his stance as now, more forcefully, he repeated his demand for the password.

A flurry of dialogue between the two Greeks passed quite literally over his head. Their tone as untroubled as any mundane conversation over coffee eventually produced the word he was looking for. The dark figure approached, and what at one point Richard had thought to be a machine gun, he now saw was a bundle of green shoots cradled in the man's arms. Turning, he could see that the second man had also been gathering the same, and looking up into their grinning faces, he recognised them as two of the Greek soldiers from their party. Both were highly amused at the anxiety they had caused.

Richard's stony expression prompted the first to explain in rudimentary fashion the purpose of their actions. Waving the shoots in front of Richard's face, he pointed up to the vineyard, then began to chew on one.

'*Kalo* … good.' He explained, then thrusting some into Richard's hands, squeezed past him to join his friend. Together they ran on to rejoin the others, their laughter mapping out the many twists and turns of the track ahead, leaving Richard to follow. Both out of curiosity and as an endeavour to halt his racing adrenalin, he began to chew upon the vine shoots. The taste was not unpleasant, if a little astringent, and hurrying on, he too caught up with the party.

Leaving the track now, they came upon a wider road, that climbed in sweeping curves up the hillside. At its crest the road delivered them into a small village square, where the menfolk were gathered in a simple *kafeneon.*

Manolis marched in to prise out more guests and as the party spiralled off to wind its way along the narrow alleyways of the village to his house, so it increased in size, as friends and relations responded to his invitations until, arriving at his door, he waited to usher the 'Capitaines' personally into his home.

He called out for his wife to leave her kitchen and greet his guests. Dusting her floury hands upon her apron, she hurried to the door, a broad smile upon her careworn face. As Richard and Jim presented themselves in turn at the door, she bustled them inside, chattering away, oblivious to the fact that neither of them spoke a word of her language. To which fact Manolis tried several times in vain to apprise her, but she simply nodded happily and continued to fuss over her guests. Richard turned to Manolis for help.

'She greets you … *Kalos orisate* … it means welcome.' Manolis explained, leaving the rest of his congregation to file into his house.

'What should I say in return, to thank her?'

'*Kalos sas vrikame.*'

Richard stumbled over the foreign words, but obviously succeeded in getting the message across, as Manolis' wife shrieked with delight at his efforts. She then flung her arms around him and escorted him across to a chair, shooing out its previous occupant, before disappearing back into her kitchen from where her shrill voice could be heard in excited conversation with others of her sex, who occasionally peered out for a glimpse of the foreign 'Capitaines.'

They took in their surroundings. The room was simply furnished. A large table dominated its centre with numerous chairs surrounding it. Several more, borrowed for the occasion, lined the walls. A sideboard, chest, and settle were the only other items of furniture, each covered with finely embroidered cloths that spoke of long evenings' labours under the flickering oil lamps that stood upon them. Brushwood crackled in the simple open fire. The only pictures to decorate the otherwise bare stone walls showed the family's ancestors, glaring down proudly at the assembled company. A faded wedding photograph adorned the sideboard.

All eyes were fixed upon the 'Capitaines,' who sat with equally fixed smiles, wondering what they should say.

'Something smells good!' ventured Jim, who fortunately did not have to wait long before discovering the origins of the tempting aroma, as a pretty young girl appeared from the kitchen, carrying a tray of hot cakes and several small glasses, brimming with a clear liquid.

'Delicious' he mumbled through a mouthful of rich doughy pastry, discovering its creamy cheese filling. The young girl smiled shyly at his compliment.

'They are called *kalitsounia*,' Manolis explained, taking a glass, 'and this is *tsikouthia* … *raki* from my own grapes … Cretan brandy! *Yamas!*' He downed the glass.

Jim raised his glass and gave the girl a broad grin, 'Cheers pet!' Things were looking up at last he thought.

'This is my niece Maria, the one who is to be engaged.' Manolis continued, the latter piece of information reaching Jim's ears mid-swallow, with distressing effect.

Richard gave Jim a good slap on the back and raised his own glass. 'To Maria!'

Taking a carafe from the table Manolis refilled their glasses, and when he was satisfied that all in the room had a full glass, he called Maria and her young man, Dimitri, to him and the hubbub of chatter stilled. All that could be heard was the crackle of twigs smouldering in the smoky fire.

Taking out a small brown envelope from the sideboard drawer, Manolis withdrew a simple gold cross on a chain and fastened it around the young man's neck. Then as Manolis' wife brought out an icon of St George from their bedroom, he blessed their exchange of rings and the room burst into life again as everyone toasted the couple.

They could be little more than fifteen thought Richard, as he raised his glass and watched Maria and Dimitri take their place at the head of the table. Manolis urged his guests to draw their chairs closer to the table as the women began bringing out steaming plates of soup.

'Are you the local priest or something?' asked Richard.

Manolis laughed. 'No … for an engagement, no priest … only for the wedding … whenever that will be.' His smile slipped away as the outside world began to encroach upon the happy event. He gazed at the couple for a moment, before explaining. 'I do this for her father, my little brother … he died … in Albania. That is his wife.' He nodded to the young widow, dressed in the black she would wear for life. Then, as suddenly as the mood had descended upon him, so

Manolis brushed the matter aside with a sweeping gesture. 'Now … eat!'

His guests needed little encouragement, the soup of chicken and rice with its distinctively flavoured egg and lemon base was rich and satisfying. To stomachs hardened on short rations, this alone would have been ample, but there was more to come. The soup plates, once drained, were replaced by others, heaped with macaroni and freshly grated goat's cheese, while in the centre of the table there was an enormous dish of lamb.

The 'Capitaines' lost little time in emulating the local guests, who, having unsheathed their knives, proceeded to spear their choice of cut. The wine, like the *tsikouthia*, came from Manolis' own vines and he would not see a glass empty. For all there it was the first decent meal in months, and scant breath was wasted in talk. Food, Richard knew, had also become a serious problem for the civilians, and he wondered how Manolis and more to the point his wife had managed to lay on such a spread.

Finally, when everyone had had their fill, the women cleared the main table for the men to carry outside. An elderly Cretan picked up his lyra and with a liberal dispensation of *tsikouthia* at hand to oil his bowing arm began to fill the room with an urgent rhythm, summoning the young couple to dance.

Manolis knelt to clap out the time as his niece and her fiancé began to trace the intricate footsteps of their forbears. It was an art of which they were rightly proud and one which the young couple had enjoyed for much of their short span, so that now, beyond a first fleeting embarrassment at being the centre of so much attention, they settled into their ritualised motions with an accomplished air of confidence that belied their tender years.

'You'd think they were born dancing, these Cretans!'

Finding Jim's sentiments echoing his own thoughts, Richard nodded, content to succumb to the potent combination of the music and *tsikouthia*, both of which were bringing for the first time in months some welcome relaxation and a general sense of well-being.

A plaintive, discordant note held on the lyra was the cue for the young couple's dance to end and their efforts were applauded enthusiastically. The boy urged his new uncle to dance for them now.

Manolis needed little persuasion. Exchanging places with them he stood, arms spread in universal embrace, motionless, waiting for the music to take its hold. A hush fell upon the room as the old Cretan drew out a haunting melody from his simple instrument. All eyes fell upon the majestic, immobile figure before them.

Slowly, imperceptibly almost, the statue came to life. Richard marvelled at the grace with which the rugged, blustering bulk of a man shrugged off time's ravages from his frame. Scorning gravity's claims, he was as one with the music. Gradually the partnership quickened their pace, urged on by enthusiastic shouts from their audience until, leaping as high as his room would allow, Manolis smartly slapped the soles of both his boots before returning to earth, repeating the trick several times to roars of approval from the delighted assembly.

One by one, others stood up to join in the dance and Manolis entreated Richard and Jim to join them, but neither of the 'Capitaines,' despite the emboldening effects of the *tsikouthia*, felt brave enough to take up the challenge. Manolis, however, was not to be dissuaded, and grasping Jim pulled him into the circle.

Richard also found himself hauled to his feet by the two Greek soldiers he had encountered in the vineyard. Aping his grim, rifle-poised stance, they related the episode to the assembled company drawing suitable guffaws, but their humour was good natured and any discomfort short lived, for they were keen to show their Cretan cousins that they knew a step or two themselves. Arms entwined, they drew their foreign guests into their circle, slowly pacing out the steps for them to follow.

Just when the 'Capitaines' finally thought they had the hang of it, the pace inevitably quickened and they sought valiantly, both to keep up and at the same time steer clear of the flailing boots, as one after another led the circle with his own acrobatic speciality.

Grasping a bottle, Manolis stepped into the centre of the rotating circle, thrusting it to the lips of each dancer as they passed. And so the circle spun round and round, as indeed did the vineyards, when much later Richard and Jim retraced their footsteps back to camp, leaving the Greeks with their Cretan hosts to carouse on into the early hours.

TWELVE

To Richard it seemed no time at all before the following day was upon them. Stand to was accompanied by the now well-accustomed attentions of the daily dawn bombing raid. Whether this day's raid was actually heavier and more vicious than usual, or it was simply his aching head that made it seem so, he was unaware, being thankful only that an hour or so later they ceased, in time for him to reflect on a very unappetising breakfast by comparison to the previous night's fare.

No sooner had he summoned up the courage to tackle some food though than another wave of bombers appeared, sending them all scurrying back into the slit trenches. The sky above gradually turned black with an unprecedented mass of planes, and as bomb after bomb fell around them ploughing up the earth, so fighter planes followed in the wake of each pass, strafing those rooted out and fleeing for better cover. Richard now knew for certain that this day was not to be like any other.

'Something's up.' He muttered to Jim, crouched now behind him.

'Yeah … my breakfast!'

A stick of bombs ripped into a nearby trench beneath a group of olive trees, scything down the trees along with its sheltering occupants and deafening the rest with its shock wave. Richard had seen the two Greek soldiers he had danced with heading for the trees moments earlier, and now feared the worst. Brushing off the mantle of debris that showered upon him, he realised with growing revulsion that it was not only earth that covered him, but the continuing *blitzkrieg* gave him no time to dwell upon the grim discovery.

Incessantly the bombs thundered about them, confounding their senses until, some thirty minutes later there came a lull in the activity, but peering above the trench, Richard was able to see precious little. Everything was swirling dust and smoke. The bombers could still be heard attacking the airfield, but the dark shapes Richard now saw as he strained to peer through the murk were not bombers. Barely visible, yet clearly not so very distant, the noiseless, looming shapes made no sense. For a moment he was convinced that he had gone deaf, yet the hubbub of distant battle still rang in his ears. Then he recognised the silent intruders.

'Gliders!'

Rising above the discordant drone of the Ju52's triple motors, Werner's strident tenor voice outshone Dieter's baritone in the final rousing chorus of '*Rot Scheint die Sonne.*' Competitive in every single thing since childhood, the boyhood friends, like the sixteen other crack parachutists of the elite *Fallschirmjaeger* seated alongside them in the rattling Junkers transport plane, were pumped full of adrenaline. The shots of caffeine and sodium salicylate they had each been injected with, along with the amphetamines, prior to boarding the trusty, corrugated *'Tante Ju'* transports, were working their magic. The obligatory glass of lemonade quenched some of the thirst, but more importantly, its fruit acids were guaranteed to kickstart the rush. There were more amphetamines packed in their specialist uniforms, but there would be no need for them: such was the might of the *Fliegerkorps* that was about to descend on the tiny island of Crete.

Ten-thousand paratroopers had been kept primed for this assault, considered vital to deny the Allies control of the Mediterranean. For weeks they had been under orders of strictest secrecy: their parachutists' sing-songs banned, paybooks replaced by identity cards, unable to wear even their hallowed parachute badges as they congregated at their newly captured airfields in mainland Greece.

Werner proudly fingered his own badge, now reinstated, of the plunging eagle, framed in its oak and laurel leaf garland, beneath his heavily padded over-jacket. Dieter read his thoughts and grinned at his friend. Their talk for days had been of nothing else but this, and now the moment had finally arrived. Corinth lay behind them and they were part of the spearhead for Group West. Their objective: to storm the Maleme airfield.

He adjusted his rubberised kneepads, and re-tightened his helmet straps, before checking his pistol one final time.

'No cheating now Werner!' he gibed at his friend, 'Only definite kills count!'

Werner laughed. 'I won't need to cheat. I've autographed every bullet, so they'll know just whose it was that killed them!'

Dieter had watched his friend while away the long hours of waiting, carefully engraving spirals on every round of ammunition: the same spiral that adorned the butt of his luger pistol.

'Don't forget, triple points for one with the knife!' Werner brandished the long blade.

'Well while you're busy sticking pigs, I'll already have got to the big guns!' Dieter boasted, nodding to the weapons canisters, their static lines already attached to the cable above.

'Let's just hope the assault gliders have left us something to do!'

Werner and Dieter knew that the bombers would already have softened up what pitiful defences the Allied troops had left, and at this very moment dozens more '*Tante Ju's*' would be freeing the first wave of assault gliders they had towed from the mainland with their elite attack troops onboard, preparing the way for their own parachute assault. It would be a simple case of mopping up. They pictured their comrades springing out from the silvery gliders, weapons blazing.

The alert halted their reveries and the men lined up after their officers, attaching their lines to the cable above as the cabin door was secured open. The rush of air heightened their senses still further and they looked down eagerly at the landscape slipping by beneath them.

Flying low, they could clearly see the terrain, pockmarked and smoking. The bombers had done their work well. Werner moved up the line as the officers jumped first — their pale crimson chutes bursting open as they leapt out spreadeagled. White chutes of other ranks followed, interspersed by the camouflage chutes that marked the weapons canisters they would head for. Behind them would be the yellow chutes of the medical supplies. Not much need of them judging by the devastation below.

Werner stood at the door, one hand on either side rail, felt Dieter's friendly slap on his arm, and leapt into the air. He felt the tug of the static line pull at the harness between his shoulder blades and struggled to focus through the billowing smoke that clouded his goggles. The smoke cleared. Ahead, he could see the falling chutes of the previous group as they drifted to earth. Though he could not hear the shots ring out, he saw their effect as one by one his comrades fell limp under their chutes, some crashing into trees as they hit the ground, others tumbling to earth as their chutes billowed into flames from incendiary tracers. Gunfire seemed to be coming from all around them and then the familiar din of an anti-aircraft gun reached him, and he heard the shells rip into the following transport plane above, sending men plummeting past him, disgorged from the rending of its belly.

Werner tried to reach for his pistol. This should not be happening. The defences were supposed to have been wiped out. He felt the bullet lodge in his spine, but strangely there seemed to be no pain, no sensation. He watched, almost hypnotised as the ground sped up towards him, he had to swing his legs forward — be ready to roll — but his lower body was paralysed. Skimming down past an olive tree, a branch snagged his chute, jerking him upright.

His feet met the ground, legs buckled underneath him, and he heard but still did not feel the bones break beneath him. The chute flurried to a rest above him, still snagged upon the tree, leaving him sitting — bolt upright — unable to move.

As the dust began to clear he saw an old woman running towards him. His mind flashed back to the old farm where he and Dieter had played as children. She reminded him of Aunt Elfrieda, always around to patch up their grazes. Elfrieda would help him now. He managed to remove his goggles as the old woman reached him, just in time to see her raise the heavy wooden scythe, before hurling its shiny, steel blade down into his face. As the blood obscured his vision, and beyond his own screams, he was sure he heard his name being called — one last time.

'Werner!'

'Werner!' Dieter howled his friend's name, horrified at the sight. Struggling to free himself of his own parachute, gunfire forced him back down into the undergrowth preventing him from rushing directly to his friend. Firing his own pistol in the direction of the shots, he made for the cover of another nearby tree. From there he could still see Werner. A man had now joined the woman and was stripping Werner of his weapons.

Dieter took aim and fired, one shot at the woman, one at the man. His first shot rang off the blade of her scythe, throwing both of them out of range of his second. The pair rapidly disappeared into the undergrowth, but not before the man had delivered a final shot from Werner's own luger, convulsing his body, leaving him slumped, head down, lifeless. Rapid gunfire and shouts from his commanding officer forced Dieter to abandon his friend and head for the weapons canister.

'One day …' he sobbed through gritted teeth '… one day!'

'Like shooting ducks at the fairground!' Jim shouted, picking off one after another of the wave of parachutists, floating down towards them. Having been relieved of his bren gun, he was now like Richard equipped with a rifle and it was rapidly becoming his new best friend.

'Tell your men not to fire all at once,' Richard shouted over to Manolis. 'Get them to save their ammo. Each pick a man … aim for their feet!'

To the west, they had watched the gliders come to rest around the dry river bed, some carrying on to safer ground further westwards, but many had landed right in the middle of the New Zealand defences. Their occupants had been swiftly machine gunned down, most unable to even get out of the planes.

Below and to the east, the anti-aircraft battery sited on Hill 107, though struggling to cope with the low approach of the enemy transports, steadily took its toll. Despite the appalling attrition, wave after wave of planes in triple formation continued to drop more paratroopers.

Like seeds blown on the wind as they left the planes, one by one, the parachutes blossomed and billowed open, leaving the *Fallschirmjaeger* dangling at the mercy of their gossamer canopies, the elements, and the hostile reception awaiting them. In the distance Richard could see more troop gliders landing on the beaches, while just below, groups of surviving paratroopers were scrambling to organise themselves.

'They're all heading for the canisters.'

'Schmeissers!' said Jim as rapid fire began to be returned. 'We'll have some of those!' Grabbing a few of Manolis' men, he headed for a stray weapons canister that had landed nearby. Richard and the others kept the handful of survivors pinned down until the canister was retrieved.

'That's more like it,' said Jim, pulling out a submachine gun among the carefully stowed rifles and ammunition. 'let's see how you like some of your own medicine!'

Across the plain, as the day wore on, several more weapons canisters fell into Allied hands, re-arming the defenders and decimating the invaders, cut down by their own weapons. But by the afternoon, it was obvious that a significant German presence had established itself to the west of the Tavronitis river, threatening the airfield, while a determined group of surviving paratroopers had finally managed to dig themselves in against the company holding the slopes of Hill 107.

Later still that afternoon, keeping watch on the stalemate on the slopes below, Richard and Jim's attention was drawn to an offensive being mounted by the company guarding the airfield, as they endeavoured to drive the Germans back beyond the Tavronitis.

'They're bringing out the I tanks as well as the Bofors.' Richard handed Jim the single pair of field glasses they possessed.

'That should push the buggers back.' Jim watched the two light tanks that were the sum total of the remaining armoured fighting vehicles head off, covering the advance across the open airfield. 'Christ! There's only about forty Kiwis at best … it's seething with Krauts on the other side of the river!' he passed the glasses back to Richard to see for himself.

Richard watched as they managed to reach the edge of the airfield, when one of the tanks ceased firing and came to a halt. 'I don't believe it, there's one turning back!'

'Bet the bloody two pounder's jammed, what about his machine gun?'

'Nothing … now the other's packed up altogether …the Kiwis are all turning back.'

'Let me see …' Jim grabbed for the field glasses. Richard found himself happy to hand them over, relinquishing the sight of the retreating infantry being cut down on the open airfield as they did their best to withdraw. Jim's silence told him all he needed to know.

As night fell, an uneasy quiet finally descended upon the carnage.

'Penny for them?' asked Richard, aware that Jim himself had fallen unusually quiet.

'Our response. Just thinking about my old man. He took me down to Newcastle to buy us a last pint before I left with the Hussars. Made me stand in front of this bloody great monument … 'The Response' … fine thing mind. Angel up above, blowing the call to arms with all the lads like him below … that they'd raised for the Northumberland Fusiliers marching off to the Great War. He never talked much about his war … didn't then either really… I just remember him saying, "Do what you have to son, just make sure you come back." Most of his pals didn't.'

THIRTEEN

The dawn bombing raid lacked nothing of the previous day's intensity, but from their viewpoint Richard and Jim could clearly see how today's efforts were now far more accurately targeted on the New Zealand defences. The paratroopers had laid out a codework of symbols with yellow and white strips: signals to the pilots above, informing them not just of who to target and who to avoid, but also showing exactly what was needed in the way of equipment and supplies.

'Canny bastards!' Jim pointed towards the cluster of three parachutes: their combined payload a lightweight, field artillery gun drifting gently towards its requested drop zone, along with numerous other canisters of equipment. 'Ah now you're taking the piss man!' He watched in disgust as a motorcycle followed. 'What's next … *bierkellers*?'

'It gets worse …' Richard pointed to the airfield, where despite the hail of defending fire, the first of several Ju52's began to touch down, rapidly disgorging troops and equipment before promptly taking off again.

Alerted to the danger, all available weapons were quickly brought to bear on the transports and their reinforcements.

Soon, crippled planes began to litter the landing strip, but it was not very long before they were shunted away with the captured I tank, along with any other vehicle that could be repaired and put to use, and the reinforcements resumed as dive bombers continued to target the defender's gun emplacements.

Closer by, the detachment of paratroopers that had dug in the night before on the slopes below, were mounting an attack on the New Zealanders holding the foot-slopes of Hill 107.

'Why aren't their chums at the top helping out?'

'Because they've gone!' Richard answered Jim's query, his field glasses trained on the now abandoned anti-aircraft emplacement at the head of the spur.

'What the…?'

Jim's intended profanity was cut short by the breathless arrival of a runner from HQ.

Twenty minutes later, Richard and Jim found themselves contemplating the dismal probability of a second evacuation within the space of just a few weeks, assuming of course that the Royal Navy would be in a position to facilitate this. They, however, were currently attempting to thwart the combined element of the invasion — the German fleet now approaching the coast.

Having cut their field telephone lines, the paratroopers had succeeded in isolating the individual companies, so that HQ had been forced to rely on hastily retrieved information which, mistakenly, had led them to believe that the companies guarding the airfield and the foot-slopes of 107 had been overrun. As a consequence, the Company assigned to Hill 107 itself had been ordered to withdraw and regroup with the other remaining companies in a line defending the HQ and Pirgos village to the east.

There would be further attempts to retake the airfield, the runner had told them, but, sceptical that he or others would be able to relay any further news to their band of irregulars, the advice was to head towards Chania. From there any evacuation, if there was one, would have to head towards the south, across the White Mountains to Sphakia.

'You'll be able to hook up with your chums,' the runner had told Richard, 'There's still a detachment of the Rangers over there ... and some of your anti-tank lads too ...mostly infantry now though,' he aimed at Jim before heading back.

'Perhaps it is best you should go ...' Manolis' voice broke into their thoughts. 'I can send one of my men to guide you ... this fight is for us now.'

Any contemplation on the matter was pre-empted by a salvo of rifle fire from behind them, followed by an outburst of Greek issued with equal urgency.

'They're coming up towards us!' Manolis' translation galvanised the three men into action, joining their comrades as they tried to repulse a group of paratroopers working their way up the slopes to their own position. A volley of stick grenades sent them diving for cover, but determined now to have their vengeance, the band stood their ground, and as the paratroopers leapt over their defences — fully expecting their foes to have scattered — they were cut down point blank with everything the Cretans and their Greek compatriots had to offer, caring little whether it was Italian bullets or vintage Turkish musket shot that brought down the invaders.

'Time for the grenades ...', Jim hollered. Manolis' translation was redundant, as the missiles began to fly headlong into the rush of still advancing paratroopers. Unprepared for such a level of defence, the paratroopers were stunned into inaction as the grenades began to detonate among them. Both they and the beleaguered defendants froze like startled rabbits, as the advance of a paratrooper wielding his flame thrower was brought to a dramatic standstill. The grenade exploding at his feet triggered an inferno from the ruptured fuel tanks strapped to his back.

Taking hold of the situation, Manolis urged on a charge from his men.

'Go for it... now!' Richard urged, 'they're all bunched up.' He had spotted the weakness and they all now took advantage of the situation, pushing the invaders back down until they had no further source of retreat. Heedless of their lack of ammunition, the Cretans pressed on, resolute in a bayonet charge. Suddenly the paratroopers arms were thrown skywards — even the elite of the *Fallschirmjaeger* could not deal with this patriotic zeal.

'Halt! Hold your fire ... they're surrendering!' Jim and Richard's cries served only to halt the dispatch of a handful of remaining paratroopers. 'STOP!' they screamed.

'*Malakas*!' spat one of the Greek soldiers, 'Kill them now ... you leave them ... they will kill us ....'

'They have surrendered. They are our prisoners ... we have a duty.' Richard stepped between the Greek soldier and the paratrooper kneeling in front of him. Looking towards Manolis for support, Richard felt a bead of sweat trickle into the corner of his mouth. For a moment Manolis said nothing, weighing up the situation. Richard stood his ground.

Manolis issued a command, and his men surrounded the remaining paratroopers. As the Greek soldier spat his disgust, Manolis' men began to disarm and search the paratroopers. Richard sensed the relief course through the paratrooper's body beside him.

'*Ich danke ehnen*' he heard him gasp, as he turned to search him. Surprised at the amount of equipment concealed within the paratrooper's uniform, Richard added a printed leaflet from the trooper's jacket pocket to the growing pile of arms and sustenance gathered from their prisoners before instinct made him retrieve it. Pocketing it instead, he hauled the paratrooper to his feet. Now face to face, Dieter thanked Richard once more.

'*Danke schoen.*'

Diane relaxed into Eddie's embrace, following his effortless lead as he swept her around the Assembly Rooms dance floor. Tomorrow he would be gone. His own posting imminent, it was unlikely he would have any further leave. Caught in the swirl of emotions engulfing her and still not knowing where Richard was or what had happened to him, Diane had been unsure whether she should accept Eddie's invitation for a farewell at their local dance hall.

She and Eddie had always danced together so easily, but back then it had always been the three of them, yet Richard had usually left them to it, 'Two left feet,' his oft repeated excuse. Even on the couple of occasions they had all pitched up at the Assembly Rooms after their wedding, he had appeared genuinely happy to see Eddie wheel her through the steps he knew were alien to him.

Diane knew she could not let Eddie leave without a good send-off. Relaxing now into the rhythm of the band, she was glad to see him so happy. Nestling into his shoulder, she wondered when she might feel Richard's embrace again. Or Eddie's. A wave of despair swept over her at the prospect that she might never again hold close her two dearest childhood friends.

The blitz had been kind to them so far that evening and the dance was in full swing.

With each dance their small talk slipped away. Content to let the music be their guide, neither wanting the warmth of their embrace to end, they were among the last to leave.

Walking Diane home arm in arm, Eddie welcomed the easy silence between them. If they started talking now, he might not be able to keep his thoughts to himself any longer.

Finally, they were at her door.

'Well ducks, if I can't get my boots on tomorrow, I'll blame you for treading on my plates all night!'

'Take care Eddie.' Diane gave Eddie a hug. Embarrassed at the tears welling in her eyes, she accepted his handkerchief and hurriedly composed herself, before offering it back. Closing her hand around it, he took a step back.

'Bye ducks!' he gave her hand a last squeeze but found Diane's hand drawing him back to her. She struggled to find the right words, but there were none — knowing only that she could not let him leave without kissing him — a brief, urgent kiss that left both standing, foreheads touching, as if the racing thoughts in both their minds might somehow replace the words neither could find. Eddie's hand gently sought the nape of her neck, and easing her head back, he returned her kiss.

As the runner had predicted, no further news arrived and it rapidly became obvious that the counter-attacks on the airfield had failed, with plane after plane-load of German reinforcements landing unopposed throughout the day. Richard and Jim knew they had little alternative but to head east to Chania.

The problem was their prisoners. If they left them behind with Manolis, who was determined to remain and protect his family, they at least stood a good chance of not getting lynched by a determined group of the Cretan irregulars, who were as keen as the Greeks to be rid of them. But would the advancing Germans be as lenient to him when he handed them over?

On the other hand, if they tried to take the four men back towards Chania, not only would they be slowed down, they would become easy targets for any enemy groups they might run into along the way. Both Richard and Jim knew deep down that the slender authority they had been given as 'advisors' to the irregulars would very likely soon be challenged by the disaffected Greeks with whom they would be travelling.

It was Manolis in the end who came up with the solution. 'This is Fanouris. He takes his wife and boy back to his village … the same where I was born, near to Irakleio. He show you the way to Vrises, better than to go near Chania … many

Germans there.' He turned to Fanouris, '*Vrises, konta stin Georgopoulis. Xereis*?' Satisfied that Fanouris understood the plan, he turned back to Richard. 'From there you go South to Sphakia … he go on to east.'

Richard cast an eye towards the four paratroopers. Manolis continued.

'Two hours walk, then there is …' he struggled for the word, 'where water comes …'

'A spring?' suggested Richard.

Manolis shrugged, 'Water, anyway…' and rapidly conversed again in his own language with Fanouris. 'He knows this place. You leave the Germans there. They have water … it is easy they are found.'

Richard shook his hand. '*Efkharisto Manoli* … for everything.'

'*Sto kalo na pate, agori mou* … go well … but go now Capitaines … not many time!'

As they reached the spring, Richard could see the reasoning behind Manolis' suggestion. Several trees stood over the rough stone trough that captured the fall of the mountain spring water trickling down though green ferns from the rocks rising above it. The prisoners could be tied to the trees here with access to water and, on what passed for a main road, would soon enough be found.

Richard passed a couple of the ropes Manolis had given them to Jim, who muttered under his breath, 'Don't much fancy their chances if it turns out to be a few locals who find them first! They'll be trussed up for slaughter like this.'

'I know. Put a couple of slips between the knots … half-an-hour and they should be loose, then they can look out for themselves.'

As Richard finished tying the paratrooper he had earlier disarmed, he withdrew the printed leaflet he had retrieved. 'My German isn't up to much … but make sure you treat these people fairly,' Richard pointed to the ninth, on the list of ten exhortations from the *Wehrmacht*, for the conduct of their fighting elite, the *Fallschirmjaegers*. 'They are 'honest foes' as well.'

Dieter met Richard's gaze impassively, though as Richard suspected, he understood him perfectly well and knew without needing to look the command to which he was referring: 'Fight chivalrously against an honest foe; armed irregulars deserve no quarter.' Instead Dieter's gaze travelled over to Fanouris, waiting with his son and wife, her few meagre possessions and food for the journey now wrapped in a cloth bundle, which she had slung on the end of her long-handled scythe.

'It's their country, remember.' Richard stuffed the leaflet back into Dieter's jacket pocket and together with Jim followed the example of the Greek soldiers topping up their water bottles from the spring. From all accounts there was a tough journey ahead of them. Setting off, they were relieved to find the Greek soldiers content to leave the prisoners behind, without questioning Manolis' orders.

Fanouris led the way, his wife and son at his side. They followed the winding road onwards for a short while, before heading off on a smaller trail leading into the woods. As they passed into a small clearing, they heard Fanouris' raised voice and saw him railing at his son, landing him a clout around the ear. He held up the son's empty water bottle in explanation.

'*Pende lepta ...*' he said, holding up his hand to indicate five minutes to Richard and Jim, brushing past them as he headed back to the spring. About to follow, Richard found himself quietly restrained by Jim.

'You've done what you can.'

Fanouris' wife continued to chastise their son, '*Ilithios Michaeli ... Gaidaros!*'

The group settled down to wait as idle conversation between the Greek soldiers was occasionally interspersed by the crack of Michaelis' cheeks receiving further chastisement.

Eventually Fanouris reappeared, brandishing the full water bottle, and as Richard glanced at the soaked sleeves and front of his jacket, he mimed having slipped at the trough, making light of the resulting abrasions on his face and neck. Pushing on through the gathered soldiers, he took the lead once more.

Bringing up the rear, Richard nodded down to a patch of damp earth, where Fanouris had originally called the halt. Jim understood his suspicions, but knew he had to shrug it off.

'Better hope young Michaelis just pissed himself. Like I said, we did what we could.'

FOURTEEN

Diane struggled to answer the child's cries, willing herself to rise from the bed, but her body would not respond. Still tangled in the web of her dreams, the urgent complaints persisted, as did the semi-conscious paralysis of her limbs. In her mind she could visualise leaping from the bed to soothe — whom — whose child? As the dreams began to dissolve, she struggled to look back to that other child she had held, another daughter — another father — another partner, from some other far distant time that now rapidly eluded her mind's grasp.

Ellie's screams finally pierced her sleep's cocoon and Diane awoke to the reality of her hotel room — the sweat now cooling on her skin, as the colours of twilight faded outside the window informing her just how heavily she had slumbered. Thankful both for the glass of water she had remembered to leave on the bedside table, and for Catherine's soothing tones from next door, she heard Ellie's complaints diminish until a welcome silence prevailed.

Diane decided to risk swinging her legs round and slowly sat up, fully expecting to suffer a hangover, but was surprised and grateful to find she had escaped with nothing more than a raging thirst. As she did so, the earring that she had fallen asleep holding, slipped from her lap to the floor. She picked it up, instantly regretting rising so quickly and sat for a moment to recover and reflect on the few remaining fragments she could recall of the strange dream.

A strong image of the child's father persisted, flowing black locks, the glint of golden adornments in his hair. She struggled to picture the child again — their child. Had the girl been wearing the earrings in the dream, or was she now reconstructing it?

Amused at what the combination of a museum trip, two glasses of wine, and a fertile imagination could provide, she nevertheless felt the urge to jot down a note or two about it. Seldom before had she dreamed so vividly.

As she momentarily recalled the threat of the smoking volcano, she pulled out her diary from the bedside cabinet drawer. From it tumbled a shower of notes and receipts. Normally secured by a broad elastic band that held an envelope to the backboard of the diary, they now scattered freely to the floor. Diane checked the diary — the elastic band was still there — as was the envelope, but it now sat redundantly between the frontboard and the first page.

Diane knew full well that it would take a lot more than two glasses of wine for her to have broken such a long-established habit. She contemplated the only obvious alternative — someone else had been through her diary — someone who had not taken the trouble to cover their tracks properly.

She was not overly worried about any information that could be gleaned, it was mostly mundane stuff, otherwise she would have taken it with her. Diane was not the 'Dear Diary' type.

She looked at the remaining contents of the drawer. She could not be one hundred percent sure but felt — though nothing seemed to be missing — that not only had the contents been searched — they had also been specifically rearranged. Her suspicions were confirmed when she checked the shelves in the wardrobe. Again, nothing had been taken, but the contents of each shelf had been switched.

Diane sat back down on the bed, one hand on the hotel telephone as she tried to decide what to do. Instinctively, she knew she had to report the intrusion. Just as instinctively, she knew who was behind it. But what could she say? Nothing had been taken. To say what she suspected might have been the object of the search could lead to all sorts of problems. Her deliberations were cut short by a gentle tap on the door, and she turned to see Catherine enter, quietly closing the door behind her.

'I've only just managed to get her down. It took me ages to find her night things, you didn't move them did you Mum?'

It was not only Michaelis Serides' ears that were burning: the whisky seared its way through the acidity in his stomach as he looked for some clarity of thought that sobriety no longer offered him. The cold, sober light of day only brought sweat-ridden anxieties. Juggling of bills and unpaid debts. No saint himself, there were those he now owed, who would wait only so long, and he also knew what the consequences would be if he failed to settle very soon.

Pouring another, he was tempted to upend the bottle — not that much left anyway — but then he remembered he had to go up the village tomorrow and clear his father's house of the last of the furniture before the sale was completed in the next few days. Not that he would see any of the proceeds. It was the last of his assets he could sell to prop up his failing business and the bank would swallow that up straight away. He was one stumble away from bankruptcy and a pair of broken legs. Unconsciously he rubbed the old wound above his knee.

Cursing his luck for the millionth time for not having been smarter about the first earring, he now tried to hone his plan to get the other. This time he would not be so foolish. This time he knew where he would take it to get a fair price. But first he had to get it. He had not really expected it to have been left in their rooms, but it had been worth a chance, and he was pleased with his 'rearrangements'. That would shake them up. He was confident they would not go to the police and risk the dire consequences he had already painted. But what should be his next step? An invitation perhaps? An invitation to dinner at the club. The lure? Information of course! Information about her husband.

But as Michaelis considered just what he might say, he could not help but wonder as to what really did happen all those years ago. It was a lifetime away now. Some things of course remained acutely clear in his memory, but others were just a blur. How was it that this English woman had the other earring? And then there was that Xenakis bitch and her ridiculous accusations … that's all they could be … ridiculous … it was impossible. He drained his glass. 'Bitch!' Worse still. '*Poutana!*' There had been a time though when he had felt very differently about her.

FIFTEEN

Fanouris Serides was a practical man. He liked things simple. Which was not to say that he was in any way simple himself. Far from it. He had the cunning of a wolf. And like a wolf, he carried few regrets. It still rankled that he had only managed to slit three of the four German prisoner's throats back near Maleme. The rib that had cracked under him in the struggle with the fourth over the stone water trough was a daily reminder. Still, at least he'd had the satisfaction of seeing the young German's startled expression as he had pulled out the looted pistol.

To his credit though, the German had not turned and fled. Instead, the sight of one of his own comrade's weapons being levelled against him had curiously enraged him and he had lunged for the gun, but Fanouris had quick reflexes and had been able to bring the butt of the pistol hard down on the German's skull, sending him crashing back against the trough. He would have finished him there and then, had he not heard more soldiers approaching and considered his own safety more vital. If only the stupid Englishmen had made a better job of tying them up in the first place. They, of course, were his main regret.

He blamed the mainlanders for slowing them down, with their insistence on rest breaks. But for them, they would have reached the evacuation columns in time. Instead, they had found their escape route barred by advancing German patrols. Unable to agree on a plan, the mainland Greeks had scattered leaving him saddled with the two Englishmen.

He blamed his idiot son Michaelis for suggesting they go with them on to Heraklion, to try their chances of getting away by boat from there.

He blamed his wife for suggesting it would be safer for them to stay in the village until they could be sure who to trust.

But most of all he blamed himself. Not only for agreeing to go along with all of it, but for deciding to offload them onto Manolis' brother. It had seemed a good idea at the time. After all, it was Manolis who had landed him with the problem in the first place. Manolis' brother Vasilis also had the largest house in the village with several outbuildings. It made sense. It was practical. Simple.

The problem was Litsa — Evangelitsa Petrakis, Vasilis' only daughter. The daughter that Fanouris was determined his son would marry. The daughter that would bring with her a dowry of the best of Vasilis' olives and vines. The same daughter that was now making doe eyes at one of the Englishmen.

Before they came, it had all been going to plan. Michaelis had needed no persuasion at all to carry out the part of suitor, she was a pretty enough girl, or would be when she'd got a bit more meat on her for Fanouris' own liking. Michaelis practically fawned on her, and she had not been totally averse to his attentions. There were only a couple of other likely contenders in the village and Fanouris would take care of them, one way or another. All he needed to do was toughen Michaelis up a bit more. He was still too soft. God knows he'd tried often enough to beat some sense into the boy.

He looked at him now, sulking in a corner of Vasilis' courtyard, glaring at Litsa and the soldier in his new Cretan disguise, now known as Yiannis. He was probably only two or three years older than Michaelis, but the difference in maturity seemed far greater. It was time for the wolf to use some of his cunning.

Leaning back against the rough stone wall of the house, Richard watched the sun slowly sink down beyond the darkening mountains and took a welcome swig of Vasilis' wine. The sun's rays lingered on in the rosy amber hues that he swirled in the simple glass. It had been a long, hard day, but it was satisfying to know that the grapes he had helped gather that day would soon become next year's wine. He ran his fingers through the three month's growth of beard that contributed, along with his borrowed Cretan clothes and boots, to the illusion of his new alias: Yiannis.

'It won't grow if you keep playing with it … unlike certain other things!' Jim's Geordie tones broke the spell of his own assumed identity: Yiorgos, whose burgeoning moustache was threatening to outdo even some of the locals. Richard welcomed the banter. He hadn't seen much of Jim lately.

It had been considered prudent at a gathering of the village menfolk, that along with their new identities, they should be housed separately, in the hope that one odd fish might just escape suspicion, while two together would be highly unlikely. Richard had been given shelter above Vasilis' donkey shed, while Jim had similar arrangements in Manolis' old house on the outskirts of the village, where his sister cared for two elderly relations. Forbidden to disclose their real names, they had been given their aliases. The less anyone knew the safer they all would be. News of German reprisals for harbouring Allies had spread rapidly: propagated in the first instance by leaflet drops from the enemy planes, spelling out just what would happen to anyone foolish enough to do so.

It was a threat that weighed just as heavily on Richard and Jim. Eager to free their hosts of their burden, they had been keen to head down to the coast at once and take their chances of finding a boat off the island, but the build-up of German troops had made it an impossibility. Word came that groups of Allied soldiers were gathering at a monastery near Preveli and that some had been helped to escape on boats during the night. More attempts would be made, but they were told to wait. With the occupation complete, the Germans were scaling down their numbers. The assault and paratroop divisions were being flown on to other missions. Engineers remained to secure the defences. Captured Allied soldiers were being transported off the island to distant prison camps.

Then came the news that the Germans had discovered the escape route at Preveli and closed the operation down, but there were also rumours circulating that a small group of British commandos had landed and were trying to organise the local resistance groups. A few of the soldiers in hiding were opting to stay and fight alongside the locals, others were being spirited away on fishing boats as and when the opportunity arose.

Many who had taken to the hills close to starvation decided to throw in their lot and turn themselves in to the remaining makeshift prison camps. At least they would be fed. Richard and Jim would be given word, when the time was right. For now, they could only wait. Working made the waiting tolerable and was a way of repaying their hosts' selfless generosity.

Richard looked down at the calloused hands cradling his glass with a certain pride. It had taken him some time to come to terms with village life, but slowly he had come not only to understand and respect its rhythms and routines, but to feel that the shared labours gave him a curious sense of belonging that he had not experienced before.

Vasilis who carried himself with the same dignity as his brother Manolis had been a patient teacher and was appreciative of Richard's help. His had not been the easiest of lives. As the eldest son, he had inherited a good number of his parent's vines and olive fields along with the main house. Manolis and their younger brother Christos had not been left short, but with Christos now lying in an Albanian grave and Manolis living on the other side of the island with his wife, the upkeep of all the family estates fell squarely on Vasilis' shoulders.

Spread out as they were in patchwork parcels of land dotted across the area — a plot acquired here, another exchanged there — passed on down through the generations, they were a considerable burden. A burden his twin sons might have helped him with, had they not died in childbirth taking his wife with them and leaving him alone with Litsa, then just eight years old.

That had been ten years ago and the woman she had become seemed far more than the sum of her years. There had been other help. Income from the fields had enabled

Vasilis to employ workers occasionally — but now, in such uncertain times — what revenue might there be to support them? Her life had been just as hard, helping her father with every chore, but he had not neglected her own needs ensuring she had a good education. He encouraged her to assist the local doctor, from whom she had also learnt some English. This had been a lifesaver for both Richard and Jim, whom she had steadily coaxed into learning more than just the handful of Greek words they had already picked up.

She returned from the house now with plates of cut tomatoes, cucumber and olives, while Vasilis passed around a large carafe of his wine to refresh the weary workers who had gathered to harvest one of his best fields for the pressing. Some like Fanouris and his son would be paid for their labours, others knew that Vasilis would help with their own harvest in return.

No longer dressed in her drab working outfit of shirt and loose trousers, Litsa moved confidently in the dress she had made herself, brightening Michaelis' expression as she passed the plates around, before ending her circuit in front of Richard. He made to get up from his patch on the ground where he had flopped after the pressing was finally over.

'*Kathiste, eiste kourasmeni.*' Litsa pushed him back down gently, handed him a plate, then brought a chair to sit by him. Happy to accept her invitation to remain seated, Richard thanked her in his best new Greek — lied that he wasn't tired at all — and tried to piece together an enquiry about tomorrow's work.

'*Avrio … ti kanoume … ti thoulia?*'

'More grapes to be picked.' She answered, sparing his weary brain. 'But these not for wine … these to eat, when dry.'

'Sultanas?' Richard suggested.

'Yes … the same in Greek!' she said, pleased to have added to her own vocabulary, as Jim dragged his chair over to join them. *'Yiorgo! Ti kaneis?'*

As Richard left Jim to battle his own way through his Greek responses urged on by Litsa's patient coaching, he tuned out of the pair's conversation just above him and thought back over the long day's harvest, which had culminated in the pressing. Expecting at least some rudimentary kind of machinery, he had been surprised when all the workers had upended their baskets into a long shallow concrete trough, raised up to waist height, in one of the larger outbuildings.

Vasilis and Litsa had then stripped off their footwear, and trousers rolled up around their thighs, feet and legs thoroughly washed, climbed up into the trough. Pausing above him as she swung one leg over the sill, Litsa had looked down at Richard with a smile he had come to know too well and held out her hand, 'And you.'

Hurrying through the preparations, he climbed in. Sinking beyond his knees into the mass of grapes, he followed their lead, slowly wading up and down through the juicy fruit, feeling the grapes strip from their stems between his toes. Slowly, the juice began to trickle from the spout set at one end of the trough and other workers began filling barrels and large jars. As the mass of fruit decreased below him so the juice began to pour at a rate the others struggled to keep up with. Eventually the flow began to cease, but still the work was not over. All the remaining stems and crushed pulp were then gathered and put into two huge earthenware jars.

'For the *tsikouthia* …' Litsa told him, explaining that the contents would be left in each *pithos* to ferment, until the final juices were then distilled. Richard remembered Manolis' *tsikouthia* only too well!

Right at this moment, however, it was Litsa's shapely leg poised over the sill that lingered in Richard's mind, and as the hum of the continuing conversation above him re-entered his consciousness, he realised that he was presently at eye level with those same shapely legs, now crossed before him.

Swiftly taking a drink, he vowed to get up and join in the conversation, which he did. But not before once again admiring those self-same legs — from glimpse of thigh, past crook of knee, down the slim, delicate calf — to the slipper suspended from her toe, as Litsa bobbed her foot in time with her conversation.

Any hopes that the sultana vineyard might be reasonably close by quickly evaporated, as Richard followed Litsa and Vasilis' lead, heading up out of the village to steeper slopes in the crisp morning air. Brushing away the flies that seemed equally as keen on him as Vasilis' basket laden donkey, he dug in for the climb as father and daughter cajoled the beast up the rocky trail. He might have developed the perfect disguise he reflected, but it would only take one observant German to spot who the flies and mosquitos consistently headed for.

Pushing aside from his mind the thousand-and-one itchy bites that Vasilis' rough shirt and trousers now aggravated, he adjusted his own load and followed the trail that led up through ancient olive groves and past steep escarpments, until finally surfacing to a steeply banked plateau of vines. Vasilis tied the donkey up under the shade of a tree and started unloading the equipment.

Thankful that their journey was at an end and now used to the routine, Richard picked up a couple of baskets and was about to start gathering the grapes.

'*Ochi!*' warned Vasilis.

Litsa explained, 'These are not our grapes ....' Richard had already understood that today it would be just the three of them working Manolis' field for him in his absence, but why was Vasilis telling him not to pick them?

Litsa piled several more baskets into the couple he was already holding, balanced a roll of old, bundled netting on top of them, and carried on enigmatically, 'Now it is we who are the donkeys!' And as Vasilis lashed an old oil-drum to his back and grasped a jerrycan in either hand, Richard once again followed their lead as Litsa gathered up the remaining bundles, and father and daughter began to make their way up the slippery path to the left of the field of vines.

A ragged hedgerow beside the path offered brief glimpses of the distant mountains beyond. Richard followed on with his load struggling to keep his balance. Reaching the top corner of the field, there seemed nowhere else to go, then Vasilis grasped the slim trunk of a bush that marked the end of the hedgerow and swung around it, dropping down and vanishing from sight. Litsa followed as with some difficulty did Richard, realising now that the hedgerow had concealed another lower terrace spreading out and dropping away from them.

Across the field, an identical hedgerow marked its border, concealing an even steeper drop beyond. He scrambled down a series of steps, roughly hewn from the rock and earth. Before him was an irregular, roughly triangular shaped plot, the high, broader end of which, where they stood, was planted with vines now overburdened with their fruit. Below he could see the plot tapered down to a flatter band of bare, untilled earth. Beyond that, it was obvious that there was a sheer drop. Down below, he could see the donkey where they had left him, rooting around under the tree.

Vasilis carried his load down to the lower end of the plot and began pouring liquid from the jerrycans into the oil-drum. Litsa took the bundles of netting from Richard's arms and unrolled them on the gentler slope of the bare earth. She looked around for some rocks to hold the netting down and Richard found more for her. Satisfied that the nets were secure, she turned her smile on him again handed him two baskets and explained the process.

'You pick … my father washes for the grapes to not go bad … I lay them out to dry.'

Richard headed for the nearest row of vines. Again he heard Vasilis' grumble of warning.

'*Ochi!*'

'You start from the top.' Litsa explained, 'It is easier later … you will see!'

As midday approached Richard understood Litsa's advice only too well. Looking down the field, he judged that he had picked somewhere between a quarter and a third of the rows of vines, but at least the rows were now narrowing and the length of climb and descent diminishing. Vasilis had taken a turn to give him a break and he had enjoyed working closely with Litsa, decanting the baskets of plunged and drained trusses of grapes onto the nets for her to arrange, joking about the ungainly rubber gauntlets both wore for the process. He hadn't understood exactly what it was they put in the liquid that kept the grapes free from infection but realised it probably didn't do much good for skin.

Back on his turn at picking the grapes once more, he tried to make sense of the strength of feeling he was now experiencing for Litsa. From the start he had let it be known that he was married. Jim had tried making overtures to her several times but had got nowhere. She had always been pleasant with both of them. She never flirted and treated all such approaches from the local boys with the same polite detachment. Unsurprisingly, given her childhood experiences, she was very much an independent woman.

And what of Diane? He knew he should — and did — feel guilty about these feelings. He had thought over and over again about the strange distances that had developed between them in their short time together, but he knew he was looking for excuses. If it was only just physical. If it was only just that — but it was more — he felt totally at ease for the first time in another woman's company. Again, there was that odd sense of belonging.

With Diane, he had always been too eager to please, to impress, to make her laugh as Eddie did. Deep down, he suspected that Diane had chosen him for his prospects. He had studied, Eddie had doodled in the margins. There had been much talk of how their future would be planned. She had mapped out careers in teaching for both of them, brushing aside his preferred interests.

Hauling the baskets up '*dio, dio*', one on each shoulder

as Vasilis had shown him, he set off down to Vasilis at the drum, waiting while each basket was washed before handing him another.

He carried one previously washed and drained basket over to Litsa, his thoughts still a swirl of confusion. Squatting down as he waited for her to finish laying the last pile out, he was suddenly struck an unexpected blow on the back of the shoulders.

Picking himself up he turned to face Vasilis, standing branch in hand, who then pulled him up by his shirt front, thrust baskets into his hands and roared at him to get back up the hill. Shaken into submission, he took the baskets but stood frozen by the guilt of his thoughts. Vasilis continued a tirade of incomprehensible Greek — now face to face — his spit hitting Richard's cheeks. He struggled to understand what had happened. Vasilis could not possibly have read his thoughts. He had not actually done a single inappropriate thing. Vasilis roared even louder and clouted him across the head.

Bellows of laughter from below brought the answer — an understanding also urged into him by Vasilis' earnest, wide-eyed look — at odds with the continued insults. Richard played the idiot he had become and muttered his agreement, *'Ne … Ne kyrios!'* and scurried back up the slope, feigning ignorance of the two German soldiers he had now finally glimpsed down by the donkey under the trees below.

Sheltering under the shade, gorging themselves on handfuls of looted grapes, the two soldiers were in no hurry to go anywhere. With a pantomime playing out above them, a couple of bottles of local wine they had appropriated, and a donkey to taunt, they were more than content to spin out their tour of duty in comfort for the time being.

And so Richard, Litsa, and Vasilis toiled on. Ordinarily they too would be sheltering under the trees by now, to eat and sleep awhile until the midday heat was over. It did not take long before the soldiers discovered the cloth bag Litsa had hung on the tree holding the lunch she had packed. Helping themselves to the contents, they waved for Vasilis and the others to come down and join them. Vasilis indicated he was far too busy — too little time to stop. The soldiers shrugged and settled down to enjoy their wine and free food. Richard wondered just how long they would be content to do so before becoming suspicious as to why they weren't stopping themselves. His disguise had held up so far — but at close quarters?

An hour slipped by, and much of another. The wine, fuelled banter between the two soldiers died down as they stretched out to doze a bit. Vasilis signalled Richard to slow down, take it easy. They were all exhausted. The go slow had not lasted for long, however, when one of the soldiers abruptly got up, selected a good vantage point, unbuttoned his fly and urinated, tracing a high arc over the landscape below. Alerted by his actions, the other rose and decided to pick out a path up to their vines to see just exactly what was going on up above.

Vasilis said nothing, continuing with his chores, knowing full well that they could not climb directly up the steep escarpment. Eventually the soldier toppled back to the ground, cursing. His comrade added to his embarrassment with a hearty laugh. Angry now, he shouted up to Vasilis, demanding to know how they had got up there. Since Vasilis spoke no German, and they no Greek, it was not difficult for him to show at first that he didn't understand what it was that they wanted. But he could see the German's temper rising nevertheless and knew that to evade his request any longer would only further infuriate him. He had no choice but to point to the route that led up to their vineyard.

As the two soldiers gathered their weapons, a shot rang out. Richard instinctively ducked down — the basket he was moving spewed out its contents. Alerted by the sudden movement, the soldiers swung up their rifles. Another shot followed, but all recognised now that the shots were coming from further down the hillside.

Hurried conversation between the two soldiers prompted one to sling his rifle over his shoulder, leaving the other with Richard in his sights. As his comrade headed off down the slope, the other slowly and deliberately mimed shooting first Richard, then Vasilis, and finally Litsa. In the still air, they clearly heard him mimic the sound of each bullet as he toyed with the trigger, '*Peeaaow* … *Peeaaow*.' one each for Richard and Vasilis. A wolf whistle followed for Litsa.

A shout from his comrade and a further gunshot in the distance below finally drew him away and they heard his laughter ringing down the slopes as he ran after his friend. All three sank to the ground in exhausted relief.

After resting a short while, with only their own grapes for a late lunch, Vasilis suggested they pack up for the day and finish the field tomorrow. It was Richard who persuaded him to carry on for another couple of rows, to leave just a comfortable half day's work the following day. Knowing the amount of further work that lay in store for him over this busy period, Vasilis was grateful and was only too aware of the sense in Richard's plan. Pity he already had a wife; he couldn't see any of Litsa's prospective suitors having half the wit or stamina.

By the middle of the second row, Richard had already reduced his load to single baskets. Everyone was content to ease back on the pace. The toll of their continued labours under the full heat of the sun, included a throbbing headache for Richard, which merged as a tight knot in the back of his neck that now joined together with the constant ache in his shoulders. Slithering down past the hedgerow marking a sheer drop to the path below serving further terraces, he did not argue as Vasilis told him to gather up the remaining baskets and call it a day.

Leaving one basket tucked under the vine he had last picked as a marker, he headed further back up the field to collect a couple of remaining baskets, pausing to add the odd bunch of grapes that had escaped his attention earlier in the day hidden under the spreading leaves.

Brushing beside the hedgerow on his right, he squinted down the narrow, slippery path that headed back down beside the rows of vines leading off to his left. Satisfied that he could see no further missed bunches he swung the baskets up onto his shoulder and set off back down the steep path. By now he was used to the way the dry, crumbly earth skidded beneath him, but he was totally unprepared for what happened next.

The crumbles of earth continued to roll down before him in their familiar way as he slithered down each step, but then he was totally thrown off balance as the earth suddenly gave way beneath him. He felt the sharp graze of a bush in the hedgerow at his side flash by as did the briefest glimpse of the terrace way down below, before his face met the wall of earth that had been his path disappearing above him. Showers of earth filled his eyes as he struggled to grasp hold of something — anything. The baskets he had been carrying slammed down onto his head, as he sank further down into the earth. The initial fleeting fear of toppling down the steep escarpment was quickly replaced with a still more frightening one — that of being buried alive.

For the moment, he was jammed tight. One arm reached skywards around the baskets that now rested on his head. The other was twisted deep into roots of the hedgerow trees. His legs seemed suspended in a void. Gingerly, he reached around with his one free hand above the baskets. He could feel the crumbled sides of the hole he was in, but there was nothing he could get a hold on.

Trickles of fine earth continued to cascade around him, building up around his shoulders, past his neck, his chin. Spluttering, he wriggled to free some of the earth, which he now felt working its way down the back of his shirt. A sharp pain in his elbow spoke of some equally sharp rock caught in the roots, wedging his forearm and hand, uncomfortably twisting them in against his own ribs. If he could just free his hand, get a purchase on those roots then …

With a final shower of earth, the glints of light that briefly shone through the wicker baskets above him vanished, as he plunged into the darkness of the void.

SIXTEEN

Even through closed eyes, the brilliance of the sun's rays lit up both the inner, physical curtain of her daydreams, as well as her mood. Secure in the knowledge that Ellie was safely in 'granny's' hands for a few hours, Catherine had finally begun to relax on the sun lounger.

At first it had been difficult. The busy rows of sunworshippers on the hotel beach were a world apart from the secluded picnic of the previous day, but in time she had managed to ignore the surrounding chatter, even almost succeeding in her efforts to suppress the knee jerk reaction to respond to any infant shriek. And with lunchtime approaching, several of the beds began to be abandoned in favour of other needs. Conscious that she should also limit her own exposure in the full heat of the day, she shifted around onto her belly, promising herself just another half hour or so.

Delving into her bag for more sun lotion, she found the driftwood carving that Antonis had made for Ellie. Tracing the body of the artfully realised crab brought renewed admiration for the skill involved, accompanied by an intense regret that their outing had ended so awkwardly. She knew she should care more about resolving the dead end that her questioning on her mother's behalf had brought about, but also knew full well that what really mattered to her was Antonis himself. She had been sure that it would be a long time indeed before she would be prepared to think about anyone else after Robert.

In recent months she had found herself 'bumping' into friends of friends at get togethers, as well-wishers had endeavoured to steer her towards another partner, while other friends had also made it clear that they themselves would not be averse to seeing their friendship develop in a different direction: 'After all … she would need a man in her life more than ever now that she had Ellie to care for.' Catherine had not been remotely interested in any of the various proposals, though the one that came from a close girlfriend, was not only a complete surprise but mildly intriguing.

A tiny pebble slipped into her palm from the knotted roots of the carving, and she could feel once more the silken sensation of those countless timeworn beads slipping between her toes — like water itself — at what had now become her 'secret' beach. The memories flooded back as she buried her head into the pillow of her arms. His easy smile, his lithe, tanned body close to hers as they crouched by Ellie, his fingers deftly shaping, then burnishing the driftwood. And then there was the polite coolness as her enquiries had struck some deep, hidden nerve.

Damn Mum and her problems! A deep sigh accompanied her wish to put aside the whole troublesome mess her mother had become embroiled in. There had still been no proper discussion about this missing husband of hers. And with all the fuss of the previous day's break-in, there had also been no opportunity to raise the nagging question that now lingered unanswered in her mind. Instead there had been the unsavoury business of reporting the disturbance — witnessing her mother wriggle her way around the full facts with the hotel manager, who had been all too ready and willing to dismiss the maid responsible for attending to their room, until Diane was forced to save the girl by confessing that she suspected she knew who the intruder might be.

In which case it was a matter for the police — and would have been, but for the timely appearance of the distinguished gentleman seated at a nearby table, who had overheard their conversation and came to their aid. The hotel manager instantly deferred to his arrival and introduced them to the owner of the hotel, who, in impeccable English that held just the barest trace of his native Germany, assured them that he would take care of matters. The hotel safe was at their disposal — they could be assured of complete confidentiality. He would make his own enquiries about Michaelis Serides, a name and reputation that he was obviously already familiar with. They were to relax and enjoy their stay.

Catherine particularly remembered the calming effect he had upon her mother, as he took her hand very formally and presented her with his card, instructing her to address all future concerns, however insignificant they may seem, to him and him alone. Not usually the easiest person to mollify, Diane had succumbed in an instant. 'Thank you,' she had said with genuine relief. 'Thank you, Mr Brandt.'

'Dieter,' he had answered, 'please call me Dieter.'

Polishing out the tiny smudge on the corner of the silver frame, Dieter loosely folded the silk handkerchief before replacing it in the breast pocket of his linen jacket and then returned the photograph of Hannelore to its customary place on his desk. The colours had begun to fade he noticed, but his memory of her was as clear now as the summer day they had first met, when her family had visited his own, at his parent's country estate in Bavaria. Briefly savouring other tender moments, the inevitable, final memory of her loss, as always won through.

Their love had survived the war, the recrimination and rebuilding, even the stillbirths, but both had been powerless to halt nature's final cruelty as the disease had relentlessly worked its way through her tiny frame, bringing her life to an untimely end. Shutting out the painful images, Dieter reflected on his impending appointment. It was uncanny how much this Englishwoman and her daughter reminded him of his wife. The mother was much as Hannelore would now have been had she survived, and as for the daughter, they could have been twins.

And then there was the matter of Michaelis Serides. He had had his suspicions for some time now. Looking across to the black and white photo on the other side of the desk at the two young tearaways at loose on the farm, he remembered another wound — older, in some ways even deeper — but now so long ago. Yet in all the years that had passed, there had never been a friendship to match Werner's. But he was tiring.

At first it had been a mission. A sworn promise to exact revenge. As the decades passed, reunions had begun to be staged on the island, as compatriots had gathered to relive the sunny summers of their former occupation. Distasteful as he often found them, Dieter had sometimes joined their gatherings, in search of any information he could find, even though his own experience of the war had been quite different. Having been transferred with the reformed paratroop divisions to the Russian front, he experienced the humiliation of capture for a second time. Surviving the prison camp, he finally made it back to a very different homeland.

But old money always won through, and the family construction business had not found itself short of rebuilding work. Eventually finding himself at the helm, he had been able to pursue his quest while constructing a chain of hotels on the island. He had, however, all but given up hope of tracking down Werner's killers.

Besides, time and familiarity with the Cretans he now traded and lived among, had brought a healing dose of understanding and respect, to the point that he now regularly contributed to various charities that had been set up for reparation. Nevertheless, the guilt he appeased was, he felt, communal and not personal. He carried no qualms about his own conduct. That he was still alive, he knew had been from the mercy of others and that knowledge had slowly shaped the man he had become. Yet still he could not fully free himself from the need to seek out and confront the culprits — if indeed they had even survived the war or later hardships.

With Hannelore gone, Dieter had settled in the penthouse of the hotel, occasionally returning to the estate to attend to necessary business, but never for very long. There were too many memories.

The expected knock at the door eventually came, as did the strange mix of memory and fascination as Diane entered. There was a moment's silence as she took in the luxurious surroundings of the penthouse. 'This is beautiful.'

'Thank you. May I offer you a drink?' Dieter took Diane's hand and led her out onto the terrace. Diane found herself in an uncharacteristically biddable mood.

'That's very kind of you, but I do hope I'm not disturbing your evening?'

'It is by far the most pleasant disturbance I have experienced in a long while! Would a gin and tonic be acceptable?'

'It would, thank you!'

While Dieter went to fetch the drinks, Diane took the opportunity to explore the terrace. It quickly became clear that the penthouse occupied the entire top floor of the main hotel building. To its western end, the lengthy terrace opened onto a private pool, screened from the front of the hotel by arboured gardens. A scent of jasmine lingered in the air. The rattle of ice in the glasses of the drinks tray signalled Dieter's return. Pouring the gin into the glass, he measured the tonic to her liking and handed her the drink. She paid him another genuine compliment.

'You have the perfect place to watch the setting sun.'

'It is my favourite time of the day, to relax and reflect. Please, take a chair, share the moment with me.'

Again, Diane was content to put aside the purpose of her visit and accept the invitation. They both sat in comfortable silence as the sun eventually slipped from sight and then, as the reddish hues of the sky slowly turned towards the velvet of evening, concealed lights around the pool obeyed their timer's command. The welcome period of quiet reflection in his company had not only calmed the initial hesitancy Diane held about the favour she was planning to ask of Dieter, but it also now persuaded her to confide in him. She didn't know whether it was his manner, the power and responsibility of his position, or some other indefinable quality that her antennae had picked up on, but she instinctively felt she could trust this man. So it was with some surprise when she had unfolded the whole story, relating every last detail to him, that she found him refusing her request.

'I'm sorry … I shouldn't have presumed …' Diane put her drink down, readying herself to leave. Dieter gently handed the glass back to her, a wry smile on his lips.

'Let me be clear about this. You have received a letter from Michaelis Serides, inviting you to dine with him at his club, where he promises to give you information about your husband?' He paused for a moment for Diane to agree. 'And you would like me to supply a member of my staff to accompany you discreetly for your security?' He pushed on ahead of Diane's imminent interjection. 'And yes, I am aware … you wish to pay me for the services of my employee ….'

'It's only fair,' Diane cut in, 'I didn't want to impose on my daughter again and I wouldn't expect …'

'But it would not be fair to me ….'

'I'm sorry, I don't understand.'

'Even if my staff were for hire, why should I give some paid minion the pleasure of your company, when I would be only too delighted to accompany you myself for free?'

'No really … I couldn't expect you to….'

'Why not? I could say that I would consider it my duty. In truth, it would be a pleasure.'

Diane struggled with an equal measure of relief and anxiety. 'I know it sounds ridiculous, looking for one missing husband … but I did make it clear that I have another that I'm very content with back in England?' Dieter nodded. 'Please don't be offended, I don't want to sound rude, or ungrateful … but I do want to make that clear.'

'You have and I understand perfectly. I can assure you that my intentions are entirely honourable. As I have already mentioned, I have my own reasons for keeping an eye on Mr Serides. Now, may I get you another drink … perhaps some champagne before dinner?'

'Well, that's extremely kind of you but shouldn't we be thinking about getting ready to leave? I know I haven't given you much notice, but Mr Serides is expecting me at nine.'

'And you shall be there at nine exactly. Tomorrow! Rule number one — keep them waiting — no matter what it is they are offering, or how much you may want it. May I see the invitation?'

Diane handed it over. Dieter gave it a cursory, distasteful glance before inviting Diane back to his study, seating her at his desk with pen and paper and dictating a brief reply indicating that she was otherwise engaged this evening, but would be happy to attend the following day, if agreeable. He then called reception to alert his driver that there was a message he wanted delivered.

Her secretarial duties completed, Diane admired the sweeping, organic curves of the Art Nouveau desk with its graceful galleried shelves that held one photograph to either side, illuminated by the integral lamps that swept up above them as if they had grown there.

'This is quite a desk!'

'Henry Van de Velde. Belgian, late 1890s ... the chair as well, naturally.'

'*Natürlich* ... naturally.' Diane winced at her involuntary translation, but Dieter seemed untroubled and smiled reassuringly before continuing.

'My late wife,' he explained, as Diane's gaze fell upon the photograph.

'It's incredible ... she's so like...'

'I know.' And then as Diane's gaze travelled to the opposite side, 'My best friend Werner, on our farm before the war ... he died here on the first day.'

'I'm sorry.'

Dieter sensed her discomfort. 'You may think me an unlikely ally in your search, but I will do my utmost to be of assistance. You have my word.'

'Thank you.' She knew the simple words were insufficient to convey the relief she felt at finally being able to share her burden. Relishing, but strangely embarrassed by the unaccustomed security she was experiencing, Diane relaxed back into the chair and glanced around at the paintings on the study walls.

As Dieter noted her reactions: approval here, surprised recognition there — occasional indifference — the word she had used earlier when defending her marriage lingered on in his mind. '*Content?*'

'Now, I believe I mentioned champagne.'

Diane's had not been the only invitation received that day, though Catherine's had been far less formal. Antonis had left word at reception that he would be finishing that day's shift at six, if she happened to be free. Catherine needed no tuition in 'treating them mean and keeping them keen.' Six o'clock would be a totally inconvenient time given Ellie's requirements. Besides, the remaining half-hour's musings on the sun lounger had led Catherine to question the whole situation.

Despite her fierce independence, she knew well enough that she was almost certainly a prime candidate for a rebound romance in this heady climate. And what of Antonis? Easy-going, handsome, with a captive audience of holidaymakers coming and going every week or two. She would surely not have been the first to fall for that smile. He probably had a wife tucked away in that village — that would explain the sudden cooling when her enquiries had dug too deep. If she hadn't been so wrapped up in her mother's problems, she would certainly have been digging in that direction as well. And so the reply she left at reception was short and not entirely sweet.

SEVENTEEN

Landing abruptly on a mound of the same soft, crumbled earth that continued to shower around him, the impetus of Richard's fall spun him off the slope of raised debris and onto cold hard rock floor, which jarred his already bruised ribs and arm.

Disoriented, he squinted back up into the rain of dust. Tiny pinpricks of light continued to pierce down through the base of the wicker basket now firmly wedged into the hole above. Judging it to be some twenty or more feet above him, he despaired of the notion of trying to climb back up. He could see little of the cavernous dome enclosing him and doubted in any case that the friable earth would support an ascent. His only chance would be if there was another entrance to this place.

Knowing that there had been a steep drop down to a lower path beyond the hedgerow, meant that he could not be far from the outside. Perhaps there had once been an entrance to this cave from the path, but in which direction did it lie? He tried to remember the sun's position — perhaps he could judge the direction from a slant in the light? But the sun was obviously already too low, the pinpricks of light were, as far as he could tell, quite vertical.

On hands and knees, he began to explore around the central mound of earth, pressing outwards until he came to solid rock. Eventually the dust cleared a little and his eyes became accustomed to the gloom as he slowly circled the dim column of light and a mental picture of the confines of his imprisonment began to form.

Settling back down on the even section of rock floor where he judged he had first come to rest, Richard weighed his options. So far as he could tell from the initial exploration there was no obvious exit. If he called out for help and *if* his cries were heard by Litsa or Vasilis, they too would be in danger of falling through. They would be bound to wonder what had happened to him though and would almost certainly spot the abandoned basket. He would have to wait and hope he would hear them approach, then try to warn them.

They might of course think he had just got fed up and wandered back to the village on his own — in which case he could be there for some considerable time. He wondered for a moment if any of the grapes from the basket had toppled down as well and ran his hands around the loose debris around him, slowly circling the mound of earth on his knees like a crab.

He had nearly completed what he judged to be another full circuit, when his foot lodged against what he took to be a small rock behind him. He tried to skittle it out of the way. As he did so, the sound it made, as it clattered over the irregular surface, told him instantly that it was no rock. He could tell that it was hollow.

Backing up, he followed the mental path the sound had lodged in his brain and turning around, swept the ground ahead to see what it was. As he advanced, he stumbled into a bundle of what felt like dry sticks, snapping beneath him. Instinctively he picked up one that seemed stronger than the rest. It had a knurled end that fitted neatly into his palm, while the opposite end, where it had snapped, was sharp. Any tool was welcome.

Then his hand bumped into it. He felt it spin away slightly before resettling by his fingers. Picking it up he assessed the flattened oval shape with his hands and confirmed it by holding it against the faint, dusty plumes of light from above. It was a stoppered clay flask, no bigger than his own hand, with two small lugs at either shoulder. He felt the remnants of some disintegrating cord or leather strap fall away from one lug. Was it some ancient water flask? Would anything be drinkable after such a time? He shook it. It was not empty but did not sound as liquid should. Trying to tease the stopper out, fragments of old fabric wound around it came away in his fingers, then suddenly the plug of cork slipped out.

As he tried to catch hold of it, something cool slithered across his wrist from the flask and fell to the floor. He shuddered irrationally, almost dropping the flask. Something else was rattling inside, but he decided to find whatever it was that had dropped first and began searching the floor again. Finding the stopper, he replaced it in the neck of the flask, pocketing it, so that he could concentrate on his search, sweeping around with the stick.

Voices from above broke his concentration. He could hear Litsa calling his name. Springing to his feet he instantly abandoned the search.

'Stay away,' he yelled up, 'it's not safe … you'll fall as well!'

Again, he heard her calling. She had not heard his warning. Suddenly a shower of earth told him that she was almost directly above. He screamed out another warning and heard it echoed by Vasilis, as rocks now began to tumble down amidst the rain of soil. Again, both men cried out.

A flash of light pierced down upon him as he saw Litsa's foot stab through the canopy, and he heard Vasilis' groans as he tried to hold on to his daughter. Her fall arrested, Richard saw the tree roots he had previously been caught in, slide in to the centre of the hole. He knew Vasilis had a hold on the tree and was dragging Litsa back out.

As her foot disappeared, so the roots shuddered, dislodging rocks they had clung to for decades. Richard threw himself back against the furthest wall of the cavern away from the debris raining down around the tree above. A grunt of relief told him that Vasilis had succeeded in pulling Litsa to safety.

With a final shudder, the tree finally lost its own grip on the surrounding soil and plummeted down towards Richard. For a moment, when the dust began to clear, it seemed that there might at last be an exit route — if he could just clamber up the fallen tree, now wedged against the opposite wall — but no sooner had he started towards it, than the ominous creak of another tree straining above, made him press back again into the natural alcove of the cavern.

Without any further warning an entire curtain of rocks, trees, vines, and soil came tumbling down sealing the shaft completely. This time not the slightest glimmer of light remained to light the swirling clouds of dust that stung his eyes and filled his lungs. Nor was there any sound from above. Gasping for air he sunk to his knees, coughing and choking, hacking up the dust, only to be forced time and again to take another deadly breath.

Taking off his shirt, he tied it around his face to mask the worst of it, but still it penetrated his laboured breaths. If he could wait it out, the dust would settle. He slumped back against the cavern wall, trying to regulate his breathing. Sweat began to drip from him as he fought against the instinctive desire to gag on the soil in his airways.

The cool of the cavern rock against his back seemed a comfort in the stifling atmosphere. He could feel the sweat pooling at the base of his spine and shivered involuntarily, bringing on another fierce bout of gagging and choking. As the worst of the coughing subsided, yet another shiver coursed through him as he sensed something slipping over his right hand, on the floor beside him.

Recoiling to his left, he froze for a second, listening for any movement. He knew he had put the stick down beside him when he had taken off his shirt and carefully searched around for it now with his left hand. It must be somewhere nearby.

Breathing a sigh of relief as he finally found it, he transferred the stick to his other hand and began sweeping the area where he had felt the disturbance. Suddenly a chill swept across his wrist, and he realised what it was he had felt before — air — the faintest of breezes was filtering in down by the wall at floor level. First with his hands and then, having drawn back the improvised mask — with his face — he located the source of the breeze and lay for several minutes, inhaling the fresh air and clearing his lungs. When his strength had recovered, he began to feel around the base of the wall. Where he had been sitting was solid rock. To his right was a mix of both rocks and loose earth.

Scrabbling away in the darkness, he managed to loosen some of the rocks and could tell that the air was blowing up through them. In his mind he pictured a cavity — a passage — a tunnel perhaps. Surely the path at the foot of the terrace must be somewhere beyond? Slowly and methodically, he began to excavate the hole he had begun, scraping away at the earth with the stick and prying out rocks of all shapes and sizes.

The flask in his pocket began to dig into him as he settled into the work, so he set it aside with his shirt on the level rock beside him. It rattled once more as he pushed it towards the wall, but there was a greater curiosity to satisfy first. Before too long he had dug out a sizeable cavity — in which he now squatted. Convinced by now that an entrance to the cave had been sealed up long ago, he pressed on, but the solid rock of the cavern wall continued downwards until, withdrawing a final cluster of rocks and earth he also reached solid rock beneath him.

Dispirited he sank back on his haunches. Had he been fooling himself? Would he ever escape this place? Yet still the faint breeze whispered up through the rocks beside him, refreshing both body and mind. Though he could not see a thing, he knew he was sitting on an unnaturally flat piece of horizontal rock that butted up against a similarly unnatural vertical face. It had to be the work of man. He tried to visualise the possibilities.

The air was still coming from ahead and below him. Was this the first in a series of steps, leading down and out? There was only one way to find out. Pushing on for what seemed like hours, Richard eventually managed to clear his way down two more distinct levels. He was not wrong, they were large, rough-hewn steps, but how many? How long could he last in here?

Thirsty and exhausted, he found his shirt and curled up to rest. With no concept of time in the darkness, he neither knew nor cared how long he slept, but on waking, resolutely set back to the task. Eventually, he reached a lintel above the fourth step, limiting the length of the trench he had so far dug through.

Before long he had again reached solid rock ahead of him, but soon reasoned that the passage must make a turn into the rockface — a turn towards freedom. To his delight he found that to be the case. Sensing he was nearing his goal he tried to speed things up, cursing as unseen rocks tumbled down upon his feet. Exhausted by the labour of carrying the debris back up to the cavern, he now tried to stack the rocks at the sides of the previously excavated steps, narrowing the access in so doing and hindering his progress. Slumping down in the turn of the steps, he gave in once more to a brief restless sleep.

On waking again, he reluctantly cleared a wider path up one side of the steps, heaping the spoil back into the cavern. After all, he had no idea how many more there might be. Finally returning to the task, and with a further two steps excavated, he became aware of a rock face sloping down in front of him. As he dug deeper, he gradually found himself more and more constricted by the solid sheet of rock, narrowing down to the lowest step. Tracing the contours of this curious, slanting roof, the awful truth began to dawn on him — this was one huge boulder that had sealed the exit. Was all his effort for nothing? There was no way he could hope to move such an enormous sheet of rock.

Forcing himself not to give in to the desperation he felt was about to consume him, Richard felt around the edges of the rock, searching once again for the elusive draught of air. Eventually he rediscovered it around shoulder height, on the left flank of the wall. He could still feel some loose rubble close to the rock above and began to scrape away with the stick. A shower of debris fell from just above him and the draught grew stronger. Elated, he paid no attention to the blood he could feel trickling from his temple and prodded away furiously with the stick, instinctively ducking and shielding his closed eyes each time he heard further rocks dislodge — then as he opened his eyes — it was light, not dust that briefly forced them back shut. A bright shard of sunlight pierced the roof of his prison.

Squinting up, he could now see the outline of the great boulder above, where it met the natural slope of the rock face. Raking out as much loose debris as he could, he managed to dislodge a large piece. Just a little more and he would be able to squeeze through. Glimpses of trees beyond tantalised him, but the rocks would not shift. Lifting up a dislodged stone, he started to batter away at the side of the disintegrating rock face. Slowly, chunks of the rock broke free, as did others from above.

He began to time his hits with a leap back after each, to allow for the falling shower of debris resulting from each blow. Hauling himself up, he tried to squeeze through the gap. The sharp rock began to lacerate his bare chest. He would have to enlarge the hole still further. Deciding to retrieve his shirt before the next attempt, he also remembered the flask and scrambled back up the steps into the gloom of the cavern once more. From below he could hear further falls of rock.

Quickly locating the flask, he slipped it back into his pocket and hurried back down the steps. Earth and smaller rocks were still falling in around the boulder. Armed once again with the stick and a usefully sized rock, Richard patiently picked away at the opening until he could see a fracture in the rock. One good hit and the hole would be large enough. He dealt it a good blow, but the only rock that fell was once again from above. Tucking the stick in the top of his trousers, he picked up a heavier rock with both hands. The angle and constriction of the passage made it difficult to get a good swing, but he felt the splintering rock face yield a little to his blow. When the showers from above had stopped, he tried to push the remaining spur of rock away from the fracture. Again, he could feel it give, but it would not break free. One more hit.

It took three, but finally the rock tumbled outwards and Richard hauled himself up into the opening. Still, it was an awkward squeeze. The nature of the opening meant that he had to edge out of the gap on his side. Wriggling his upper body through, he found an obstruction jamming against his hips. Below him, the stick still tucked into his trousers was preventing him from escaping, as was the flask in his upper pocket. Reaching down, he managed to grasp the stick from beneath him and with its aid then prised himself free.

He tumbled out into the open air and lay spreadeagled for a moment, grateful to be alive. Reflecting that so simple an implement as a stick had proved such a lifesaver, he took his first proper look at it in the daylight. What he saw chilled him to the bone — for it was exactly that — a human bone. Now much worn from his abuse, it was nevertheless unmistakeable. He recalled stumbling on what he had thought had been a bundle of twigs. The truth shamed him, and he felt impelled to return the bone to its resting place.

Leaning on a large rock adjoining the gap by the boulder, he suddenly felt it give way and heard the clatter of rocks now falling continuously inside. He had only an instant to react, dropping the bone back inside before leaping back, as the huge boulder tilted perilously towards him — before collapsing inwards — triggering a landslide from above and re-sealing the grave with a final permanence.

He toppled back further still as the blast of air expelled from the cavern by the huge slab of rock was followed by another cascade of rubble. Scrambling back onto the path, he heard shouts from above, and saw Vasilis and two other villagers peering over the edge of the escarpment. First staring in amazement, they then broke into broad grins of relief. Vasilis leant wearily on his pick axe, while the others raised their mattocks and shovels in the air in celebration. Richard caught a brief glimpse of Litsa's face, before it disappeared again. Shrieks of delight plotted her course back down from the vineyard.

Moments later she came running up the path to him as Richard struggled to his feet, only to be almost toppled back to the ground as she threw her arms around him. His own arms enfolded her as she buried her face into his chest, squeezing him tight until the pain in his ribs forced him to acknowledge the discomfort. Startled into release, she burst into a torrent of unintelligible Greek enquiries, fussing over every scrape and graze. When she had finally ascertained that he was not about to expire, she stood back, looked him over, summoned her best English and said, 'I think you are a very dirty boy!'

Several hours later, as the shadows of the trees began to lengthen, scrubbed to within an inch of his life and dressed in Vasilis' best trousers and shirt, Richard found himself being propelled along the path that led up to the little village church, Litsa to one side, Vasilis to the other.

'*Doxa to Theo, Yianni!*' The old woman crossed herself, and leaving the open doorway of her house, fell in behind them, to join in the thanksgiving that Litsa had insisted upon. She had prayed for him in the church the previous night and those prayers had been answered. Now thanks must be given. By the time they had reached the church, their number had doubled. Litsa led the way, and one by one each paid their respects, thanking God for Richard's miraculous escape. Under Vasilis' watchful eye, Richard found himself making the sign of the cross as he offered his prayers. Even though the little church with its byzantine frescoes was a far cry from St Mary's and his own sporadic Anglican upbringing, he knew it would be the same God he should be thanking, yet still he could not help but feel a strange sense of fraudulence going through the unfamiliar motions.

Vasilis stood in one of the side stalls, leaning his arms on the rests provided to keep the chanters supported during the long services and motioned Richard to do the same as Litsa lit candles and prayed. Though he had slept off some of his exhaustion through a good part of the afternoon, his mind was still weary, and he struggled now to concentrate on the thanks he knew he should be giving.

Random fragments of Sunday school memories, of Diane and their wedding, tangled hopelessly together with the traumas of the previous night, the war, and this strange new life he was now a part of. Who was this Yianni he had become — this man in foreign beard and clothes? This man who even now in the sanctity of this church was secretly coveting another woman: the same woman who had stripped and washed him — as simply and innocently as she would have done with a child — whose delight that her prayers had been answered must surely mean that she shared some measure of similar feelings?

He closed his eyes, shutting out the slender form of her body as she knelt in prayer, only for it to be replaced by the memory of her dark hair tumbling around his face when she had dressed the wound to his forehead before he slept. He could still feel the softness of her hair.

'I will wait outside for you.' Her voice broke through the reverie, and he opened his eyes to see her face once more in front of him. Embarrassed that she had assumed him to be deep in prayer, when the reality was so very different, Richard nodded and took a moment lighting a candle himself as Litsa and Vasilis left him alone in the church.

His embarrassment was further compounded, emerging from the church to a chorus of congratulations. Vasilis took the long bell rope from the side of the whitewashed church and moving away towards the nearby tree, he planted his foot on the stone, set deep in the ground, and began to haul down on the rope.

Richard looked up to see the heavy bell slowly swing into motion. Vasilis let it swing back and forth until it had gained momentum and then pulled down hard, ringing out their gratitude across the countryside. One of the village elders briefly tried to stop him, raising his concerns about the

Germans. Vasilis' reply needed no translation. He gave the bell another three resounding peals, then handed the rope to Richard, but try as he might, he could not master the knack of timing the swing. Much to everyone's amusement, the bell remained stubbornly mute. Insisting that everyone return to his house to continue the celebration Vasilis rounded up the small gathering.

Litsa hung back. *'Pende lepta Patera.'* Vasilis looked at his daughter, then at Richard, and nodded his consent,

'Pende lepta!'

Left alone with Richard in the church courtyard, Litsa headed for a stone bench near the tree, still lit by the last of the sun's rays. They sat together in silence for a moment.

'Thank you. I'm amazed you came here and prayed for me.'

'Anyone would … I'm sure your wife does.' The silence settled in once again until Richard remembered, announcing that he had something for her. Withdrawing the flask from his pocket, he shook it, provoking Litsa's curiosity. 'Where did you get that?'

'I found it in the cave last night.'

'And what is inside?'

Insisting she should close her eyes and hold out her hand, Richard emptied the flask for the second time that day. He himself had been amazed at its contents when he had earlier emptied the pockets of his soiled clothing and waited now with keen anticipation for Litsa's reaction to the pair of earrings that dropped into her palm. She was indeed surprised.

'They are very beautiful,' she said with a sad smile, 'but I cannot take them.'

'Why not? They belong to you in any case … I found them on your land.'

'My uncle's,' she corrected him, 'or maybe no one's …' remembering where she had seen him land at the edge of the common path.

'I want you to have them,' Richard insisted.

'You don't understand … if you were to give these to me, then it would mean …' she waited for him to understand. 'You are already married … you must keep these for your wife.' Litsa handed him back the earrings and took the flask, turning it over in her hands, trying to make sense of the designs engraved on the side. There was a mountain with clouds above and a boat leaving a harbour below. On the other side was some ancient writing and symbols she did not recognise. Seeing her interest, Richard urged her to keep the flask at least.

'This I will take,' she agreed, tracing the outline of the tiny boat, 'to remember Yianni … when he has sailed back to his wife. I shall keep …' she struggled for a moment, recalling long, candlelit evenings at the doctor's surgery spent poring over old herbals, learning their English names. '… *Ne!* … rosemary … for 'rememberings'. I shall keep rosemary in it' She leant towards Richard, planting a kiss on his cheek. '*Efkharisto* … Thank you for my gift.'

'*Tipota* … it's nothing.' Richard attempted to return the kiss, but Litsa forestalled him, deciding to check the dressing on Richard's forehead instead.

'Better this comes off now!' she announced, peeling the gauze away from the dried wound. 'Don't cry!' she teased as he winced. Then collecting her gift, she sprang to her feet.

'Come, or there will be no *tsikouthia* left!' Richard followed slowly behind as she skipped out of the church courtyard. He looked at the glittering earrings left in his hand, a welter of emotions spinning in his mind, wondering briefly who had owned these beautiful things and what exactly it was that had also slipped out from the flask, now buried once more in the cave?

His mind already clouded with a different guilt and confusion, he reflected that he should really have returned these as well, along with the remains he had so unceremoniously disturbed. He quickened his pace to catch up with Litsa and returned the earrings to his pocket. It was too late now.

EIGHTEEN

Twenty-four hours had altered Catherine's frame of mind considerably. Not only was the invitation she received today for a far more suitable time — eight-thirty, and now specifically a dinner invitation, her suspicions as to Antonis' character and possible marital status had also mellowed in the intervening hours — mainly because she had thought about little else and wanted the truth to be favourable. It was entirely possible that he could still be single and unattached — unlikely perhaps — but possible. She wondered if he still lived with his mother? There had been no mention of a father.

Her decision to accept this evening's invitation had also been partly prompted by the curious annoyance and dissatisfaction she had experienced last night, spending a thoroughly uneventful evening in her hotel room with just Ellie's gentle snores for company, only to discover that her mother, on arriving much later, had not sorted out her problems with the nightclub owner as planned. Rather, she had been wined and dined in the luxurious surroundings of the hotel owner's penthouse, every single detail of which she now felt she knew intimately.

Accepting Antonis' invitation would mean she would have to use the hotel's babysitting service again, since her mother would finally be going to the club with her charming new escort at much the same time. She would rather it was not the case, but it had not dissuaded her. Besides, as her mother had assured her, the meeting with Serides would only be brief. Dieter Brandt would see to that. Diane would be back with Ellie in no time. Despite her earlier resolve that she too deserved a good time, Catherine nevertheless felt unusually nervous as she walked down to the hotel lobby for her rendezvous.

Antonis' familiar smile, however, eased her tension considerably, and the small talk about the fish restaurant he was driving her to, not far along the coast from her 'secret' beach flowed easily, the more so when Antonis received a favourable reply to the question he had forgotten to ask until they had almost arrived — yes, she did like fish.

The initial frustration Michaelis Serides had experienced on receiving the postponement to his own invitation had also mellowed a little with the passage of time. Time he had put to good use up in the village. He still had use of the house for a few days more. He may still need it. Hopefully it wouldn't come to that — it was a huge risk — but if the woman refused to agree, well he would just have to go ahead with it. At least the house was now prepared.

The plan had come to him towards the end of the second bottle of whisky, after the previous night's anger and vengeful thoughts had been compounded by a late night visit from one of his creditors, or rather their messengers, leaving him in no doubt whatsoever that time was no longer on his side. While both the cold light of day and the accompanying hangover argued overwhelmingly against the wisdom of such a reckless plan, the pains in his ribcage from last night's 'reminder' told him he had to get that earring somehow. Get it, sell the damn thing, and be done with it. And if that involved carrying out the full plan — he'd already worked out how he could implicate the Xenakis bitch and her bastard as well. It paid to keep a close watch on everyone's movements, even if it added to his expenses.

At least there was a decent crowd in tonight to pay for it. He pulled aside the curtain screening the view down into the club from his office. Still no sign of the woman, but it was not yet nine and, reassured that the club was filling up nicely, Michaelis poured another whisky and settled back into his chair. Time to run over the plot; the hook had already been baited. *Give her a little taste ... name the price ... offer a split. Everybody's happy. Unless she refuses to see sense ... then a couple of veiled threats ... and if that doesn't work ... she only has herself to blame.*

Michaelis took a final swig of whisky and pulled back the curtain. Nine-o'clock, on the dot, she certainly was punctual.

A ragged ribbon of twinkling lights delineated the outline of the coast that swept away into inky darkness beyond the low, whitewashed wall of the restaurant terrace. Lemon scented geraniums and a host of other plants tumbled from the recycled containers placed upon it. Simple homely decoration that mirrored the wholesome fare being served. The lively chatter from the other tables was entirely in the native tongue. Local people enjoying good local food.

The temperature had soared that day and now a soft breeze coming off the sea brought welcome relief to the sultry night. Catherine looked out at the moonlit reflections on the waves lapping at the shore down below the terrace that jutted out from the low cliff and watched a couple picking their way along the shoreline, chatting quietly, hand in hand.

Her own conversation with Antonis had reached a lull, but it was comfortable. They had exhausted the usual second date enquiries about one another and both had been quietly pleased to learn that there were no other partners on the scene. Antonis did, as Catherine suspected, live with his mother, helping her with their olive groves and vineyards in the village, while juggling his driving duties at the hotel and taking on some joinery work during the winter months.

He had been fascinated by her own independence. Intrigued that she was able to earn a living from her graphic design work, he listened with genuine interest as she shared her aspirations to concentrate on illustration. She in turn had encouraged him to take his carving more seriously. He obviously had a talent. He had confessed to a deep satisfaction in bringing the wood to life but could not see it as being anything more than a hobby.

His hand brushing hers, as he poured more wine from the carafe into the glass she held, brought Catherine's attention back from the shoreline. She smiled warmly, welcoming both the wine and the contact.

'Thank you, it's a lovely wine.'

Antonis nodded. 'The owner's ... but not as good as mine ... you will see!'

'I'm looking forward to trying it!' Catherine knew that the opportunity to do so was already agreed upon. Whether it would qualify as another date would remain to be seen, but once again, Antonis had apologised. This time for ending their picnic abruptly over her enquiries. Having let his mother know about Catherine and Diane's interest in Serides and the earring, she now wanted to meet them both. Catherine had little problem agreeing to a meeting for the following day.

She wondered now how Diane had got on at the nightclub. Whatever she had or hadn't learnt, it seemed that Antonis' mother was keen to talk to them. Maybe that would be an end of it. Determined to put all that to the back of her mind, she raised her glass to Antonis again.

'Cheers.'

'*Yamas!*' he replied, his easy smile rapidly turning to puzzlement as Catherine laughed.

For some time now she had been aware of the generously proportioned woman, seated with her partner further along the terrace behind Antonis. Scarcely drawing breath between mouthfuls, she had kept up a garrulous conversation, whilst busily shelling prawns — blithely tossing the discards over the wall, oblivious of anyone down below. An angry shout had now caused only the slightest of pauses and an imperious glare down to the unfortunate recipient.

Taking Antonis' hands, Catherine drew him close as she quietly explained what was happening behind him and they both enjoyed the continuing spectacle as he swung his chair around to 'take in the view.'

The moment's closeness confirmed Catherine's desire. She wanted him close again. She wanted him to kiss her. Though he turned his attentions back towards her and the conversation flowed freely along with the wine, she longed to be free of the formalities and restrictions of the restaurant terrace.

Knowing that her 'secret' beach was somewhere nearby, Catherine proposed a walk before they returned to the hotel. Antonis happily agreed and drove the short distance down to the little bay. Following the same path down to the water's edge, she stood, sandals in hand, gazing out over the moonlit ripples waiting for Antonis to join her — waiting for him to make the first move. Standing just behind, he watched and waited with her. Clearly, she would have to get things going.

Stepping back as the waters slipped over her toes, she bumped into him and turned her body towards his. Reassured by his welcoming embrace, she buried her face into his chest, savouring his scent. Acquiescing now, as he lifted her face to his, they kissed, and as he ran his fingers up the nape of her neck and into her hair, she tossed her sandals further up the beach, to do the same.

The first, gentle exploratory kisses soon became ardent, hungry, searching ones as their hands followed mutually agreed paths. Catherine's fingers traced the contours of his shoulders before slipping down to the base of his spine as she felt him cradle her own cheeks. She could feel his arousal mirroring her own and she drew him in tighter.

Leaving her own, his lips brushed across her closed eyes, and she felt the warmth of his breath pass her ear — the kisses continuing down her neck as he began to unbutton her blouse. Leaning back, she scanned the surrounding area as first his hand then his lips found her breast. A moment's doubt and hesitation engulfed her, not just at the prospect of their being seen, but the very notion of what she was doing so soon.

Yet in so many ways it felt so right — so natural — as if she had known this gentle man for so long. Raising his mouth back to hers, she kissed him deeply and led him back to pick up her sandals.

'Let's walk a little.' Her sandals in one hand, his hand held tightly in the other, they walked in slow, contented silence, deeper into the secluded shelter of the bay. Shutting out the confusion of voices in her head, Catherine willed herself to relax. The gentle rhythm of the waves lapping onto the fine shingle began to replace the voices. The breeze had softened and still the warmth of the day clung into the night. Such a perfect night, alone with this man under the stars in the half light of the moon. There may never be such a perfect time again.

The moment the thought slipped into her mind, she knew she would be powerless to resist the impulse of this intoxicating evening. Catherine relaxed her grip on Antonis' hand then dropped the sandals. As he bent down to retrieve them, she carried on walking, slowly unbuttoning her blouse before letting it too drop to the ground. Running her hands through her hair, she revelled in the freedom, as the gentle breeze played around her breasts. Continuing, she was aware that Antonis had stopped by the discarded blouse and for an instant, self-doubt momentarily threatened to overcome her, but she was not prepared to surrender this newfound liberation and determination won through.

Slipping out of her skirt, she tossed it high up on the beach. Again, the momentary glimpse of reality had informed her that she would probably be travelling back in a damp blouse. Choosing modesty over wet knickers, however, she waded out into the water, gasping at the first chill. Persevering, she swam out a short way before turning to look at Antonis.

Reassured by a flash of white that she knew meant he was smiling, she watched him drape her blouse over a rock, together with her skirt and sandals, before taking off his own shirt. Undoing his belt, he slipped trousers and underwear down in one move.

'Cheat!' she called out through chattering teeth, wishing now she had had the courage to remove her own. Bobbing out of them, she threw them to him and watched as he retrieved them from the water's edge, rinsing the fine pebbles out, before wringing them dry and adding them to their abandoned clothing.

As he walked about, she once again admired his lithe and toned body, now free of any encumbrance and with his own growing admiration for her only too evident. Wading out to join her, she pulled him to her, eager for his warmth — tentative kisses finding the reassurance they sought as they gently bobbed together in the ebb and flow of the tide. Again Antonis' hands cupped her cheeks, but this time as the water lifted them both up, she came back down to rest upon him.

Holding his gaze, Catherine slowly relaxed her grip on his arms entrusting her body to his. Secure inside her, he steadied her waist, encouraging her to lay her head back on the water. Trusting in his hold, she allowed herself to float, arms outstretched and lay back, gazing up at the stars as his fire burned inside her. She had been right. It was the perfect time.

NINETEEN

'Idiots! Why pick a moonlit night?' He chuckled, savouring the scene now brought sharply into focus through the binoculars. For once, the information had been exact: The right place, the right time. They were his for the taking, but he knew he must wait a little longer, let the scene play out. He had everything covered. He could afford to wait.

Huddled into the rocks at the edge of the beach, they gazed out over the moonlit ripples. The breeze had dropped, and they had been sure they had heard movement nearby, but there had been no further sound for several minutes now. Their own silence allowed each to dwell on their own thoughts — everything had been so sudden and now things were about to change forever. Just three days before, Richard had been celebrating his subterranean escape, yet here he now was on the southern coast of Crete Litsa to one side of him and Jim to the other, as they waited for a boat to slip round the bay and take them from the island.

The celebrations in Vasilis' courtyard had been brought to an abrupt standstill by the sudden arrival of Dimitris, barely recognisable as the young groom to be that Richard and Jim had toasted in Manolis' house. Though bruised and scarred from earlier beatings, the immediate concern had been the blood he was losing from a recent gunshot wound to his abdomen. It was he who had been the target of the gunshots all had heard the previous day, as he had tried to make his way back to the village.

Sending word for the doctor to be called, Litsa had tended to Dimitri's wounds as best she could, while he recounted the horrors he had experienced when a troop of Germans had arrived at the village to mete out retribution for the assistance and harbouring of Allied soldiers. He and Manolis had been rounded up with the other men to be marched off for execution. Believing they would be safest inside, Dimitris had urged Maria to stay hidden in the house with Manolis' wife, but he had underestimated the thoroughness of the revenge the Germans had planned.

Breaking away from the column of prisoners as they saw the first flamethrowers begin to torch the houses, both he and Manolis were beaten to the ground, howling their protests in vain as their own house erupted into flames. The piteous screams of their women trapped inside tormented their ears and neither man knew which of their partners it was that they briefly saw hurtling from the doorway, wreathed in flames, before they themselves were beaten senseless.

The beatings had saved their lives, however, for the soldiers left them abandoned, unconscious on the ground, to carry on rounding up the rest of the men who had fled into the hills. By the time the execution party had been regathered, Manolis and Dimitris had vanished.

Recognising the 'Capitaines', Dimitris had warned them that both they and the rest of the villagers were at risk from similar reprisals. Manolis was already meeting with contacts in the resistance arranging for a fishing boat to take them and another party to Egypt. Someone would be needed to guide them to the rendezvous point at the beach. Litsa not only volunteered, but insisted — maintaining that if stopped, the presence of a woman would make the party less suspicious and so Richard now found himself by her side with Jim, awaiting their passage to freedom.

Having retrieved their meagre personal belongings from their hiding places, they had traded their rifles with the resistance contact for less conspicuous small arms. Richard absent-mindedly fingered the Italian pistol in his jacket pocket. A half-written letter to Diane nestled in the other, along with some bread and olives and a couple of field dressings from his kit. Into one he had slipped the pair of earrings that yet again Litsa had refused to accept.

Once at the tiny beach, her duty done, Richard had urged Litsa to return, but she had insisted on waiting for the boat to be sure they got away safely. Now all three waited nervously. With a moon barely a couple of days into its wane, the night was far from ideal. But the hope was that any Germans in the area would be caught off guard, assuming that no escape attempts would even be considered in such circumstances. Their anxieties were compounded by the fact that they should have been joined by another resistance worker bringing three more escapees, but there had been no sign of them. There was no question they had the right beach. Litsa knew it well, she had cousins nearby. It was another reason she had been entrusted with the task.

'There!' whispered Jim. 'Beyond those rocks.'

Richard peered into the night, trying to make out what Jim had seen. Gradually, he managed to discern the dark silhouette of the little caique, breaking cover of the rocky bluff. As it slipped in silently towards them, Richard felt Litsa's hand take his own. There was so much he wanted to say — yet he could not find a single word. As Jim headed down towards the water's edge, Richard turned to Litsa. A glint of reflected moonlight hinted at the tears welling in her eyes, but she gave him a brave smile.

'It is time, you must go.' Silencing any reply with her own finger held to his lips, she met his gaze briefly before letting her finger drop and kissing him tenderly. Then pushing him ahead, she urged him on to join Jim, who was catching a rope the skipper had thrown to him from the caique.

Hauling the boat towards him, Jim heard the old fisherman hiss at him to stop. It was close enough. He did not want to risk the boat being beached. Wading out to the caique, Jim threw back the tail of the rope to Richard, following on behind him. Catching it, he turned for one last farewell to Litsa only to find himself suddenly blinded.

A searchlight seared into life from the rocks above the bay and orders rattled out in German from several directions. For a moment everyone froze — then a shot from Jim's pistol drew the searchlight towards him — promptly followed by a hail of gunfire. Hauling himself into the boat, Jim scuttled backwards, desperately retreating from the pinpricks of light that dotted the prow of the caique as the bullets peppered the hull. The diversion gave Richard the opportunity to draw his own weapon, and steadying his aim, he shot out the searchlight. In the glare of the light and confusion no one had noticed the arrival of clouds that now briefly obscured the moon. Angry shouts from the Germans pinpointed their positions, but for Richard or Jim to fire now would only give away their own.

'Come on!' Jim's urgent plea was reinforced with an arm thrust down towards Richard, who was trying to see if Litsa had made it back to the safety of a group of nearby rocks. He had glimpsed her making off in that direction as the light was shot out. 'Now!' Jim urged again as a volley of shots resumed in their general direction.

Richard waded towards Jim's outstretched arm, but as he found himself being hauled up alongside the prow, he saw another searchlight flare into life, briefly illuminating the German's own position, before sweeping the shoreline. He caught a fleeting glimpse of Litsa darting between the rocks. The Germans had seen her too and shots rapidly followed the course of the searchlight. He heard her scream ring out into the night, rising above the gunfire. Once again, he tried to shoot out the light, but the bobbing of the boat threw off his aim. His fire, however, did at least draw the attention away from her as the searchlight began to rove the water again, seeking out the boat.

Looking up, he could see the clouds beginning to clear from the moon. In no more than a few moments they would all be only too clearly visible. He knew he could not leave her. Reaching into his pocket he hastily pulled out a letter together with the opened field dressing packet, into which he had placed the earrings for safety. 'Get these to Diane for me.' Pressing them into Jim's hand, Richard slipped back into the water and pushed hard on the boat's prow, turning it out to sea. With a final heave at the stern, he called up to Jim, 'Tell the skipper to use the motor once I've taken out the light.'

Wading back toward the beach, far enough to get a decent stance, Richard took aim and managed to put the second searchlight out of use. Diving immediately to one side he side-stroked along the shoreline towards the rocks where he had last heard Litsa's cry, as a hail of gunfire sprayed his original firing position.

Hearing the caique's motor start up, he steadied himself in the water again, and emptied the chamber in the direction of the German gunfire. An agonised cry told him he had found at least one victim. Again the gunfire intensified around him as he heard bullets zipping into the water close by. He tried to put as much distance behind him as he could, with as little disturbance to the waves, now sparkling again in the full glare of the moonlight.

With the caique now clearly visible once more, all guns but one were brought to bear on the little boat as it steadily left the shoreline behind. One lone rifleman had kept Richard in his sights as he continued sidling along the shoreline. Single deliberate shots traced his path, anticipating his progress as he now slipped in and out of the waves. Richard imagined himself behind the sights, finger curled around the trigger, waiting for the swimmer to rise at given intervals along his path.

Abruptly he slipped deeper beneath the surface and twisted his body out into deeper water and saw the bullet slice through the water where his original path would have taken him. If he could just keep moving out into the bay below the water for a few moments more — but his lungs were bursting.

Rising as quietly as he could, he gasped for air and sank beneath the surface again. With luck, his hunter had assumed he had scored a lucky shot. Surfacing again, he could see the caique disappearing out of range as the gunfire petered out and hoped that the absence of any sign of Jim or the skipper meant they were simply keeping their heads down.

Looking back to the beach, he could see the Germans now moving down from their positions. He had to get back to the shoreline and find Litsa before they did. Slipping beneath the waves once more Richard headed back towards the rocks. Emerging once, then twice for air, he could see he was making good progress, but as he surfaced for the third time, the rifle shot bit into his side just below the water. This time it was his turn to let out an involuntary cry as the hunter found his mark. Sinking back deep beneath the surface, he could see his own blood blackening the water around him, but beyond the searing pain of the wound, he sensed that it was not a vital one and he swam for all he was worth as further shots spiralled through the eerily moonlit sea.

Rising as infrequently as possible, Richard adopted a zig-zag course that slowly brought him nearer to a large rocky outcrop that bordered the bay. The overhanging rocks would give him some shelter from the moonlight and a chance to get ashore and find Litsa. Pushed up against the jagged rockface by the pulse of the waves, he was grateful for the jacket he had previously been cursing for slowing his progress.

Steadying himself against the swell, he sidled into the cover of the stone canopy and waited. All firing had ceased.

Thankful now that he had cried out in pain, he prayed that the rifleman believed it to have been a mortal wound. He could hear the Germans' conversation as they searched the rocks, accompanied by occasional flashes of torchlight sweeping here and there. At least that meant Litsa had so far not been found.

A sudden loud splash at the shoreline alerted everyone — gunshots rang out and torches were brought to bear on the scene of the disturbance. Richard froze, dreading that he might see Litsa's body revealed in one of the wavering pools of light. Instead, it was her hand — very much alive — that startled him, cupping gently around his mouth lest he betray her stealthy approach through the waters beside him.

Leading him further out around the rocky outcrop, she pointed down to a hollow in the rock face before diving into it. Watching her feet disappear before him, he took a deep breath and followed suit. Using his hands to guide his progress along the narrow underwater tunnel, he was soon aware of the moonlight once again filtering down from above, before he was finally buoyed up by the push of the waves through the blow-hole.

Scrambling up a rough path in the rocks, it became clear how Litsa had been so easily able to surprise him, having first created a diversion by hurling a large piece of flotsam over to slap into the water by the shallower rocks at the shoreline. Hugging the profile of the rocks, she now led him down to the sands of an adjoining bay and as she tried to run Richard could see the cause of her own outcry. She had twisted one ankle and was hardly able to bear any weight on it. Accepting his support Litsa slipped her arm around his waist, only to discover his wound.

'A fine pair we make!' he joked to ease her fears. Then as he noticed the moon disappearing behind clouds once more, 'At least it looks like Mother Nature is back on our side again.' Leaving the beach behind them they slipped into the safety of the wooded hillside.

When the last of the shots had died away in the distance, Jim reappeared from behind the sheltering crates and made his way back to the skipper, who was lying down, one arm on the rudder, keeping watch over the stern.

'That was a close one!' But Jim's thanks died on his lips as he gave the skipper a hearty slap on the shoulder. Rolling off the rudder onto his back, one eye stared blankly up at the moon, the other was a pool of darkness: a grim portal for the bullet lodged in his brain.

Settling the old Greek to one side, Jim looked back at the shoreline. He could see faint flashes of light and feared for Richard and Litsa's safety. Gradually the coast seemed to slip sideways, and he realised he needed to take hold of the rudder, now flapping idly, freed from the skippers grasp. Bringing the little beach back to the centre of the stern once more, he watched it slowly fade into the distance as the motor puttered on.

Eventually as the beach became indistinguishable from the black outline of the island, Jim turned his thoughts forward and began to take stock of his situation. Despite being a Tynemouth lad, his own childhood had given him no experience in sailing whatsoever. Still, at least he had the motor — for now — but how long would the fuel last? He had better check for spare — but that would mean leaving the rudder.

It did not take him long, however, to find the weathered rope the skipper used to tie off the rudder, and he searched the little boat as best he could in the cloudy half-light of the moon. What he found did not inspire him. Of the two cans he had discovered — one for fuel and the other water, neither appeared to have more than a cupful left. The boat and its contents had been riddled with bullets. Thankfully most, so far as he was aware, were above the water line. But it was not looking good.

His search for a compass finally ended in the skipper's pocket — at least he had that, and he knew that Egypt lay more or less due South. He looked at the sail furled along the boom and contemplated the task ahead. A task for tomorrow he concluded, tiring now in the small hours of the night. Checking the compass, he adjusted the rudder, tied it off firmly, and tried to settle down beside it until — conscious of the companion close by who would never wake again, he realised he had one last duty to perform.

Keeping the old fisherman's knife, Jim put the few coins he found back into the skipper's pocket for luck and gave him his thanks as he watched the body slip beneath the inky waters.

Hushed conversation filtered into Richard's consciousness, conspiring with the bright rays of the early morning sun, to prise him from the realms of his dreams. Stirring on the hard palliasse of straw, with a coarse blanket chafing against his bare skin, he was rapidly reminded of his present location.

Rhythmical grinding of teeth and an unmistakeable odour confirmed the donkey's presence below the raised wooden platform that had served as his shelter for the night. Litsa had led them to her cousin's house, and as the memories flooded back, he examined the only thing he wore: an improvised dressing around his waist. She had confirmed that the bullet had passed clean through the fleshy area, just above his hip. In one grip, he could feel both where the bullet had entered with his finger, and where it had left, with his thumb.

Attempting to sit up, the toll of the torn muscles brought out an involuntary groan. He heard the conversation outside cease. Rising quickly he looked about for his clothes, but they were nowhere to be seen. Footsteps on the simple wooden stairs froze him, clutching the blanket around his waist.

'An interesting dress …' Litsa teased, appearing with his clothes, 'but these might suit you better!' Richard struggled to take them without losing his grip on the blanket. Litsa laughed at his predicament. 'It is not as if I haven't…'

'I know!' Richard cut in.

'Twice now, if I am not mistaken. You will have to stop getting into trouble! Now sit back down, I want to look at the dressing before we go.' Satisfied with her inspection, she handed him the clothes. 'The jacket is still not dry, but the rest are not so bad.'

Richard began to empty the pockets, shaking the pistol dry, more from force of habit since he had no further ammunition. Then taking out the sodden cloth bundle of bread and olives, his wrist caught on something sharp.

'Damn!' He looked at the pinpricks of blood forming on the scratch.

'What now?' said Litsa, archly.

'It looks as if they don't want to leave you … well, one at least!' Richard held up the offending earring that had snagged in the lining of the pocket. Holding his hand open, he offered it to her. Litsa looked at it for a moment, before looking back up at him.

'Why did you stay?' she asked.

'You know why … I couldn't leave you.'

'You should have.' Litsa folded his hand back over the earring. 'We'll see …'

'Breakfast then?' Richard unwrapped the sodden parcel.

'No time!' Litsa replied, taking an olive, nevertheless. 'My cousin has given us some food to take. But we must leave. The Germans must not find us here.'

'Yes, you're right.' Richard began to hurry into his clothes. 'You know they were waiting for us on the beach?'

'Yes, I do.'

'And you know what that must mean?'

'Yes … someone has betrayed us.'

Staring down at his own breakfast, Jim wondered just how long he might have to make it last. The motor had run dry during the night and by the time he had woken, the little caique had succumbed to another course, drifting slowly eastwards.

Rationing himself, he took a couple of sips from the meagre remains of the water can. Hunger might turn out to be the least of his problems. Time then for his first sailing lesson. He had everything he needed: a boat, sails, and a vast expanse of sea to practice in. He was missing only one thing — wind.

Diane's breakfast was interrupted by an unexpected visitor.

'Not too early for you I hope … just got off the night train!'

'Eddie!' Diane flung her arms around him. 'What on earth are you doing back here? Come in. Leave your things in the hall and come through. There's tea in the pot. Mum and Dad are out.'

'Yeah, hoping mine are too.'

'Why, what's wrong?' Diane waited patiently as Eddie took a swig or two of the tea.

'Discharged.'

'What … why?'

'Medical grounds.'

'But you're as fit as a fiddle!'

'Thought I was … ticker … that's what it is … dodgy ticker ….'

Diane struggled to find the right words. 'So, what will that mean … do you have to have an operation?'

'No, no … no. Just means I'll have to do something else … take it easy … do something that doesn't involve …' Diane watched him fidget uneasily with the cup and saucer. Drawing her chair closer to him, she took them, set them back on the table and took his hands in her own.

'It'll be alright Eddie.'

'Course it will ducks, course it will.' He tried in vain to shrug off the despondency, choking back his emotions, before letting it all pour out. 'Ah bollocks! It's not my bleeding heart. It's my nerves. I couldn't think straight with all that screaming and shouting going on in my head, day after day. I kept doing the wrong thing, time after time. I wanted to get it right Di. They think I'm simple ... or spineless ... neuro ... psycho ... something or other they said. I can't tell Dad! *I can't tell him*!"

'You won't have to.' Diane squeezed his hands hard. 'No one has to know. It's our secret. You say exactly what you told me first. I'll go to the library and look up some fancy name for it, then no one will be any the wiser. I'll look after you, I promise.'

'Will you Di, will you?'

'Of course I will. Now you need a fresh cup of tea and something to eat. And tonight, you're going to take me dancing, right? That'll cheer us both up!'

TWENTY

Though weary from their long trek back from the coast, Richard and Litsa waited patiently in Vasilis' courtyard for the meeting to begin. It had taken them the better part of three full day's steady walking to reach the rendezvous beach and nearly double that to return, slowed down by their injuries, though their pace had quickened as the swelling lessened and Litsa's ankle began to heal. Despite the ordeal, Richard had relished the opportunity to have Litsa's undivided attention and their conversations had been spontaneous and enjoyable.

Once again, however, decisions had to be made and there were serious matters to address. Looking around as the numbers grew, Richard recognised most of the faces: Vasilis, of course, Manolis, and Dimitris now thankfully in better shape. Present also were Fanouris and Michaelis, Pavlos, Lefteris and Christos, together with his son Andreas who had helped with the harvest, old Gregori who kept the goats with his son Yianni, as was his wife Stefania, intent on knowing what was happening rather than waiting with the majority of the women who were gathered in a huddle at the courtyard gate. If Litsa could remain, why not she? There were others he knew by sight but whose names escaped him, if ever he had known them, among the myriad Yianni's and Yiorgo's, but two strange faces stood out — faces he did not recognise.

As the meeting got under way, however, it became clear that they were resistance workers. After Richard and Litsa had recounted the events at the beach, the discussion became heated and he was unable to follow the rapid exchanges, though it was not too difficult to follow the gist of the conversations, along with occasional translations from Litsa.

First there was general outrage at the knowledge that there had to be a traitor in their midst. An intense interrogation of the resistance worker who had been charged with guiding the other escapees to the rendezvous beach followed, but it became clear that they had never showed up at their original meeting point. Nor had they been seen since.

Wary of trusting someone from a village other than their own, Manolis and Fanouris were reluctant to bring an end to the questioning, but Vasilis intervened on the man's behalf. He knew his family and did not believe he could be responsible. Grudgingly they let the matter drop and speculations and accusations continued to circulate among the group for some time.

Eventually, with no resolution to that particular problem in sight, Vasilis called the meeting's attention to the remaining matter in hand and Richard found himself the centre of that attention. It was left to the second resistance worker to decide on Richard's fate. Having kept aloof from all of the earlier accusations, and without revealing a name, he now took control of the meeting. Richard sensed that this was a man accustomed to being obeyed. Someone used to more than just village life.

There was a cave some two or three miles distant from the village. The man waited until the entire assembly acknowledged they knew the place, casting his eye to one and all including the women at the gate. Richard was to be taken to the cave at once. The sooner he was away from the village, the less risk there was to all. He would spend that night there alone. The following evening, he would be collected by the resistance worker himself along with two young volunteers he had recruited from a nearby village.

A flurry of appreciation spread through the gathering, applauding their neighbouring village's commitment to the cause, but all fell silent as he then asked for two more to join him from their own number. Andreas and Michaelis felt the man's gaze fall on them. Proud that he should be considered worthy, Andreas looked to his father for approval. Christos studied the boy gravely for a moment before nodding his assent.

'Michaeli?' Andreas entreated his friend to join him. Wriggling free from Fanouris' covert grip on his jacket, Michaelis stepped forward ignoring his father's warning hiss. Taking the two boys to one side, the man briefed them on what they were to bring the following night, and as he sent them off to make the most of their last night, the meeting began to disperse.

Turning his attention to Richard and Litsa, he spoke in English, 'You have understood?'

'Yes.' Richard stood to address him. 'Yes, perfectly. It's the best solution. I can't put these people in any more danger. Besides, I'm sure I could be of help to you with your cause.' The man eyed him impassively.

'We shall see. Now who is to take you to the cave?'

'I will of course.' Litsa sprang to Richard's side, only to find herself now the subject of the man's measured gaze. Vasilis interjected, insisting she had done enough and should rest and leave it to someone else, but his daughter was adamant. The resistance worker shrugged.

'It is of no consequence … take him if you wish, but soon!'

Summarily dismissed, Litsa and Richard watched him lead her father over to his colleague, seated now at Vasilis' little table by the house door. All three entered into an earnest discussion.

Litsa turned to Richard, 'You will need water and food … and a blanket. I will get them'

He watched her hurry into the house, pausing briefly to reassure her father. Though he had been a part of the household for little more than a matter of months, it felt to Richard that he was leaving a true home. There had been no time for reflection on his previous departure and he knew there was little now, so sat quietly awaiting Litsa's return, embracing the scene. It was one he feared he may never see again.

Diane had been relieved to see the Eddie she knew of old, coming to life on the dance floor as he swung her through their routines, but it had proved a fleeting respite. In the days that followed, she sensed him slipping deeper and deeper into a quiet despondency. True to her word, she had unearthed an obscure heart condition in the reference library: one that did not call for immediate intervention but would effectively rule him out of active service.

A stalwart of the 14 -18 war, Eddie's father had not taken the news well, regardless of cause. It had been his dream that his son would finish the job he had started so long ago. Only briefly enquiring whether it meant Eddie was likely to drop dead at any moment, he too had withdrawn into morose reflection, despite reassurances that Eddie was likely to be around for a good while yet.

She had managed to cajole Eddie into going with her to the picture house one evening, but neither had particularly enjoyed the event. Not having heard a word from him since then, she now found herself at the front door of his parent's house, steeling herself to face his father, as she lifted the cast iron knocker.

Breathing a sigh of relief as Eddie himself finally opened the door, Diane triumphantly held up the bag of broken biscuits. 'Let's put the kettle on!' Breezing past him, she headed for the kitchen calling out for Eddie's mother.

'She's not here Di.' Responding to Diane's enquiring look, he explained, 'She's gone down to her sister's in Kent … taken Alice with her as well.'

'And your dad?'

'Drowning his sorrows in the boozer, I expect.' He filled the kettle and handed it to Diane, who lit the gas. Settling the kettle over the flames, she asked the question, regardless of the growing suspicion that she already knew the answer.

'What's he got to be sorry about?'

'He'll be worrying what his mates think about his shirker of a son. Reckons he's already heard a couple of them whispering about conscientious objectors.'

'That's ridiculous!'

'That's why Mum's down in Kent with Alice … trying

to talk Nell into taking me on at the farm. Keep me out of the limelight.' Diane busied herself, swilling out the teapot, warming it with a little water from the kettle, before realising she had taken complete control of the kitchen.

'I'm so sorry … maybe you wanted to get another brew from that?'

Eddie laughed and handed her the caddy. 'Not likely, the last cup was like gnat's!' Eddie let Diane continue with the tea making and set out a tray. 'Let's go up and see if we can get any news on the crystal. Still no news from Rich?'

'Another letter from Crete, but it's ages old … I do hope he's managed to get away.'

Finding himself back in the role of consoler rather than consoled helped to keep Eddie's spirits up as they set the tray between them on Eddie's bed. Laughing at the groaning springs, Eddie apologised for the lumpy mattress. For a while they listened briefly to snatches of news and foreign music, one ear each to the bakelite headphones on the pillow between them arguing over next choice from the bag of misshapen treats, but eventually the conversation returned to Eddie's future.

Trying to gauge his mood, Diane decided to broach the subject of Kent once more. Clearing away the tray from the crumpled bed, she straightened out the bedspread, while Eddie put away the crystal set and replaced the pillow they had shared. 'Would you want to work on a farm, Eddie?'

'Could do worse, I suppose.'

'But you'd be so far away still.'

Well … maybe that's for the best …'

'Take no notice of your father, Eddie, you're a grown man now.'

'I know. That's why I've already made up my mind.'

'To do what?'

'There's plenty of call for drivers, even if you girls are snapping up most of the jobs!'

'That's a splendid idea Eddie … your father won't be able to moan then. You'll be doing an important job, whether it's ambulances or the fire …'

'He can moan all he likes. I won't be around to hear it.'

'What do you mean?'

'I've got a chum up in Coventry, they're getting it pretty bad up there. He's going to put me up for a while, until I get myself straight ….' Eddie shifted uncomfortably, then got up and looked out of the window.

'When?'

'Tomorrow … I'm getting the train up tomorrow, Di.'

'You weren't going to tell me?'

'Course I was ducks … course I was. It's just … difficult.'

'I don't understand.'

'Well, it's bad enough my old man thinking I'm a conchie … but … being here, with Rich away … and you just round the corner …'

'But that's good Eddie … we're here for each other … we've always been best friends.'

'Best friends … yeah!'

'Well, aren't we … Eddie?'

'What if … what if being best friends wasn't enough Di?'

It was Diane's turn to display discomfort. 'I don't understand.'

'Yes, you do Di.' Eddie turned to face her, 'I have to get away. You know it makes sense. I can't stay here any longer … seeing you and keeping it to myself. For God's sake, you must know how I feel for you … always have felt … I love you Di.'

Even though Diane had indeed known, to hear Eddie finally speak the words still came as such a shock that as she rose to join him at the window, she found her reply was as much of a shock to her as it was to him. 'But I love you too.'

The cave though not so very far from the village was not an easy find. Richard could see why it had gained a reputation as a safe hideout among the locals. Perched high above an escarpment, dotted with spiny shrubs and what few trees had the tenacity to force their roots in the crevices of the rocks, he could not even see a glimpse of the opening that Litsa endeavoured to point out for him as they faced the final climb. He saw the overhanging brow of rock, which would make an approach from above almost impossible save for the most experienced or foolhardy of climbers. Richard simply had to trust her word that behind the solid sheet of rock, which was all he could see below it, there existed an entrance to the cave.

'Stay here then and talk me up to it. You don't need to come any further, I can see your ankle's playing up again.'

Litsa looked up at the final climb. He knew she was in pain, but he also knew her answer.

'No! I will do the talking … you can do the pulling!' Shooing him ahead, she held out her hand for him to haul her up.

Clinging on to the sparse foliage they picked their way around long-displaced boulders, among narrow gullies that snaked their way down the slippery hillside, until their path ended abruptly at a narrow ledge. Briefly wondering whether Litsa had misjudged the route, Richard felt her press close to him as she edged around him over the drop below and took hold of a stout tree root, knotted into the face of the rock where the path petered out.

'No more pulling,' she smiled 'now you push!' Hitching her skirts around her, she took a hold on the roots and planted her good foot up on a grip in the rock face waiting for Richard to push her up. 'Don't tell me now you're shy Mr Englishman?'

Richard obliged and hauling himself up beside her, found himself on another wider ledge, the sheet of rock facing him. To his right he saw the ledge once again peter out to nothing as it met the vertical curtain of rock. Looking up, he could see no further footholds, or any other way off the ledge.

Litsa smiled at his puzzlement. 'Trust me!' Sidling along the ledge that dwindled into nothing more than a toe-hold as it met the sheer face of the rock, she slipped her hand around the edge and before he could voice his concerns for her safety, she was gone.

Her name escaped as little more than a croak from his throat but was instantly rewarded by Litsa's face grinning around to him from behind the rock face, followed by her arm.

'Pass me the things.'

Richard slipped off the bundle of provisions Litsa had tied into the blanket and swung them round to her. Warily following their course, he found he was able to step around to another open ledge.

Like a giant arching wedge of cheese, the seemingly blank rock face concealed a low, dry cave that extended back some ten or twelve feet — the rough, dusty floor terminating in a raised slab of rock that met the inward slope of the cave's roof. Spread with old bracken and straw, it had obviously eased many a fugitive's night. Richard was about to set the bundle down.

'Not yet!' warned Litsa taking a couple of sticks from a pile beside the blackened pit close by the entrance. Slowly prising up the dried bedding with one, she explored the dusty slab with the other and quickly found what she was looking for.

Scuttling away from the light, the scorpion met its end as the second stick came crashing down upon it. Satisfied no others were still lurking there, Litsa swept the remains from the slab of rock and sorted out a few suitable candidates to redress the bed. 'We'll need some fresh ones as well.'

Richard responded to her request, looking around the ledge and scrambling up onto a little slope that continued above the cave. By the time he had returned with the fruits of his foraging, Litsa had swept out the floor of the cave, evicted another pair of scorpions and stacked the old bedding for future use as kindling by the firepit.

Laying the final fronds on the makeshift bed together, each slowed their progress, rearranging them, reluctant for the shared task to end — both acutely aware of how little time remained. The sun had already set. Taking the frond she had already twice moved from her, Richard set it aside and held her hands, as she turned to face him

'Litsa … I want you to know …'

'You don't need to … I do know … and it is the same for me.'

'But I have no idea …'

Again, Litsa pre-empted his thoughts. 'No one knows what is going to happen.' Tracing her fingers around his face, barely visible now in the pale shaft of moonlight, she ruffled his beard. 'Who are you really my Yianni?' Seeing Richard about to answer, she held her fingers to his lips. Taking them, he kissed them and felt a shiver run through her.

'You're cold?'

'A little, but you will warm me won't you Yianni?' Litsa slipped her hand into Richard's jacket pocket and finding what she had expected withdrew the single earring. She looked at it for a moment, glinting in the moonlight — her future resting in her hand. Her eyes firmly on Richard's, Litsa put on the earring.

The words he had never imagined he could possibly ever hear still hung in Eddie's ears as he gazed at Diane in the fading light. Her expression was as surprised as his own — an expression that was brought into sudden illumination — as a light came on in the opposite back extension window.

Eddie promptly drew the flimsy curtains that refused to close completely and turned back to Diane, expecting the moment to be shattered, gone, never to have happened. Yet there she stood. The expression of surprise though had turned to concern, confusion. Feelings he knew only too well.

About to draw down the blackout linings, Diane stayed Eddie's hand, and as a shout from the rear terrace secured its demand, the glow of light through the curtains of the opposite window vanished as instantly as it had arrived, and once again

Diane's face was illuminated only by the faint light of the crescent moon filtering through their own flimsy curtains. He wanted her so badly, yet still found himself telling her, 'I have to go. It wouldn't be right … think of Rich.'

'You think I don't? I think of him every single day, not to mention the nights … and do you know what's funny? I think of you too. I thought that once I was married, it would all fall into place … that the feelings I had for you would change, slip away, turn into something else … that some part of growing up, being a married woman … would make it all different. But it doesn't … I'm just the same silly girl who dreamt she'd always have her two boys.' Diane moved closer to Eddie resting her head on his chest. Of course I'd never want to hurt Richard, but it doesn't seem to matter what I do ….' Raising her head, Diane's eyes searched Eddie's. 'You can't just kill love.'

Though barely one quarter of its monthly majesty, the moon's impassive gaze still reached far and wide. From London terrace to Cretan cave, three thousand miles was as nothing. An insignificant fraction of the globe that held it captive, whose occupants nightly cast their dreams up into its beam, each so very different, each so very much the same.

Drawing her face to his, he ran his fingers through her hair, breathed in the scent of her, and traced the contours of her face, whose every detail had long since been burned in his memory. Slowly, so slowly — to savour forever — this first real kiss — his arms enfolded her. And when their breathing had steadied to an easy unison through barely parted lips, she felt his hand slip from shoulder to elbow, where it paused, seeking passage up along her inner arm, across her breast. Holding his hand cupped to her breast, she sought out the other, to do the same.

Then slowly easing back from him she began to undress. He had wanted this for so long and for a moment could only stand admiring her body. Comfortable in the pale moonlight, she turned towards the bed both had just prepared and sat awaiting him. She did not have long to wait. Lying back, she drew him into her embrace and as his kisses explored her body, she closed her eyes, pushing aside the giddy swirl of confusions in her mind, oblivious of the discomforts of the bedding beneath her. Another brief discomfort quickly giving way to a deeper pleasure as she welcomed him. In all too short a time she felt his body arch and fall still, content to rest in her embrace, while over his shoulder she watched the moon edge out of sight and wondered what their futures might hold.

TWENTY-ONE

'I must go!' Easing herself gently from his embrace, Litsa gathered her clothes and dressed. Conscious of his gaze, she threw his own clothes at him. 'You'll catch a cold lying there!'

He laughed, but quickly dressed. She was right. Vasilis would be worried.

'You'll be alright … getting back in the dark?' he asked, only to endure Litsa's dismissive laughter.

'Of course! But you can help me down to the ledge.' She moved to the entrance of the cave and turned. Richard watched her, silhouetted in the opening, as she took out the earring. Unable to see her expression, he then found her pressing the earring into his shirt pocket. 'Keep me there … close to your heart. If you come back, I shall wear it forever.'

Before he could reply she had slipped around the rockface. Joining her on the narrow ledge, she drew him to her for one last lingering kiss, before grasping the knotted tangle of roots with one hand, holding out the other for Richard to lower her to the ledge below.

Letting her down, he watched as she scrambled back down the rocky slope slowly disappearing into the gloom. Briefly catching sight of her once more as she rejoined the dusty road below, he glimpsed one final wave and then she was gone.

Swinging back around the rockface to the entrance of the cave, a match suddenly flared in the darkness above him.

'Pretty girl!'

Briefly illuminated by the lighting of his cigarette, Richard recognised the resistance worker, squatting on the rough slope that led up above the cave. Startled as much by his appearance as to what he may have witnessed, Richard stood speechless as the man slithered down to join him.

Holding up the dying match, he inspected the cave. 'Very cosy, a pity you won't be staying!'

When finally he did lay down to sleep that night, Richard found himself in very different quarters. Huddled onto a rough wooden bed that still held the scent of past goat-herders as well as their charges, unable to sleep, he too lay gazing up at the moon, now far higher in its orbit, piercing through the broken shutters of the crumbling stone hut.

In moving him far from the original cave, where everyone expected him to be, the resistance worker hoped to safeguard both Richard's and his own interests. Now only he and his volunteers would be privy to the rendezvous they all would keep as soon as darkness fell the following day.

Beating down mercilessly over the Libyan Sea, the sun was at its zenith. Huddled below, in the shelter of the tarpaulin,

Jim drifted in his own private no-man's land, somewhere between sleep and semi-consciousness, praying for night to come again. How many nights — how many days? He had lost count. The torment might ease a little with the night — along with the thirst.

The first two days had not been so bad as he had learnt to handle the little craft, but as the water ran out so did his strength. His blistered body succumbed to the relentless toll of juggling opposing winds and currents in the full glare of the sun, and he learnt to save his energies for the cooler hours, but still no shoreline greeted him, as time and again he peered above the compass needle.

Squatting down at the front door, Eddie reached through the letter flap and found the string tied to the lock. Pulling the key through, he could see his father's broad shoulders hunched over the paper spread out before him on the kitchen table. Letting himself in, he hung his jacket on the hallstand and sauntered into the kitchen happily whistling a tune he knew would irritate the old man. 'Picked a winner yet?'

'What are you so bleedin' cheerful about?'

'Why wouldn't I be cheerful? It's a lovely day out there.' As pleasant as the day indeed was, the sunshine merely reinforced the elation Eddie had felt since waking that morning to realise that for the first time, his constant dreams of Diane were no longer just a fantasy.

'Well don't think you'll be swanning the streets for much longer matey … you need to pack your bags. Got a letter from your ma … Nell says she'll find a use for you on the farm.'

'Fraid she'll have to manage without me Dad. I start at the dairy tomorrow morning!'

'Dairy? What are you talking about?'

'Got me self a job. Deliveries. Can I borrow your alarm clock?'

'You … a bleedin' milkman?'

'No worse than digging spuds!'

Taking down the saline drip, the medical officer drew the sheet over the man's blistered face. It was not an unfamiliar sight. His had not been the first boat that had finally come to rest on the nearby shore. There had been a chance he might recover — moments of lucidity — but in the end the dehydration had proved too much.

Remembering the letter the man had pressed into his hand, the doctor withdrew it now, to write down the details. He would file a report and in due course another widow would be told of her fate. The letter would also eventually make its way back to her.

He had no idea why the man had also thrust the field dressing with it, probably just the delirium. Recalling his words, 'Tell her … Richard didn't make it …' he filled in the name and briefly inspected the dressing. Too soiled to make further use of, he threw it into the waste bin. His pen halted over the report, however, as his mind queried the metallic clink the packet made as it hit the container. Retrieving it, he saw a gold hook protruding from a slit in the wrapping. Withdrawing the earring, he now saw why the man had wanted the dressing to accompany the letter to his wife —

most probably a souvenir from one of the bazaars bought while he had been training.

Turning it over in his hands, he wondered what to do with it. Sent through the usual channels, it would probably never reach his widow. Slipping the earring back into the dressing, he set it aside, noticing as he did so, that it was much the same size as the cardboard box beside it, that held glass slides.

Opening the box, he took out the remaining couple of fresh slides, inserted the dressing in their place along with a couple of redundant slides and wrote the address on the lid of the box before finally placing the letter inside on top of the slides and tying the box ready to be posted. If it made it back to her all well and good, if not — well he'd done his best — there were other things to attend to.

Breaking off the fresh green sprig of rosemary, Litsa carried it back into the house, poured a little water into the flask and putting the rosemary into it, set it on the stone window sill. Outside, the last vestiges of sun-tinged colour faded from the sky as twilight took hold and familiar stars began to stud the darkening sky. They would be setting off now, Andreas and Michaelis, the resistance man, and his other two volunteers. She knew without asking that she would not be allowed to join them — to see him one last time. She knew she should not in any case — already there had been whispering. Tracing the outline of the tiny boat on the flask, she wondered whether she would ever see him again.

Lighting the little oil lamp, she started to occupy herself with preparations for the evening meal. Her father was already cleaning up outside. Pouring a little *tsikouthia* for him, she set it ready for his arrival, alongside some dried bread and olives, before rinsing the wild greens she had gathered earlier. There was still some rabbit left from the previous day. It would be enough; she had little appetite herself.

Settling into his chair, Vasilis sipped his drink and watched as his daughter went about her work. Noticing the little flask of rosemary on the sill, he was about to offer some word of consolation, when a gunshot echoed from the distant hills.

The bowl of greens crashed to the floor as Litsa swung round in alarm. Before Vasilis could utter a word, she had fled through the door. Jumping up, he followed her into the courtyard, shouting out for her to return, warning her of the dangers, but she was already weaving through the village streets heading for the road up into the hills.

Following as fast as he could, Vasilis came to the fork in the road, where one trail led up towards the cave. Heading up it, he suddenly heard muffled voices alongside, coming from somewhere close by. It had to be the other path. Quietly retracing his steps back to the fork, he saw two shadowy forms in the dim light. Recognising his daughter walking back towards him, he saw that around her shoulders, she held the arm of the second, limping figure she supported. As they came closer Vasilis realised it was Michaelis.

Pressing the bottle of *tsikouthia* to his lips, Litsa held Michaeli's gaze. Feeling his grip tighten sharply on her own hand as the old doctor pried the bullet from his leg, she heard it finally drop onto the table and Michaeli's hand relaxed a little, reluctant however, to let go completely.

Handing him the bullet for a souvenir, the doctor took the bottle and sprinkled some of the alcohol onto the wound to sterilise it before pouring himself a generous glass to keep Vasilis company, while leaving Litsa to bandage Michaeli's leg.

Methodically dressing the wound as she had been taught, Litsa's mind was far away in the hills, as she ran over what Michaelis had recounted. The change of rendezvous confided to them, they had not travelled far along the new path, when there had been a single gunshot from a wooded area above the trail. At first the group had scattered, each seeking what shelter they could, but in the ensuing calm, they had broken cover to find no trace of the assailant. Finding his friend wounded, Andreas had been charged with accompanying Michaelis back to the village, while the others pressed on. Shortly afterwards they had met Litsa, and Andreas hurried back to rejoin the others.

Drawing up a comfortable chair for him, Litsa seated Michaelis by her father and the doctor then refilled the little bottle of tsikouthia.

Vasilis turned to ask for more olives, but Litsa had gone.

She knew the old hut they must be heading for and for the second time that night she ran for all she was worth, through the village — up the road to the fork — on past where she had met Michaelis and Andreas. Eventually her laboured breaths forced her to slow her pace. Wary also of making too much noise, she pushed quietly on. What she would do when she got there, she had no idea. All she knew was — she had to be there — had to know that he was safe.

Approaching the brow of a hill, she paused in the

shadow of its dark profile, the starlit sky sweeping up above it. Knowing that the hut was only a short distance beyond, she crept up quietly into the cover of a bush from where she could look down the opposite slope.

She could just see the dim outline of the hut, but little else — no movement — no sound. Concerned now, as much for her own safety as for Richard's, she nestled down into the bush, unsure what to do next. Time slipped by and her mind wandered back to the previous evening. To those precious few minutes they had shared together. Her thoughts were interrupted by a noise: a brief, faint sound she could not identify. And as she strained to hear it again, began to wonder if she had really heard anything at all. But then she saw it — a flash of light in the trees beyond the hut. Now both vision and hearing became finely attuned upon the little hut.

So suddenly that she could not help but let out a startled shriek, all was cacophony and mayhem. The yellow flares of machine gun fire spitting into the hut had barely registered before the deadly staccato reached her ears. Stifling her own screams, she watched the torchlights penetrate the little building, and heard five more individual, unequivocal shots, that pierced her own soul.

Choking back her tears, she willed her sobbing frame to be silent but the easy conversation and laughter that drifted up from the little hut told her that she had not been heard. Before long the soldiers headed off back into the trees — their torches mapping out their path.

Waiting until all sight and sound of them had disappeared, Litsa slowly emerged from her cover and hesitantly made her way down to the little hut, pausing at the threshold, not wanting to see what she knew she had to see.

Looking inside she could dimly make out the tangled sprawl of bodies. She could see the resistance man, still seated grotesquely on the wooden bed. The gunfire had left him splayed out, half propped against the wall behind. On the floor just ahead to her right must be the two volunteers. Now her eyes accustomed to the gloom she could see Richard lying face upwards, close to the door. Just beyond was Andreas, slumped in the space between him and the bed.

Sinking to her knees, she let out her grief. Huge sobs shaking her body. Her tears splashing onto his face. The warmth was still in his body, and she hugged him close to keep it there. Tiring eventually, she let him sink back to the floor as her tears began to subside. Still kneeling, she was about to smooth back his hair when she was startled by another sound nearby. Someone was coming. With nowhere else to hide, Litsa scrambled behind Andreas' body, forcing herself into the tiny space between him and half under the low bed. Once more willing herself into silence, she tried to steady her breathing as a shadow loomed at the doorway.

Assessing the scene for a moment, the figure then withdrew something from his trouser pocket, something small — a folded wad of paper, she thought — and as Litsa held her breath, she watched as the man stooped down by Richard and pulled open his shirt pocket. About to put the paper in, the hand paused as the owner's fingers discovered the earring inside. Litsa watched as it was withdrawn.

A torch sprang into life as calloused hands examined the find. As it was pocketed, the torch swung back down to Richard's shirt pocket once more and she saw that the wad of paper being slipped into Richard's pocket was money — folded banknotes — foreign notes she did not recognise.

For a moment the light illuminated Richard's face and Litsa could not stifle an intake of breath. Blinded, as the light rapidly swung into her own eyes, she hardly saw the fist that swung down into her face knocking her head back against the frame of the bed. Then there was darkness.

Voices echoed deep within her brain. At first distant, muffled, then louder and louder, until she seemed totally surrounded by them. Once again light stabbed into her eyes. But this time the hand that appeared was gentle, appealing, it was familiar. A hand she recognised. Then she heard her father's voice 'Litsa … *Litsa mou* …'

Another light, an oil lamp flaring into life, dwarfed the torch-beam, and she heard Christos gasp as he recognised his son beside her and fell to his knees. Lifting his lifeless body to his breast, Litsa saw the pain in his eyes and her own grief flooded back to her. Taking her father's outstretched hand, she crawled from her hiding place — past Andreas gently rocking in his father's embrace — and into her own father's arms.

TWENTY-TWO

'You can see now why I did not say anything before ... I did not want to upset you unnecessarily.' Michaelis placed the photo of Richard on the table, between himself and Diane, who sat silently, staring down at Richard's image, trying to take in what she had just been told.

Even he felt a twinge of remorse at the effect his recollections had brought about and tried to soften the blow a little. 'It may not even have been your husband, though it was definitely not the other Englishman who got away. He was quite different. We never knew their real names, they were given Greek ones. As I say, I cannot be certain that the man responsible was the same man in your photograph ... your husband ... it was a long time ago.'

'What was his name ... his Greek name?'

'Yiannis.' Michaelis watched as Diane picked up the faded photograph. 'The name means something to you?'

'Maybe.' Diane struggled to remember the last letters she had received. A cartoon Richard had scribbled came to mind. A joke to be passed on to Eddie, of him on a beach. What had it said? Something like ...*Greetings from Yianni, the Cretan Castaway* ...? She kept her thoughts to herself and took a sip of the wine Michaelis had poured for her. It was the first she had taken so far refusing to his annoyance, anything else. Replacing Richard's photo in her bag, she looked quietly for a moment at Michaelis, before summoning the courage to confront him. 'I don't believe you.'

Michaelis shrugged. 'It is what happened ... I cannot change it.'

'You expect me to believe that Richard would have betrayed the very people who were helping him?'

'The German money was in his pocket. Who knows why....'

'He would never have done that!' Diane insisted.

'Then it must have been someone else. I have told you as much as I know. Now, about your other problem ....'

'I don't have any other problems.'

'I think you might have ... you see, I had a visit today.' Michaelis poured himself another whisky. 'A visit from a very inquisitive member of the antiquities department. He was very anxious to find someone ... someone who had been making enquiries about a certain earring.'

'I know it was you who searched our rooms the other day,' Diane countered.

'I'm sorry ... you think I ...?' Michaelis feigned his heartfelt disappointment that she should think so poorly of him, before brushing the accusation aside and continuing with his tale. 'This official has said he will return tomorrow ... with the police. I am very worried. For some reason he thinks I know this person. Of course, I said nothing about our meeting, but it is difficult to be sure who may have been watching. I have tried to protect you so far, but I have my business to think of. I cannot protect you indefinitely ... you must see that?'

Diane took another sip of wine as the thinly veiled threat began to sink in. She was sure he was lying but didn't doubt that he could indeed land her in a lot of trouble if he chose to. She glanced across to the busy table Dieter had booked for a group of his friends. Was it time to give him the signal? Reassured by his watchful eye, she decided to bide her time as Michaelis, oblivious to the party that had gathered behind him at Dieter's table, continued.

'There may be a way we can resolve this however ....' Michaelis poured more wine for her. 'It is possible this man has a price ....'

'And what is yours?'

Again feigning surprise at her ill-concealed opinion of him, Michaelis protested, 'I am only trying to help. Supposing he could be bought. Paid off to drop the enquiry ... do you have money to do this?'

'I wouldn't even consider it!'

'But you should ... you are not in your own country now.'

'That shouldn't make any difference!' Diane's airy tone belied the tension that was building inside her as Michaelis leant forwards to press home his point.

'But it does. Things work very differently here, Miss Diane. You could be in very serious trouble ... very serious indeed. But as I said, I may still be able to help. Of course, if you're not interested ...'

'I'm sure I can guess, but please do tell me exactly what you had in mind.'

'There is a man who would pay a lot of money for the other earring. Unfortunately, I did not know him when I had the first one ... if I had ...' Michaelis took a deep swig of whisky, pushed the wasted opportunities from his mind, and got back to the point. 'His money could make all your troubles disappear.'

'And no doubt some of yours as well?'

'Naturally. It is business after all. You have the earring, I have the contact. Fifty, fifty?'

Diane pretended to weigh the offer, wondering what more she could gain from this meeting before she gave the signal. 'I need to know more first. I don't believe you have told me the truth about my husband. He would never be a traitor. Nothing makes sense. How did your father come by the other earring?'

'I've told you already. I have no idea.'

'Who found the bodies?'

'Half the village. The bitch's father led them there.'

'What bitch?'

Michaelis' eyes narrowed. His fingers stopped playing with the worry beads and he held out his hand. 'Show me the photograph again …'

Diane took it from her bag once more and handed it over warily.

Michaelis looked at it for some time — his own alcohol clouded mind sifting through the possible ramifications of what to say to her. Sensing that she was stalling for time and would refuse his offer in any case, any former trace of consideration for her feelings evaporated. He hadn't really cared whether Yiannis had been her husband or not. As to the earring, he had been telling the truth when he had said that he had no idea how his father came by it — knowing his father, though, he could well imagine how — but was this the soldier who had ruined his own chances with Litsa?

He twisted the picture in the light. A formal portrait. A young man, scarcely older than he had been, but without the beard and moustache? There were similarities — very likely it was him. In fact, now Michaelis very much wanted it to be him. The old heartaches briefly came surging back, only to be rapidly replaced by the long-nurtured hatred.

As it began to crumple in his hand, Diane snatched back the photograph. Michaelis downed another whisky. He had tried to make it easy for her — given her the chance to walk away believing that it might not have been him — but no she had to keep picking at the scabs. Well then she could have what she wanted. 'Yes, it's him … I can see it now definitely!' Michaelis relished the pain in Diane's eyes, waiting quietly, concealing his eagerness to add to that pain — first she had to ask for it. 'I'm sorry what else was it you wanted to know?'

Diane steadied herself. 'You said …' hesitating for a moment until she saw the smile begin to curl at the corner of Michaelis' lip, she then demanded to know. 'What bitch, whose father?'

'Ah, the father, yes. Vasilis Petrakis, pillar of the community … and his darling daughter Litsa … Evangelitsa Petrakis. Your husband's whore … the one who bore his bastard son!'

Drawing her shawl around her shoulders, Diane resisted the urge to get up and run away from the nightmare — to escape the poison pouring from this drunkard's lips. Steeling herself, she continued to confront him. 'And is she still alive to confirm your story this Evangelitsa Petrakis?'

'Oh yes!' Michaelis gloated, 'Though she doesn't use the name she soiled any more … calls herself Xenakis now, after the name she gave her bastard … Antonis Xenakis. I'm sure you'll both have plenty to talk about!' Michaelis drained the bottle into his glass, took one last swig and slammed the glass down in front of Diane. 'Enough of this! Accept my offer now, or you will regret it!'

'Is that a threat I've just overheard?' Appearing at Diane's side, Dieter sat down at the table, proprietorially adjusting the shawl that had been Diane's signal.

'Who the hell are you?' Michaelis glared across the table.

'Brandt. Dieter Brandt.' Michaelis ignored the proffered hand. 'I do sincerely hope I was mistaken, for if I thought for one moment that you meant any harm … any inconvenience whatsoever, to my friend…'

'Do you have any idea who you're talking to?' Michaelis staggered to his feet, about to summon his staff.

'Unfortunately, I do Mr Serides. In fact, I've been having a very interesting conversation with some people who also know you only too well.' Dieter glanced briefly over his shoulder.

Looking across to the group at the table Dieter had left, Michaelis paled.

'Yes, I should sit down if I were you Mr Serides, unless you'd care to have an out of hours chat with the governor of your bank? He's having such an intriguing conversation at the moment with some of your creditors. Such a small world! Oh, and by the way, the two gentleman to his side … they are extremely interested in your premises … one has something to do with hygiene, I think … and the other, planning permissions. You see Mr Serides, if I chose to, I could have you closed down tonight.' Dieter waited a moment for the message to sink home, as Michaelis fidgeted nervously with the worry beads. 'So, are we clear then?'

Reluctantly, Michaelis sat back down. 'May I?' Dieter held his hand open, inviting Michaelis to hand over the beads.

'What do you want with these … they're just…'

'*Komboloi* … I know. Curiosity, call it.' Dieter examined the bullet threaded in with the rest of the beads that had caught his eye. And what of this?'

'I've already told her … she'll tell you, she knows … that's the bloody bullet the Germans shot me with … the reason I wasn't able to go with the others. The reason I haven't been able to walk properly ever since! Bastards!' Michaelis fell silent as Dieter continued examining the bullet in silence. Finally he turned his gaze back to Michaelis.

'What … what is it?' mumbled Michaelis.

'It's a very distinctive design … the spiral carved into this bullet … you haven't noticed it before?'

'Of course I have. What of it … pathetic Nazi scribbles!'

'Pathetic? Perhaps. Yes, you may well be right … but Nazi? No!' Dieter handed the beads back to Michaelis. 'I would be very interested in finding the pistol that fired this bullet.'

'Why ask me? How on earth should I know where it is? Ask your countrymen … it's a German bullet, fired from a German gun!'

'Yes … I do know that … from a Luger to be precise, a Luger P08 that had the same markings engraved on the handle, but I very much doubt that it was fired by a German soldier.'

'I don't understand … what are you talking about?'

'Your father … his name was Fanouris?' Thoroughly confused and amazed that this man should know his father's name, Michaelis merely nodded. 'And I gather from your associates that he died, a widower, not so long ago?' Michaelis nodded again. 'Very well.'

Offering his arm, Dieter waited until Diane had risen and gathered her things before looking Michaelis squarely in the eye. 'I do sincerely hope you have understood my warning Mr Serides. Unlike some, I am not in the habit of making idle threats. I trust therefore that our paths will not cross again ... unless of course you should happen to come across a Luger P08.'

Depositing his card in Michaelis' shirt pocket, Dieter escorted Diane from the club.

Reluctant to let go of the evening's memories, Catherine slipped quietly into her room fully expecting to find both Ellie and her mother fast asleep. The absence of any sound from Ellie's cot confirmed one part of the supposition, but she was surprised to see her mother seated by the window, gazing absently at the night-lit view. A dim pool of orange light from the nearby lamp imbued the monochrome photograph lying on the table beside it with a vibrancy enhanced still further from the golden diffractions of the earring placed upon it.

Diane did not turn from the window, commenting simply, 'It's late.'

Checking on Ellie, Catherine resisted the urge to bridle at the remark, but nevertheless could not help but feel like a guilty teenager. Determined to let nothing spoil her night, however, she asked brightly, 'How did you get on? Did Mr Serides say anything?'

'Mr Serides said a lot of things!'

'Such as … Mum?' Sensing Diane's reluctance to continue, Catherine became concerned. 'What happened Mum … tell me … are you alright? I thought Mr Brandt was going to be there.'

'He was. He was very helpful.'

'Then what's wrong?'

'There was another woman it seems … Richard and a woman from the village.'

Beginning to understand, Catherine tried to find some way of comforting her mother. 'It must have been difficult, I suppose … being at war ….'

'You have no idea. I don't mean that unkindly Cath … but really, you don't.'

'Serides may have been lying … or just mistaken. How can you be sure?'

'I can't … at least not until tomorrow.'

'Why? What happens tomorrow?'

'That's when we meet your bus driver's mother isn't it?'

Catherine had barely begun to process the query forming in her mind as to the tone of her mother's distaste for Antonis' occupation before making the connection. 'You mean…'

'Yes … apparently, he is Richard's son. First, his mother wanted to see me, and now it seems, I need to see her.'

So far the night had held only one single, niggling cause for concern for Catherine. Now, as she relived the moment, it became magnified a thousand-fold. He had promised to be careful and had been. But there had been a moment as he set her free when his footing had slipped in the swell of the waves. Both had been relieved and amused at the phosphorescent trail glinting in the moonlit seawater. *But what if...?*

Now the other nagging question that had gone unanswered in Catherine's mind over the previous days finally found its voice with a renewed urgency: 'Who is my father?'

'What?' Diane's own startled confusion rapidly dissolved as she too began to read between the lines. 'I don't believe it! You mean you've already ... the bus driver!'

'His name is Antonis.'

'You couldn't even wait for...'

'I asked you a question mother. One I've been trying to ask ever since you dropped your bombshell the other night. This first husband of yours, Richard ... is he my father? Now I really need to know. Tell me ... is Antonis my brother?'

'Of course not! Why would you think that? You know who your father is!'

'Do I? You had me in June 1942.When exactly did this Richard come to Crete?'

'May 1941. So, you see you couldn't possibly be...'

'Oh yes ... I see! Didn't take you too long either then, did it?' The slap across Catherine's face startled both women into a brooding hiatus. Eventually Diane tried to explain.

'As you said Cath ... being at war...'

'I thought I didn't have any idea?'

'Don't be childish! We were close ... we grew up together: your father, Richard, and I. When Crete was evacuated and still there was no word ...'

'You don't need to explain.'

'I want to ... I need to. For years I've blamed myself, when all along ...'

'Wait until tomorrow, Mum. There's no point until you know what really happened. Even if it does turn out to be true … so what? It happens all the time. Is he still alive?'

'No.'

'Then it may take a while to come to terms with it, but you will Mum … and I do know that! So what if he did have an affair? Had a son? I know you're bound to feel betrayed…'

'Apparently I'm not the only one he betrayed!'

'I don't understand … there were other women?'

'Other lives. According to Serides, my husband took money from the Germans to betray the resistance but didn't live to spend it.'

'And you believe that?'

'Of course I don't! What time do we meet the mother?'

'After Antonis' shift tomorrow … he said he'd drive us up there around one, one-thirty.'

'Get the address from him tomorrow and tell your friend we shall be travelling with Mr Brandt.'

'But I've already…'

'Tell him we shall be there at two-o'clock. Please don't argue Cath. I'm tired and the only person I feel I can trust here is Dieter.' Diane headed towards the door. 'Let's see if we can get some sleep … I'm so sorry I dragged you into all of this Cath … I had no idea ….'

'You don't need to apologise Mum. I'm sure it'll all look better tomorrow.'

'Well, it can hardly get any worse!'

Michaelis bolted the club door, and switching off the last remaining lights, made his way back up to his office. Since losing the apartment it had also served as his living quarters. Pulling aside the makeshift curtain he rescued the bottle of Black Label from his desk, before tumbling onto the bed to count the bundle of drachmae in his pocket. At least the bloody German had paid in cash, tipping handsomely too, just to rub his nose in it no doubt. He flicked through what remained of it. That was the only trouble with cash, the bloody staff always wanted some.

Lying back, Michaelis took a long, deep swig at the bottle and wondered what he could possibly do now. *Screw the German! And to hell with the English bitch too!* If he tried anything now, they'd know it was him straight away. It had been a stupid, drunken, desperate plan in any case. In a way he was relieved that he couldn't carry it out. Even if she had handed over the earring, she would probably still have gone to the police in any case. Now she knew far too much — about him — about the Xenakis affair — even the bloody German seemed to be involved.

Michaelis reached over for the bottle of sleeping pills and threw two back with another long swig of the whisky. *Shut it all out … deal with it in the morning. Go up to the village. Get rid of the stupid makeshift cot. Could still burn the club … disappear. Why disappear with nothing though? Maybe it could still work. Maybe … maybe ….*

TWENTY-THREE

Litsa dried her hands nervously in the folds of her apron, before taking it off and hanging it behind the kitchen door. Antonis would be here any moment now. Surveying the simple room, set to receive her guests, she found herself wishing for their sake that she could have entertained them in her father's house. But it was a brief and fanciful thought, quickly dismissed. To dwell on it would bring back too many painful memories.

Her father's door had long since been closed to her, as had his heart, poisoned by Fanouris' devious whisperings when she had refused Michaelis' offer to make an honest woman of her. He had made certain that no one believed the word of a harlot carrying a traitor's child. In the beginning, many of the villagers had been prepared to accept her word, that she had seen the German money planted on Richard's body, but as her belly grew, so his guilt in both matters seemed confirmed.

The village had made up its mind. Even the birth of a healthy grandson did nothing to alter Vasilis' deteriorating mood. The once proud and respected landowner now found himself shunned by those he had counted as friends, and he began to spend his solitary hours drinking the fruit of the vines he now neglected. With the end of the war came peacetime celebrations that passed Vasilis by, as did the endless kafeneon discussions of the ensuing civil war that plagued the mainland.

While blackening his family's name behind his back, Fanouris had slowly wheedled his way into Vasilis' affections, sympathising with his distress, encouraging him to continue drowning his sorrows in drink — banish his daughter if she insisted on remaining independent — and accept Michaelis' help in the fields. And as the once profitable vineyards and olive fields strangely failed to yield their usual harvests under Michaelis and Fanouris' care — one by one — they were 'grudgingly' accepted as payment in lieu of services rendered. Neither Litsa or Manolis, who had taken her and the child into his own care, could reason with him or make him realise what Fanouris was doing.

Only once many years later, when Litsa had visited him as he laid in bed suffering the agonies of an unexplained bout of food poisoning, had he asked about the boy. She saw the pain and regret in his eyes for the way he had treated her, for the loss of his own daughter and grandson, but she also saw fear. Michaelis had now installed himself as manager of those remaining lands he did not already own. Three days later Vasilis died of a heart attack.

As devastating as it was, it came as no surprise to learn that Vasilis had left his entire estate to Michaelis. Wealthy in his own right now, Michaelis speedily slipped Fanouris' leash and abandoned the labours of the fields, borrowing against the lands and property to finance his dream of a nightclub in the burgeoning city. For a while Fanouris and his wife strove to maintain the estate, but their own health and advancing years soon limited their endeavours. Vasilis' house fell empty and Litsa was forced to watch her stolen birthright fall into disrepair.

Her son grown into a man, his own childhood traumas of growing up branded the bastard son of a traitor long since settled in playground fisticuffs, Litsa continued to nurse her uncle in his old age while Antonis took on the responsibilities of Manolis' vineyards and fields — neither mother nor son bowing to the shame cast their way. Willing his estate to Litsa, Manolis died knowing he had at least set right some of his brother's neglect.

Standing in her doorway now, Litsa looked along to the end of the street where she could see, as she did every day, the dilapidated gates of the courtyard of her former home hanging crookedly from their posts. More often than not a child would be swinging on them, secure in the knowledge that no one would stop them.

Whenever she passed the house, she had to restrain the urge to take a broom to the old courtyard. Two years ago she had approached Michaelis to see if he would consider selling the property back to her, only to be asked an exorbitant figure. Now if rumours were to be believed he had lost everything.

Though this gave her some measure of satisfaction, she would have no lasting peace until Yiannis' name was cleared. Quite apart from the natural hatred she had come to hold for both Michaelis and his father for their treatment of her family, she had long been convinced that it was Fanouris who had left the German money to incriminate Yiannis. The sudden reappearance of the earring merely confirmed it. But still Michaelis denied everything, and she could prove nothing.

But now Antonis was bringing someone else who was also interested in the earring. How did they know anything about it, this girl he had met and her mother? There had been some talk of an archaeologist, but why go to Serides? Why not the museum? Perhaps it was not just the earring they were interested in. Feeling a wave of nervousness wash over her as she heard Antonis' pick-up approaching, Litsa gave the room a final glance and belatedly thought to check her own appearance as the pickup came to a halt outside.

Sitting in the simple, old upright chair that permanently resided on the little balcony, Michaelis wondered why his father had never thought to get himself something more comfortable. He had spent his entire life relentlessly pursuing wealth with every connivance and trickery he could think of, yet had done nothing with it, seemingly content in the knowledge that he had deprived others.

He could have moved into Vasilis' old house and would have been far more comfortable in his last years, but stubbornly chose to remain where he was. He had won. That was what was important. Gazing out over the countryside beyond the village as his father had done throughout his life, Michaelis realised it had been many years since he had taken the trouble to do the same. Of course he had come and gone dozens of times, more so as his father had neared the end, but to actually sit and look — to really see the country that gave birth to him — this was the first time in a very long while.

Long since discarded pistachio shells ground beneath his shoes as he shuffled on the hard seat, bringing his father to mind once more. There were no pleasant memories. Even so he felt the need to spend a few minutes more. The litter of shells prompted him to go inside the house in search of his father's raki and something to go with it — he would toast the old bastard one last time — before he gave the keys to the bank.

As with the chair, there was nothing left of any value in the house. There had been the odd piece of furniture, the discovery of a few looted items that had raised a few drachmae — and of course the earring — wrapped in an old handkerchief, forgotten for years at the back of a drawer.

Taking the bottle of raki from the cool of the pantry, Michaeli wiped out a glass, spat out a stale pistachio, and taking a handful of sultanas instead, left the gloom of the house for the welcome daylight of the balcony. Being an urban night-owl by nature, he felt a curious surprise at the unexpected sense of relaxation that came over him as he settled back into the chair in the afternoon sun and poured a glass.

Having originally woken in the early hours of the morning stinking in the sweat of his own whisky-fuelled nightmares, he had showered and contemplated the bottle of sleeping pills beside his bed. Would that be the final answer? Draining a glass of water, he had taken another pill. If he could just sleep, then he might find an answer in the morning.

Any answers the morning may have held though remained firmly within his dreams, for it was well beyond midday before the clatter of kitchen preparations from below had roused him from his slumbers. Refreshed in a way he had not felt for some while, he had shaved, taken a good breakfast, and driven out to the village. And all the time an answer was finally forming in his mind. The germ of it had already been sown in the previous night's rambling deliberations — and now it was turning into a resolution.

He *would disappear*. Say nothing to anyone and just vanish. He had nothing left to lose. There was nothing to gain by staying. No one to stay for. He still had his car. There were also a few odds and ends tucked away with a bit of emergency cash, as well as an expensive watch and a couple of gold bracelets that he could sell along the way. He would take whatever extra cash came in from the club tonight and get the dawn ferry to the mainland. Let the bank and his creditors fight it out among themselves — he was sick of it all anyway.

Perhaps his father had the right idea after all. Why not find another out of the way village where nobody knew him? A little, old run-down house — what more did he need? Pouring another raki, he made a mental note to clear the bar of as much stock as he could carry as well.

The sound of an approaching motor briefly materialised into a glimpse of the Xenakis boy's pickup as it swung round the bend of the road below him. He mentally followed its path on around his father's house, past the little alley between and heard it pull up as expected outside old Manolis' house — the Xenakis house now. His relaxed mood allowed him to drift back, to remember better times. Times when Litsa had been his whole world — before the war — before the bloody Englishman. It could have been so very different.

At first, despite her rejection of him, he had felt shame at the way his father had cheated Litsa out of her inheritance, but eventually he allowed himself to believe she was getting exactly what she deserved for sleeping with a traitor who had betrayed her own people. Her loss was his gain — she could still have even had both, but no she was too proud. Even now she was still trying to get her lover off the hook, trying to shift the blame onto his own father with all this talk about the damned earring.

He had first thought her accusations following the newspaper reports to have just been opportunistic. A chance to fit some publicly acknowledged item to her old, fabricated tale of someone looting the Englishman's body and planting the German money. But now there was the soldier's wife. He knew from her stunned reaction the previous night that she had known nothing about Litsa — and yet she had the other earring. The connections were there, but even in his more rational mood Michaelis still chose to push them aside, and downing his glass resolved to make a start on tidying up the place.

Litsa's surprise that Antonis was alone in the pickup gave way to a heightened sense of nervousness as she saw a sleek, black Mercedes draw up behind him. Her anxiety was not eased either on seeing Antonis' demeanour as he got out of the pickup — a far cry from his usual, confident air.

Seeing that there was no time for explanations, she nodded for him to help their visitors from their car and decided to stand her ground in the doorway to welcome them to her house. Guessing that the distinguished looking driver who was now also helping the ladies from the car must be the archaeologist Antonis had spoken of, she quickly weighed up the two women. Fashionably dressed, the elder woman was obviously younger than herself. Litsa again wished she had paid less attention to the house and more to herself. Though she had always refused to wear the widow's black, it had been some time since she had treated herself to anything new.

Turning her attention to the daughter, now busy lifting her child from the car, she was surprised to see that she too was a mature woman, though her casual dress reflected an independence that still bound her to the younger generation. Since Antonis had already told her that she had a young child, Litsa had automatically assumed that she would be a fair bit younger than him, but looking at her now, she realised there probably wasn't much in the age difference. Turning her attention back to the mother, she was forced to revise her opinion of her age and once more regretted that she had not set aside more time or consideration for herself. But it was too late now. Still looking sheepish, Antonis escorted the gentleman to her and made the introductions.

'*Mitera* … this is Mr. Brandt, the owner of the hotel. Mr Brandt … my mother, Evangelitsa Xanakis.'

Taking his hand, Litsa's mind raced with confusion — had Antonis lost his job because of this girl?

'*Kalos orisate* Mr. Brandt … you are welcome to my house, and your guests are my guests.'

'*Kalos sas vrikame kyria Xenakis* … your English is excellent!'

'You are very kind, but no … it has been a long time … your own English, however, certainly is.'

'Ah! The accent or the name? I trust you do not have a

problem. I know it can sometimes be difficult ... I would understand ...'

'As I said Mr. Brandt, you are welcome. Please introduce me to your guests ... they will be hot outside, please bring them in.'

The formalities over, and now finding herself seated alongside Catherine on the modest sofa, Diane's own tensions began to simmer inside as she juggled the glass of cordial and sweetmeats she was offered, trying to read this woman now comfortably occupied with observing the familiar traditions of welcoming guests. She seemed the very model of respectability, hardly the whore that Serides had painted. Had it all been lies? Or if true, how had it come about? She would surely have been older than Richard. *Perhaps that explained it ... she had been past her prime. No one had wanted her ... she had seen a chance ....*

'Would you prefer some tea?'

Litsa's enquiry interrupted her thoughts, but Antonis cut in before she could reply.

'They won't like the mountain tea ... that's only for stomach aches!'

'I know ... I do have some English tea as well, Antoni.'

Diane found herself refusing, in spite of the fact that a cup of tea would actually be very welcome, wondering how she was going to broach the whole subject. Instead smiling politely at Antonis, she asked him to tell her about the mountain tea, and as she listened to his explanation of the various herbs it contained, she searched for Richard. The eyes certainly, they could so easily be his — the wayward hair too. But there was also something about his manner. A quietness that resonated most of all with her. Sensing her discomfort as the conversation petered out, Dieter came to the rescue.

'*Kyria Xenakis*, thank you for your hospitality. I for one am very partial to the Cretan mountain tea, it can be extremely refreshing. Perhaps we could prevail upon you a little later for some, but please do sit with us now. There is something we would like to discuss if you are agreeable?'

'Of course.' Litsa sat patiently, waiting for Dieter to continue.

'It is a delicate matter, and we don't wish to offend in any way, but...'

'Did you know this man?' Diane handed Richard's photograph to Litsa.

As she looked at his likeness for the first time since that terrible night, the tears that began to well in Litsa's eyes made any reply redundant. Surprised and concerned at his mother's distress, Antonis tried to comfort her and in response to his questioning look, she handed him the photograph. 'Your father … Yianni.'

'Richard.' Diane's automatic correction was made quietly, in spite of the confirmation of his betrayal. 'Richard Anthony Forrest … my husband.'

'I'm so sorry,' Litsa's choked response came with no excuses.

Making no acknowledgement of the apology, Diane brought out the earring from her bag and placed it on the table in front of Litsa. 'What do you know about this?'

Litsa afforded a wistful smile at the memories her recognition stirred, before telling Diane, 'You were meant to have both.'

'He told you he was married?'

'Yes ... he was not to blame.'

'I have been told that he was to blame ... for something far more serious.'

'That is a lie!' Litsa pointed to the earring. 'And this will prove it. He gave this and a letter for you, to his friend who escaped on the boat ... but later, he found that the other one had caught in his pocket.'

'Why wasn't he able to escape as well?'

'He tried to ... but the Germans were shooting at us...'

'Us? You were there?'

Litsa nodded. 'I led them to the beach.' Seeing the hurt in Diane's eyes, Litsa repeated herself. 'The Germans were shooting ... he wasn't able to get up into the boat before it left.'

'But he was able to hand this and the letter over?'

'Yes, but only just ... it was so difficult...'

'He stayed for you.' Diane's raised hand silenced any denial. She had heard enough.

Breaking the awkward silence, Catherine smiled at Litsa and referred to the earring.

'You said this would prove Richard's ... Yianni's innocence ... what did you mean?'

'The other earring was in his shirt pocket the night he died. I followed them up to the hut. I saw the German soldiers come and then I heard them all being shot. Later, when they had gone, I went inside ... and found them all dead ... but then I heard someone else coming and I hid. I saw a man put money into his pocket ... when he tried to push the money in, he found the earring and took it. He heard me and made me blind with a torch before he knocked me down.'

'Do you know who it was?'

'I didn't then, but I do now!'

'Fanouris Serides?' Dieter asked, quietly.

Litsa nodded. 'Yes. Him! He was responsible for Yianni's death and all the others. And then he spent the rest of his days stealing my lands and ruining my family's life. No one would believe me … I couldn't prove anything. But when he died … when Michaelis found the earring … then I knew for sure.'

Catherine's intervention had disturbed Ellie, who had previously been content to doze in her mother's arms. Tired and in strange surroundings, she now gave vent to her feelings, demanding to be fed.

'I'm sorry, is there somewhere I could …'

'Of course.' Litsa showed Catherine through to her bedroom. 'Let her sleep there a little afterwards.' Returning to the others, Litsa repeated her offer of tea, which this time, was accepted. Antonis helped his mother with the preparations, while Dieter allowed Diane to sit in quiet reflection, before doing his best to engineer small talk during the tea. Responding to Litsa's concerns, he reassured her that Antonis' position at the hotel was in no danger, pointing out that, on the contrary, he was a valued employee. Diane eventually broke her silence.

'What happened to … where is Richard … Yianni … buried?'

'Here, in the village.' Litsa set her cup down. 'At first some of them did believe me, they knew what your husband was like … he had worked together with them. They knew he was a good man. Christos and his friends persuaded the others to let me bury him in a corner of the cemetery … It is a nice place … under a tree. Would you like me to take you there?'

'Yes, if you would?'

Dieter rose with the two women. 'I assume it is close by?' Litsa nodded. 'Then why don't you both go, and Antonis and I will take care of things here?'

Holding the door open for them, Dieter watched the two women walk off down the dusty street together, then helping Antonis clear the crockery from the table, he paused for a moment picking up the photograph. He had already suspected, and now he knew. Settling back down on the sofa, Dieter struggled with his own emotions as he looked at the face of the man who had twice saved his life.

Through the open door Dieter could still see Diane and Litsa nearing the end of the street. Was it just that she reminded him so much of his own, long-lost Hannelore he wondered? Surely that was not the only reason he felt such a strong attraction to Diane, this woman he had known for such a short time? He knew he had enjoyed playing the white knight more than he should. After all, she had made it clear enough there was a husband waiting in England, yet he also sensed her own ease and pleasure in his company. Reminding himself instead of the nightmare both she and Litsa were now unravelling, Dieter dismissed his own fanciful yearnings and looked back to the photograph, silently vowing to do what he could for those that Richard had held dear. Rising, as Antonis reappeared, Dieter smiled warmly and handed him the photograph.

'Your father was a man to be proud of, Antoni.'

Back in the gloom of the old house, looking now at his father's bedstead pushed sideways up against the wall — the two planks lashed from one side of the tall headrails down to similar rails at the foot of the bed — Michaelis shuddered at the stupidity of his ill-conceived, desperate plan. Untying the boards from the improvised cot, he wondered how he could have thought he would get away with it: to have the little girl kidnapped from the hotel by the old gypsy woman pretending to be Antonis' mother — get the earring — plant the key to the house in the Xenakis woman's place next door and hope to claim no knowledge of any of it?

Roughly nailing back the boards he had previously removed from the panelling at the upper end of the staircase, Michaelis pushed the iron bedstead back into its place in front of the panelling, cursing as the castors caught on a rug to one side. Pulling out the rucked material he gave the end of the bed a final heave and slammed it up against the staircase.

He let loose another curse on hearing the clatter of something falling behind the small bedside cabinet by the foot of the stairs. Pulling it out, he discovered that what he had heard was nothing that had fallen from the cabinet, rather it was a triangular piece of panelling that had slipped out of place from the stair-panelling behind it.

About to replace it, he noticed something glinting within the cavity. Reaching inside, he found an old tin caddy, and as he pulled off the lid, a broad grin spread across his face as he tipped out the contents. *'Efkharisto Baba!'* Thanking his father, he unrolled the bundle of drachma notes. Exactly what he needed right now.

Setting the money aside on the bed, he knelt down and reached back, deep into the cavity under the stairs, hoping for more bounty. Tucked up against the side of the panelling, he felt a cloth bundle. He could also feel that it contained something solid, something hard, metallic. Withdrawing it and sitting back on the bed, Michaelis shook off the dust and began unfolding the cloth, rapidly aware from its feel, even before he had finished unwrapping it of what it was he had found.

The pistol fit neatly in his hand and for several moments he sat looking at it, reluctant to make the next move, but he knew it was one he could not avoid. Tilting the butt of the gun up towards him, he found what he was dreading, and traced the finely engraved spiral with one finger. Emptying the chamber, Michaelis looked at the single remaining bullet — also engraved with the spiral markings — identical to the one threaded among his worry beads.

There was no longer any escape from the truth, nor the pain that came with it.

Diane read the name on the headstone, 'Yiannis Xenakis.' Litsa had been right, it was a quiet, peaceful corner. She had tended the grave carefully and there were rosemary bushes growing nearby. Diane watched her gather a few sprigs, before turning her attention back to the headstone. There was no date of birth, only the date of death, confirmed as the 9th of September 1941. It was a date she was only too familiar with, being just one day after that of Catherine's conception.

'I suppose Antonis' birthday is in June?'

'Yes … June 12th.' Noticing Diane's pained smile, Litsa asked, 'Why?'

'It's not important. Why did you never report his death to the authorities?'

'I did … but we never knew their real names….'

'What! Even when you slept with them?'

Litsa ignored the barb. 'Later some people came to the village from a … *commission*? They were moving all the bodies of soldiers who had been killed on the island to a big cemetery at Souda. So much time had gone by … I knew you must have known he was dead. I said I didn't know anything and sent them away. I didn't want him to be someone without a name … I didn't want to lose him … I'm sorry.'

'Why Xenakis?'

'It means stranger or foreigner. He had been a stranger to me … and after his death I became a stranger to everyone here. As Diane fell silent, Litsa's own curiosity came to the fore. 'You asked me about Antonis' birthday … how old were you when you had your daughter?'

Diane hesitated a moment, before adding a year, and lying in response, 'Twenty-one.'

'Life has been kind to you, I was only eighteen. Shall we go back?'

Seated once more on the balcony, Michaelis poured another raki, heedless of the clear liquid overflowing from the brimming glass onto the bleached wooden table, his concentration focused instead upon the Luger pistol beside it. Eventually reacting to the pool of liquid gradually accumulating around the gun, he ceased pouring and absently threw back the glass, before automatically refilling it. His mind was numb. However, as if amplified by the discovery that it had been his own father who had shot him in the leg, the dull, constant ache just above his knee seemed now to throb in earnest.

Massaging it, he tried to come to terms with all that the discovery meant. In many ways the fact that his father hadn't thought twice about seriously wounding his own son did not surprise him. It was merely the gravest in a long list of brutalities. In an odd way, Michaelis reflected — it even showed he cared — sparing him from a worse fate. But the fact that he knew what that fate would be was the worm that now burrowed deep into Michaelis' conscience — one that had been wriggling on the sidelines for some time now.

Attempting to play the devil's advocate with the nagging thoughts inside his head, Michaelis continued to drain the bottle of raki, vacillating wildly between both piteous shame and callous disregard for Litsa's sufferings. But what of the others who had died? Andreas his best friend had been killed by his own father's betrayal. Old Christos and his wife were still alive — *what if they found out* — but then how could they? Only he knew the truth. Litsa suspected it of course, but she had no way of proving it — or did she? Michaelis had seen the German and the English women following Antonis in the black Mercedes. At the time he had simply been pleased that the bitch would be having her face rubbed in her husband's infidelity, but if she had the earring with her, the earring Litsa had accused his father of taking, then?

Springing up from the table, Michaelis took hold of the pistol and heading back through the house let himself out of the rear door that gave onto the little alley separating his father's house from Litsa's. There had been many a time after old Manolis had taken her into his care that he had spied on her through the little bedroom window. Sidling up to it now, he could hear voices from further inside the house. Pausing for a moment, he listened; weighing up the situation and picturing the scene within. Litsa's voice needed no recognition and within seconds he knew for certain they were all there: the bastard Antonis, the woman and her daughter, and the bloody German. Easing back the casement, he looked in and saw the child asleep on the bed, and through the half open door of the bedroom, he could see the low table in the centre of the main room beyond. All that was visible of the room's occupants were seated legs and the occasional hand reaching down to the table. But there on the table itself, he could clearly see the earring. At times, he had even doubted the woman really had it, but now it was there for everyone to see.

His mind racing with all of the available options and their possible consequences, Michaelis struggled to make his decision. He had already sunk to the depths of considering becoming a kidnapper to get the earring and now here was the very child at his mercy — and the earring in plain view. All he knew was that he needed that earring now more than ever.

Catherine's scream, on seeing him at the window as she looked in to check on Ellie, startled him into action and he found himself levelling the gun at her. Then as the two men rushed to join her, Michaelis shouted for them to get back. Pointing the gun at Ellie to emphasise his determination, he repeated his demand, 'I said get back!'

Dieter took the opportunity to pull Catherine out of danger and motioned for Antonis to stand back.

'Stay where I can see you all.' Michaelis felt the dryness in his throat clip the words and sweat began to trickle down the sides of his temples.

'I see you've found your father's gun.' Dieter's comment drew Michaelis' attention as well as the line of fire back to himself. A raging curiosity burned inside of Michaelis' head. How could this man possibly know about the gun? Pushing the confusion from his mind, he ignored the taunt.

'I want the earring.'

'Of course, why not?' Dieter turned to fetch it.

'No! I want Litsa to bring it to me ... and you will all stay where I can see you!' Michaelis pointed to Antonis, who had been edging towards the front door, waving him back into the centre of the room. His shouting had now woken Ellie, who was crying and working her way towards the edge of the bed.

Collecting the earring, Litsa entered the bedroom.

'Michaeli, let me see to the child first.'

'No! Leave her. Bring the earring to me.'

'She will fall Michaeli!'

Ellie's cries grew even more shrill and Michaelis was tempted to let her have her way, just for some quiet, but he did not want to give any advantage away.

'Bring it to me, then you can see to her,' he insisted.

Moving towards him, Litsa suddenly saw Ellie slip, as she tried to pull herself up to the bedpost. Ignoring Michaelis, she grabbed the falling child and passed Ellie back to Dieter. Turning back to face Michaelis, Litsa calmly walked up to him and held out the earring.

'Here! Your father stole the first one ... now you can steal the other. That's all you Serides are good for!'

Closing his hand around the earring, Michaelis met Litsa's eyes. His entire being crawled with an innate instinct to utter some obscenity in return for her insult, but his mouth could only offer, 'Litsa …I'm…' The apology unfinished, Michaelis darted back up the alley.

Dieter rushed to Litsa's side and bringing her back into the main room made sure that the rest of the women were alright.

'Where's Antoni?' Litsa rushed out of the open front door, followed closely by Dieter, who made to head up the narrow alley. 'No!' she shouted instinctively, 'He will be leaving from the other side … Antonis would know that.'

Running around the donkey sheds and garden that surrounded the house, they could see Michaelis' car still parked by the courtyard. Litsa screamed out Antonis' name, and as they both came to the courtyard gate, Christos also appeared from his house opposite wanting to know what all the commotion was.

'Stay inside Christo, Michaelis has a gun,' Litsa warned.

Dieter pushed Litsa back towards Christos' care and stepped warily through the open gateway. 'Michaelis?' There was no reply. 'Antoni? Leave him … it's not worth it.'

A scuffle from inside the old shed stopped Dieter in his tracks and as he turned, he saw Antonis retreating from the open doorway. In his hands he held a long wooden scythe, the rusty blade pointed towards Michaelis, who now appeared — the pistol levelled at Antonis chest.

'Leave it Antoni … let him go … it's over.'

'He doesn't deserve to live.' Antonis stopped retreating and stood his ground, inviting Michaelis to do his worst. 'You ruined my mother's life … stole my grandfather's house and his life too … I'm not letting you go!'

'I'll do it!' Michaelis warned, steadying his aim with both hands.

'Of course you would, you murdering bastard.'

'No … no … not me …that was my father … but I didn't know, I swear! I never thought, I couldn't believe he would ever … not until…'

'Until you found the gun.' Dieter walked calmly towards Michaelis.

'Stay back!' Michaelis screamed.

Dieter slowed his pace but continued to position himself between Antonis and Michaelis, who was now visibly shaking but still clasping the gun with both hands. 'There have been too many deaths already Michaeli.'

'Who the hell are you anyway? How could you possibly have known?'

'I've already told you who I am. As to how I know that your father shot his own son with the gun you are holding … that is because it belonged to my best friend. His name was Werner. I watched him carve those spirals on his bullets and on that gun. I have been looking for it for a long while. He and I were in the first wave of the parachute landings.'

Michaelis struggled to take in what Dieter was telling him, trying to concentrate on keeping Antonis at bay with the pistol. Ignoring his plight and the threat he faced himself, as Michaelis made it clear he would fire at either of them, Dieter continued.

'I watched your father take it from Werner and finish him off. Perhaps he was doing him a kindness, though I doubt it … you see Werner was dying from the wounds your mother had already made … most probably with this very scythe.' He took the weapon from Antonis and contemplated the rusting blade. Aware that Michaelis was now firmly aiming the gun at him, Dieter slowly moved closer to the old house, drawing the line of Michaelis' fire away from Antonis and the others, now gathering at the gate.

'What did you expect? You invaded our country … it was war … your bloody war!'

'You are right … absolutely. But that was not my only experience with your father. There were four of us … we had been taken prisoner … and for expediency, we had been bound and left for our own troops to find. Do you remember Michaeli? Under the trees? I remember you … filling your water bottles at the spring … you, your mother, and your father, along with the Greek and British soldiers who had tied us. After everyone had left, your father returned. I watched him slit my comrades throats one by one … I saw the pleasure in his eyes as he did it … and the fury when he realised I had escaped my bonds. We fought, and he threatened me with that very same gun, but he heard more troops coming, so I felt the butt of the gun instead. By the time I came round, he had fled.'

'It doesn't make any difference … none of it does … you're not going to stop me!'

'No one is Michaeli … you are free to go. You are not responsible for your father's actions. There is nothing to be gained by holding you here … everybody knows the truth now.'

Michaeli looked over his shoulder, beyond Antonis still to his side, to the small crowd pressing at the gate, where Litsa, Diane, and Catherine, clutching Ellie to her, had been joined by Christos and his wife along with a growing number of others from the village.

Seeing the panic in Michaelis' eyes, Dieter tried to regain his attention. 'If you put down the gun, give back the earring … there will be nothing to answer for …you will be free to go. No one will stop you. I give you my word.'

'I can't …' Michaelis whimpered, his whole body now shaking. 'I need to … I need …'

Seeing the stain spread down Michaelis' trousers as he turned to face the others, Dieter urged him desperately, 'Give me the gun Michaeli. I'll do what I can to help … Michaeli?'

Aware that Michaelis was now heading determinedly towards Litsa, Dieter dropped the scythe and followed, intent on restraining him.

Distracted by Dieter's approach behind him, Michaelis glanced around briefly, before turning towards Litsa once more. Oblivious of the cracked paving in front of him, he stumbled, sprawling forward, his grip automatically tightening on the trigger of the gun as the single shot rang out.

TWENTY-FOUR

The searing pain that tore within her clawed desperately for release, while her screams reverberated around the operating theatre, only momentarily eclipsed by the tray of instruments sent crashing to the floor by her free hand lashing out in despair. With the grip on her other hand tightening automatically came a different pain, as the cannula twisted in her vein. Above her, nervous eyes signalled instant, earnest apology, before rapidly seeking aid from the other gowned and masked figures that hovered in front of the bright lights, distorted by her sweat-blurred vision.

She had already been told that complications were to be expected and now found herself co-operating in dull, resigned compliance as her body was manipulated into position, knowing full well what was to follow. Numbing relief gradually followed the insertion of the second needle, and as tubes were taped to her body, she heard another tray of implements being prepared. A gentler squeeze on her hand now came with a look of encouragement from above as she was made ready. The first pains, slowly diminishing to dull, stubborn aches, were replaced by disconnected, tugging sensations as the surgeon's knife began its work.

Tears mingled with the sweat in her eyes, and she found them being wiped away by yet another disconnected hand. Then suddenly her whole body seemed to tremble in spasm, as with one last exhausted, uncontrollable groan the life was pulled from her.

The scream now filling the room brought a totally different response — one of absolute relief for Catherine, as she finally saw the glistening, healthy body of her newborn son held aloft for her.

Distant muted sounds of early morning activity emanating from the corridor eventually roused Catherine from her slumbers, and she woke to see her mother still seated in the chair by the window, now framing another dawn over London. Her mother's absent gaze, however, was trained neither on the view or Catherine, but on the cot beside her bed.

As grateful as she was for her mother's support, her presence inevitably carried with it unwelcome reminders of the endless arguments that had marred her pregnancy. At first, enduring the depressingly familiar entreaties to consider a termination and then the onslaught of advice and opinion that had followed her refusal. Perhaps, now her son was finally here, Diane would warm to him. There had never been a problem with Ellie, but since their return from Crete, Diane's mood had been withdrawn, morose, and strangely negative. Studying her now, as she looked impassively down at her grandson, Catherine tried to imagine her mother's thoughts.

'Pick him up if you like, Mum.'

Diane turned to Catherine. 'You're awake! How are you feeling?'

'I'm fine … seriously … give your grandson a cuddle!'

'Better not dear … don't want to risk him catching anything … not until he's stronger.'

'He'll be fine … won't you Vangeli?'

'So that's decided is it … Vangelis?'

'You know it is Mum … after Antonis' mother … it's the way they do things … I don't suppose you'd have preferred Yiannis or Richard? After all, it should really have been the grandfather's name for a boy.'

'I don't see why you needed to follow any traditions … it's hardly a conventional relationship after all!'

'Mum, please don't start. I like Vangelis … it's a good strong name.'

'And the surname?'

'Xenakis of course.'

'So that's decided as well. And will the father be appearing anytime soon do you think?'

'You know perfectly well he will … and you also know why he couldn't be here. Quite apart from the baby coming early, Litsa's only just getting out of hospital.' Catherine watched her mother turn away at the sound of the name, briskly gathering her things together.

'Well, I can see you're fine here darling. I'd better get back and see how your father's coping with Ellie.'

'Alright. You must be exhausted. Thanks for staying Mum. Give Dad and Ellie my love … and don't worry … everything will be fine.'

'That's what I'm supposed to say isn't it?'

Diane leant over and kissed Catherine, before giving a final wave and smile of encouragement to her daughter, who could not help but notice nevertheless as she watched her mother disappear behind the door, the absence of any acknowledgement of her grandson.

Easing the Mercedes past the straggle of goats that followed in Christos' wake, Dieter swung the saloon into the now familiar village, slowing to a crawl as he approached the door of Litsa's house.

'Where's Antoni? He said he would be waiting for us,' Litsa queried from the rear seat. 'He should be ready to welcome you.'

'Why me? You're the patient.'

'Ex-patient!'

'That's right, free at last.' Dieter glanced at her in the mirror, the months of operations, infections, and further procedures had taken their toll since the stray bullet from Serides' pistol had punctured her lung, but Litsa was a survivor, if at the moment a rather irritable one.

'Where is the boy … and why aren't you stopping?' she asked as the Mercedes rolled on past the door.

'I thought we might take a little drive instead … not far …' he teased, continuing slowly up the dusty road before finally bringing Litsa alongside a grinning Antonis, leaning on the newly painted gate. 'You see he is waiting outside your house … just as he said he would!'

'What do you mean … my house? What have you done?'

Dieter applied the handbrake, turned off the engine and

glancing briefly in the mirror at Litsa's startled expression, smiled, got out of the car, and came round to her door, opening it as Antonis swung open the courtyard gate. 'I took the liberty of arranging for the bank to transfer your father's property back into your name.'

'Arranging ... how?'

Dieter brushed her enquiry aside. 'The place was a little run down ... I do hope you'll be happy with the renovations ... if there's anything you don't like ...'

'I don't understand ... I can't possibly ... why have you done this?'

'Why? Because ... you deserve it. Because I want to ... and because I can! You were not the only one to recognise the face in that photograph. But for the man you knew as Yiannis, I would not be alive today. So anything I can do to help those he cared for...'

'But how can I repay you?'

'There is no need ... as I said, it is I who am entirely in your debt. So please ... Evangelitsa ... accept this small gesture and let Antonis welcome you to your home.

Lukas Economides surveyed the bare shelves of his office and rechecked the drawers of the desk, but his packing had already been thorough, reflecting his nature. There was nothing forgotten, nothing left behind. He would not be sorry to see the back of the cramped workspace, but his dreams of promotion and a move down the corridor of the Antiquities Department to the Assistant Director's office had not been realised. Instead there was a transfer, a promotion of sorts, to a new department on the mainland, while another higher flying candidate — doubtless with connections he did not have — was being drafted in for that appointment, along with another subordinate to fill Lukas' shoes.

His tenure had not been without some merit, however, and he took a moment to thumb through the file he had prepared for his successor, to ensure that he was fully briefed on the status of ongoing projects. The labours of the last six years flicked before his eyes, bringing a mixture of satisfactions, irritations, and finally an overriding resentment that he would not be able to reap the fruits of those labours with the recognition he felt he deserved.

Pausing at one case he had felt sure could have developed into something far more substantial than the not inconsiderable finds they had already proved to be, he flipped open the ring binder and took out the notes. First one, and then the match of the pair had turned up, yet still they had no definitive explanations as to the whereabouts or nature of the discovery of the earrings. Serides had vanished. The Englishwoman's account merely confirmed the likely date of discovery, but his enquiries were still on hold because of the Xenakis woman's hospitalisation. Certainly the fact that both she and Serides came from the same village would suggest the probable area, but where exactly?

Slipping the notes into his briefcase, Lukas flipped the clamp back down and closed the binder. If his successor was in any way worth his salt, then he would make the necessary connections for himself and follow things up in due course. If not, then there might be an opportunity for him to feather his own nest and pursue a little out-of-hours investigation at some time in the future — once he had settled into his new post — when the time was right.

Sitting at the table in the kitchen of her father's home once more, Litsa looked at the one thing that had not changed. Antonis had placed the little flask with its fresh sprigs of rosemary on the window sill. He would have known her habits full well by now of course, but what were the chances of his placing it there, exactly where it had been the night she had heard the gunshot and ran out into the dark so many years ago?

She sighed deeply at the passage of so many years and the losses they had brought, but even such a simple effort instantly reminded her of her own wound and its lasting effects. It would be some time still before she could expect to regain anything approaching her former strength. The past months had been a seemingly endless nightmare and she had often despaired of returning home at all — but to be here now — sitting in the inheritance she had thought lost for good was something she could never have dared to envisage.

She would call Mr. Brandt to thank him again on the new telephone he had installed for her, but she would need to calm herself first, be sure she had thought carefully what to say. Though what could she say that could possibly express the gratitude and overwhelming swirl of emotions she was experiencing?

Wiping away the tears that threatened to overcome her, she wished for a moment that Antonis was with her, to get to know the old place again together, but she took some comfort at least knowing that he was now finally on his way to England to see his son, the son he was naming in her honour — Vangelis.

TWENTY-FIVE

'Why can you never back me up on anything?' Diane vented her anger — throwing the damp tea towel in the direction of the washing machine.

Eddie finished putting away the dried dishes, before scooping up the towel and depositing it into the drum. Moving Diane away from the drawer she was leaning against, he took out a clean towel and calmly laid it over the draining basket before answering her accusation.

'Backing you up has nothing to do with it ... I simply feel they're making the right decision.'

'For them!'

'Of course, for them, who else? It's their life.'

'Catherine doesn't know what she's letting herself in for ... and she should be thinking of Ellie as well ... what kind of life is she going to have growing up among foreigners?'

'They won't be foreigners. By the time she does grow up she'll be just like one of them.'

'And that's supposed to make me feel better?' Diane snapped. 'Anyway, it will all be over long before then ... just wait and see. I'd give it a year at best, and he'll be back to his old tricks, picking up more rebounds on his magic bus!'

'I don't agree. I don't think he's like that. You've seen how they are together.'

'It won't last.'

'Why not? I haven't seen Cath so happy for a long time and he's great with both of the children. They can't stay cooped up in the flat for ever.'

'There's nothing to stop him getting a proper job over here instead of those occasional handyman jobs he picks up. We've already said we'd help out with the deposit for a mortgage.'

'It's obviously not what they want though, and from the sounds of it, this Dieter chap seems to be looking out for them … giving Antonis a promotion and paying for a house to be done up for them in the village. And Cath will have his mum around as well, if she needs help with the kids. She sounds a good sort … Litsa.'

'Everybody's a good sort to you aren't they Eddie? Just how you want them to be … turn a blind eye … keep the peace … don't ruffle any feathers. Everybody's pal … used car Eddie! If you had any balls at all, you'd back me up and persuade your daughter to see sense … but no! You let everyone walk all over you … even your own daughter!'

'Well, I've had plenty of practice living with her mother!'

Pounding up the hill, Eddie checked his pockets for keys and wallet and was thankful to find both. It would have been a pity to have had to return for either and thus spoil the satisfaction of the resounding door slam he had departed with. The 'used car' taunt was familiar territory, but Diane's highbrow opinions didn't much bother him anymore. He knew full well he hadn't lived up to her expectations for him and that didn't bother him either. He was content with his lot — and he reckoned it wasn't such a bad lot either — he had built up a high-end dealership from scratch, with a profitable servicing business attached, in a damned good area. Add to that a fine house that was pretty much paid for — most women would be happy with that — but Diane wasn't like most women.

He slowed his pace a little and tried to fathom her latest outburst — and there had been many since she had returned from Crete. Whereas once he had never been at a loss for the right thing to say to her, these days it seemed the complete opposite. A prime example had been the revelation of Richard's affair. To Eddie it had come as something of a relief. Finally, he felt that he had been let off the hook, and in an odd way he had been pleased for his old friend, but such sentiments had not gone down well with Diane. Richard's fall from grace had been a grand betrayal and no consideration of her own failings would detract from that. Far from it. Instead, an anger had begun to grow. A resentment it seemed of all the wasted years of guilt.

As for Cath and Antonis. Who could possibly know how things would turn out? Despite Diane's scorn of his opinion, he had a good feeling about the lad. He hadn't minded lending a hand in the workshop — always seemed cheerful — and most importantly always seemed to be looking out for Cath and the two kids.

In many small ways he reminded Eddie of Richard and he had enjoyed talking to Antonis about his father. But it was hardly surprising he wanted to get back to his own country.

From what he'd told him there was a pile of work waiting for him on his mother's lands, as well as his old job to get back to. And Cath didn't seem like she was being pressured to go — if anything she seemed eager to give it a try. Of course, they would miss them — but there would be visits.

Pushing open the door of the Prince, a familiar voice greeted him.

'Hello Eddie! … Usual? … Seeing a fair bit of you these days!'

Diane skipped back as the pathetically short lob sailed down towards her, already relishing the satisfaction the final smash would bring. No better way to finish a match. She had needed a victim and Jack's pretty new girlfriend had been easy pickings. She could see him approaching now, as she consoled the girl at the net, retrieving the ball that had bounced high over the fencing from the venom of her stroke. Throwing the ball back into the court he continued towards them to rescue the girl.

Exercising her skills had gone some way to clearing the dark clouds of her mood, but the victory had been too easily won. The angry fire still burned inside her — the hunger still unsatiated. She wasn't finished yet.

'Show me that grip again Jack … I still don't feel I'm striking the backhand just right.'

'It seemed pretty good to me!' bemoaned the girl.

'I did warn you she takes no prisoners!' Jack gave his girlfriend a reassuring hug before taking Diane's racquet to demonstrate the grip once more.

Retrieving her racquet and practising the grip, Diane turned to his girlfriend. 'Anyone will tell you … Jack gets amazing penetration with so little effort! No … I'm still not sure that's right … it's so difficult to visualise, back to front. Come behind me Jack … I need to see it from your perspective.'

Drawing his arm around her, she fumbled with the grip until Jack was obliged to bring his other hand around her waist as well to adjust her fingers. 'That's better, I think I'm getting it now!'

Satisfied that both were suitably embarrassed, Diane slipped out from the embrace. 'Now young man, I think your friend could do with a lesson or two herself!' Slinging her bag over her shoulder, she beamed at them both. 'Speaking of lessons … don't forget that assignment I gave you Jack. You'll be back up to Oxford soon. Important year.' And as the flush of her victories began to fade, she added before leaving, 'Your last article was excellent Jack … really … you'll do well.'

Reflecting on her behaviour as she idly wound the lemon and ice cubes around the glass, Diane's mood rapidly slipped back to its former level. Ordinarily she would be up with the rest of the crowd perched on a favourite stool at the bar, but instead found herself preferring to sit alone at one of the tables by the clubhouse window. She could see Jack and his girl still out on court. At least they were still playing, if perhaps not talking.

And would Eddie be talking to her when she got back? He didn't understand. Nobody understood. Did she even?

Her world seemed to have changed so rapidly and yet no one else seemed bothered. The man whose place in her heart she had nurtured for all these years, raised up because of her own guilt, had left her for another woman. How could she not feel angry?

And now her life was to be inextricably linked to this other woman, her own daughter making a life together with that same woman's son, Richard's son. First she had taken her husband and now she would take her daughter and grandchild as well.

Even Dieter, whose considerate manner and many accomplishments had made such an impression on her, had stopped calling. There was no real reason why he should of course now that everything had been settled. But if she were honest, she missed his easy company. Now he was obviously only concerned with caring for the fragile and precious Litsa. She had even asked Dieter to stand as godfather for the new baby. She had it all.

TWENTY-SIX

Though it had seemed she would never have everything ready in time, Catherine finally found herself with nothing left to do. There was not a picture unstraightened, a display that had not been rearranged, or a glass left unpolished. Pushing open the glazed entrance door, she stepped out onto the broad pavement and absorbed the bustle of the evening traffic beyond the line of parked cars, winding its way past the church and on down to Kalokerinou. It had been ten years since she had first explored Heraklion's streets. Ten life-changing years that now found her about to host the opening reception of her own gallery.

Turning her back on the whining scooters, she looked at the gallery now — the bright lights of the newly refurbished premises illuminating her work. The move to Crete with Antonis had initially all but brought her graphic design work to a standstill. And raising Ellie and Vangelis had occupied much of her energies in any case. But as the children had grown, she had secured a few local commissions, including some illustration work, which had encouraged her to make further use of her newfound spare time.

Enthusiastic experimentation with various media had led to several series of paintings, pastels, and sketches, which now formed the core of the new gallery. Eirene a friend she had made at the children's school was a gifted ceramicist. Her work was an ideal complement to Catherine's, and Eirene had also been instrumental in bringing another friend on board who specialised in contemporary jewellery. Between them, they had found little difficulty sourcing a number of other craftspeople, only too eager to find an outlet for their work.

Nervously checking her watch, Catherine took one last look at the main window display. Antonis would be here soon with his mother and the priest, who would give his blessing to their enterprise. Eirene was bringing the children. Dieter was bringing Mum from the hotel. *Why the hell wasn't Dad coming?* She knew things had been difficult between them lately, but surely, he knew how much this meant to her? And then there were the guests. For so long, it had just been a dream. Something to talk about — to wish for one day — but now it was about to turn into reality. Catherine shivered a little in the autumn air and offered a prayer of her own that Antonis' unfailing support and belief in her would not be in vain.

When he had heard of their plans, Dieter had offered to help and invest in their scheme, but Antonis had quietly insisted that this would be their own venture. Though appreciative of Dieter's good intentions, a desk job had not suited Antonis and in any case, managing his mother's regained estate had soon required that he give it his undivided attention Over the years that attention had paid off. Sink or swim — Antonis and Catherine would go it alone.

Looking through the display into the gallery itself, Catherine briefly relived the past few hectic weeks as they had worked together night after night, painting walls, fitting the place out, assembling display cabinets, hanging paintings, adjusting lights. Her focus returning to the display itself, she looked at the central piece — the one that in a way gave her more satisfaction and pride than everything else put together — the result of months of continued badgering, prodding, and gentle nagging — an impressive, original woodcarving by Antonis Xenakis.

'This is letting the side down a bit, isn't it?' Diane's tease was emboldened by the couple of gin and tonics she had already shared with Dieter. 'Buying British?'

'I thought you might appreciate it,' Dieter replied, holding open the door of the Jaguar for her. 'Of course, we could take the bus if you'd prefer?'

'What do you generally pick Litsa up in?'

Dieter smiled, as much to himself as to Diane, closed the door and walked around the car, taking his time settling into the leather seat before answering. 'So you're still convinced I'm carrying a flame for Litsa?'

'Well, aren't you?'

'No … I never have. Which is just as well, since she seems happy enough with the company of her doctor from the hospital. They see each other from time to time. I gather it is a mutually agreeable companionship.'

Though it had been several years since he had last seen her, Dieter found his attraction to Diane unchanged.

Unwilling to compromise her marriage, he had kept his feelings to himself, yet within moments of meeting again, both had found themselves slipping back into each other's company with a disturbing ease. Unable now to let the betrayal of jealousy pass, Dieter pulled away from the hotel, eager to play Diane at her own game.

'Litsa is adorable … a truly remarkable person … and an excellent friend.' Dieter paused briefly sensing Diane stiffening in her seat before firmly settling the issue. 'But she is only a friend, and I wouldn't want it any other way. Of course, you would know that yourself if we had seen more of you these past few years. By the way, how is Eddie … are you still … 'content'?'

'Eddie's not so well I'm afraid … I haven't said anything to Catherine yet … I didn't want to spoil her evening.'

'I'm sorry Diane. Truly. Is it serious?'

'His heart … it seems he did have a dodgy ticker after all! He needs a bypass.'

'If you want a good specialist, I know an…'

'No, it's fine, thank you Dieter, he's already booked in for the day after tomorrow.'

'So we won't have your company for long this time either?'

'No … I'm afraid not.'

'That's a great pity. I know the children were really looking forward to spending some time with you.'

'I doubt that!' Diane scoffed. 'I can't imagine they would want to spend much time with grumpy old gran.'

'You'd be surprised … and why has gran been so grumpy?'

'I don't know … put it down to late menopause!'

Dieter laughed, grateful for the release that hid a genuine disappointment. Brushing aside an inner irritation that he had allowed feelings he thought long buried to surface at yet another inopportune moment, he nevertheless took Diane's hand as they waited for the lights to change. 'Don't let the past rob you of your future Diane, they're wonderful children. Vangelis is basketball crazy and Ellie's never without a sketchbook in her hands. Her mother's daughter without a doubt … and her grandmother's!'

'Don't be ridiculous! I could never draw.'

'I know it was difficult for you coming to terms with what happened … but Litsa is a good woman … and I'm sure there is the best of Richard in her son … and now his grandson. Don't be a stranger to your grandchildren. After the operation … bring Eddie to the hotel for a month or so to recuperate and get to know them better'

'I … don't know how he'd feel about that.'

'Well, you won't if you don't ask him … it would do you both good. Why not spend Christmas here in Crete? You can have the penthouse.'

'How come? Where will you be?'

'I'm spending more time back at the estate these days … getting to know the old place again. Things tick over well enough here without me. You're always welcome there as well if you would like to visit … anytime.'

'Thank you, Dieter.' Realising they had stopped, Diane looked around. 'Are we here?'

Dieter nodded and pointed beyond the line of parked cars he had pulled up by to the gallery beside her. Diane looked at the crowd of people gathering at the brightly lit gallery and read the illuminated sign above.

'Ariadne!'

'I'll let Catherine explain that to you.' Dieter grinned, giving a light toot on the horn.

'There's nowhere to park … do you want me to…'

Dieter placed his hand on her arm encouraging her to relax, as a man appeared from a neighbouring establishment jumped into the car parked directly in front of the gallery, and pulled away to let Dieter in.

'Is there anything you don't think of?'

Parking the Jaguar, Dieter smiled. 'I don't know … I can't think of anything at the moment … but I'm sure you'll let me know if there is! Get ready …you've been spotted!' Dieter pointed to Ellie, pulling Eirene's daughter in her wake and making for the car. Diane was greeted by the rush of her excited granddaughter — burying herself into her embrace.

'*Yiayia!* This is Sophie, my best friend!'

'Hello Sophie … it's lovely to meet you.'

'Come on …' Ellie pulled at Diane's hand. 'The priest is about to start!'

Diane noticed her grandson sitting gloomily on some steps at the side of the shop. 'What's the matter with Vangelis?'

'He bust *Yiayia* Litsa's pot … the one she keeps her rosemary in … I told him not to keep bouncing his ball in the house!'

'I'll take them in.' Dieter nodded for Diane to go over to Vangelis as he led both the girls back into the gallery.

'Hello Vangeli … I heard about the pot.' Vangelis nodded morosely. 'I'm sure it can be stuck back together again.'

'That's what *Yiayia* Litsa said … she didn't seem too angry … but Mum and Dad are mad at me.'

'I'm sure they won't be for long. What sort of pot was it?

'Old.' He shaped the flask with his fingers. 'Sort of round with a hole at the top … it had a ship on it.'

Diane looked around. Across the road she could see a souvenir shop. Among their displays were a selection of Greek painted vases. Taking Vangelis' hand, she led him through the traffic. 'Come on … let's get Litsa another one.' As they stood in front of the window, Diane encouraged Vangelis to choose one he thought she would like.

'There!' He pointed excitedly. 'That one has a ship on it … it's a bit bigger though?'

'That's alright … she'll be able to fit more rosemary in it, won't she?' Diane indicated the vase to the shopkeeper, who retrieved it from the window display and handed it to her for her inspection.

Showing the vase to Vangelis, Diane slowly rotated it so that he could see the ship and the other pictures of fighting warriors. His cheerful smile made any further query redundant. This was obviously the one to have. Responding to her raised eyebrows as Diane found the price tag, the shopkeeper tried to reassure her.

'Genuine reproduction!' Then, as Diane puzzled over the contradiction. 'Certified museum copy.' he explained.

'Very well … just make sure you don't break this one as well Vangeli!'

With the vase bought and wrapped, Vangelis gave Diane a hug.

'Thank you *Yiayia.*'

'You're welcome, Vangeli. So shall we give this to *Yiayia* Litsa now?' Vangeli nodded. 'So, I suppose I'm *Yiayia* Diane?'

'Oh no … you're *Yiayia* Londino!'

As they waited for a gap in the traffic, Diane reminded Vangelis of the scene on the vase.

'You know it tells a story about the ship and the people on it? I expect it's Jason and the Argonauts … you can get Mummy to tell you the story before you go to sleep.'

'I mostly read myself now, but will you tell it to me?'

'Yes Vangeli.' Diane smiled, 'Yes, if there's time I'd like that.' Crossing over to the gallery, Diane pushed Vangelis forward to seek out Litsa among the busy throng admiring her daughter's work. Dieter, she realised, had quietly worked his magic, persuading many of his influential colleagues to attend. Catherine was already busy at the cash register.

Accepting the glass of wine she was offered as she entered the gallery, Diane took a sip and prepared to lay the remainder of her ghosts to rest.

TWENTY-SEVEN

It had been good to catch up with all of Jack's news, and his invitation for Diane to lunch with him at the Oxford and Cambridge had somehow seemed to mark a rite of passage in their relationship. He had, as she had foretold, done very well at Oxford and he had been generous in acknowledging her discreet help with his dissertation. Her influence, however, had not stopped there. For on the sporadic occasions that they had met up over the years, she had encouraged him to push for his dream and set up his own publishing house. It was a modest venture but was steadily becoming respected.

Now comfortably seated in his club, Jack's confident demeanour as they watched the limousines glide along Pall Mall below them, seemed a world apart from the shy young man she first remembered. Over the intervening years, their roles had begun to be reversed, as he began to be more often the one helping her, recommending occasional clients whose son or daughter needed a bit of private tuition to help them over a particular hurdle. It had eased her retirement. The occupation often more welcome than the remuneration, since things were in no way difficult. Obliged to take things easier, Eddie had sold the dealership at a good price.

'So … what's been happening?' Jack pulled Diane's gaze back to the table. 'Oh yes, you mentioned earlier that your grandson Vangelis was coming to stay with you?'

'God, yes!' Diane's anxiety flooded back. 'He's eighteen now. What am I going to do with him, Jack? Stop grinning, I'm serious, he's going to be here for a month … four whole weeks! What am I going to do with him?'

'Do what you do best I suppose … get him to realise his potential! I'm guessing that's why Catherine has sent him over for the summer.' Jack poured the last of the wine into Diane's glass and gestured for the waiter to bring over the dessert trolley. 'What's Ellie up to? Summer camp again?'

'No, they're past all that now. She's already finished her second year of Uni. She's off to Rhodes. Sophie has relations there. Vangelis will absolutely hate being here I'm sure …. He's bound to prefer being at home with all of his basketball pals.'

'Still wants to join the Harlem Globetrotters, does he?'

'No … some Greek team I can't pronounce. Apparently it's either that or he's going to become the next Indiana Jones! He sees himself backpacking across the globe, solving all the world's archaeological riddles singlehanded. University, though, doesn't seem to figure anywhere on his horizons.'

'Sounds like a trip to the British Museum is in order.'

'Yes, I've already inked that one in.' Diane declined the offer of dessert.

'Go on!' Jack urged. 'Might as well have one … I'll finish it off if you don't manage it!'

Diane eyed Jack's waistband pointedly. 'You shouldn't be having one either! The publishing lifestyle is obviously suiting you far too well! I'll wager you haven't been out on a court for ages.'

'Au contraire … I got thrashed only the other day!'

'Well, if you cut down on the business lunches, I'm sure you'd be the one doing the thrashing again! Maybe you could take Vangelis out for a game or two sometime?'

'Of course.'

'And … I know it's a bit of a cheek to ask, but perhaps you could bring him here … I'll pay of course … but it might be good to give him a taste of what having a university education could do for him?'

'Could turn him off it for life!' Jack warned, nodding towards a pair of elderly members, one absorbed in scooping out stilton, while his companion dozed, oblivious to his continuing conversation. 'Don't worry I'll organise a few culture shocks. I'll take him to the Bodleian, and we'll unearth a few lost civilizations together! He won't stand a chance … between the two of us he'll be enrolling before he knows it!'

So far it had been a very good year. His promotion had finally brought Lukas the office he felt he deserved. It had taken the better part of two decades to achieve, but no one had pulled the rug from under him this time. Crete had been much on his mind of late, not just because of this latest move, which had brought unpleasant reminders of that earlier lost opportunity, but also because of the old case notes he had unearthed at the bottom of his filing drawer, where they had lain forgotten since his arrival.

With his pay grade and pension now at a level he was unlikely to better, Lukas' thoughts were already focused on an easy glide into semi-retirement and if he could combine that with a successful excavation on the side to add a little glory and extra income, so much the better. He just hoped he hadn't left it too late — the woman had been in hospital at the time — was she even still alive? He would know soon enough. Flight and hotel were already booked. He was looking forward to his trip back to Crete — a couple of weeks of well-earned rest and relaxation, and hopefully, a profitable bit of digging of the sort that didn't require a spade.

Pulling the courtyard gate closed behind him, Antonis already knew from the pangs in his stomach just how late he was. Lunchtime had long-since passed, and if he needed any further reminder, there was Catherine already outside their house loading the car to drive in for her evening session at the gallery. This much was no problem. She was well-accustomed to his timekeeping and understood the vagaries of managing his mother's estate. They would share the events of their separate days later on.

What concerned him was the presence of the stranger in the village — a short, stocky man, even at this distance visibly uncomfortable in the afternoon heat, loosening his tie and shrugging off his jacket as Catherine evidently tried to explain something to him. As she pointed in his direction, Antonis could see her relief on seeing him at the gate. She waved, turned the man towards him, jumped in the car and with a toot was gone.

Left alone, the man began walking towards Antonis — stopped suddenly in his tracks, remembering and retrieving his briefcase from the hired car — before hurriedly locking it and heading off at a renewed pace back towards Antonis, eager to halt his own approach.

'Kyrios Xenakis?' Thrusting forward his hand, the man introduced himself. 'Lukas Economides. I was just explaining to your wife ... how refreshing it is to have a conversation in English again!'

Antonis accepted the limp, damp handshake, wondering why Catherine hadn't answered the man's queries in Greek, which she spoke fluently. Clearly keen to demonstrate his own command of the language, the man continued in the same vein. Antonis decided to humour him.

'I do apologise for turning up unannounced, but I am only here for a short while.' Flashing his card, 'Department of Antiquities ... over from Athens.' Lukas tried to steer Antonis back in the direction he had come. 'It was your mother I came to see, I gather she has moved from her old house?' Antonis stood his ground. Lukas looked at the imposing building beyond the courtyard gates. 'A very fine house ...a change of fortune, perhaps?'

'What is it that you want?'

'Just a few moments of your mother's time. I'm trying to clear up some old case notes that should have been catalogued years ago by the local office.'

'My mother is resting, she has not been well.'

'I'm very sorry to hear that ... it really would only take a moment or two...?'

'I've already said...' Antonis' response was interrupted by Litsa, who had appeared at the gate.

'It's alright Antoni, I couldn't settle.'

Lukas seized his opportunity and left Antonis' side to address Litsa at the gate, 'I am impressed ... such perfect English, from the whole family!'

The early morning call arranged, Lukas replaced the receiver and decided to treat himself to a nightcap from the mini-bar in his room. Taking his drink out on to the little balcony, he settled into a chair to reflect on the day's events. All in all, not a bad result. He had persuaded Kyria Xenakis to spare him five minutes, and once seated together at the courtyard table in the shade of the awning, had managed to spin this out for a good forty-five more.

With her son dispatched to bring them cold drinks, Lukas had lost no time in getting to the point. What did she know about the discovery of the earrings? Did she know exactly where they were found? Was any other jewellery found?

Struggling to keep pace with the flow of his questions, she had begun to tell him a long-winded story about a soldier she had met during the war. Deftly steering her back repeatedly to the relevant points, Lukas began to piece together the facts, establishing that it was the British soldier who had discovered them after falling into a cave near their vineyard.

Lukas allowed himself a self-congratulatory smirk at the recollection of his performance when the son had returned, cautioning his mother against revealing the location — it was one he had played out several times before — gravely reminding them that all such finds were the property of the state, regardless of whose land they were discovered on, before outlining and exaggerating the possible penalties they might bring upon themselves, should they choose to withhold information and obstruct a state official in his duty. Usually, it fell to his assistant to take the terrified interviewee aside and explain that it needn't come to that — all they had to do was show a little co-operation.

His skilful switch from bad cop to good had persuaded the woman to have her son agree to show him the site the following day, hence the early start. A price the son had extracted in return, saying that if he was going to have to take him that far, he might as well get a day's work in the field out of the journey.

As to whether anything else had been found, Lukas couldn't quite make up his mind and pondered on it now. He counted himself a pretty good judge of people, and while the woman seemed eager enough to please, he didn't trust the son and felt sure he was hiding something. He had asked again how they had managed to move to such a fine house and had been fobbed off with something about an inheritance. There was something they were not telling him. Lukas knew his artefacts. The chances were that such a fine pair of earrings would be part of a set. Had the rest been sold off to pay for their new lifestyle, he wondered?

Also the old woman had struggled to recall a conversation she had had with the soldier — about something slipping from a pot — something like water. It didn't make much sense. Neither had her answer to Lukas' query about this pot, telling him she kept her rosemary in it on the window sill.

When he had contrived to pay a visit to the bathroom, he had taken the opportunity to look it over: an obvious reproduction from totally the wrong period. The rosemary clearly wasn't doing much for her memory. She was definitely losing it!

Having originally considered whether he should be intentionally late for the early morning rendezvous in order to lend weight to his own authority, Lukas had decided upon the opposite tack, intending to beat the son at his own game and rouse him from his breakfast. He was somewhat disgruntled therefore to find Antonis and one of his workers already awaiting his arrival, seated on a traktoraki loaded with equipment.

Indicating that he was prepared to follow them, Lukas found Antonis signalling his refusal, and as the young lad vacated his seat and climbed into the rear, it became obvious that he was to join them.

'Your insurance won't cover you where we're going!' Antonis explained, hauling Lukas up onto the open bench seat beside him before gunning the noisy engine into life.

Lukas soon understood his reasoning as the little three wheeler quickly turned up onto a rocky trail leading out of the village, and he clung on nervously as they seesawed their way up the path, the young lad wedged into the trailer section behind him among the baskets and nets. 'Since you seem happy speaking English Mr. Economides, we'll continue to do so. It will be helpful for me ... you see I had a long conversation with a good friend last night about your department's obligations as well as our own ....'

Antonis paused as he swung the traktoraki into another bend on their upward climb, enjoying Lukas' discomfort as he nearly slid off the seat before continuing to add to it, 'He explained all the legal terms to me, in English … about public and private digging rights … compensation … that sort of thing. Everything I need to know really. So you see I shall be able to understand exactly what our legal position is … I wouldn't want there to be any … 'misunderstandings' … in English or in Greek.'

Lukas gave Antonis a fixed smile, reluctant to acknowledge the warning shot that had been sent across his bows, or his continuing trepidation as the little agricultural vehicle sent stones skittering down the drop beside him. Eventually, Antonis brought the traktoraki to a halt.

'Ah we've arrived!' Lukas was unable to conceal the relief in his voice. Antonis shook his head pointing to the donkey tied up at a nearby tree. Lukas' face dropped, as he saw another young worker scrambling down a steep slope towards them, while the one in the rear began handing over the equipment to his colleague. Viewing the climb he began to have serious regrets, but steeled himself nevertheless and was about to follow the two workers, who were now clambering back up the slope with their loads, wondering whether he was supposed to mount the donkey, when Antonis whistled to him.

Lukas turned to see Antonis, once again seated on the traktoraki. Joining him Lukas expressed his confusion.

'They're going up to work the field … you could help them if you'd prefer?' Lukas smiled a polite refusal as Antonis urged the little vehicle on over a hillock and down again onto a wider track skirting around below the upper vineyards. Stepping down as Antonis pulled up to one side of the track, Lukas looked up at the crest of vines perched high above. A steep slope of scrub-covered scree terminated in a huge rock boulder embedded in the hillside.

'There you are,' Antonis pointed up to the vines at the edge of the drop. 'That's where my father fell through into a hole somewhere beneath those vines. Apparently, he managed to dig his way out lower down before this whole hillside caved in.'

Lukas' face dropped for the second time that day as his long-nurtured vision of a comfortable director's tent adjoining a nice level dig site disintegrated. They were out in the middle of nowhere, with no known settlements of any archaeological significance anywhere nearby, and he was facing the prospect of a massive engineering project to uncover — what? The likelihood of there being any structure of any importance was virtually nil. At best there might be the remains of a natural cave, but again, its remote location effectively ruled it out as anything more than a wayside shelter. As far as he was aware there were no ancient thoroughfares through the area that could have lent it any great importance.

Relishing the ill-concealed expression of disappointment in evidence on Lukas' face as he surveyed the area, Antonis began to list the difficulties that would confront any excavation. 'I would imagine that as soon as you disturb this lower area, the whole terrace up there will collapse. I've asked the boys to check the number of vines that we'll lose … if you leave me your card, I'll have my friend's solicitor send an estimate for the likely compensation.'

Lukas waved Antonis' suggestion aside — attempting to deal with it in the same manner as the flies buzzing about his perspiring forehead. 'That may not be necessary after all …

I was hoping …' He turned back to Antonis, warily. 'You're positive this is where the earrings were found?'

'Absolutely. The solicitor will send you an affidavit along with the estimate.'

'I've told you already … there will be no need for any estimates,' Lukas snapped.

'But if you're intending to excavate …'

'There will be no excavation! You've brought me to the middle of nowhere to look at a crumbling hillside. There's not one thing here to suggest that this could possibly warrant the expense of a further investigation.'

'I can't help that,' shrugged Antonis, 'you asked to be shown where they were found. Shall I take you back to the village?'

'Yes!' snapped Lukas, before suddenly changing his mind. No! No, not yet. I need to take some pictures first … make a record of the area for my files. I shan't be very long,' he added hastily as Antonis appeared ready to head off up towards the vineyard.

Instead, Antonis settled back on the traktoraki and watched as Lukas photographed the area, waiting patiently as he viewed it from all angles and jotted down notes in a small pocket book.

'There! That's everything recorded,' Lukas said in a more measured tone as he climbed back onto the traktoraki. 'Now if anyone should attempt an … 'unauthorised' dig, we shall know about it!' He tapped the camera and looked pointedly at Antonis. 'And I would be grateful if you were to send me that affidavit.'

'No problem … I'll drop it into the local office.'

'Ah … no … if you don't mind, please forward that to me directly.'

Antonis held out his hand for Lukas' card noting the hesitation, before it was reluctantly parted with. Observing the address, he queried Lukas' original statement. 'I thought you said you were from the Athens office?'

'Flying from Athens, I think I said.'

'This address is a bit out of the way to be dealing with a case over here, isn't it?'

'One of the quirks of administration we have to put up with I'm afraid.' Lukas stared straight ahead, clutching his briefcase, waiting to be taken back.

Antonis eyed Lukas for several moments, before he started up the engine, and smiled disarmingly, as Lukas shuffled on the seat beside him. 'It's been good to clear the air. I think we understand each other much better now, don't you Lukas?' Then as he swung the traktoraki around, he warned him, 'Hold onto your seat!'

TWENTY-EIGHT

Scanning the bleary-eyed passengers appearing from the customs hall, as they wearily endeavoured to point their luggage trolleys towards the quickest possible exit, Catherine spotted him. A shoulder bag slung over one arm, the other trailing a lightweight case on wheels, he weaved a path through the tangle of trolleys and gave his mother a broad smile: his father's smile.

Catherine had become accustomed to the long periods of separation. The university years, the placements, graduations, ensuing employments and excavations that had kept him away from Crete. What she never seemed to be able to overcome was her surprise at his altered appearance on each return. Were it not for the fact that he so closely resembled his father, she might very well wonder who was this handsome, mature young man approaching her? It was hard to believe he would not be a twenty-something for very much longer.

'Thanks for coming darling.' Catherine gave Vangelis a long hug, which said all she needed to about how much she had missed him. 'Was the flight dreadful?'

'No, not too bad … a fair bit of turbulence coming in,

but I gather the worst of the storms have mostly blown themselves out now.'

'Yes, they have. It's still very windy though. I hope your coming won't make things too difficult for you at work?'

Vangelis shrugged. 'No problem. Thanks for turning out at this ungodly hour!'

'Also, no problem. I know it keeps the costs down. We'll help with that anyway.'

'There's no need Mum, … really. How's *Yiayia*?'

'Not too bad … she had seemed to be getting over the last infection, but she's gone downhill again pretty quickly since those torrential rains.'

'It looked dreadful … they showed it on the news. Was the village badly flooded?'

'Nothing too serious really, but to her it seems like the end of the world!'

'Aren't you parked over there?' Vangelis queried, as Catherine veered in the opposite direction outside the terminal.

'No, Dad's hovering at the drop off area … at least that's one benefit of turning out in the middle of the night! How's Anne?'

'She's fine … couldn't get time off at such short notice, but she sends her love. Hey! What the …?' Vangelis stopped abruptly as the door of a new, four-wheel drive pickup swung open into his path. Catherine laughed as Antonis stepped out and lifted Vangelis off his feet, his cases dangling in the air.

'The old one gave up the ghost a few months ago,' she explained as Antonis finally set his son down and looked him over.

'Nice wheels Dad!' managed Vangelis, regaining his breath. 'Very nice!'

Waking in his old room, Vangelis reached over and checked the time on his mobile. Having managed to ignore the crowing of the village cocks, he had slept on, and it was now just gone eleven. Slumping back, he looked around the room — largely unchanged since his departure for university — only the odd overly enthusiastic poster had been removed to spare visiting guests the embarrassment of teenage obsession. Despite all the reminders of his own boyhood possessions surrounding him, however, it now felt that he was the visitor. Home had been somewhere else for so long now. Hauling himself out of bed he resolved to make use of this visit, even if brief, to have a good clear out.

Making his way down to the kitchen, Vangelis caught up with the alterations that he had barely noticed upon his arrival in the early hours. The little room he remembered had been much enlarged and was now dominated by a sturdy cooking range. Heading for its welcome warmth, he looked around at all of the new cabinets and fittings, which while contemporary still maintained the cosiness of the country kitchen of his youth

'Good timing sleepyhead!' Catherine appeared at the door. 'I'm just about to put the kettle on.'

'Thought you'd be at the gallery, Mum.' Vangelis gave Catherine a hug and settled down at the kitchen table.

'Ellie's holding the fort. I've been getting on with some framing in the studio.'

'How's all that going? I know you said things were getting tougher.'

'They are … for everybody. The whole economy is in a mess, so it's not surprising. People have to eat and pay the bills first … our little luxuries come last, if at all these days.'

'Will you have to close?'

'Probably … we'll see it out until the lease review, but then …' Catherine shrugged off the inevitable. 'We had a good run … better to cut our losses sooner rather than later.'

'What about Ellie … what will she do?'

'Oh, Ellie will be fine. Her photography is really taking off. It's one of the few things that are keeping the gallery going right now. She wants to travel, build up a portfolio. Uncle Dieter has already given her some contacts, people to visit … places to stay. She's also going to spend some time in London with Gran as soon as she's better, so you'll both be able to catch up some more then as well. But she'll tell you all about that herself, she'll be back for lunch. Eirene is taking care of the gallery later on, so we can all spend some time with *Yiayia*.

Vangelis struggled for a moment to find the right words, 'You don't think she's going to get better this time?'

Catherine also took her time to reply, resisting the initial urge to gloss over the question. She remembered only too well how much her own father's death had affected him. Coming only a few weeks before Vangelis' finals, Grandad Eddie's heart attack had come as a shock to them all, but it had put Vangelis into a real tail-spin, so close had they become in his later years.

Catherine fondly recalled her mother's efforts, putting aside her own grief to ensure that Vangelis didn't blow his chances. 'I really don't know Vangeli. She's a fighter, but the damage to her lungs makes it so much harder for her to get over each infection. She's been a little better since I called you ... mostly because she knew you were coming I think. She kept saying that she'd had these dreams and wanted to talk to you.'

'Why me?'

Catherine shrugged. 'Who knows, but when we had the floods she became really insistent. I thought it was best to call you for both your sakes. It's probably nothing and as I say, *Yiayia*'s a fighter ... she even managed to make you some of your favourites!'

'*Kalitsounia*?'

Catherine nodded. 'Want some now? Dad will be back soon, and I know there's something he wants to show you before we take lunch over to *Yiayia*'s!'

The winds had finally cleared the sky of scudding clouds and Vangelis was grateful for the late October sun now warming them as Antonis steered the old traktoraki up the familiar paths that wound through the olive groves

'I'm amazed you've still kept her going!'

Antonis shrugged. 'She's easy enough to repair and she does the job!'

Vangelis prepared himself for the swing around the big old olive tree as the trail wound on upwards. Sitting with his father on the old traktoraki brought a host of childhood memories flooding back — so many summers spent picking grapes — winters collecting olives. Once again, he was reminded of how long he had been away, and looking at his father now he could not help but feel a certain guilt at the seasons he had missed. Antonis was still a fit, healthy man, but Vangelis knew that it could not be getting any easier for him. 'How are you managing with the harvests Dad ... are you still able to get people to help you?'

'It's more difficult these days. All the youngsters have left the village ... most of them don't want to know about working the land anymore. But there's always someone looking for work down at the gate ... it used to be just the Albanians, now they're from all over! Every year it costs more to make less, but we get by.'

'Wouldn't it be easier for you if you sold off some of these higher fields? They're so difficult to get to.'

'Which means we'd probably get next to nothing for them. No ...we'll manage until we can't ... and deal with it then. Anyway, you might not be so keen to sell, when you see where I'm taking you!'

'Well, I'm guessing it's the field where your father found the earrings. Why what's happened ... has that man you told me about been back? That was ages ago. I thought he'd said it was a waste of time looking for anything there?'

Antonis eased the traktoraki to a halt. 'He did.' Dismounting, he held out his arm for Vangelis to follow as he set off down the trail. Slapping his arm around his son's shoulder and steering him onto the raised bank edging the trail, which had become a quagmire from the rains, he continued, 'Yes, he did ... but that was then.'

'So what's different now?' queried Vangelis.

'This is what's different now.' Antonis kicked aside the gnarled and tangled litter of roots and foliage strewn across their muddy path and pointed up to where the terrace of vines had lined the crest of the hillside.

Looking up, Vangelis could see that the vines had completely disappeared. The hillside he remembered as a steep, shrub-covered slope, seemingly propped in place by the huge boulder at its foot, had itself all but vanished. Now a vertiginous drop, capped by a few solitary vines, ended in a wide flattened mound, just above the boulder which had been toppled sideways along the bank of the trail.

Clambering up onto the giant stone, Vangelis took in the scene, picturing the devastating force the rains had inflicted as the water had sheared off whole sections of the hillside, before washing away the bulk of the debris. A low recess, arcing out from the left of the mound of earth caught his eye. Sloping inwards away from the almost vertical main face, it was unmistakeably the remains of a cave now uncovered.

Looking for some foothold to get across and inspect it more closely, he saw below him something which excited him even more — a flat, level slab. Stepping down onto it, he could just see beneath the sloping earth rising ahead of him, the outline of the edge of what appeared to be another slab — another step. This may very well have been a natural cave, but someone, at some time in the distant past, had taken the trouble to construct an entrance, and now as he stood almost at eye level with the great spreading mound of earth, he was also aware of its own level base. Another clear sign that an artificial floor had been cleared.

Sweeping the damp earth from the edge of the next step, Vangelis felt something obstruct his hand. Freeing it from the clammy grip of the soil, he knew almost at once what it was that he had found. Wiping away the remaining earth, he examined the human femur. From its size, he could roughly guess that the thigh-bone probably belonged to a young adult, and his mind could not resist the temptation to wonder — would it prove to be female — was this the owner of the earrings? Staring at the mound of earth before him, Vangelis' mind raced with speculation as to what else might remain to be discovered.

'Started digging already?' Antonis appeared above him. 'I'll bring some shovels up tomorrow if you like. Found anything interesting?'

Vangelis held up the bone. 'You can forget about digging for a while, Dad ... there's a hell of a lot of that needs doing first before we can begin to think about that! And we certainly won't be using shovels until much later on!'

Despite the pleasure of having the whole family seated around the table in Litsa's dining room, the conversation had not been as upbeat as Catherine had hoped. 'It sounds like we've got a bit of a nightmare on our hands then?' She passed around plates encouraging everyone to help themselves to fruit after the lunch. 'We thought this could have been an opportunity for you.'

'It is Mum,' Vangelis leaned back on his chair. 'It's an amazing opportunity, but as I've said, I can't just go wading in there on my own.'

'No, I understand that. I know it has to be reported to the local authorities first, but if we have to go to all the trouble of protecting the site ... and I know you explained we'll get reimbursed for the expense eventually ... but if it is down to us to take that responsibility because we own the land, how is it that you may not even be allowed to do the excavations? You're a qualified archaeologist now.'

'We may own the land, but we're only the holders of anything that might be found there, we don't own them. Nevertheless, we're obliged to protect them until an excavation can be agreed upon. And to be able to supervise a dig you need a certain number of years' experience, depending on how the site is eventually classified. Even if, as is most likely, it's classed as a rescue excavation and probably only of minor importance, I'll still be just short of the three years needed … pre-grad. stuff doesn't count.

Assuming the directorate doesn't decide to expropriate the site … in which case it would be completely out of our hands, the best bet might even be to get attached to one of the foreign schools and persuade them to take it on as a permitted dig … they each get three a year. But that could take some time.'

'What about private sponsorship?' asked Ellie.

'Well assuming we could get it, I'm not really sure how that would work or whether it would be allowed. We'd still need someone with enough experience to direct the excavation and submit all the necessary scientific competencies, and they would also be the ones who would have to send the reports.'

'And get the glory I suppose?' Ellie enquired, receiving the expected confirmation.

'What about the man who came sniffing around from the mainland?' suggested Antonis, 'Could he be of any use?'

'I doubt it … I don't really understand why it wasn't someone from the office here on Crete. They would be the ones who would have to instigate anything.'

'I expect he was on the glory trail as well ... he must have thought there was some way he could sidestep all the red tape you've been talking about,' Ellie suggested.

'Perhaps,' Vangelis agreed. 'Who knows?'

'I bet uncle Dieter would!'

'Pack it in Ellie, you can't go pestering Dieter for everything.'

'Why not?' Ellie giggled, pouring another glass of wine. 'You may be his godson, but I'm his protégée now!'

Her daughter's high spirits aside, Catherine could see some sense in what she was saying. 'Dieter certainly came up with all of the right answers for you to deal with that awful little man last time. Antoni ... what do you say ... shouldn't we run it by him at least, to see if he's got any suggestions?'

'Don't disturb him now,' Litsa's unexpected voice broke into the conversation. Though seated at the table with them, she had almost been forgotten in all of the excited discussions. 'I expect he'll be taking an afternoon nap ... which is what I need right now!'

Vangelis got up to help his grandmother. 'I'm sorry *Yiayia*, we've been ignoring you ... that's dreadful! After all, it's your lands we're talking about.'

'Don't worry about that.' Litsa steadied herself at the table and added with a twinkle in her eye, 'I've done enough digging on that field already! You decide among yourselves what you think is best. Everything will all be yours to worry about soon enough anyway!'

Vangelis dismissed the suggestion. 'Nonsense! I'm counting on you to help me out with all my reports when the dig's completed!' Helping Litsa to her room, Vangelis remembered his earlier conversation at breakfast. 'I forgot,

Yiayia … Mum said you wanted to talk to me about something … some dreams you've been having?'

'Oh, that will keep … after all Vangeli, I don't think you'll be going anywhere in a hurry now … will you?' Litsa gave Vangelis a knowing smile as she closed the door for her nap.

TWENTY-NINE

The breakfast table resembled a campaign map, as Vangelis and his father considered how best to secure the site. A napkin suspended from condiments covered the bread basket — serving as the huge tarpaulin required to shelter the mound from further rainfall, while a wall of cereal packets represented the line of fencing that would be needed along the bank of the trail.

'It's a good job there's a deep ditch within the bank. That will have caught a lot of the overspill in case anything of interest has already been washed away,' mused Vangelis.

Antonis grunted, more consumed with his fencing calculations.

'That's my access gate!' Vangelis complained as Ellie appeared, helping herself to cereal and settling down at the table.

'Don't worry, I'll close it behind me! Where's Mum?'

'She's gone to the gallery.'

'I thought I was supposed to be going. Damn! I'd have stayed in bed if I'd known!'

'Your talents are needed in the field, dear sister. We're going to do a proper survey of the site. Dad and I will measure it out and we'll be needing a photographic record, so no sneaking back upstairs. As soon as you're ready we'll be off!'

'Not before I've woken up!' warned Ellie. 'And if you're so keen to get going, you can save some time by making my coffee, little brother!'

'Delighted to!' Vangelis busied himself making a full pot for them all.

'I thought you were going down to report it to the authorities today?'

'Dieter suggested delaying it for twenty-four hours until he's made some enquiries. Besides, surveying the site and submitting a plan to secure it can only count in our favour. I'll go down to the office tomorrow once we've got everything together.'

'Weren't you supposed to be flying back tomorrow?'

'Postponed it.'

'Won't that cause problems at work?' asked Antonis.

'They'll manage without me … and they'll need to get used to it anyway!'

'What do you mean?' Antonis set aside his pen and pad.

'I'll be handing in my resignation. I will have to go back sometime soon to sort things out, but you're going to need help with all of this Dad.'

'Damn! Just when I was going to turn your old room into an extra studio!' teased Ellie. 'What's Anne going to say about all of this … think she'll join the madhouse?'

'I don't know. I'd like her to.'

'Maybe it's time to pop the question then!'

'Not exactly the best time to do it though is it? Just when I've packed in my job!'

'Coward!' Ellie lobbed a screwed up napkin at Vangelis as he settled back into his chair.

'Now look what you've done … you've just wiped out the whole fence!'

'I don't know why you're bothering. If you ask me, it would be better to just leave everything as it is. Sling a tarpaulin over the main attraction, chuck a load of earth over it and nobody will be any the wiser. If you stick a bloody great fence up, then you might as well go the whole hog and add a neon sign saying 'Dig Here'!'

Neither Vangelis nor his father could quite manage a suitable reply, but both were reluctantly thinking that Ellie might indeed have a very good point.

'You should rest Mr. Brandt.'

'Yes, thank you Monique, I shall. But I do need to check some emails first.'

'Surely they can wait? It can take some time to get used to dialysis. This was only your third session. You must expect to still feel very tired.' Monique could see that her new employer was in no mood to heed her advice. Freed from the shackles of the newly installed home haemodialysis unit, Dieter Brandt was keen to get back behind his desk.

Cleaning up after the session, as she watched him leave the dedicated treatment room, Monique reflected on both her new position and employer. So far she was very satisfied with both. Her accommodation in the huge, rambling house was very generous, if a little dated, and her duties, beyond the couple of hours of daily dialysis, minimal. A little secretarial help that she would have been prepared to take on without further reward, but for which he had insisted her salary be adjusted accordingly. Rather than have too many staff around him, Dieter Brandt preferred a chosen few he could trust.

The agency had told her this would be a prize position to land, and they had not been wrong. She had been warned, however, that more than a dozen of their candidates had already failed to get the job and had feared that her German might not be suitably up to scratch, but both parties had been comfortable settling upon a middle ground of English, though he seemed equally at ease conversing with her in her native French. What it was that had tipped the balance in her favour, she didn't know.

Whereas with most live-in positions she had held before, she had either been expected, or preferred, to keep to her own quarters. However, Mr Brandt — Dieter — as he kept reminding her to call him, had made it clear she was welcome to have the run of the house, dine with him, or in her rooms as she chose from day to day. All she had to do was let Gudrun the housekeeper know a few hours in advance. The previous evening had been the first occasion she had chosen to accept the open invitation, and she had been agreeably surprised at the easy flow of conversation and his genuine interest in her life and opinions — their considerable disparity in age proving no obstacle.

Pausing now at the open door of his office, Monique called out to see if there was anything else he needed. Silhouetted by the glow of the monitor at his computer desk, Dieter swivelled around on the chair, attempting to rise, before suddenly collapsing back into his seat.

'Dizzy …' he mumbled.

'And starting a temperature, by the feel of it.'

The cool of Monique's hand reminded Dieter of his unfinished task. 'I must send this email.'

Monique reached over and tapped the keyboard. 'Done!' she said. 'Now you really do have to rest. I need to see that temperature come down, or you could end up back in the clinic.'

'But I hadn't finished …' Dieter complained.

'It will all keep, I'm sure,' she reassured him. 'As I said, it does take time to get used to the treatments. It may be that the dialysate balance needs to be altered, or you might find overnight treatments suit you better …. I know you didn't want the equipment in your room … but it would mean only three nights a week that way.'

'No, we'll keep things as they are.' As Monique had guessed, Dieter wanted to keep any reminders of this recent challenge to his life firmly locked away. Out of sight and out of mind. Seeing him turning back to the computer, she was about to continue her remonstrations but was pleased to see that he was only shutting the system down.

'I'm coming!' he agreed, 'But please remind me, I do need to get back to my godson.'

'I shall,' Monique assured him. 'But only when you've rested, and that temperature is back to normal!

'Mind if I use your computer again Ellie?' Vangelis asked, 'Dieter said he'd email the various options once he'd checked things out with his contacts.'

'Sure. Leave it on when you're done and I'll download the site images.' Ellie dumped her camera bag on the table and headed for the kettle. 'What do you want Dad, tea … coffee?'

'No … something stronger!' Antonis helped himself to a glass of *tsikouthia* and put the bottle and more glasses on the table. It had been a long but productive day, measuring and photographing the site, and while the cold spell had meant they had been able to carry out their survey without disturbance, Antonis needed warming up. He had enjoyed working alongside both his son and daughter once more and was beginning to take to the idea of this new project.

'Toasting a successful day, I hope?' Catherine quickly closed the door on the gusty wind that accompanied her arrival.

'You're back early, Mum … what's up?'

'Nothing. I didn't go to the gallery, Eirene's covering. *Yiayia* wasn't too well, so I stayed with her this afternoon.' Hanging up her coat, Catherine saw Vangelis coming back down the stairs. 'Perhaps you can pop over and spend a bit of time with her later, love … see what it was she wanted to talk to you about?' she suggested.

'Yes … fine,' Vangelis acknowledged absently, absorbed in the printout he was holding.

'From Dieter?' asked Ellie. Vangelis nodded. 'And?'

'A bit odd … he talks about the people he's spoken with … mostly what we'd already guessed and then says he doesn't think he can help ….'

'That's it … no suggestions?'

'Nothing at all, no good wishes … very abrupt, not like him at all … doesn't even bother signing off.'

'Perhaps we shouldn't have troubled him … my fault,' said Catherine.

Antonis disagreed. 'No … he seemed really excited about it yesterday … keen to see who he could get on board to help.'

'Well, it's back to plan A then. I'll go down to the office tomorrow … hand in the survey … see what they say about protecting the site … and just hope I can get included in the excavation.' Screwing up the printout, Vangelis binned it. 'I'll go and see *Yiayia* now before it gets too late.'

Despite his breezy exit, Catherine could sense her son's disappointment. He could not have had a better godfather — indeed, they all had much to be grateful to Dieter for, and she probably should not have suggested calling him, but she knew how much this excavation would mean to Vangelis.

Letting himself in by the front door, Vangelis knew from the direction of Litsa's troublesome cough that she had already retired to her bedroom and called up to her.

'Hi *Yiayia*, it's only me … would you rather I came back tomorrow?'

'No …' Litsa struggled to catch her breath. 'No Vangeli … come up and see me … I'd like that.'

After he had fussed over her for a while, Litsa persuaded Vangelis to settle in the armchair beside her and tell her about his life in England — about Anne, about his hopes and plans for the future. Inevitably the conversation wound its way back to the cave and the excavation that would eventually follow, as well as Dieter's odd behaviour, and Vangelis' anxiety that he could end up not even being able to get involved in a dig that was on their own land.

'I expect your *nonos* was just tired, I'm sure you'll hear from Dieter again soon. But I was right, wasn't I?' Litsa asked. 'You are going to stay?' Vangelis nodded. 'Then it will all work out in the end. I feel it. I knew something was going to happen. I knew you'd stay.'

'What do you mean, you knew?'

'Ever since that man came here asking questions about the earrings … saying there must be something else in the cave up there. I've had the dreams since then …. I knew one day something would happen … and then when those dreadful storms came … I knew!'

'What dreams *Yiayia*?'

'Your grandmother in London had them too. She told me once … she saw a little girl wearing the earrings.'

'She's never told me that,' Vangelis' expression betrayed his disbelief.

'It's true,' Litsa insisted. 'You can ask her. She said she felt as though she was the child's mother.'

Vangelis could not imagine his grandmother Diane ever being so fanciful but decided to humour Litsa. 'What did you dream *Yiayia*? Did you see this child as well?'

'No … no I never see anybody, just the waves. Huge waves … throwing the ship about and the sky is black with smoke from the mountain behind us … just like it was on the pot.'

'The pot?'

'The rosemary pot.'

'You mean the one I got you with *Yiayia Londino*?'

'Yes … no! The one before that … the one that was broken! You said you were going to glue it back together for me. Do you remember?'

Vangelis remembered a lingering guilt at never having got around to fulfilling his promise more than the pot itself, but he did recall that there had been a ship on it — the reason for choosing its replacement.

'What does the pot have to do with the earrings?'

'They were in the pot Yiannis found in the cave … I've told you that already!'

'I don't remember that.'

'And they keep telling me I forget everything!'

'Do you still have the pieces?'

'Yes … they're wrapped up in a drawer somewhere … I'll have a look tomorrow.' Vangelis resisted the urge to suggest he help Litsa search for them immediately. Sensing his impatience, Litsa cautioned him. 'Don't get your hopes up. It's not much of a thing. Not anything you would call valuable … more like a flask for water, than a proper vase … you obviously don't remember it well.'

'It may not be valuable *Yiayia*, but we do need to document everything.'

'That sounds like I shan't be seeing much of it, if you ever do get round to putting it back together. Never mind … I've done without it for long enough now!'

'So, in your dreams you're on that ship?'

'Yes … always frightened … always trying to get away …'

'From what?'

'From the mountain, from the black clouds … the waves are so big, I'm sure we'll drown before we reach the shore.'

'Who's we? You said you never see anybody.'

'No, I don't … but someone is looking after me … my mother, I think ….'

Catherine's appearance at the door made them both jump. 'What's up with you two?' She laughed at their startled expressions. 'Been telling tales?'

'*Yiayia*'s dreams.' Vangelis explained. 'You didn't tell me your mum had dreams about the earrings.'

'God! That was before you were born. She'd had too much white wine if you ask me!'

'Well, I don't drink,' Litsa insisted.

'Probably just your medicine then!' joked Catherine, before brandishing a night tray of medications. 'On which subject …'

'I'd better let you get some rest *Yiayia*. I hope you don't get bothered with any more dreams.'

'No, I think I'll sleep well tonight. It's been good to talk Vangeli. We'll talk some more tomorrow, and I'll find that pot for you. And if there's anything else you want to know, just ask … I can't give you any answers when I'm gone!'

THIRTY

As exhausted as he still felt, Dieter nevertheless relished being back behind his own desk. Back once more in control of his life and free at last from the confines of the private clinic. Another two-and-a-half weeks had been lost to an intermittent haze of delirium, while interminable speculations over adverse reactions, underlying infections, antibiotics, formulas, procedures and prognoses drifted in and out of consciousness around him. But he had been lucky, he had pulled through, the treatment plan had worked. Life would slowly get back to normal — as normal as it could be in the circumstances.

Monique had collated the printouts of the email correspondence she had maintained in his absence. Brought over from the computer workstation, there were two neat stacks to his left — the larger, business related; the smaller: personal. To his right, lay a handful of unopened post.

He had fanned the letters out and pulled two from the deck. Their origins were familiar, and he had known even before opening them, what would lie within — the blunt facts had already been clear from the emails. Before him the single sheet of handmade writing paper was blank, the fountain pen poised as it had been for some while. There were times when only a handwritten letter would suffice — but how to begin — how to encapsulate the emotion of so many years?

Monique discreetly placed a small tray of tea to his side and turned to leave.

'Please stay Monique. I want to apologise.'

'There's absolutely no need….'

'I must! Please … draw up that chair … sit with me for a moment while I explain. It was unforgiveable of me to have been angry with you. You did exactly as I asked of you … you weren't to know …'

'I did check at the clinic … whether I should tell you or not … but they also thought that it would be better not to upset you, not until you were stronger.'

'I understand. And I'm grateful for the sympathetic way you have dealt with the correspondence. I made things extremely difficult for you when I forbade you to tell anyone I was ill. I appreciate there are only so many variations on, 'He's away on business and will get back to you soon,' that you can be expected to come up with, especially when …' Dieter was reluctant to say the words — to acknowledge the bereavement that had been kept from him.

'You were very close?'

'Yes. My adopted family really.' Dieter pointed to the group of framed photographs lining the central galleried shelf of the desk. 'Vangelis my godson, and Ellie, his sister. Catherine and Antonis, their parents. And then the grandparents, Diane in London… and Litsa.' Bringing down Litsa's photograph, Dieter placed it at the head of the blank sheet of paper. 'Goodbyes are difficult enough … it's knowing what to say to those left behind that is always worse.'

Vangelis cast a last glance over the site before tossing the shovel into the wheelbarrow. Already largely hidden from the trail by the huge boulder, the remains of the cave had been further disguised by a heap of brushwood and debris, which in itself secured one of three large tarpaulins that had been needed to protect the remaining mound of earth and the series of steps leading down to the boulder. As Ellie had suggested, these in turn were now disguised with barrow loads of the topsoil, rubble, and uprooted vines that had washed down the trail. The ostensible altruism of their efforts at clearing the trail for one and all, concealing their need to preserve the site, as well as providing the material itself.

Wheeling the barrow back to the traktoraki, he and Antonis lifted it into the rear. Neither spoke for a while as they rattled back down to the village. Passing the courtyard of the now empty house, Antonis pulled his mind away from their recent bereavement.

'What time is your flight?'

'Not for hours yet. Don't worry. I'll be back before you know it, but I have to tie up things in England.'

'Of course, I know that. Take all the time you like. I don't think our friends down at the department are going to be making their minds up anytime soon!'

'Doesn't look that way,' Vangelis agreed, reflecting briefly on the cursory assessment of the junior the department had recently dispatched to examine the site, and his gloomy pessimism that there was no funding available to do anything whatever the case. 'I was thinking of the olives though … I'll be back in time to give you a hand.'

'Well that would be good, but look after yourself first. Spend some time with Anne.'

Vangelis flashed an encouraging smile of agreement but was not looking forward to the conversations he knew they must both have. She had come for Litsa's funeral and had been genuinely moved by the warmth of the family's pleasure at seeing her again but had been taken aback by Vangelis' abrupt decision to leave England. Understandably she would need time herself to decide whether she could, as he had suggested, accompany him.

Topping Vangelis' glass up, Jack set the Cotes du Rhone back down in the corner of the grate and continued warming his rear in front of the fire as he summed up the situation.

'So, you and Anne haven't really seen anything of each other since you were over the last time ... before you went back to help with the olive harvest. She doesn't want to give up her life here, yet in spite of the fact that you're obviously still besotted with her, you seem intent on heading back to Crete sooner rather than later. You're mad boy! Can't lose a woman like that. Why not spend a week or two here at least? Give her time ... let her come round to the idea. Better still, make an honest woman of her! Haven't been to a good wedding in ages! I know you had to give up your flat, but you're welcome to use the spare room for as long as you like.'

'Thanks Jack. It's not as if I haven't thought about it, but the trouble is I really do need to be there in case anything does finally get decided about the site.'

'I thought that was all on hold.'

'As far as the department's concerned, it is. With the economy going the way it is as well, they're being squeezed hard enough even to keep up with existing commitments. But Dieter is trying to put together a privately sponsored package with the archaeologist I came over to see. If he can apply for the permits through his connections, then we're hoping they will at least be happy that someone else is picking up the bill and give us the go ahead.'

'Sounds as though that could take some while ... why the rush to get back so soon?'

'Someone else has been sniffing around with ideas of his own.'

'Well can't you just inform the department?'

'That's the problem ... he is the department! Or part of it at any rate. He was a junior in Heraklion when the first earring was discovered. Now he's head of another branch on the mainland. For some reason he's always kept tabs on the case. He's about to retire and wants to go out with a bang. He's also trying to pull together a sponsorship, and with his contacts ...'

'Odds-on favourite,' Jack sympathised as they both took thoughtful swigs. 'Well, I can understand why you're keen to get back. Still ... stick around till the weekend ... eh? I'm thinking of having a bit of a do!'

'Stop grinning Mum!' Vangelis' embarrassment was compounded by Ellie's look of mock adoration. 'Tell them Dad!'

Antonis shrugged, a barely concealed smile on his own face.

'I can be happy that my baby's finally getting married, can't I?' Catherine broadened her grin to annoy him some more.

'But I told you three hours ago!'

'Oh, the effects will last for a good while yet!' Catherine promised. 'Now … tell me all about it again!'

'She would have been pleased you've chosen the little chapel. She never stopped going up there, even though the new one is so much closer.' Catherine pushed open the front door and propped a chair by it to keep it ajar, before opening the windows of Litsa's house one by one to air the place.

Vangelis helped her. 'It wouldn't be the same in the new church, it's far too big … we'd just rattle around in there … there aren't that many on Anne's side either. Anyway, it's where you and Dad were married, so we'll be keeping the tradition going. I want Anne to really feel she belongs in the village that she's a part of a community. I'm sure Dad wanted the same for you.'

'It wasn't that simple I'm afraid. There were a lot of bridges to mend … but we got there eventually.'

'You've never said much about those days … you or Dad.'

'I suppose not. Well, we'll put that to rights … but not here … not now.'

'Why … do you think she can hear us?' Vangelis teased.

'Of course she can … I talk to her every day!' Catherine rolled her sleeves up. 'We should have made a start on this a long while ago … it just never seemed to be the right time … but now it does! Bring in those boxes and let's get cracking!'

'And you're sure … you and Dad … about this?'

'Well, where else are you and Anne going to live? We can't all be on top of each other down there. And don't worry, we'll look after your sister, she won't be forgotten. Not that she's likely to be hanging around here for very much longer. I can see the wanderlust getting stronger by the day. And don't expect too much too soon from Anne … or yourself for that matter. You're both used to much more exciting lives in the city. I doubt that there'll be enough to keep you here when all this business with the dig is over and done with. But whatever you choose, you'll always have this to come back to. Now let's start sorting things out!'

It had been a long and tiring day for all of the family, finally sorting through Litsa's possessions. More often than not, the physical effort had been outweighed by emotional tolls, as decisions over what to keep and what to throw inevitably dictated the pace. But tiredness was not the only reason Vangelis had retired to his room for an early night.

They had found, as Litsa had said they would, the remains of the broken flask carefully wrapped in the bottom of a drawer. Vangelis had recognised the paper bag at once. It was the same one that had contained the replacement vase he had carried from the souvenir shop all those years ago. The evening meal over, he could wait no longer to examine it properly.

Clearing a space on his old desk, he carefully withdrew the bundle of tissue paper that Litsa had reused to wrap the broken shards and slowly spread them out before him. His excitement was soon tempered, however, as he began to realise just how costly his childhood clumsiness had been. The flask had shattered into numerous small pieces. This would be a jigsaw that would take some considerable time to reassemble. Nevertheless, he methodically started working through the fragments, rotating each piece, searching for matches, and before too long had managed to lay out the more obvious and recognisable components — the neck and shoulders of the flask, the lugs to either side. But the central body of the vessel had taken the worst of the damage and was proving to be a much more difficult task.

His tiredness finally getting the better of him, Vangelis switched off the desk lamp, having at least pieced together what he felt sure was part of the ship he remembered. Resolving that he would attempt the restoration of the flask himself, he set about compiling a mental list of requirements. He would need suitable conservation adhesive, bead box, and various other odds and ends to support the reconstruction. It would be impossible to examine the flask properly otherwise and make sense of the intriguing fragments — he was sure that some of the symbols he could partially make out were Egyptian — yet the flask was clearly Minoan.

Settling down for the night, he pushed the jumble of fragments and their curious contradictions from his mind, idly wondering if he too would soon be dreaming of Litsa's ship on the waves, but a deep sleep of contented exhaustion soon swept over him instead.

Waking as Catherine settled on the end of the bed, he was about to reach for his mobile.

'Gone eleven!' she said, anticipating his enquiry. 'I thought I'd better bring you up a cup, or you'd be here till lunchtime!' Noticing the fragments of the flask laid out on the desk, she smiled, 'That takes me back. It's a long time since we did a puzzle together.'

'You can help if you like,' Vangelis suggested, pulling himself up as he took the cup.

'No time I'm afraid ... and neither have you ... you need to see the priest. Dad's already spoken to him. The date is fine, but there are forms that need to be filled. And the department rang ... something's finally happening!'

THIRTY-ONE

Having spent so much time treading water while awaiting the department's decision, Vangelis yet again had cause to regret his own indecision in not having proposed to Anne sooner. With the dig now in full swing and the wedding almost upon him he was feeling the strain, as he tried to give equal attention to the seemingly endless preparations required for what both had agreed was to be a relatively simple ceremony and reception, while knowing that his presence was needed elsewhere.

'You were the one who wanted an old fashioned reception in the village square,' Anne reminded him. 'It doesn't just take care of itself. I still think we need to order a marquee in case it rains.'

'It's June,' Vangelis pointed out. 'We're in Crete.'

'And it's never rained in June before?'

Vangelis sidestepped the question declaring, 'I guarantee it won't!' at the same time praying that no freak of nature would hold him to account. 'We won't need a marquee.'

Anne shrugged. 'It's on your head!'

Once again hoping that it wouldn't be, Vangelis sidled towards the door.

'Alright … I know you're itching to get up there … the rest can wait, I suppose!'

Slinging the rucksack over his shoulder, Vangelis tried to make his exit less indecently hasteful than his inner urgency dictated, giving Anne a tender but brief embrace. Not fooled by his guile, she reciprocated with a lingering, passionate kiss, holding on to him tightly until he began to squirm.

'Go on … get out of here!' she grinned, finally releasing him. 'Not even married and I'm already an archaeologist's widow!'

Gunning the trail bike into life, Vangelis sped off towards the site. At least he would be there in next to no time: the pair of ex-rental bikes they had picked up cheaply had proved a godsend for himself and Ellie. Once agreed upon, the excavation had gone ahead rapidly, and they were now steadily working their way across the levelled floor and had already cleared one-third of the remaining mound of earth.

In the end, a compromise had been reached between themselves, the department, and Lukas Economides. Holding most of the cards, he had been the driving force, but his own impatience to reach an agreement had allowed Dieter's lawyer to extract the best possible terms in return for their share of the sponsorship. While the excavation would be supervised by Lukas and his senior archaeologist, there were places on the team for both Vangelis and Ellie: he to assist in the excavations, and she to continue the photographic documentation she had already very capably begun. Waiving compensation rights for loss of any use of the land during the excavation had also ensured that there would be a guarantee of shared rights to use Ellie's photographs in any future displays or publications. The main reports, however, would be the preserve of Lukas' archaeologist, Simon Eliades.

Thankfully Vangelis had found that he and his team were easy enough to get along with, and the dig had progressed both amicably and professionally without any onsite wrangles or rivalries. Little of any great significance had so far come to light, but all were hopeful that as they worked their way into the central area the situation would change.

Parking his bike next to Ellie's, Vangelis climbed up the newly constructed ramp to the site, wondering why everything was so quiet. Usually there would be a barrow being wheeled to or from the spill pile. Reaching the top, he could see why — everyone was gathered around one spot. The flash from Ellie's camera confirmed his immediate suspicion — they had found something — and he had missed the moment.

'Where the hell have you been?' whispered Ellie, adjusting the tripod before focusing the camera on the cleared square below. 'You've missed the fame and fortune pics. I'm just getting some last close-ups before they lift it.'

Vangelis cursed under his breath, but his disappointment soon evaporated as he too was drawn into the excitement of what had been found. Coiled on the floor lay a necklace. Still partially embedded in a fine tilth, it was nevertheless instantly recognisable. This was almost certainly the companion piece to the earrings.

'Magnificent, isn't it?' Simon handed him a sable brush. 'Here, get yourself on the record before it's too late!'

Acknowledging his generosity, Vangelis began teasing the last remaining particles of debris from the necklace.

Entranced as much by the delicacy of the workmanship as the enduring nature of the piece, he watched the untarnished gold spring back to life in the sunlight. When cleaned, the lapis lazuli would rival it in brilliance and contrast. Ellie seized the opportunity as Simon had suggested to fire off some shots of her brother examining the find.

As she added in the flash gun on the last couple of pictures, Vangelis noticed a reflection not just from the necklace itself but from a small area surrounding it. Pointing it out to Simon, he asked Ellie to fire the gun again and they both witnessed the white halo that briefly appeared. Gently clearing a narrow band of the fine tilth beside the necklace down to the original surface of the floor, a fine whitish powder was evident.

'Ash?' Vangelis queried.

'Possibly.' Simon motioned for his assistant to bring over the tray he had readied for the necklace. Easing the necklace from the soil onto the waiting tray, a white coil remained beneath, starkly delineating the outline. 'Get some close ups of that for me would you Ellie? With and without the flash. Then I think we'd better get a sample of that powder Vangeli. Well spotted.'

'I knew there had to be a companion piece … I told you!' Lukas crowed to Simon. 'This must be what your grandmother was talking about when she said your grandfather felt something slip from a pot, Vangeli. Perhaps there was some kind of powder in it too?'

'I'm afraid there's no way of knowing now … she kept rosemary in it for forty years or more!'

'Well, it certainly wasn't the one I saw in her house when I visited.'

'No,' agreed Vangelis, 'the original was broken many years ago.' He had been wondering for some time, exactly how and when to break the news that he had been working on the flask, and rapidly concluded that this was as good an opportunity as any, even though he still hadn't completed the restoration or fully deciphered the inscriptions he had found on it.

'But I do have some good news that I've been meaning to share with you all. When we cleared my grandmother's house recently, we came across the pieces of the original flask. I was amazed that she'd kept them for all these years. I've almost finished restoring it … don't worry it's fully reversible, if necessary.' He assured Simon hastily before issuing a general invitation. 'I'd like you to all come up to the house at the end of the week and Ellie will have a set of prints ready for everyone.'

Ellie shot him a covert look of surprised annoyance, before giving a somewhat forced smile of agreement to one and all. Vangelis inwardly breathed a sigh of relief, as the buzz of anticipation transferred away from him and back to the necklace as it was carried off to the tent for cleaning.

'Thanks for the warning!' sniped Ellie as she set the camera back on the tripod.

'Sorry,' grinned Vangelis.

'I don't know what you're smiling about … you're getting married at the end of the week … or had you forgotten?'

'I'm running out of time Jack. I know there's something I'm not seeing here … and I know it's something important.'

'Can I?' Jack looked to Vangelis for permission to pick up the flask and study the completed restoration, comparing it with the pile of sketches lying beside. 'Nice work ... I can see how it kept you busy ... so many drawings.'

'I needed to make sure no piece was locked out during the reassembly.'

Jack knew from Vangelis' cursory tone that he wasn't in the mood for compliments or any discussion of conservation practices, and so set to analysing the painted decoration.

'Alright ... so we have a ship on a pretty lively sea ... stormy looking day, judging from the clouds above the mountain behind ... couple of dolphins skipping along the side of the ship?' Turning the flask over, Jack looked briefly at the inscription centred on the reverse, before promptly handing it back to Vangelis. 'That's the end of my two-penno'rth ... my ancient Minoan isn't up to scratch I'm afraid.'

'Nobody's is Jack. Linear A still hasn't been deciphered.'

'Looks like you're buggered then!'

'I would be, except this isn't Linear A ... it's hieratic, the script that evolved from hieroglyphs.'

'Egyptian then?'

'The inscription certainly. The Minoans did have their own form of hieroglyphics, some of which make up Linear B, but that's not what we have here. Nor is this.' Vangelis pointed out a lozenge-shaped seal impression below the text. 'The Minoans used seals, though usually only on tablets for records or for sealing goods ... but this isn't Minoan, it's also Egyptian. A scarab seal, like a small cartouche ... almost certainly a name ...'

'What! We're talking pharaohs here?'

Vangelis laughed. 'No, it's likely to be a private seal, or possibly an official of some kind.'

'So how did an Egyptian flask end up here?'

'We know that there was trade between the Egyptian and Minoan civilizations. Examples of imported pottery wares have been discovered in both countries. So in that sense, it's not totally out of the ordinary ...'

'But?' Jack urged.

'I don't believe it is Egyptian ... the painted decoration is undoubtedly Minoan.'

'The painter could have settled in Egypt.'

'Yes ... I'd considered that ... but even the clay used looks Minoan. And there are other things that just don't add up. For a start, the size and shape.'

'Yes, it does look a bit deformed. I did wonder at first, whether you'd got all the bits back in the right place!'

Vangelis ignored the taunt and continued to explain. 'Basically, it's similar enough to other thrown, globular flasks that have been found here on the island. They're usually a good bit larger than this, but most importantly they don't have this flattened distortion. I'd guess that this particular flask must have fallen onto its side before it was fired, giving it this flattened area where the inscription is ... and you can see how the opposite side has also indented slightly as a result of the impact.'

'It does have a familiar shape nevertheless,' Jack commented. 'A bit like a travelling water flask?'

Vangelis agreed. 'Yes, you're probably thinking of a pilgrim flask. But then we'd be talking much, much later, even for Mycenaean originals, or those made in Egypt around the same period. The point is this should have been a reject. Slapped back down while it was still wet, put back on the wheel and started again. Yet they've carried on with the painted decoration and someone — most probably an Egyptian official to have used hieratic script — has added an inscription and his own seal. Extremely unusual to say the least, but it just doesn't make sense. Who puts their name to shoddy goods?'

'Perhaps, for whatever reason there wasn't time to make another … or perhaps it fell over later … maybe in the firing, after it had already been signed?'

Vangelis shook his head. 'If it had survived that, which I doubt, the inscription would be distorted and there would be all sorts of foreign matter from the kiln embedded into it. You'd be closer with your first guess I'd say. I'm no ceramicist, but there do seem to be signs of it having been fired before it had properly dried.

'Then there's what was found inside. The earrings and necklace. Extremely expensive things … was this made to disguise them … or is it just a simple water flask? And then … how did they end up in a deserted wayside cave on the northern side of the island? It's not an impossibility I know, but the trade routes with Egypt, apart from Kato Zakro, right at the eastern end of the island, are all from the south.'

'Well, what about the inscription? Surely that can tell us something about it … how is your ancient Egyptian these days, Vangeli?'

'Not a great deal better than your Minoan, I'm afraid! I can make some of it out … it would appear to be wishing a woman and child safety on their journey … which ties in with the decoration, but there's more that I don't understand. Neither do I have any idea whose seal it is. You can only do so much over the internet. I need to get back to London and start researching.'

'Well, as I've said before, you know you've got somewhere to stay.'

'Thanks Jack, but there just isn't time. I've kept the flask to myself so far, but I've got the whole team coming over this evening, so then it'll be a free-for-all … which is only fair … but I had hoped I might be able to crack it first. Then of course, it's the wedding tomorrow. Thanks again Jack, for coming over and agreeing to do the honours.'

'Wouldn't miss it for the world! Anyway, save the thanks until after the speech … who knows what I'll come out with after a few! But getting back to this little problem, why don't you slip back after the wedding for a day or two.'

'Honeymoon,' Vangelis reminded him.

'Of course. Where?'

'Santorini.'

'Talk about a busman's holiday! After that then?'

'It gets worse! We've just uncovered our first bones at the site … things will slow down a bit for that, so I'm hoping I won't miss too much … but I've already had to persuade Anne to make Santorini just a mini break until the site is cleared, and then I'll be under pain of death to take her on a proper honeymoon.'

'No pressure then! I'm assuming you've got photographs of the inscriptions and seal?'

Vangelis nodded, 'Yes, of course. Ellie's taken loads.'

'Well, if you're happy to let me do so, why don't I email a couple to a chum of mine at Oxford. Can't guarantee anything of course, but I'd be very surprised if he wasn't able to crack your inscription for you. What do you think?'

'I think that's bloody fantastic!'

'Good. Let's get on with it and then you can pour me a good stiff drink!'

THIRTY-TWO

Relaxing at last, in the welcome quiet of the now almost empty hotel bar, Vangelis shared a final nightcap with Jack and wondered if Anne had also finally managed to escape the gathering of friends and relations back at the house. Knowing what lay in store for her the following day — when half the female population of the village would turn out intent on helping to dress the bride — he hoped she was getting the rest she would certainly need. He knew full well that he had the better of the deal, spending the night in peace at the hotel leaving both houses at their disposal.

'Sorry if that was a bit of a tame stag do for you Jack!'

'Well, it certainly was original ... can't say I've ever spent one surrounded by archaeologists arguing the toss over an old pot before ... mind you, I suppose it's put being a tosspot into a slightly better perspective!'

Vangelis grinned, as Jack stretched back on the hotel sofa. 'Want another?'

'Not unless the groom-to-be still wants to make more of his last night of freedom?'

'No ... I'm going to head up ... I should really do something about a speech.'

'Good idea!' Jack held out his hand for a pull-up. 'Well, if the rest of your colleagues feel anything like I do …. It'll be a fortnight before their heads are clear enough to make any sense of your mystery flask … cunning strategy! Oh, and please … do apologise again to that sweet little assistant who came late … I was sure someone had organised a stripper!'

'We won't be waiting in the church then?' Jack allowed Vangelis to straighten his tie, wishing he'd had less brunch and more coffee to prepare for his afternoon duties.

'You know you should be doing this for me, don't you? You're getting off lightly … in the old days, you would have had to shave me as well!' Satisfied with his appearance, Vangelis answered Jack's question. 'We wait outside the church, but first you as my *koumbaro* …

'Best man.' Jack let Vangelis know he was keeping up.

'That's right, along with Nikos …'

'Another best man.'

'Yes … we get as many as we like here … but don't worry, you're still my favourite! Both of you will escort me from the village square to the church, as we follow the musicians.'

'Who'll be playing The March to the Gallows, I presume?'

'It will be the gallows if we forget the flowers! They should have been delivered ready for us to take down at reception.'

'Doesn't Anne get to carry flowers?'

'Yes, the ones I'm bringing to her … now let's be sure we've got everything else …. Ellie and the other girls are dealing with the *koufeta* and the candles… do we have the *stefana*?'

Jack tapped the box. 'Yes, I can't wait to see you both in these dinky, little white tiaras!'

'Crowns. And you remember what you've got to do with them? Keep an eye on Manolis, he'll tell you when they need to be exchanged. Same as with the rings. You do have the rings … envelopes for the priest and the band?'

Once again, Jack nodded — patted his pockets dutifully — and gave Vangelis a confident thumbs up, holding the door open for him.

'These might come in handy!' Vangelis dropped the car keys into Jack's hand.

'You mean we're not taking the donkey?'

As the late afternoon sun began to tint the whitewashed houses of the village, arms linked, Jack steered Vangelis towards the church, Manolis at his other elbow.

'I can see why they do this … not much chance of doing a runner now, matey!'

'Don't worry … even if he does give us the slip, there are plenty of guns in the village!' Nikos advised them cheerfully. 'He won't stand a chance!'

With the last minute dash back to the hotel for Jack's speech and the resulting hectic drive up to the village now just a distant memory, the trio finally relaxed to the strains of the lyra and laouto as they followed the musicians leading the wedding procession through the winding streets.

Arriving at the old chapel, Vangelis stood at the door to await his bride as the wedding party continued to fill the courtyard until the customary delay fulfilled, he saw Anne escorted by her father, with her *koumbara* following, making her way up towards them. Stepping through the gate into the old courtyard, she moved slowly through the dappled shade of the trees, emerging into the glow of the late afternoon sun that irradiated her dress, where she waited for Vangelis to present the bouquet he had carried for her.

Leaving his friend's side, he whispered, 'You were right Jack ... I couldn't let a woman like that get away!'

It had only been a handful of days, but for Anne and Vangelis, time had finally stood still. Removed from the swirl of emotions surrounding both the dig and their wedding, they had both rapidly succumbed to Santorini's charms. Perched high on the clifftop, they had nestled among gleaming white buildings and iconic, blue-domed churches, looking out at the arms of the caldera encircling the deep blue sea far below.

Discussion of work had been off limits and not only Anne, but Vangelis himself, had been surprised at his ambivalence towards unopened emails. The world had managed without them.

Inevitably, however, the wheels of time began to revolve once more and they found themselves seated in the stern of the boat on their passage back to Crete, reluctantly watching the clifftop houses of Thera slowly diminish as they left Santorini behind — each entertaining very different thoughts — Anne wishing there had been more time to laze on the black volcanic sands — Vangelis admiring the different bands of colour that revealed the cycle of the volcano's activity in the stratification of the cliffs. Just how huge the original volcano had been became clear, as they sailed through the flooded caldera past the new volcano dwarfed by the remnants of the main island, the broken chain of Therasia, and on past the tiny cape of Aspronisi.

Passing the multicoloured cliffs Vangelis could not contain his enthusiasm. 'You can see the entire history recorded there!' He pointed out the different layers. 'Just above the waterline there … is the dark, ancient lava flow … then above that, the red cinder fall of the Minoan eruption that were followed by masses of pumice and lighter ash which raised up these huge cliffs. Three-and-a-half-thousand years in a single snapshot!'

As the boat slipped past the cape and out into the open sea, Anne snuggled closer. 'It looks like we got the best of the weather … I thought you said it never rained in June?'

Vangelis looked up at the gathering clouds. 'It'll blow over. Want to go inside?'

'No, I'm fine,' Anne took a final look at the receding island before pulling Vangelis to his feet, 'let's walk a bit.' Taking his hand, she led him along the side of the boat, until the spray coming off the bow halted their progress and they leant against the rails, watching the waves roll by below. 'Any news from Jack?' she enquired.

'No idea,' Vangelis replied. 'Even if his chap has got back to him with a translation, he'd know not to bother us until we got back.'

'And you still haven't checked your emails?' Vangelis shook his head. 'I'm impressed! Thanks for leaving work behind, it's done you good, you needed a break.'

'We both did. And once the dig's complete I'll make sure we have a proper honeymoon.'

'Look!' This time it was Anne who could not conceal her excitement. 'Dolphins!'

They both marvelled as a pair of striped dolphins raced alongside the boat, leaping playfully in and out of the bow waves. Finally tiring of their game, the dolphins slowed their pace and Vangelis watched as they gradually slipped behind, by the side of the boat.

Beyond them he could still see the outline of Santorini in the distance, now slowly becoming shrouded in lowering clouds that hovered above the truncated island where the towering volcano would have been.

'Idiot!' he exclaimed as the momentary sensation of déjà vu crystallized into realisation. Suddenly, both the dreams Litsa had recounted and the scene on the flask combined as one as he continued to stare at the receding island. 'It wasn't Crete or Egypt they were travelling from ... they were fleeing the eruptions of Santorini!'

THIRTY-THREE

'I would have thought that with a recession underway, this was hardly an appropriate time to be opening an art gallery, particularly in such a fashionable part of London!' The criticism in Diane's comment was only marginally softened by the look she gave Dieter, which told him she knew how indulgent he had been.

'She'll still have to work hard for it,' he countered. 'It won't just be her works on these walls that will keep it going. She knows that. Running Catherine's gallery in Crete will have opened her eyes. And if you want to attract good artists to a gallery in London, then you need to be in the right place.'

'And know the right people! Thank you, Dieter. Ellie said the opening was a great success, I wish I could have made it.'

'How are you now?'

'Oh fine.' Diane brushed any further discussion of her health aside.

Seated in a quiet corner of the main gallery area, Dieter and Diane were ideally placed to observe the first of the guests begin to arrive. The central display of Ellie's new gallery had been rehung for the evening with images from the dig in Crete, to coincide with the book launch she was hosting for her brother.

He and Jack fussed over display copies of the book propped beside the pile Vangelis would hopefully be signing, while Ellie and Anne greeted the new arrivals, steering them towards the drinks table at the rear. Diane struggled to reconcile these self-assured adults with her own grandchildren.

'It's hard to believe they're the same children … it seems only yesterday that Ellie was tumbling out of Catherine's gallery and poor Vangelis was sulking on the steps.'

'Yes, a great deal has happened since then. Not just for us but for everyone.' Dieter's eyes stayed on the bustle around the table, but his mind was far away. 'Back then I was sure that Greece had seen the last of her troubles: the wars, the junta. Now they fight a different battle just to keep their heads above water. It must seem to them that the enemy no longer wears a soldier's uniform but a banker's suit.'

'Very few countries are free of difficulties Dieter, but yes, they're definitely getting the worst of it, while I'm sure we'll get by with a bit more belt tightening. I suppose it's probably very true that 'We never had it so good.' Nowadays there seems to be far too much to have … to want. So much talk of 'rights' … so little thought for what is really needed. You've done what you can Dieter. I heard about your Foundation … no more penthouse in Crete then?'

'No that went a good while ago, I sold the chain to someone I know will look after the staff and hopefully the Foundation will ensure help is given where it is needed most. Talking of hopes … I had hoped after seeing you again at the wedding last year, that you might have taken me up on my offer…?'

The arrival of Monique, bearing champagne flutes, interrupted the conversation.

'Ellie insisted I bring you over some of the 'good stuff' before it all goes … but I expect you'd probably prefer some tea … I can make some if you'd like?'

'Nonsense! Turn down good bubbly?' Diane laughed, taking two and passing one on to Dieter. 'We have to toast the success of the book!'

'I was just attempting to persuade Diane to come and visit us, Monique.'

'You should,' she agreed. 'It is a beautiful place. You would love it.'

The sound of Jack's glass being struck with his fountain pen stilled the gallery, once again precluding any response from Diane. Having seen Catherine and Antonis arriving, he was keen to get the evening under way.

'Ladies and Gentlemen … Mesdames et Messieurs!'

Launching into a brief introductory speech, Jack spent a few moments warming the gathering up, before handing over to Vangelis.

'Thanks Jack … and not just for the introduction. There are also many others here this evening to whom I am deeply indebted: without whose help and guidance this book simply would not have been possible. I'll try and spare their blushes and not tire everyone else by keeping those thanks to a minimum. But before I do that, I have come to realise that there are two very special people that deserve more gratitude than I am able to give. A mother and child whose lives were brought to such an untimely end, and whose possessions have not only fired our imaginations, but helped us to understand their plight as clearly as if it had happened only yesterday.'

Slipping in between her parents, Ellie put an arm around each waist, and Catherine and Antonis held her close, their pride in their children only too evident as they listened.

'Whether it is the yearning to decipher long-forgotten tongues, the need to walk in the footsteps of our ancestors, or simply an interest in and appreciation of their craft, be it a simple earthenware utensil or the finest jewellery, we share an innate desire to breathe life into these artefacts. But what of the lives that breathed their last to satisfy this curiosity?

'What of the child, whose locks were the living framework for the golden spiral ornaments we can now admire? Her hair now long since vanished, its adornments the only remaining testament to those tresses. Or the young mother, whose embrace comforted her daughter in their final moments. What an opportunity was lost to name these poor unfortunates, when an Egyptian official neglected to give us the identity of what we can only speculate to have been his lover and child.

'Identified from his seal upon the flask he must have commissioned, we know from existing records that he was already serving his pharaoh as a delegate, trading with the people of Crete and Thera ... the Keftiu, as the Egyptians knew them. Both pictorially and in hieratic script, he tells us of the eruptions and earthquakes that were shaking Thera. It is tempting to surmise that the original damage to the flask was brought about by just such a tremor before its decoration was completed.'

Anne handed Jack a glass as he joined her at the rear of the gathering, and both raised a silent toast as Vangelis continued addressing his guests.

Querying Anne's knowing smile, he whispered under his breath, 'You're looking even more than usually pleased with yourself!'

'So will you be,' she replied, 'I took your advice and had a long talk with Diane.' Satisfying Jack's raised eyebrow, she continued, 'You may just get the book you really wanted after all!'

Jack gave a her a congratulatory squeeze and both quietly raised their glasses a second time, before turning their attentions back to Vangelis.

'Was the flask intended to conceal the earrings and necklace as currency to ensure their future welfare on reaching Crete? If it had been filled with water and not the jewellery would they have survived? It seems unlikely. Examination of the lowest steps at the entrance of the cave have now revealed significant layers of ash-fall and what remains of their clothing suggests that they were also covered with it, which must have been their reason for seeking shelter in the cave.

'It seems the cruellest twist of fate, that having escaped the horrors and destruction of Thera — survived raging seas to reach Crete — they then travelled inland, seeking shelter from the ash raining down from above, only to be entombed as aftershocks brought the cave walls tumbling down around them. We can only hope that their end was swift.'

'Amen,' Diane's softly whispered agreement brought Dieter's gaze back to her. 'It's what I always prayed for Richard.'

'And it would have been,' Dieter reassured her.

'Yes, I know. At least that was one consolation Litsa gave me. Oh, don't worry,' she assured him in turn as Dieter took her hand, 'I came to terms with everything a long while ago. It's just that talking about it all today with Anne brings everything back so very clearly. That and these ….' Diane opened her handbag and withdrew the slim bundle of yellowing letters.

Seeing the wartime censor labels pasted at the ends where the letters had been resealed instantly confirmed for Dieter who they were from. He waited in silence as she slipped one very crumpled letter from the ribboned package. This one bore no censor's label, nor any postal marking: only Diane's name and address.

'His last,' she explained. 'It was in the packet with the earrings.' Extracting two small pages from the grimed envelope, she afforded a brief smile along with a lightly breathed sigh as she unfolded the pages, handing Dieter the letter to see for himself the cartoon drawn on it. 'That would have been for Eddie … he and Rich were always joking about opening up a bar in some sunny place when the war was over.'

Dieter also smiled as he looked at the scribbled drawing of a hairy castaway sitting in front of his shanty bar on the beach. A driftwood sign nailed to the bar read 'Yianni's'. A hammock slung between the bar and a palm tree had only just been begun to be sketched in and although there was space left at the bottom of the page, no message had been written.

'The letter is unfinished as well,' Diane said as Dieter turned to the second page before recognising its personal nature and promptly offering it back to her.

'He must have thought a lot of Eddie.'

'He did ... as you'll see if you read the letter. It's fine, I don't mind.' Diane pushed the letter back to him. 'We were so close, the three of us ... before the war ....' Diane continued, softly reminiscing as Dieter reopened the letter.

Reading the beginning brought back a flood of memories as Dieter recalled his own letters to Hannelore. The years slipped away in a flash, and he paused briefly to look at Diane still wrapped up in her own thoughts. The words could have been his own.

Reading on, the script changed from pen to pencil, as did the tone. Now a resignation seemed to have set in. Though he still spoke of his good fortune of having Diane's love to hold on to, he reflected that Eddie was not so lucky. There was obviously another break before a final hurried sentence had been scribbled in. 'Darling Di,' it read, 'if something should happen to me, look after our old chum ...' As Diane had warned him, the letter remained unfinished.

Dieter quietly refolded the letter and replaced it in the envelope. 'It must have helped ... knowing you had his blessing.'

'Not at the time,' Diane observed wryly. Seeing Dieter's confusion, a look of respect spread over her face. 'She never told you ... Litsa? She must have known I lied to her ....'

'About what?'

'My age. She had to have known they shared virtually the same birthdate.' Seeing Dieter at a loss to understand, Diane explained. 'When Litsa showed me Richard's grave, the one thing that I couldn't get out of my mind was the date he had died ... or rather the day that came before it. That was the day Litsa said she and Richard had...' Diane took a moment, before continuing, 'It was the day Antonis was conceived. Exactly the same day as Catherine's conception. I lied about my age, pretending I'd had Catherine a year later, but the truth was I had been just as unfaithful as her ... but I couldn't admit it. I was just so angry ... after all those years of guilt ... not even the letter when it finally arrived could take that pain away.'

Taking both of Diane's hands in his own, Dieter's reassurances were cut short as Jack once more stilled the gathering for Vangelis's concluding remarks. Diane grimaced, lest her own discussion had been part of the disturbance, gave Dieter's hand a squeeze of thanks and turned her attention back to her grandson — as did Dieter — but not before noting with some satisfaction that Diane's hand stayed comfortably resting in his own as Vangelis spoke.

'Even if we are now able to link some dates and reigns of known individuals with the Theran eruption, conventional dynastic dating still remains at odds with the latest carbon and ice-core samples by as much as a hundred years. I trust that one day an answer will be found to explain the mystery behind these missing years.

'Were it not for a young mother and her child, who perished more than three-and-a-half-thousand years ago, we would not be able to share in these precious gifts today. But which is the more valuable? The fabulous jewellery, or the simple, broken flask with its own unique record of time? Or is it perhaps, time itself ... whether a missing century ... a moment shared ... or a final breath?'

As Vangelis wound up his speech, Diane became aware of Dieter's eyes upon her.

'I was remembering a particularly beautiful sunset, a long time ago, on that penthouse terrace in Crete,' he explained. 'I'd just met an equally beautiful lady that day.' Dieter handed Diane her glass. 'We shared a quiet drink and enjoyed the sunset together.'

Diane smiled. 'I remember it well. I said you had the perfect place to watch them.'

'These days I see them from the palm house in my gardens … perhaps not quite as spectacular …' Dieter paused for a moment, taking Diane's free hand gently back into his own. 'Come back with me Diane … let's share them together.'

'I don't know how many sunsets I have left Dieter.'

'Nor I … so why waste anymore? I should have asked you so many years ago, but there never seemed to be the right moment. Your grandson is right. Time is the most valuable thing we have. We've both had good and bad in our lives, and we have been blessed with long lives. Why spend whatever is left, alone, wrapped up in the past, when we can share happiness together?'

Dieter raised his glass, inviting Diane to accept his proposal.

'You once told me your intentions were entirely honourable,' she replied, raising her own. A twinkle in her eye, she gave his hand another squeeze. 'I hope that's changed!'

ACKNOWLEDGEMENTS

The most frequently offered piece of advice to writers is perhaps: 'Write what you know.' Undeniably sound advice. However, the leaps of imagination that carry us to so many different worlds would never have come into being if such advice was followed absolutely to the letter.

While *Lost in Crete* is a work of fiction, the backdrop to it is the 1941 invasion of Crete. Not having served myself, I was determined to be as thorough as possible in my research; to respect all those whose lives were forever altered or lost in the struggle. My first and most important acknowledgement therefore is to those whose courage and bravery were not fiction, but only too real.

It follows, therefore, that I must then thank the staff of The Imperial War Museum, whose patience, as I scoured microfilm footage and requested numerous copies of The London Gazette, was admirable. Given that this was in the 80s, and many will have now retired, my thanks are very much belated, but I am sure their good work carries on.

Similarly, to the Wandsworth Library branch, long since closed, which had an exceptional collection of WWII books. My gratitude naturally extends to their authors.

Personal thanks. Where to begin? This story would never have come into being had I not met my former wife Katerina. She knows I will never stop thanking her for our two beautiful daughters Gabrielle and Juliette. Their patience and support, along with that of my wife, Gaye, as I sought their opinions on every instalment, was indispensable.

The same goes for my second family: clan Mansfield. Also for Roula's enduring kindness, as well as 'Las Chicas' — Aileen, Deirdre, and Margaret. And to David and Tony, for valiantly trying to curb the habits of a misspent youth; persuading me not to pebbledash my prose with superfluous commas and misplaced possessive apostrophes!

Last but certainly not least, special thanks to Veida, not only for her editorial input and for weeding out still more commas in proofing, but also for a lifetime's encouragement.

This book is printed on paper from sustainable sources managed under the Forest Stewardship Council (FSC) scheme.

It has been printed in the UK to reduce transportation miles and their impact upon the environment.

For every new title that Troubador publishes, we plant a tree to offset CO_2, partnering with the More Trees scheme.

For more about how Troubador offsets its environmental impact, see www.troubador.co.uk/sustainability-and-community